# THE FOOL, THE LOVERS, THE DEVIL

# Tarot card reference

**THE FOOL.**

Innocence, freedom, originality, adventure, foolishness, carelessness, idealism, spontaneity, lack of commitment, new beginnings

**THE DEVIL.**

Detachment, independence, overcoming addiction, freedom, revelation, reclaiming power, reasserting control

**THE LOVERS.**

love, soulmates, kindred spirits, relationships, major choices, romance, desire, sexual connections

# Special Thanks to:

Iliandra Alvey

Claudia Cangini

Stacey Dean

Kate Waverly

Gennifer Ulmen

Meredith Trapp

J Raven Wilde

Priscillah Bancy

# Contents

# THE FOOL, THE LOVERS, THE DEVIL

RILEY QUINN

**Mary and Addison**
*Illustrated by Claudia Cangini*

# I

# Call Me By Thine Own Name

Waking up in a new place is scary. Adding a headache makes it scarier, and the fear factor maxes out when doing so naked.

Any hope I would spend the morning lazily getting moving evaporated as I tumbled out of the unfamiliar bed. I needed to escape. Fuck, if I had asthma, I'd stress myself to death. What a way to go, tangled in a random dude's sheets.

My bra, panties, and jeans were easily extracted from their impromptu clotheslines. I prayed to any power listening that my purse hadn't gotten lost.

I held my tangled brown hair behind my head before resuming my panic. Nice priorities, Addison. Shirts are optional, but hair in your face? Unacceptable. Fuck the purse. One problem at a time.

My mind worked in overdrive trying to glean some clues about whatever guy I had slept with last night. How did this happen? The only one I remember talking to was the birthday boy himself,

Joshua. I figured I should be happy this wasn't his house. Was this a house? The bedroom was only a little too big to be a hotel room.

Still, the situation wasn't truly dangerous. The room, while unfamiliar, wasn't unwelcoming. The bed had an actual frame, and, despite the lived-in vibe, the room wasn't messy or smelly. Again that either meant a clean man, a hotel room (unlikely), or... a girl? Nonsense. I wouldn't sleep naked for a slumber party.

"It could be worse," I told myself. He decorated the room at least. I scoured my mind for details of the previous night. I got tipsy at Joshua's twenty-eighth birthday party and hit it off with his friend Mary, but not once did that involve my mysterious one-night stand. I pushed down the fear he had kidnapped me and pulled on my shirt.

I pulled at the front to inspect the graphic. This shirt seemed unfamiliar, but it felt like one of mine. Mary would wear this sort of thing.

Now that I wasn't naked, I noticed the bedside table. A box of painkillers and a bottle of water stood out amidst the alarm clock and lamp. This gave me pause. It wasn't a glass of water, and it wasn't a bottle of pills. I snorted at the bougie water brand I couldn't pronounce, "Uisce Beatha". Unbearably pretentious, but still tamper-evident like the blister-packed painkillers.

Part of me wanted to exercise the most extreme caution, but I erred on giving my drunk self the tiniest bit of faith. I took the offering. Everything indicated my one-night stand was decent. Or the clean sort of psycho.

Besides, between my headache, dry throat, and strange lingering dreams of Mary, the chance to have one or two fewer things to think about was welcome.

I defaulted to prayers again as I wrestled with the needlessly complex water bottle. Nothing articulate, just "please" over and over again. As though politeness in beseeching the universe would make all the difference.

The living room was oddly familiar, the place must have made some impression because I had the distinct feeling my dream used scenery from here.

"I can't believe I got black-out drunk." I muttered as I looked around the living space. I let my feet skim the carpet, walking on the balls of my feet out of habit.

Ordinarily, it shouldn't have been hard to find my purse. The peeling faux leather and dyed canvas were normally distinctive, but here it was practically camo. I circled the couch in the living room area once, resisting the urge to stop and count the candles cluttering the coffee table. With the computer desk also a bust, all that was left was the kitchen. I frowned at the row of bottles across the top of the fridge and cast around across the abandoned mugs and snack containers until I found my prize.

A basket of fruit and a box of granola bars sat on the kitchen counter next to my purse, so I again indulged in the unspoken offering. For a guy, he continued to impress. I didn't hook up often (pronounced "ever"), but I wished I remembered this one.

My shoes and socks were by the door among a modest boot collection, and, with the last of my essential belongings accounted for, nothing was keeping me here. I kicked the floor outside the door to fix my sock just so and stepped over to the railing of the hotel-like terrace. At this point, I knew it wasn't a hotel (score one for clean boys), and I pieced a few things together as I looked down. This must be Tristan Tower. It was the closest to the bar we'd been to last night, and it was the only multi-floor building in the metro-ish area that wasn't office space. I returned to the door, hit the electronic lock button, and jiggled the handle to make sure it latched.

I snapped a picture of the door number on a whim before returning to the brushed brass railing. Apartments lined the exterior in levels, tables decorated the foyer below, and a coffee bar sported a short line of caffeine junkies like myself. The place had a theme for crying out loud. Everything from the tile in the foyer, carpet in the halls, and walls with their accents adhered to a deep green palate. It was lucky I hadn't checked this place out when I moved to town a couple of years ago, or I might have bought into this place for the colors alone...- and the granite counters... Already the awe and intimidation I felt at the scale of this place started to outweigh the panic from before.

So I woke up away from home, big deal. The danger had largely passed so the crisis could stew on the back burner for a bit. I tore open the wrapper of the granola bar and picked a direction to search for an elevator.

My phone reported the night's notifications as I walked. Joshua left several messages. First, he wished me goodnight because I left without saying goodbye- wow, that was rude, Addison- After that, the messages turned cryptic. Something about baseball? Batting for the other team? Had there been a game on at the bar? That didn't sound right, but I know I hadn't been focused on the TVs.

I disregarded the nonsense and sent my birthday wishes again. It wasn't Joshua's fault I'd woken up in his buddy's bed. I didn't want to worry him. But of course if it was his fault, there would be hell to pay. To be fair, Joshua was a good one. Easily my longest term friendship since we had met in college. Even if he *had* fixed me up with one of his work friends it would in general be better than whatever judgment calls I would have made to arrive here. Shit, he might as well have set me up with someone. I trust his judge of character more than my own after the Richard debacle, Especially when everyone was drinking. Fuck, I was clingy when I got tipsy.

By the time I got to the coffee bar, I had caught up on my emails and group chats. I considered ordering my usual, but the advertisement for the oat milk latte caught my eye. I could stand to branch out. Just because almond milk was so yucky to me didn't mean I wouldn't like oat milk. I liked oatmeal. Kinda.

As I Idly scanned the foyer, a woman with bright red hair caught my eye. Mary was reading at a small table next to the fountain. My memories of last night were hazy— but she wasn't.

I wasn't sure I was actually happy to see her. Talking to attractive people was intimidating and, had she not taken this moment to look up, I would have sooner snuck out of the tower than strike up conversation. even from a few tables away I could see her smile. She seemed to brighten the entire foyer, even when dressed in almost all black. Like last night, she had jeans and a t-shirt, but she had forgone the bright plaid over-shirt she had last night. I guess with hair dyed that brightly she would never be short on color, even if she was pale as a ghost.

She waved, friendly as ever, so I decided a quick 'hello' wouldn't hurt more than I could bear. I managed not to run into any chairs as I meandered over to her, she was still looking at me, so I probably wasn't misreading her interest in talking. By the time I got to the table she had finished packing up and was slinging her messenger bag over her shoulder.

"Good morning sleeping beauty." Her smile was smug and her eyebrows rose as she looked at my shirt.

"Good... morning?" I sounded a little less enthusiastic than I would have hoped as I puzzled over her wording halfway through my automatic response.

"I would have woken you, but you were sleeping soundly. I wasn't very quiet getting up, and you snored through it all, so I decided it was best for you to get your rest. I honestly didn't expect to see you up so soon."

Oh.

Oh fuck.

My face burned as the final piece of the picture fell into place.

Her eyes widened. "Hey, it's okay. I wouldn't have minded if you slept till dinner."

She laughed but I struggled to find the humor, much less act amused. My whole body burned now and I was fighting my flight instinct. It was so obvious now, and yet I thought I had applied logic so well...

I twisted the cardboard ring on my cup. "How long have you been up?"

"Just a couple hours. I ran to the bookstore and then decided to hang out here until lunchtime."

I managed a nod but words escaped me. Fuck, I'd been staring at my coffee too long. I looked up and combed my fingers through my hair.

"Is everything alright, Addie?"

My heart fluttered. A nickname? Even Joshua called me Addison. My thoughts struggled to settle as I took a deep breath. It was fine. She could call me Addie if she wanted. Whatever. Maybe I liked it better? Who could say? Shit, she asked a question. Yes or no. Easy.

"Y-yeah."

I hadn't convinced her. Fuck. I opened and closed my mouth as she continued to psychoanalyze me.

"Sorry. It's just --" The right words weren't coming to me. How did I frame this?

"I've never..."

She nodded.

Her posture didn't show judgment, so I managed to reboot my thoughts. Starting over gave me deja-vu. I wondered if there were long-term effects from emotional shock therapy.

"I thought I was straight-- I mean I think I'm straight? I'm straight."

She pursed her lips. She must have had this conversation before.

"How are you coping with uh... that?"

"Honestly?" I huffed a half-panicked laugh. "I'm not really processing it yet? Does that make sense?"

"Do you regret --"

"Nononono no," I cut in. I hardly remembered it- or rather, I remembered a lot, but I wasn't sure how much was real and how much I dreamt up... Still, I sensed telling her as much would only offend in a different way.

"That's good." She let go of the strap of her satchel and smiled.

I took another sip of my coffee and tried not to stare. Just as it occurred to me that it might have been my turn to talk, she spoke up.

"Well, uh... you know how to reach me if you wanna chat or hang out sometime."

I nodded without a thought. How would I contact her? Why did I want to so badly?

She rocked back and forth on her heels and I dug through my memorized scripts for ways to say goodbye.

"Uh, have a nice lunch." I managed a smile, proud that I hadn't stumbled over so few words.

She nodded and smiled, probably returning the sentiment but I was only focused on which way she was likely to go. I waved as she stepped past me and I looked in any other direction for an exit-y door. I didn't even think to hail a cab until I was standing in the sunlight.

Fuck.

I slept with *Mary*. I hadn't ever forgotten, I just couldn't believe that was real. My pea brain had written it off as another of those dreams. Christ, dreams were one thing but now I'd really gone and done it. And fuck had we done it.

I pulled at my hair to try and rein in my thoughts but it only sparked more memories.

Daydream turned to obsession as the night played on repeat in my mind. Every loop there was some additional detail and at some point I had to wonder if I was inventing new memories to torture myself. The fact that it had been better than I had dreamed only made my imagination all the more cruel.

When I got home, I felt the pull of habit. Saturday. Groceries. I took inventory of the fridge and nearly left before realizing I needed a shower first.

I rifled through my dresser to lay out clothes, remembered I didn't have housemates anymore, and left a trail of discarded apparel to the bathroom instead. At this point, remembering her touch left me dazed and warm. So much so, I almost didn't notice the mark on my collarbone as I approached the shower stall.

What I initially assumed must be a bruise or at worst a hickey, revealed itself to be an ink stamp. The same sort they used at events to show proof of payment or legal drinking age.

I struggled to read in reverse through the mirror, and the realization left me bemused and vexed. Mary had marked me, literally, with a custom stamp featuring her name and phone number.

# 2

# When Can I See You Again?

I had revised this blasted message at least ten times now, and I needed to get it right. Every letter had to be perfect, or I'd fuck everything up.

I'd done nothing since my shower but agonize over this message, and my alarm clock already read four in the afternoon. I hadn't even done my grocery shopping. Groceries were literally my only errand today!

I tried to scroll up to reread again and fumbled the send button. Perfect. The grand conspiracy's latest sabotage was a prematurely sent text. Et tu phone? I scanned for damage control. Worst case I would look stupid, right?

I introduced myself, okay.

I greeted her, fine.

An apology for being weird, also fine.

Lastly, I intended to ask, "Are you interested in meeting up to chat?"

Ah. It was a *goddess* fucking with me. Only a lesbian could turn that into: "Are you interested in me?"

The fucking auto-correct even added punctuation! Bitch!

A response arrived before I could react.

*Hey, it's fine, I promise. Yeah. I'm interested.*

"What?" I said aloud to my phone. It, of course, did not answer.

*Would you like to hang out tomorrow?*

"What?" I repeated to myself. Fuck she typed fast. Sure, I *wanted* to spend time with her. Who wouldn't? Should I, though?

Fuck. Read receipts were on. She knew I saw her message. Think fast, think fast.

*Sure. I'd like that.*

I said think fast, not gay, you idiot. "I'd like that"? Seriously?

Whatever. It would be stupid to say no, right? I can't turn back now. Sure, I could have claimed to be busy, but I didn't. Because I wasn't. I had never thought about how the internet would betray me this way. Fuck light-speed communication.

*Cool, I can pick you up around 5, and we can go to this ramen place I like.*

I sent my address and dropped my phone in the middle of my bed. I flopped backwards across my blankets and watched the fan spin until I caught myself staring at the light bulb. Pressing my palms to my eyes only made the spots dance.

I would see her tomorrow. Again. Already. What would I do? Did I pretend I liked girls? That wouldn't be hard. But Mary deserved better. The best policy would be honesty, and the truth was I was straight.

Maybe I was pretending I liked Mary. Being straight was far more believable that way. But was it? Even a cursory glance at my memories told me I wasn't pretending. I would never pretend to like a guy, kiss them, and go home with them if I didn't like them. Well. That wasn't true. I'd acted overly interested in a couple guys before just because they showed an interest in me first. It had been the easiest way to continue getting attention. Was I doing that with Mary?

I kissed her because I liked her. I slept with her because I liked her.

I wanted her.

I liked everything I knew about her, her hobbies, her style, the way she held me-- like a friend, of course. Fuck this.

I sat up and stuffed my phone in my pocket. (yes, the pocket is big enough. I call these jeans "unicorn" for a reason.)

"Maybe it's platonic."

Yep. I self-talked out loud now.

The thought gained traction, but my mind derailed again into a tangent. I almost passed it off as a friendly, platonic, one night stand-- and it would have passed if there was any way in hell I would do that with a guy. Whether I liked it or not, Mary was special.

I made a desperate Hail Mary (yeah, I know) and searched the internet as I left the bedroom and paced the living room.

"Can a straight girl be attracted to girls?"

I let out a breath I didn't realize I was holding. Yes. Straight girls like me had asked many times, enough that I was sure it was a nearly universal experience. I flicked through the articles. There were naysayers but also a flood of assurances. Apparently, it only meant anything if you acted on it.

Well, that was fine. If I didn't do anything, it wasn't gay.

Wait.

Fuck.

Well, that was stupid. Who were they to decide my sexuality based on my actions?

I stewed angrily at the comments before starting a new search.

"Can straight girls sleep with girls?"

Okay. Yes. A resounding yes. More naysayers than before, but there were testimonials. Books and guides on how to sleep with women as a straight woman. I wondered if such a guide would have helped me yesterday. It was interesting that I probably wouldn't have sought it out before, but now I didn't need It. I was practically an expert.

I browsed the results for longer than I'd like to admit before putting away my phone. That settled it. Mary could be attractive to me, and I could continue to... uh... act on that attraction. It still didn't mean I was a lesbian, bisexual, or whatever.

Finally, I could unfreeze. I grabbed my jacket and walked out to my car. As I started it, I got a text from Joshua.

*Did you have fun with Mary last night?*

I groaned at the winky face accompanying the message. Part of me didn't want to dignify it with a response, but I also wanted to throw his words back in his face. He was obviously going to be another naysayer, and I knew how to deal with those.

*For your information, yes. We had a lovely time.*

I didn't have to wait long for the response.

*Hahaha, that's kinda gay lol.*

I rolled my eyes. Predictable. At least I knew he wasn't teasing in a derogatory way.

*Actually, I googled it. Loads of straight women experience same-sex attraction. It doesn't mean I'm any less straight.*

I waited a minute and shrugged as nothing happened. I put the car in gear.

My phone rang over the car speaker. It was Joshua. I didn't even have time to greet him before he cut me off.

"Are you serious?" he asked. His tone was inscrutable.

"Yes?"

"Jesus Christ, what have I done?" I heard him murmur. He sounded faint, like he had moved the phone away from his face. I hardly had time for him to make this about himself.

"Was that all?"

"No... Just... don't get your heart broken, okay?"

I didn't expect that. I had answers ready for so many arguments, but not for a simple warning.

"I'll do my best."

I wondered if I should hang up.

"Can I ask that you keep an open mind? About your sexuality? Just... I get that you don't think you're gay, but it's worth considering that liking guys doesn't make you straight. Fuck. I don't know where I'm going with this...."

I rolled my eyes. Part of me wanted to blow him off or flip the script on him. How would he, a straight man, know what I'm feeling? But at the same time, he wasn't telling me what to do, arguing, getting angry at me, or even talking down on me.

"I'll try..."

"Thanks. Uh... yeah, that was all I was concerned about. Thanks again for coming to my party. I'll letcha go."

"Any time. Have a good one."

The stereo blipped as the call ended, and I sat with my thoughts. Thinking and talking about my sexuality got old fast.

*~*~*

By the time I got home, it was dark. Grocery shopping had taken twice as long as usual, and it didn't help anything that the sun was setting early. I had done nothing but fixate all day. Yesterday, Mary didn't matter; I didn't know she existed. But today, it consumed me. I changed into bed clothes on autopilot. An early night never hurt anyone. I set about my evening routine, prepping my CPAP and picking up the breadcrumb trail of clothes past-me had been *so* kind to leave for me. I froze when I picked up my shirt from this morning.

It wasn't mine.

I had taken her shirt. Obviously, I had to return it tomorrow, and I should probably wash it first, but what if I washed it wrong?

I didn't want to ruin her clothes! For all I knew, this was a special shirt too. I spent an eternity agonizing before I went and got my phone. At least breaking the ice made this easier now.

*Hey, I accidentally stole your shirt this morning. Is it cool if I wash it? I don't want to accidentally ruin your clothes.*

I didn't have to wait long.

*Nah, I'll take care of it. We can trade back tomorrow. I thought you did it on purpose.*

She sent a laughing emoji along with it, and I flushed further in embarrassment.

I nodded to myself and grabbed a plastic bag. I was already slipping back into my night routine when a thought jumped out and slapped me in the face.

Why was I hoping she would tell me to keep it? Why was I willing to trade one of *my* favorite tops just to keep one of hers?

# 3

## Seconds

My bed was a mess. I'd been cycling through outfits for the last hour, and nothing was quite right. Too casual, too formal, too colorful, or not bright enough. What if our outfits clashed? What if they looked coordinated? I had minutes until Mary arrived, but my attire needed hours of help.

I'd woken up early due to my unusual bedtime and spent the morning attempting to distract myself. Making the bed reminded me of how Mary had held me on hers. Cleaning the kitchen reminded me of the snacks she had set out for me. Doing the laundry reminded me of our scattered clothing on the floor.

Hell, I couldn't help remembering her in everything I did. I tried to relax in the bath, but I couldn't stop thinking about where she had marked me. I'd scrubbed the mark off yesterday, but now I wish I'd preserved it. As if I needed a memento. I could only see the faintest shadow of it in the mirror as I spritzed conditioner on my hair. Looking at the girl in the mirror, objectively, she didn't look all that different from Mary. I wasn't quite as pale as her, she had tattoos where I only had stretch marks, yet somehow the curves I adored on Mary were a prison to me. It made no sense. We were similar enough that I could wear her shirt without noticing, yet for some reason the features we shared were only beautiful on her. I grimaced and tried to look kinder at the stupid mirror. Why couldn't I see beauty in my own body without having to detach myself from it?

I sighed and grabbed my blue wide tooth comb. At the very least, I could look forward to a crumb of praise from my therapist over this introspection or whatever. So long as I remembered... and had the courage to mention Mary at all. I had no delusion that my self-image was rational, still, I couldn't help but wish some positivity would stick around.

Perhaps it was my difficulty looking in the mirror that left me in this predicament. I was dressed in clothes I had found in the back of my closet ten brief minutes before Mary said she would pick me up. This outfit didn't feel like a winner to me.

Sure, the boots were comfortable, but the leggings and sweater dress screamed: "Yes, I am a girly girl femme lady who is straight". What did I even know about the vibes my outfit gave me? Hell, my gaydar was so shit I hadn't considered the possibility Mary wasn't straight until I had gotten home yesterday.

My blood ran cold as the doorbell rang; time was up. She was early. I grabbed my purse and Mary's shirt. I had upgraded the plastic bag to one of those reusable shopping bags on a whim. What message was I even trying to send with that? Nothing made sense today.

My brain short-circuited again when I opened the door. I swear I'd never batted an eye at this sort of thing before, but on her, the Hawaiian shirt, ripped jeans, and short pony tail looked hot as hell. I could only see a sliver of the star-shaped tattoo on her chest, but it immediately reminded me of the half dozen tattoos I hadn't had enough time to appreciate.

Fuck shit damn, I overdressed.

She was holding out my shirt. I traded it and threw mine onto the couch. When I turned back, her eyes were still trailing back up.

I heard her greeting, and I unfroze to tear my eyes from her septum piercing.

"Hey, you're early." I tried to smile, but concern flashed across her face.

"I'm so sorry. Did you need more time? I can wait."

"No, no. It's fine. I'm just surprised, that's all."

"Used to people showing up late?"

"Or not at all." I shrugged. I regretted it when her smug look fell to sympathy. What was it about her that made me such an open book? Why the fuck did I tell her that?

I didn't have a spare neuron to pay attention to my environment as we walked to her car. What started as appreciating her outfit turned into remembering Friday night. Again. Fuck. I managed to speed up to walk beside her and focused on her car. It definitely stood out.

In my frenzy of research, I had developed the assumption she would drive something well... gay... but instead of a Sobaro, a truck, or some sort of sporty utility vehicle, she had an old sedan. I searched for the name in my memory, but as I walked around the back, the mystery solved itself. A Phoenix. I hadn't seen one like it on the road since high school, and I suspected the brand was discontinued. The pop-up headlights and hood decal were a throwback.

I was already struggling to fit "classic car enthusiast" into my impression of her as I climbed into the passenger seat. The seat cover slid and I fidgeted in vain to resituate it.

"Yeah, sorry about that. I always forget to warn people but the sun has not been kind to the upholstery. Ironic, I know."

"Ironic?"

"With the phoenix and all?"

"Right..." I habitually obsessed over whether it fit the definition of irony, probably one of my stupidest pet peeves.

She performed a pre-flight ritual, docking her phone in a suction-cup clamp and running a cable to it from a modern-looking radio. Ready at last, she held the top of the wheel. Now that I looked I could see she had sewn on a replacement cover there too. She squinted as she turned the key, and strained to hear or feel something as she executed a clearly practiced pattern.

She caught me watching and looked proud of either herself or the car. I hoped starting the engine wasn't a rare feat.

"What do you think? She's a beauty, isn't she?"

I didn't know what to say. It wasn't a junk car by any stretch. Clearly the upkeep was a labor of love. I settled for nodding, and she nodded to herself. Was that some sort of test? The parking brake clicked and thumped as she released it, and she revved the engine twice, as if testing it, before setting out. I recognized the music as a pop band I had listened to in college, but it was hard to understand over the competing road and engine noise. My car spoiled me with its relative serenity.

I blinked to catch up as I realized she was talking, but in fact, she sang along to the radio softly. She had a lovely singing voice and now that I had a sound to focus on, the background noise fell away. She sang of love lost and fear of death. And when the next song came on, she sang of toxic love and dependency. I didn't dare interrupt the private concert. We arrived at the ramen shop in no time, and the return of silence struck me as she parked and cut the engine. Neon chopsticks and noodles blinked back and forth on the animated sign, but on closer inspection it was just a TV pretending to be a neon sign.

She continued to hum as we made our way to the front of the store. I think something fizzed and sparked in my head as she took my hand in hers on the sidewalk. Hand holding? Was this a sign?

Was this a romantic thing? Or a friendship thing? Goosebumps flashed across my arms as she shifted to weave our fingers together, but I didn't pull away. Was there a point where playing along and acting natural was a bit *too* natural?

I struggled to fall in step as we approached the front door. She skipped half a step forward and before I could reach out she snagged the door and released my hand to hold it open for me.

The hostess leaned on the podium, visibly relaxing as she looked from me to Mary.

"Hey Mary, hi Mary's friend. Two?" Her electric blue hair was the perfect compliment to Mary's bright red, but she had many more piercings. Of course they were friends.

"Hi Kim." Mary stepped up beside me. "Yeah, just two."

I forced a laugh. Suddenly the date seemed more like bringing me to meet her family, particularly if she was going to know everyone here by name.

"Inside or outside?"

Mary looked at me.

I shrugged. "Either."

I tried to take in the scenery as the hostess- Kim I suppose, told us how long the wait was. I was still watching her leave when I realized Mary had disappeared from my side. I did a full 360 before realizing she had moved to sit on the bench in the little foyer, and I moved to the spot she patted as soon as I remembered how to walk.

She snagged a menu out of the pocket on the wall next to me and explained the options, providing her brief sentiment on each style as she read. Despite how closely I was listening, nothing sank in. She got to the end of the menu, and I had forgotten every single thing she had told me.

I hated making choices.

"What's your favorite?"

She flashed me a smile, but I had a sense of deja vu as she pointed to two of the bowls in turn. Fuck. I'd asked her to repeat herself.

"C-cool," I stammered. She handed me the menu to inspect for myself.

Even if I narrowed the choices down to two, it was still one too many. My thoughts turned to static as she slipped an arm around me and moved closer. The dozenth time I looked between the two choices, I gave up. I would copy her when the moment came.

"Can't decide?"

She brushed her thumb on my shoulder, and when I turned to look at her, she was very close. My eyes settled on her lips, and when I remembered to attempt to make eye contact, hers sparkled with mirth.

"No-o"

I managed not to flinch as her other hand brushed mine, and she took the menu back from me. She turned to put it back, and when she looked at me again, we were closer still.

She gave my hand a reassuring squeeze, and I read her lips as she leaned in.

"We'll just order both and you can see which one you prefer."

I agreed before I even processed what she said. Fuck. I'd agree with anything she said.

She leaned back and tore me from my thoughts as the hostess called her name. Mary led me to our table, a cozy little booth. I slipped in, and rather than sitting across from me, she followed me in. The resulting trapped sensation set off a panic, but the fear evaporated as she took my hand in hers.

She was still holding my hand as she ordered for us. When I couldn't decide what to drink, she chose that for me too. How did she know I preferred the zero sugar variety? I feared she was a mind reader or a stalker before I realized it was what I had ordered at the bar. She remembered.

I became acclimated to my hand being in hers. The touch was as natural as wearing clothes. It was comforting, securing even, as I learned to focus outside of that single sensation.

"So how's your sexuality epiphany going?"

"What?"

The words clicked halfway through the repeat.

Well, that was a bombshell of a question. Why was I afraid to tell her? I searched the scratches on the dark lacquered table, looking for answers. I loathed the idea of arguing with her, and I didn't want to disappoint her. I spent so much time obsessing and assuming today that I was all but sure she would be incredulous or offended if I said I was still straight. I'd literally planned out all the ways I could tell her and yet not one sounded right.

She rested her other elbow on the table and leaned forward to catch my eye. I fixated on her hair as a lock fell out of place and swept across her forehead.

I hadn't answered. Fuck. How long had I been staring?

"Make that a crisis, I guess."

I mustered my courage. If I framed my confession as an apology, would she be more accepting?

"I think I'm straight?"

Or a question. A question works too. Damnit.

I caught the nearly imperceptible shake of her head from the corner of my eye, and I imagined I saw the end of an eye roll.

"Okay." She brushed her hair back and smiled at me anyway.

Okay! It was okay? Everything was okay. She looked up to receive our drinks. I wondered to myself if she was ambidextrous or left-handed because she made no move to let go of my hand as she slid me my soda.

"Do you want to talk about it?"

She startled me as she broke the silence when Kim left. Had I been staring? Would anything make sense tonight? More at 9 on "Addison is fucking stupid".

"N-not really?" She raised an eyebrow. So I barreled on. "What about you? Are you a lesbian?"

"I'm pansexual demiromantic."

I blinked. Clearly, I hadn't done enough research because I expected one word, got two, and didn't know what either one meant.

"It means I can feel sexual attraction to someone regardless of their gender, and I develop a romantic attraction to people I form strong emotional ties to."

I tried to wrap the concept in my mind.

"Isn't that just bisexual?"

She laughed and shook her head.

"I'll admit it's similar, but the distinction I make is; rather than finding certain men, certain women, and certain non-binary or gender non-conforming people attractive, my sense of attraction is based on qualities that aren't necessarily correlated with a particular gender expression, --" She let that sink in before continuing. "-- and the demiromantic bit is just that I don't fall in love with people I don't already know pretty well."

"Isn't everyone demiromantic, then?"

Her smile was smug. As though I had revealed my hand in a game of poker.

"Hard as it is to believe, allegedly, some people can feel a deep desire for a romantic emotional connection with someone based on little more than their looks or expression. So, a homoromantic woman for example, may feel a desire to have sex with men, but only really feel a pull for a romantic relationship with other girls."

I stared at the bubbles in my soda as I tried to apply this to my experiences. Part of me wanted to say I'd never fall in love with someone I didn't know, but I knew I wanted a romantic relationship with Mary, even though I hardly knew her. That was something I should ask the internet about too, but I wasn't about to pull out my phone now.

I tried to think about whether I had wanted romantic relationships in the past or if I had even wanted to make a life with someone before. I struggled to put myself in that distant mindset. Was I looking for a life with Rich? Or did I just want to sleep with him? What about Adam?

"Any questions?"

She was maddeningly entertained by all of this.

"Yes and no."

She raised an eyebrow, so I continued.

"Yes, I have questions. I'm full of them. But I don't know what they are."

I stewed with my thoughts, even with how kind and patient Mary had always been, I felt like I was one thoughtless word from ruining everything.

"Is it possible... that I could be sexually attracted to men, sexually attracted to women, and r-romantically attracted to women... and still be straight?"

Mary pursed her lips and looked past me out the window. As she was about to speak again, Kim came by with two bowls of ramen. The variety and sparkle of her piercings drew me in, and my eyes remained glued to her as she walked away.

When I looked back at Mary, she wore that smug smile again.

"Which do you want to try first?" She pushed the bowls in front of me one at a time, and when she didn't move to release my hand, I took it as a challenge to figure out my napkin bundle one-handed.

The one with buttered corn and an egg was delicious, and I probably would have liked the other one too, but they loaded it with jalapeno slices. Mary laughed as I must have made a face, and she took the spicy one. I kicked myself for having such difficulty choosing when I knew my spice tolerance wasn't high.

Mary's left-handed eating distracted me, probably because her rings were shiny. Was she left handed? She always used her right on me. I sighed, barely smothering the gasp my body wanted to make. That memory came with touch, and it took my breath away. Thoughts like that always hit me out of nowhere, and recent experience only made it worse.

"What was that book you were reading?" I tried not to speak too fast as I hurried to make sure we dropped the sexuality talk. That wasn't subtle, and I think Mary knew it.

Still, she seemed happy to talk about books and music as we waited for our noodles to cool.

# 4

## Slumber Party

The conversation strayed to favorite things, and in no time, we had ordered mochi ice cream and mango-flavored sake with orange juice. Trying all her favorites became my obsession, and I was sure I would love them all.

The reality was mochi had a terrible texture, and sake mimosas, while charming, would not become my favorite drink. Nevertheless, I powered through. I didn't lie, of course. She could keep all the mochi, but the faux mimosa was not going to waste on me.

The faintest buzz warmed me as we laughed through dinner. After we paid our checks, I swung her hand in mine as we walked to her car.

"So what do you want to do now?"

I shrugged. I didn't work until ten AM tomorrow, so I had no shortage of time for further activity. I checked my phone anyway and bedtime was far away.

"Would you like to catch a movie at my place?"

I agreed. I agreed so much. "Hell yeah."

Mary laughed. "It's not going to keep you up too late is it? to-morrow being Monday and all."

I waved her off. "I can make my own mistakes thank you very much. Besides, my job in the test kitchen is mostly logistics, so I can work on those arrangements any time of day or even from home if I'm not doing inventory or something."

"As long as I'm not keeping you past your bedtime." Mary teased in a sing-song voice. "Well, it's come to my attention you have not experienced *Galantia*. And I have the perfect home theater to dust off to watch it."

"Dust off?"

"Yeah, I actually haven't used the TV as much as I thought I would. Whenever I am looking for something to do, I end up going out or reading instead. I got it when I moved in and spent waaay more than I should have on it."

"Sounds like a perfect plan, then."

I couldn't remember ever being this happy and comfortable on a date before.

I enjoyed my private concert as she drove us to her flat. Not holding her hand for the drive left a peculiar feeling of loss, but like clockwork, she retook it as we made our way from the parking garage to the elevator.

With the pleasurable company and now-familiar living space, I swiftly relaxed. I kicked my shoes off at the door and followed Mary to the couch. While she hunted down the remote, I tucked my feet under me and nestled into the corner.

However, Mary had other designs. My first surprise was that she sat next to me rather than on the left side of the couch. And in a display of confidence I could never have managed, she rearranged us so I nestled into the right corner of the sofa with my legs draped across hers.

"Is this okay?"

How was I supposed to answer that? Words? I nodded and luckily that seemed to suffice.

Her hand rested on the inside of my thigh, and I tentatively covered it with mine. Predictably, she moved to hold my hand instead and I was left to relearn how to relax as the movie began.

Part of me wanted to use the movie as an experiment: to see what I liked and disliked about each character and gauge my interest in them. The dorky main character, Tylo, made a bad first impression, but I found myself charmed by his bookish vibe. I could totally be friends with him, possibly even more. It was comforting to be reassured.

But from there, it was downhill. I struggled to both focus on the characters and reciprocate Mary's anecdotes over the movie. She gave me history and fun facts, but I focused on the femme fatale, grungy butch, and mysterious princess.

I'd try to use Tylo as a palate cleanser, but I would only find the irritating things. His cowardice and clumsiness turned me off, and I grew impatient as he stumbled through his crush with the princess. Meanwhile, the girls could do no wrong. Even as the femme fatale turned out to be evil-- and then kinda not evil? She still enraptured me.

Mary must have noticed my anxiety because she was rubbing my back. The action and tension were picking up, so I reasoned that was at least a suitable cover for my panic, but the touch still grounded me to her. I switched gears to dwell on how I felt about Mary and the things I liked about her. I wanted to know everything; I wanted to become the foremost expert on everything Mary, to be able to return an ounce of the casual intimacy she dispensed on me.

I forced myself to relax again; I had to unplug myself from the movie. I felt a buzz, but I knew for sure the small amount of alcohol I had with dinner was well on its way out of my system. No, I understood it for what it was. I was becoming aroused.

Panic and shame surged in my stomach before I remembered what I had researched. It was okay. It was fine to be attracted to Mary and not only was it okay, it was deeply enjoyable. It felt safe. Natural even.

I leaned into her shoulder as the climax of the movie no doubt approached. She kissed the top of my head and continued to rub my back. It might have soothed me if it wasn't pressing my buttons. After a few minutes of overheating, I mustered the courage to ditch the sweater. Mary at least seemed minimally disturbed by the interruption.

The weight of my mistake hit when I settled in and she resumed rubbing my back. I could feel her nails, just barely long enough to distinguish from her fingertips. The thin cotton of my tee shirt was nowhere near the protection the sweater had been. I felt her warmth now.

The princess was going full-on godmode on screen, but I looked at Mary. She was looking back at me. I wanted to kiss her again. I wanted her to kiss me again. Her eyes flicked to my lips, and I mustered all the courage I had. Knowing my odds were good made it possible for me to be bold.

"Can I kiss you?" I whispered.

She was already leaning closer, and her reply had scarcely left her mouth before her lips fell on mine.

It occurred to me that my hands were free, so I worked my left hand behind her back as my right cupped her face to mine. I felt a hand tangle into my hair as another held my side under my rib cage. Even as I leaned back she followed me another couple inches and kissed me again. The pounding of my heart made me want to fold in on myself, and I pulled her in with me.

Over time, I found myself desperate for her to explore, but she hardly moved. Her hands never strayed to my most sensitive places, and I would never do so either without permission.

Permission. That was it. I sat back and caught my breath. I had to practically bend backwards over the armrest but she gave me space. Her hand fell to my shoulder, and she sat back as I chewed my lip..

"Can I touch you?"

I feared she would ask me to elaborate or explain myself further, but she whispered yes.

I thought I was being bold, trailing my hand to her chest as she leaned in again, but she was intent on outdoing me as her left hand fell on the inside of my thigh, much further north than before.

I whimpered into her kiss as her thumb brushed my sex through my leggings. Her hand on my back had worked itself up under my shirt to pick at my bra strap. I could hardly focus on what I wanted to touch because she pressed my buttons perfectly. Like, since when was my lower back a fucking erogenous zone? I scarcely had time to wonder before she took her hand out from under my shirt and held the back of my neck instead.

I was out of my depth. If this was a competition I was losing, I suppose I was lucky it wasn't. I released her lips and rested my head on her shoulder as she pressed against me through the bothersome fabric. I was losing control of my breathing, in addition to my sense of self. To my bewilderment rather than escalating, she pulled the hem of my shirt back down and wrapped her arms around me in a simple hug.

She giggled as I groaned in frustration.

"What's up, Addie?"

I could tell she was being coy again, and it made me want to make a show of pouting. She ran the tips of her fingers under the collar of my shirt before resuming back rubs and resting her other hand on my knee.

I took my time catching my breath and squirmed far enough out of her lap that I could get my left hand out from behind her back. How was I supposed to ask? I wanted to take our clothes off and do some heavy petting, but asking flat out was absurd. I grabbed the hem of her shirt, but before I had even pulled, her hand covered mine.

"Ah ah ah," she sang, "use your words."

I sat back and gave her my best pouty face. She smiled but was otherwise unmoved.

"Can we... do it?"

"Do what?"

I kicked my feet and went back to the drawing board as she giggled and shook her head. I couldn't remember ever being this worked up before. Part of me felt sure she wanted to continue too, but her insistence on making me ask explicitly gave me pause. Was this a test? Now that I could somewhat focus, I spun scenarios in my head. If she said no, it wasn't like Mary would kick me out. We would probably rewind the movie and hang out while I agonized over the sting of rejection, but her body language told me she was on board. Hell, we had presumably done this song and dance to some degree when I was tipsy the other night.

I fought my hazy memory to remember what she said. At the bar, she'd asked, "Can I kiss you" and the whole night, I think the questions followed that energy. I grew accustomed to saying yes and being richly rewarded for it. Now, however, something was different. She needed me to be the one to ask because knowing I'd agree to anything wasn't enough anymore.

My heart dropped as I realized how justified she was. If she thought I only said yes because alcohol compromised me, she might be dealing with a weight of guilt.

Her hand was moving on my back again. I guess I was an open book after all because I had failed to hide my distress.

I hyped myself up, did everything I could to be sure she would say yes, rehearsed my proposition in my head, and turned to meet her eye.

"Would you like to g-get out of our clothes and h-have s --" I choked on my words. God, this was embarrassing. I'd never had to ask before.

"Sex," I whispered at last.

I heard her hum and she beamed at me. Her smile was so radiant I almost believed I would be okay if she said no. I mean, of course, I wouldn't. It would shatter me. But that wouldn't happen, right?

The seconds dragged, and for some reason, she was waiting on me. Had she said no after all? What did she say? Why wasn't she moving?

She tilted her head. "Please?"

"What?"

Realization flashed on her face, and she half laughed as she shook her head.

"I said yes. Would you grab me that bowl?"

I complied despite my confusion. I held the bowl in my lap as she pulled off her rings one at a time and dropped them into it. The sound gave me flashbacks to the night before last. Or was it last night? Had I *really* slept since I'd felt her touch? Anyways, I loved her rings, and her hands were alien without them. Still, I knew I'd want the ornaments off for this next part.

"Would you like to take the lead?" She took the bowl from me and placed it on the side table.

"Oh, yeah I can- uh. Yeah."

I fumbled with the bottom button of her shirt. When she didn't stop me, I crawled off her lap. She stood up as well and flicked the TV off before resting her hands on my hips. Part of me wanted to keep kissing her while I worked, but I knew I did not do multitasking. Still, the way her hands wandered made me want to rip her shirt open. I could learn to sew buttons right? I got the bottom button, changed my mind, and started working from the top down.

My eyes hung on every inch of skin I revealed, and I stalled when I got the last button open.

She pulled her shirt off her shoulders and dropped it on the couch before returning her hands to my hips. I considered working on her belt, but I guided her hands to the hem of my shirt. Rather than make me ask again, she dragged it up and over my head for me.

I struggled to figure out her belt, her lips on my neck didn't help, but she did assist me. She must have hit a hidden button, and it made a sound like a zip tie as it loosened. By the time it joined our tops behind the couch with a muffled thud, I no longer cared how it worked. I was in familiar territory as I unbuttoned her jeans and worked my fingers under the waistband. Once I had pushed them off her hips, I knelt and helped pull them from the cuff and she did the same for my leggings. Soon we were in nothing but our bras and socks.

I stepped toward her again and met her lips in a brief kiss. I shivered as she found the clasp of my bra, and she pulled back to look at me.

"Are you cold?"

"A little..." I pulled myself to her in a greedy attempt to steal some warmth, and, to my delight, it worked like a charm. Still, I couldn't be sure if she was creating the heat or me.

It was peculiar; it wasn't like I was warming myself or she was physically hot to the touch, but it felt like a weightless blanket dropped over me and blocked out any sense of cold. I could feel the air from the fan, but now it was balmy.

"Better?"

"W-what? How --"

"I'll tell you later."

With a flick of my clasp, the thought was completely out of my mind.

I undid hers a little less deftly, and she tossed our respective bras out of sight as she pulled me to her again.

"I bet nobody has ever gone down on you." we swayed as she slipped an arm around the small of my back. I shuffled, unsure where to put my feet as she pulled our hips together and eased her knee between mine. I'd never wanted to stand this close to someone before.

"N-no."

"May I?" She raised an eyebrow.

Before I could stop myself, I blurted, "I thought I was taking the lead?"

She raised both eyebrows and laughed as I dragged a hand down my face.

"You m-may."

I flushed as she guided me to sit, knelt between my legs, and eased my knees further apart. I could have still worn a shirt for this, but I tried not to be sour. I wasn't much to look at, but the way her eyes lingered communicated a difference in opinion. I loathed being seen, but I'd loathe even more to risk putting her off.

"Shouldn't we put down a blanket or towel or something?"

"Suddenly concerned about the upholstery?"

She scooted forward and situated herself between my knees. Her breath was on my skin now and speech was becoming very difficult.

"K-kinda? I'd feel bad --"

I gasped as she pressed her hand to my sex. I had the vague sense she enjoyed seeing me out of sorts, and I was still trying to continue my thought when she spoke up.

"Relax, the cushion covers are washable."

"O-oooh."

My response turned undignified as she moved her hand and nestled her face closer between my thighs.

I flailed, completely robbed of dignity, as she dragged my hips closer. I couldn't even brace myself on the floor because she had lifted my thighs onto her shoulders. I spread my legs further in hopes of catching myself but I couldn't reach the ground past her arms.

"Put your foot here."

She directed my right foot down to rest on her leg as she situated my left on her shoulder. My nail beds already protested how tightly I was holding the couch cushion.

Fuck. She hadn't even started yet.

"Comfy?"

"Yeah." I lied. She probably wasn't convinced either but it seemed to be enough for now.

She sat like that a while longer, rubbing the tops of my thighs until I took my cue to loosen up a bit.

Just as I figured out how to lean back into a pillow, she kissed the inside of my thigh.

I'm not a virgin. I *knew* that the inside of my thigh was an erogenous zone. My body, however, decided this was big and important news.

"If you keep fidgeting I might have to restrain you."

She punctuated the threat with another kiss, closer to the mark this time. My face burned. The one time I'd been tied up before had been an absolute disaster, it had quite literally ended the relationship. Now though, the terror was tempered with perverse excitement. Regardless, the threat worked and I composed myself.

I felt pride in my composure for perhaps a full second before I felt a pinch. At least she didn't scold me as she looked up.

"You bit me!"

"It was a nibble."

"It was teeth!"

"Did it hurt?"

"No-ah!" I flinched again as she made a quick move to nip again. This time she only brushed her teeth across my skin.

"Shhhhh I'll kiss it better."

I let her pull my leg back toward her and true to her word, she planted a kiss on the tortured spot.

She lifted my leg and met my eye this time as she turned a kiss into another gentle bite. I struggled to stay still as she held me there. Goddamn did I feel that.

"Good girl." she cooed and rested my foot back on her thigh.

I expected a "was that so bad?" but instead she stroked the underside of my left leg. This earned her yet another spasm.

"*Do* I have to restrain you?"

"Goddamn it Mary, I'm ticklish! You can't brush your fingers as light as a feather and expect me not to squirm!"

She sighed. "I will exercise some patience."

"*Thank* you!"

"My fingers will be more familiar, no?"

She didn't wait for my response before nudging her knuckles between my labia. Thank god I wasn't ticklish there. I jumped and bounced on the cushion, but she followed the motion and her touch was only pressing harder when gravity brought me back to her.

My hips rolled toward her but rather than teasing me, she rewarded the movement with firm pressure. She waited for me to pull back and pressed again, easing a finger in. My heavy sigh was cut short as I felt her shoulder slide under me. For some reason, my stupid idiot hips rocked into her face as I felt her lips, but she only giggled and pulled down on my thighs. Why had I been surprised? I was given every possible explicit warning that this would happen and yet I locked up again. I wasn't tense due to discomfort, quite the opposite. I wanted to struggle against her, I wanted to be held down. I wanted to be helpless, pulling and thrashing without communicating the slightest discontent.

I wasn't made to feel embarrassed. She eased her finger deeper and nudged my clit with her lips. She pressed slow and firm only a few times before sitting back and rubbing her other hand over the outside of my thigh.

"How does that feel?"

"Go-od." My voice was shaky and choked. Unable to push against her, I could only push against myself and tensing like that tended to preclude talking.

Again I feared she would pry for an articulate response but instead she curled her finger. She held my hips down until I relaxed enough to give her space before licking again.

"Oh fuck!" I tensed again, leaning toward her as she gave me another small rest.

"And how about that?"

"Jesus Christ, you're going to kill me."

"Wouldn't it be a lovely way to go?"

I didn't have a chance to remark before she resumed her attention.

I stopped trying to hold myself up. That was too much fuss. Somehow the beckoning motion she made with her fingers ripped the air from my lungs. I wanted to talk. God did I want to speak but for some reason she deserved better than profanity, and all other words were unavailable.

She pressed her mouth tighter and then she sucked. That was fucking weird. And while she had me out of sorts with that, she dragged her tongue across my clit. She kept pausing anytime I tensed my legs, so we found a compromise in me slumping and arching my back. I was about to fall off the couch into her lap, but she made no complaint.

Honestly, I don't know what she did after that. All I know is when she added a finger, she really figured out her strategy. Every sensitive place seemed to get attention and for all my curiosity I didn't have the coordination to sit up.

I was utterly fucked.

I gave up on laying still but she held my hips in place. I needed reprieve, but some masochistic part of me couldn't make the simplest effort to get it. I couldn't push her face away, I couldn't close my legs, I couldn't do anything but dig my fingers into the couch as my breathing grew loud and frantic. I tried to pull my knees back but she held me in place.

Tension wound up, beating against my skin as she executed her torturous rhythm. I wondered if this was a new type of orgasm, but she wasn't stopping and the sensation sure as hell wasn't tapering off.

Something did change though, the familiar tells arrived both far sooner and much later than I expected. Everything aligned perfectly. Heat exploded from my core and washed in waves through my spine, searing my nerves and then soothing them as the crashing wall turned to rolling waves. Still, she didn't stop until the pleasure was gone and I had to push her away to escape the over-stimulation.

At last she wasn't inside me anymore, nor was she exploiting sensitive places. I couldn't even feel her breath on my skin as she sat between my legs, holding my knees as I struggled to relax my core muscles.

"La petite mort."

Great, she fucked the language comprehension out of me.

I turned the syllables over in my head. No, that sounded like french. The... small... death. I fought the urge to roll my eyes at the cliche of dying in her arms tonight.

"Only a little." I wiped sweat from my face.

I didn't have time to sit and catch my breath before she was out from between my legs and pulling me to my feet.

"What's next? Strap? Wand? Fingers?"

"A breather?"

She laughed. "Or a break. It's important to hydrate."

I retrieved my tee shirt as she strolled to the kitchen. If she asked, I would say I was cold, but I mostly felt vulnerable.

"I've got a bunch of sodas but it's kinda late for caffeine unless it doesn't keep you up... I guess that makes your choices oat milk, orange juice, or water." She looked up as she washed her hands.

Right. It was late. I had carelessly escalated activities from "movie night and drive home" to "stay the night."

Fuck.

"I also have cocoa if you want me to make choccy milk for you."

"Uh... that sounds good."

I leaned on the bar as she collected components and stirred the concoction. The moment she met my eye her demeanor changed. She bit her lip as she handed me the cup and lingered for only a second before digging in the fridge again. She stood motionless in the doorway, gave up, grabbed a glass, and filled it from the tap. She swayed in place as she drank and I couldn't help but think she was avoiding my eye.

Was I supposed to leave now? Did I do something wrong?

"I also have board games."

I blinked as she met my eye and immediately looked away. When I didn't answer she sighed and set down her glass.

"You seem uncomfortable and I'm struggling to uh... give you security." she drummed her fingers on the counter. "I can go get dressed and I have this nice heavy blanket you can snuggle with if you like- and you're free to leave! But if you don't mind me saying, I'd like you to stay."

I did my best to think fast. I knew we would both agonize over the silence if I didn't.

"I think I need the restroom, but a blanket sounds nice."

She sprang to action and raced to the bedroom. My shoulders tensed as I heard and felt the thud through the floor, but no shouts or answering thumps came back. Despite that, the night felt like a sleepover again.

# 5

## That's Suspicious

I woke up in her bed again. This time I knew it before I opened my eyes. I had slept with Mary. Again. There were no out-of-reach memories and no doubts of how into it I really was. I had asked for or approved every activity.

And speaking of the devil, here she was, nestled in my arms and dozing. She held my left hand to her chest while her head rested on my right arm. How was I the big spoon? I wasn't actually indignant. In a way, it fit the theme. I was holding, not being held. Well, I was also being held, but you know what I mean. Goddamn she was soft.

I wiggled the fingers of the arm she had trapped under her head. It was a relief to find I still had feeling, but the action had consequences. Mary curled up and pressed herself to me. She sighed in her sleep as she squeezed my left hand to her breast, stretched her legs, and pushed her leg between mine. I found my lips pressed to her shoulder as I curled forward.

For years I had sought soft and comforting things- blankets, clothes, stuffed animals- but I wasn't prepared to be addicted to her skin.

As her other hand trailed up the arm under her head to weave those fingers together, I realized.

"Okay, you're totally awake."

I said that with the intent of extricating myself, but I pulled her closer and kissed her shoulder. I didn't want to let go, and the part of me that thought I should wasn't quite awake yet.

"Never said I wasn't." She wiggled her hips as I accidentally squeezed the hand on her chest.

"Good morning," she yawned and released my hands. I leaned back as she stretched languidly and threw off the sheet. She snuggled into me, face first this time, and brazenly groped my chest as she worked a leg between mine again. I squirmed to accommodate her as she wiggled an arm under me and pressed her ear to my chest.

She was half on top of me, but this wasn't pressing my buttons. Well, not the sexual ones. Weird.

There wasn't anything carnal about it. The scant few times I had lain with men, it either set my skin alight or made it crawl. Even as skin contact nearly overwhelmed me, no discomfort or shame registered. I took deep breaths as I struggled to decide whether to relax or revel. You would think those goals aligned, but I was only ready to focus on one thing at a time today.

She seemed to grow heavier as I trailed my fingers over her back. I felt a peculiar guilt as she hummed into my chest. I hadn't really asked, and I sure as hell wasn't doing it for her benefit. This was my greed, my need for touch, but I'd rub my fingerprints away if she let me.

"This is nice," Mary murmured.

She shifted to look me in the eye, and I half thought she would lean in for a kiss. Her eyes flicked to my lips, if I had blinked I would have missed it, but she made no move. She gazed at me as if looking for some secret hidden in my expression.

I followed as she crawled off the bed. At some point, she had collected our clothes, and mine sat on a chair near the door. I pulled on my bra and checked my phone. It would be warm, so I decided to forgo the sweater and only wear the leggings and tee shirt.

It wasn't my best look but I didn't much care what people thought of my appearance today; at least not until I got changed and went to work.

Work...

I don't think my heart beat until I checked the clock but I saw we hadn't slept in as late as it felt. I had plenty of time to get home, change, have breakfast even, and get to work. Work almost always had breakfast of course, it was a kitchen after all, but on days like today I didn't want to run the risk of going hungry until lunch just because the cooks spent the morning at the market instead.

I stretched and put my phone away. If I thought about it, missing breakfast would be less than disastrous. I habitually thought that if I didn't sleep with my CPAP, or if I was in an unfamiliar bed, then I must have gotten absolutely rotten sleep. Right now however, the morning fog had already cleared and I felt good. surprisingly good.

Strange. I was always well-rested after spending time with Mary.

By the time I had my socks on, Mary had on dark jeans and a blue plaid shirt; all layered over a graphic tee featuring an angel giving the middle finger. I smiled to myself as I focused back on getting dressed.

"Do you want to get coffee? I know this really great place."

I laughed and agreed. I wouldn't call a tent within the same building a "place"- at least not in this context, but it sounded like a nice activity regardless. She took my hand after locking the door, and at the elevator she pressed the button for the garage.

She picked up on my confusion. "It's an actual coffee place. I don't even go to that tent downstairs when I'm desperate.

I rolled my eyes. Yesterday's latte had been fine, but apparently, today's would put it to shame.

I hummed along to the familiar tunes until we arrived at the drive-through coffee shop. I'd passed this little outlet a few times, but I could easily have passed it a dozen more without knowing to stop. The brickwork had seen better days except for the clearly new sections around the drive through window where the space had been partially retrofit from a pharmacy or bank style drawer.

"You might not know the difference, but trust me, this is the crème de la crème."

I told her my usual, but she shook her head.

"Nope, you gotta try their affogato. If you haven't had it, it's coffee with ice cream."

"Sounds decadent." I indulged her but had my doubts about how coffee's bitter burnt flavor would mix with sweet cream.

"One shot or two?"

"Of espresso?"

"Or three." Mary glanced at me and wiggled her eyebrows.

"I don't do espresso."

She immediately looked disappointed so I stumbled to backpedal.

"I'll try it! But just one shot probably. I tend to get anxiety attacks on the third cup of coffee and I'm not sure how many of those a shot is worth."

"All good, all good. I certainly don't want to cause you more panic than you are already under."

"I'm not panicking!"

"Mhmm."

She ordered for us, and I squinted at her as she refused payment from me. I wanted to play at being indignant, but I supposed it gave me ammunition to pay for next time.

We parked nearby and ate our ice cream breakfast as adults do. To my surprise, I couldn't taste half the ickiness I expected from coffee. I realized a few sips in she had been watching for my reaction.

"Good, right?"

I scooped out the last nugget of cream and nodded.

"Yes, it's surprisingly good."

"I knew you didn't believe me. I knew you wouldn't the moment you got that vile concoction."

"What's wrong with an oat milk latte?"

"Normally? Nothing at all. But that god-forsaken tent makes theirs with --" she paused to shudder "-- stale drip coffee... You don't make lattes with drip coffee! You use espresso!" she half shouted, as if they would hear her and cower in shame.

I laughed at her theatrics as I enjoyed my treat. I couldn't see myself adopting her discerning palate, but I figured given time, she was bound to infect me with it.

I realized this coffee adventure had been an excellent excuse to drive me home rather than risk having her offer denied out of politeness or some notion of convenience. The gesture felt warm, perhaps even overly familiar next to my history with... uh... partners? Was there a less intimate word for what Mary was to me? Preferably other than "girlfriend"?

I hummed along again as she sang her way to my house, and I found myself wishing morning rush hour was heavier to prolong the visit. She waited for me to open my front door before driving off, and I waved as she went. I found she was becoming quite dear to me.

As I locked the door, I realized I had forgotten my sweater at her house. I initially shrugged this off as an excuse to see her again, but *that* thought slapped me in the face.

Thoughts that were innocuous at the time now stood out in my memory. I had accepted it as a date. You could go so far as to say we were dating. I was going on dates with women. And not just any woman. Mary. Intentionally. Not in an "Oh, I didn't know that was a date" way, but interested and eager to participate in that context. I had been thinking forward too. To the next date, the next time of any and everything. I wanted there to be a "next", for crying out loud! When in my entire life had I wanted another date with anyone?

My train of thought escaped me, so I fell back on my breathing exercises. It had been a long time since things had gotten this way, but hadn't this been happening since I met Mary? This wasn't like me — me, infatuated with women? Preposterous.

I kicked my boots off a little harder than was necessary, causing them to thunk against the wall next to the door. I frowned at the line of shoes, now more of a pile. This was practically a tantrum. And for what? Mary? I took a deep breath and scanned my house for things to distract me. I listed furniture items in my head, counted green items, and focused on things I could hear or smell.

I knew how to breathe, so I set about getting ready for work. The first thing I had to do was remove things that brought my thoughts back to Mary. Clothes I wore around her, for starters, but also things and places.

I had to go on autopilot to keep moving. When I got out of the shower I found a message from Mary waiting for me. It was like I was trying to make her inescapable. The absurdity of the last two days struck me; she had consumed my thoughts. Even in breakups in the past, I had hardly mourned the loss of anything but the self-esteem boost. Now I was coloring my entire life in shades of Mary.

I went to respond to the text, and I felt a perverse desire to let go. To slip out of my anxiety and respond how I wanted to. She was texting me to let me know I had forgotten my clothes, so I texted back.

*We just have to meet up again, I guess.*

I imagined her sly face and knowing expression, then her lips, her touch... Anyways, playing a straight girl as a character was a fun game. I mean, I'm straight of course, but there was a novelty to it? Whatever. Mary is fun.

I closed the message and searched for Joshua's number.

"Hey, Addison, what's up?"

"It's Mary --"

"Did she hurt you? Are you okay? Fuck. I didn't think things would get out of control --"

"No! No? What the fuck are you talking about? Mary hasn't hurt me? She's... Well, she's really cool."

"What do you know about her?"

"Uh... --" This line of questioning wasn't going anywhere good, but I went along anyway, "-- I mean. I know she's a bit of a coffee snob, she likes classic cars and small plants. She reads sci-fi and romance and knows a bunch of good places to eat out --"

"So basically nothing. Great. Perfect. Jesus Christ!" It sounded like he shouted the last bit away from the phone.

"What the fuck is up with you, Josh? You're seriously freaking me out. Besides, I didn't call to tell you how much I know about Mary or whatever. I called to... I don't know... I'm freaking out, and you're not helping! I feel like I really like Mary and I've only known her for two days!"

This time he held the phone so far away I couldn't even understand what sorts of curses he was saying.

"We better – I'm gonna talk to Mary --"

"Don't you dare!"

"This concerns her, Addison."

"I don't care! I told you – I told you that in confidence, and I will not forgive you if you blab to her immediately!"

"I don't fucking know how to tell you-- It's not my secret to tell, okay?"

"Damn right it's not your secret!"

"I mean her secret-"

"What? Does she have an STD?"

"No! She's immune! Fuck!"

"What the fuck do you mean? Immune? What the ever-loving shit are you talking about?" I mustered all the patience I had to wait for his response.

"I'm sorry, okay? This is all my fault. Is that what you want to hear?"

"What the fuck --"

He cut me off. "I practically put you two together. I hyped you up to her, I was sure you two would hit it off, but I was just as sure you would hit it off as friends. Even when you went home with her, I was holding out hope that you knew what you were doing, but you don't, okay? Neither one of you does!"

"You're doing a really shitty job of explaining yourself," I growled.

I heard a sigh. "Let me start over. Literally, everything has gotten off on the wrong foot. If your friendship with Mary is going to go anywhere, we need to sit and talk about some things. All of us."

The line was silent. What did I say to that?

It sounded like he was in a windstorm as he sighed into the mic. "Do you want to be friends with her, or do you want to get yourself hurt?"

"What kind of question is that?"

"Answer it."

"I want to be friends with her, okay? I think?"

"Okay." The relief was evident in his voice. "Let's meet at my place for dinner tonight. I'll get pizza."

"Fine."

I didn't wait for his response and hung up. I didn't even care what time he wanted me to meet. He could fucking deal with it whether I was early, late, or whatever. Fucking hell.

It took me longer than I would like to admit to realize my anger was controlling me. I half expected a message from Mary saying she'd talked to Joshua and suddenly hated me. All I got was radio silence. When did my life get so complicated?

Friday night. Two days ago. Joshua's stupid fucking birthday party.

I groaned aloud as I realized the time. I had wasted my entire reprieve before work on Mary in one way or another. I finished getting ready and stomped to my car. Nothing made sense. How did I develop an obsession with someone in two days and transform my adoration to... whatever this was.

# 6

## Pizza Time

I expected to receive a text about the time or something while I was at work, but both Joshua and Mary ended up giving me space. It was nice in a way. The weekend was completely out of my mind by lunch and I enjoyed a sort of peace until I made my way up the stairs to Joshua's apartment. I'd spied Mary's car on the way in, so I knew I would be the last to arrive. However, I doubted I had made them wait long. Five thirty was early for dinner, at least for us, so it wouldn't surprise me if they hadn't even ordered pizza yet.

I found myself glowering again as I approached his door. They were probably hard at work conspiring about me, comparing notes, getting their story straight. Mary had to be in the witness protection agency, or related to me, or secretly fifty years old.

Joshua opened the door before I could knock. Great. He was actively watching for my arrival. That didn't make me anxious at all.

"Hey, Addison," I heard Mary echo the greeting from somewhere out of sight. Joshua had the decency to be abashed, but she was cheerful.

"Hey." I brushed past him and made my way to the couch. Yep. No pizza. But the sight of Mary made it hard to hold onto my little storm-cloud of agitation.

She handed me the bag I'd given her yesterday, and I opened it to find my sweater.

"Thanks." I smiled. I meant it. God, I was weak for her. This roller coaster was going to make me sick before long.

I settled in on the other side of the love-seat from Mary. I didn't kick off my shoes this time as a little "fuck you" to Joshua. If he cared, he didn't show it. He looked like he had aged five years since Friday. He still had his work polo on, and the reddish blonde fuzz I'd seen on his face Friday had turned the corner toward full fledged beard. I wondered if he was committed to trying it out or if partying and freaking out had done this to him.

He slumped in his favorite recliner and took a long swig from his beer. It looked like he would be patient but he balled up a piece of paper and threw it at Mary. She rolled her eyes, exaggerating a lazy glance at the ceiling before letting her gaze fall on me.

"What do you know about succubi?"

I blinked at her. This was at least an order removed from what I had prepared myself for. I didn't hold back my incredulity.

"The sex demons?"

I'd read enough supernatural romance to know what came next. Now she told me she was a demon monster incapable of love, and I should run far, far away.

I did my best to stifle my budding sarcasm as she nodded.

"To put it simply, my dad is an incubus. I am a human-demon hybrid, a cambion. I'm essentially half succubus."

I looked at Joshua. There was no way he figured out a competent poker face overnight, so at the very least he was taken in by this fantasy too.

I knew my role in this script. I wasn't supposed to take them

seriously. I'd laugh at them, mock them, panic, then listen and believe their batshit claims. Or, in the reality TV version, I would
never listen and be vindicated for not letting myself get sucked into
fairy tale stories.

The doorbell rang, and Joshua got up to answer it. I zoned out
as I heard typical chatter and he dropped a couple of boxes on the
coffee table. Nobody moved to open them. I realized I was staring
at Mary. I had been for a while, but she probably expected that.

Joshua was never the sort for pranks or hysteria. I didn't believe
it, but I decided the most productive course of action would be
to suspend disbelief. Hell, I'd gotten pretty good at it over the last
couple of days.

Joshua opened his mouth to object as I grabbed a slice of pizza
from the top box and dug in. Mary followed my lead, but he grew
more incredulous by the second as he looked between us.

It was worth seeing him continue to be out of sorts, and the
silence gave me time to think. On one hand the, "my absentee
parent is actually not human" thing was alarming, but she hadn't
acted super weird. Maybe she wasn't literal? Besides, if succubi were
real it would only make sense for her to be able to seduce straight
women.

I turned the idea over. Did she violate me in some way? I ran
through the weekend's events in my head, and I didn't feel that trau-
matized. At least not by her. Sure, I didn't enjoy the sexuality panic,
but that was why we were here. This was all to prevent further panic.
The lazy part of me was on board. Sure, why not? My new friend
was a-- what had she said? Cambion? That sounded right. Clearly it
wasn't her whole identity or it would have come up by now.

"Okay," I said at last through a mouthful of pizza, "that's actually
kinda neat."

Mary smirked as Joshua grabbed fistfuls of his hair. So fucking
worth it.

"I think so too," Mary turned to Joshua. "Anything to add?" There was something velvety about the smug tone she addressed him in.

"I --" Joshua looked between us, bewildered. "You – aren't you going to ask for proof?"

"Believe it or not, Joshua, I'm not keen on having sex with *anyone* in front of you."

I finished my first slice and tossed the crust across the room into the trash bin. Mary applauded while Joshua's discomfort only grew. Oh yeah, I could tell Mary and I would get along swimmingly.

"That's not what I--" He shook his head, pinched the bridge of his nose, and slumped in his chair. "I was going to apologize for setting you two up, but now that you are teaming up on me I don't feel nearly as sorry."

Mary shook her head. "What he was supposed to tell you was that before the party he intentionally talked you up to me: all good things, of course, but he conveniently left out your sexuality. So, while he naively thought 'Wow, my friends should totally be besties!', --" She waved her hands for effect, and Joshua glowered. "--What I heard was you were both adorable and available."

I grabbed two pieces and turned them into a makeshift sandwich. I shrugged as I swallowed my first bite. "That's not entirely wrong." I turned to Joshua. "I suppose since you've given me pizza... I forgive you."

Joshua squinted at me. "They warned me," he mumbled, "they warned me not to try to make girls get along, but nobody told me they could team up!"

As Mary and I had a giggle at his expense he sat up again. He managed to look disgruntled for a couple more seconds before rolling his eyes and letting himself smile as well. It seemed his bit was over so I thought of questions I had. I didn't want to let Joshua know that I had doubts, but I couldn't help but feel that some things didn't add up. "Cambion" had to be shorthand for people that just really liked sex right? But why adopt labels of fictional beings?

"So if you feed on sexual energy or whatever, why do you eat human food? The ramen and coffee haven't been an act or something, have they?"

Mary shook her head. "So, for example, I'd say about ninety percent of my dad's diet is sexual energy while ten percent or so is physical nutrients. For me, it's the reverse. I need roughly the same amount of daily calories as any other human, but I have a sort of secondary diet? It manifests almost like an emotional need? Or like a brain chemistry thing if that makes sense? If I haven't fed with a person in a few weeks, I start to get a little physically run down, but the brunt of the toll is emotional. Sexual hunger isn't a comfortable feeling on its own and the accompanying mood changes impair focus and so on."

"Sounds normal enough I guess." That made it sound like she actually knew her father. It easily broke the haphazard rationalizations I'd made. Maybe it wasn't rational after all?

"Do you have special pheromones or like a magic charm or something to seduce people?"

Mary shrugged. "As far as pheromones go, I don't think there have been very scientific studies on cambions. It's not that we are hiding, but there's this huge misinformation campaign going on combined with a stigma that makes non-human folk a sort of closeted open secret. It's hard to tell what is real or fiction these days, even for us living among you."

She took a bite before speaking up again, "Oh! I didn't really answer your question. I don't know about pheromones, but I do in fact have a weak magical charm I could use at will, do you wanna see?"

She must have misread my skepticism for confusion. "Uh, sure." I glanced at Joshua out of the corner of my eye. I was beginning to wonder if I had fibbed a little too close to the sun on this one. Was I just going to continue to act like she was really a magical creature? Was she really? Why would she offer proof if she wasn't?

"Here, give me your hand." She rubbed her hands together and scooted closer till her knee brushed mine.

I hurried to put my half-eaten pizza slice down on the lid of the open box and tore a napkin in my haste to wipe away any grease. I held out my hand and she lifted it to press her lips to my knuckles.

I felt my cheeks flush, hardly a magical response to the display, but when I managed to meet her eye there seemed to be a challenge in her gaze. She lifted an eyebrow, and I felt her breath rush over the back of my knuckles before she lowered my hand to her lap.

The superficial heat bloomed up my arm, across my chest, shoulders, and stomach before beginning to pool between my thighs. Still, that only proved the very normal effect her presence had on me. I took a deep breath and when I let it out something in my core moved with it, goosebumps raced across my skin.

No fucking way.

I took another breath and it came out as a gasp. There wasn't anything superficial about it anymore. I couldn't have worked myself up this fast with a vibrator but she was going to make me orgasm from hand-holding? My next breath was shallow and shaky. If I didn't do something I was going to be a mess, possibly literally.

No. Not in front of Joshua. I ripped my hand back from hers, I didn't want to, god I didn't want to and the residual heat was torture as I tried to be casual about rubbing my face. Fucking unreal.

"What did you do?" Joshua sounded painfully interested.

What did she do indeed... I supposed it could have been some obscure pressure point or aphrodisiac but somehow the better explanation was that she was actually half fucking demon.

What the Fuck had I gotten myself into? Like yeah, Joshua vouched for her so she wasn't dangerous but this was all much funnier when it was pretend. Would she have gone all the way if I hadn't pulled back? I bit my lip hard as Mary scooted back to her side of the couch. Please don't tell him I nearly came. Please, please don't.

Mary took her time relaxing back, she met my gaze, and then her eyes trailed down before she turned to Joshua. "I generated some heat-- just some literal hot hands." She had a giggle at her own joke.

That relieved the embarrassment factor. It probably helped that I had acted like I'd touched a hot stove, but it didn't make me any less worked up. All I had now was anxiety and nonspecific tension. I wasn't entirely angry at her, I'd agreed to the demonstration after all, but I wasn't terribly happy either. Sure, she had helped me save face with Joshua and had let me decide when the demonstration stopped, but the lingering feeling of need hurt bad. I wasn't meant to weather these sensations without someone to hold me through them.

I grabbed one of the plush monsters Joshua had piled next to his couch and hugged it to my chest. Joshua and Mary were clearly amused at the display, but neither was cruel enough to poke fun at it. I gave myself a minute with the improvised comfort object before reclaiming my abandoned pizza sandwich. I scoured my memory for clues but I had nothing. Wasn't it bad enough to obsess over a girl without her also being so goddamn interesting?

We ate comfortably for a while, but Joshua spoke up. "So regarding your phone call earlier..." He trailed off as I shot him a glare, but it was merely a pause before he pushed on.

"Are you feeling better?"

I grit my teeth. "Yes, Joshua. I'm feeling better. Thank you." I stared him down, and he held up his hands while Mary giggled.

I turned to Mary, and she held up her hands too. "I'm just here to help. Josh has this weird notion that my parentage is a dark secret. I thought since he talked you up to me, he must have done the same for you. It didn't occur to me until he texted me today how in the dark he kept us."

"Don't put this all on me!" Joshua whined, but Mary waved him off.

"I've enjoyed hanging out with you, and I'm hoping we can continue to hang out now that some air has been cleared."

She gave me another of her charming smiles, and I wondered if this was what magic felt like. I could get used to it. Other straight girls might get icked out by this, but I, for one, was feeling pretty jazzed.

I realized I was smiling like a fool as my phone buzzed. Out of the corner of my eye I saw Joshua put down his phone and look at me. I gave him my most bored glare as I dug my phone out.

*Remember what I said, don't get your heart broken.*

I wanted to fire back something sassy but instead I spent a minute tapping randomly at the keyboard as conversation resumed. Every once in a while I looked up to see him stealing a worried glance at his phone, as though he was expected to get reamed by a three thousand word essay. At last he met my eye and I cleared the mess of spam.

*K*

# 7

# Spillover

When I got home, there was a neighborhood gathering at my house. I recognized neighbors among the party on my lawn.

I hit the button on my garage opener and the group parted to let me into the driveway. I spied the source of the interest. A thin stream of water trickled out, darkening new parts of the driveway now that the door was open. Fuck, I'd seen water in the gutter all the way to the storm drain.

Despite my frustration, I made sure to actually park my car and turn it off. One roll away had been more than enough and I didn't need to buy another bumper on top of whatever shit was being soaked.

Sherry, the only neighbor I really talked to, spoke up as I got out of my car. "I think your water heater ruptured, dear."

Last summer, the house's automatic sprinkler system got stuck on after a power outage. It had been an unfun and expensive experience, so I suspected this was the same.

Clearly, it was not.

I spared Sherry half a glance before jogging into my garage. I scowled as a neighbor I didn't even know invited himself in behind me. I unlocked the interior garage door, and the trickle along the lower seam turned into a waterfall. The water closet roared, as though I needed an audio cue on top of the water spilling out the seams. My neighbor's warning was too late to spare me from a dowsing spray of water as I opened it.

I coughed and spat as I stepped to the side. Water was spewing out onto the clothes washing machines. What was I supposed to do? This wasn't like the sprinkler issue where I could flip a breaker and presto.

Before I could even turn to address the crowd, the neighbor I had written off as rude stepped up to the door. Water sprayed everywhere as he stood up on the closet ledge and did something to the top of the heater.

"Unlucky. The leak is on the cold end."

"What does that mean?"

"We need to find the water shut off for your house. Do you know where it is?"

I wiped my hair out of my face and nodded. "Hall closet, I think."

This time nobody followed me as I splashed my way down the hall. Furthermore, I didn't get sprayed down when I opened the door and shut off the water.

When I returned to the utility room, the fountain was off. I rolled my eyes as the assembled spectators clapped and dispersed.

Sherry lingered.

"Is everything okay?"

I stared back. I gestured to the waterfall still trickling into the garage, the inch of standing water throughout the house, and my soaked clothes.

She pursed her lips.

"Do you have a plan?"

I pulled my hands through my hair and tried to find a dry patch of fabric to wipe them dry. I pulled out my phone and flicked to my landlord in my contact book.

"Yeah... I'm gonna make a few calls and see if I can't make it someone else's problem."

"Ah. Good day to be a renter."

I looked at the mess and back to her.

"Sorry, sorry." She held her hands up. "I'll be next door if you need anything."

I smiled as best I could and nodded as I brought my phone to my ear.

I splashed my way back through the house as the rental management office rang.

"GOD DAMNIT!" I screamed as the answering machine gave me the after-hours number. It was twenty fucking twenty-three, and they didn't understand call forwarding. I jabbed in the new number and dialed again as I followed the puddle from the living room to my room.

I busied myself picking up what I could; naturally, my laptop was on the floor. Because of course it was. So was a good portion of my wardrobe since I hadn't picked up from the date outfit panic. How had everything gotten soaked before I could get home?

Someone finally picked up. I paused triage to rattle off my name, address, and the problem. They had the gall to tell me to turn off the water before informing me they would send someone out in a couple of days. Fucking days. They were halfway through asking if I needed anything else when I hung up and chucked my phone into my pillows.

I struggled to execute my breathing exercises as I pulled my suitcase down from the top of my closet and stuffed clothes into it. I imagined I could already smell the mildew. I indulged in an additional duffel bag of clothes and toiletries before retrieving my phone.

Joshua picked up on the third ring.

"Hey, Addison, whassup?" He was out of breath.

"My house is flooded."

"Flooded? It's not even raining."

"My hot water tank broke or something. There's a fucking inch of water. Can I crash at your place for a little while?"

I heard Mary in the background

"Mary wants to talk to you."

"Yeah, I heard her. Put me on speaker."

"Uuuuuuh, here she is." I heard a rustle and creak before her voice came through clearer.

"Hey, Addie."

"H-hey, Mary." I clenched my fist. Did her charm work over the phone? This was ridiculous.

"You wanna crash at my place while stuff gets sorted out? My couch has a pull-out."

"Uh. Sure I guess."

I couldn't make out Joshua's interjection.

"I told him to put it on speaker, but he just doesn't listen."

"Never has been his strong suit. Give me two shakes and I can meet you at my place."

Joshua made another muffled interjection, and I heard Mary sigh.

"Three shakes."

"Like, you want me to pick up ice cream for the three of us or?"

Her laughter was musical. "No, just for the two of us. Joshua has had enough treats."

"Uh... okay, see you soon."

"Yup!" She hung up, and I shrugged.

Even as I stressed spending time with her I was relieved by the offer. Mary's bed was a lot more comfortable than Joshua's couch. Smelled better too.

I took my time scouring for further necessities and got distracted assessing the damage. Oh, to be my former roommates: vacating a short month before disaster. Maybe when I was in a better mood, I'd send them pictures to share a laugh at my misfortune. I missed them. Beyond that, there was no fairness in the world. Neither of their rooms got wet. I wondered if that said more about the absorbency of carpet or the slope of the foundation. In either case, I was bound and determined to make sure it wasn't my problem.

I pulled up one of the songs Mary had played as I locked up and ran through my mental checklist again. I set the GPS for a local dive that had pretty good custard. I considered opening a few windows in the house, but I was feeling petty. Nobody had asked me to. Fuck the house. The rental agency didn't care. I didn't either. If they thought two days was a reasonable response time, they could lie in the mildew-ridden bed they made.

*~*~*

I was feeling better already as I joined the line at Benny's. I'd waited too late to ask for Mary's favorite custard flavor, so I got both mint and peanut butter concretes. I reasoned I had given Mary enough time to get home, even if she had hung out to chat for another fifteen minutes, so I made my way to her place.

I was briefly stumped when I realized the garage had a pin pad entry, but when 1-2-3-4 didn't work, I tried 1-2-2-5. Fucking Christmas. It always worked except when it didn't. I shopped for a parking spot that wasn't numbered or labeled. I was tempted to load all my shit on a cart, but I restrained myself. My backpack was enough for tonight, and the wet clothes were the only urgent item besides. I shouldn't U-Haul into her house on my second night sleeping over.

About fifteen seconds after I rang her doorbell, I spotted her jogging down the hall toward me.

She didn't pause until she was a few feet away and waved her key to unlock the door before putting her hands on her knees.

"Sorry... hope you... haven't been... waiting long...."

I shook my head and let her lead the way in. Already, the posters and assorted crystals felt cozy and welcoming. How had I ever thought this was a man's living space? Sure, men can have nice places but if I had spared even one neuron the first time I was here I would have recognized the lesbian flag colored knit blanket over the back of the couch. Oh wait... no I wouldn't have. But besides that there had to have been *something* to clue me in. somewhere...

In contrast to her apartment, Mary looked disheveled. Her plaid over shirt was inside out, her boots had come unlaced, and I wasn't sure they were even on the correct feet. Even in this state, I found her more attractive than any movie star I could remember. Magic sure was a helluva drug.

I held up the drink carrier. "You have your choice of peanut butter or mint chocolate."

She laughed, shook her head, straightened up, and took a couple of deep breaths.

"You know I was kidding about the treats, right?"

"I know. Maybe I'm just sweet on you."

Mary snorted and took the mint concrete.

I waited until she had taken a bite to execute my plan.

"So do I *have* to take the couch or can I beg, bargain, or steal my way into your bed as long as I promise to keep my hands to myself?"

She spewed mint chunks into her hand. Yep, nailed it.

"You've gotten bold."

I stuck my tongue out and took a bite of my custard.

"What makes you think I'll keep *my* hands to myself?"

I coughed but managed to keep my mouth shut. I was expecting some sass back, but I still wasn't prepared. It should have been frustrating to be so out of my depth, but I wasn't afraid of Mary. The sense of security almost made the flustered feeling fun.

I let the jab go and filled Mary in on the bullshit from the rental management company, as well as the general damage. Once we finished dessert, I started my laundry and fished out bedclothes. She looked over the cupcake-themed set and gave me a half-lidded look.

"What do you need those for? I thought you were propositioning me."

I rolled my eyes. "I said I would keep my hands to myself. Are *you* propositioning me?"

She bit her bottom lip and made an even sillier face.

I rolled my eyes. "Okay, joke-free this time. I've never had someone that I liked snuggling with. I don't think I'd say no to sexy times, but really I'm just exhausted and looking for rest and comfort."

She blinked, and her mouth hung open. I wondered if she had been trying to cast a spell on me, but her expression was sympathetic.

She closed her mouth and looked away. "I – yeah. For sure. Absolutely."

I tossed my cup in the trash and went to the bathroom to change. I thought about switching back to teasing or sass, but the energy between us was weird. Asking to cuddle appeared to be more intimate than sex to her, but I trusted her not to consent to something she wasn't comfortable with.

I wandered the apartment while she showered and I tried not to stare when she emerged naked. She changed into bedclothes as well and I wondered if she had chosen her unicorn set to match mine in some way.

Yeah, she totally had. I watched her stroll around the kitchen, rustling in the cabinets and filling a kettle from the water filter.

"Would you like some bedtime tea?"

"Sure, that sounds lovely."

She pulled down two mugs, and I made myself comfortable at the bar while she waited for the kettle to boil.

"I must admit I wanted to pick your brain a bit more without Joshy around."

"Joshy?"

She waved dismissively. "Joshua. I like to call him that- how do you know him anyways?"

"College. We had a lot of classes in common when I was in the honors program, and even after I dropped that we still made lunch a regular thing. He just kinda ended up being my closest friend. What about you?"

Mary chewed her lip. "When I tried out live streaming video games he was one of my followers? and he recognized me at a bar one night."

"Haha, sounds like him alright. You must have been a pretty big deal."

"Not really. I never got more than twenty viewers at a time. It was kinda crazy luck."

"Wild. I wouldn't have pegged you as a gamer."

Mary opened and closed her mouth a couple times and then coughed. "I don't do that sort of streaming anymore, and I don't play video games nearly as much as he does... Anyways, what I wanted to say is that people usually don't just accept the whole demonic lineage thing. I want to check in because, not that I think you would lie, I wonder if you might have pretended for my sake or as a jab at Joshua."

"Oh, for sure. I decided to roll with it initially specifically to mess with him, but you made a pretty compelling demonstration. Besides, the more I thought about it, the more it just kinda made sense, you know?"

She tilted her head. "How so?"

"Well, there was that thing where you warmed me up and told me you would explain later, --" she nodded as if just remembering the incident. "-- and on top of that, it explains my attraction to you."

Her smile dropped. "What?"

"Like. uh. This is awkward. It's not that I think anything is somehow fake? Or that I'm being manipulated? It just explains how I'm kinda emotionally and physically predisposed in a way? I don't know the word..." Her brow furrowed and I tried not to stumble over my words. "So I'm pretty completely sure we would have hit it off even if you weren't a succubus, you know? We have a lot of interests in common and I think our personalities jive. Or something. Joshua had the right idea in that respect. To me, it feels like the magic explains how that can become sexual attraction even though I'm straight."

"I don't mean to be pedantic, but I'm a cambion, not a succubus." Her brow was still furrowed

"Right, but sex is still a big thing for you, right? I just figure there's something about that uh... I don't want to say 'messing with me' but I really wouldn't act this way with anyone else..."

She snorted. "I think I get it. I'm... really glad this is comfortable for you, regardless of the reason, I guess." The kettle beeped, so she poured our mugs of tea and placed the blue one in front of me. "Just... Please trust me that I will never ever use magic on you without your knowledge and consent. It's so utterly and completely against my values. I don't do the whole enthrallment thing."

She looked me in the eye until I nodded. I believed her, of course, and it was encouraging in a way. It was good that I could trust her not to do big magic like turn me into a newt or something, but I wasn't so worried in the first place. If she could intentionally make me orgasm with nothing more than my hand in hers, there was no telling what she could do without trying at all.

Judging by her body language, she didn't like my explanation. I decided, for her sake, I would work at developing self-restraint to overcome her charm. That way, she could know every aspect and expression of our friendship was all me. No supernatural seduction involved. I loathed to pass up the best sex of my life, but I knew my chance at a friendship with Mary would be worth it.

When we finished our tea, I followed her to bed and crawled in after her. Feeling bold-- I snuggled into her chest, nudged one of my legs between hers, and draped an arm over her waist. I hummed my contentment as she ran her fingers through my hair, and in no time, I found myself relaxed and slipping lazily toward unconsciousness.

# 8

# Maybe You Can Pay Me Some Other Way?

It was dark when my phone alarm went off. I was aware of Mary groaning nearby as I disentangled myself from the sheets to go shut it off.

I yawned as I unplugged it from the power strip on her dresser and flicked through my notifications.

"What the fuck Is that alarm tone?" Mary grumbled, and I turned to see her slipping into the warm depression I had left behind.

"It's the drowning music from an old platformer game. It's actually barely before our time, but if you ever encounter someone five or so years older than you, it will give them war flashbacks."

"Sadistic," she grumbled

I hummed my agreement and returned to bed.

"Are you telling me --" She wiggled into my arms. "-- that you set that god-forsaken alarm so much earlier than necessary so you can go back to bed?"

I let her situate the way she wanted and hummed again.

"Usually it's so I can get in a meal before work, but I'd say cuddles are a fantastic reason."

"Ill-gotten goods," Mary grumbled, but she made no move to leave

I watched with mild amusement as her lamps and light strips glowed to life. Finally, after a few minutes of simulated sunrise, the light bulb shaped alarm clock on her nightstand flicked on and grew blindingly bright.

Mary pulled back. As she stretched, I found myself admiring her silhouetted against the simulated sunrise.

"Now *that* is how you do a morning alarm." She sat up on her knees as she dragged her shirt up over her head.

I averted my eyes, but it was too late. The glow of her skin would haunt me in exquisite ways.

I realized there would be no reprieve as she crawled back toward me. I longed for the innocent comfort of yesterday morning's rest, but this was different. She lay on top of me with her nose inches from mine. Breathing became difficult but it wasn't because of the weight on my chest.

I let my arms fall on her back. What I intended to be an innocent gesture was nearly my downfall as she sighed against my cheek.

It took a herculean effort, but I reminded myself how to relax my body. I tuned out my arousal as much as I could. I wanted so badly to kiss her: to rub and tug at our clothes until nothing but friction separated our skin, but I fixated on my commitment. I would be strong for her. I would prove our friendship could be stronger than my lust.

"Can I kiss you?" her nose brushed mine.

I nodded, even as I screamed profanities in my mind. Desire forced its way to the front of my mind as my hands came alive on her back. It wasn't like we were tongue wrestling, just slightly chapped lips brushing mine. Even as chaste as it was she was so soft, and the fact that she was everywhere for me made my heart race. Still, as suddenly as it began the kiss ended. Her touch seemed to linger as she crawled off of me.

I lay paralyzed. The weight was gone but it still felt like some immovable force pinned me to the bed. The shower kicked on, and my mind continued to race. It was a success of a sort, right? I'd refrained from escalating the situation, and she wasn't perturbed. This all but proved kissing wasn't a sexual act for her.

I dragged my hands down my face as I sat on the edge of the bed. Of course kissing wasn't sexual. It literally never had to be. And that meant it wasn't something I needed to deny myself either. I considered googling it, but I decided I didn't need outside validation on this one. I could kiss Mary and still be straight. Damn it; I intended to kiss her as much as we both consented.

I took my time getting dressed as she showered and I made myself at home in her kitchen. I had the vaguest sense her fridge was fair game, but I still didn't feel bold enough to help myself to her eggs and bacon. Coffee was a safe bet, so I inspected the imposing silver monstrosity next to the refrigerator.

All said and done, I was feeling awfully proud of myself as I got the machine bubbling away. Mary appeared soon after and it took me far too long to tear my eyes away from her. Once again, she was topless with a towel wrapped around her waist and she seemed maddeningly content to go about her morning as such. half of her tattoos were covered this way, but I had a good view of the pentagram on her chest as well as her simple barbell piercings and shoulder tattoos.

"A rare treat to be served in my own home."

I looked up and took a step back as she moved past me to the refrigerator.

"I certainly wouldn't want to mooch. If it's okay with you, I'd like to do whatever I can to help out and contribute around the house...

Oh! We should probably talk about how long I can crash, and what I should pay you and such."

She raised an eyebrow and set her bottle of creamer down before leaning against the counter.

"Mkay. As far as duration goes, I think I'm comfortable checking in at... let's say two weeks. I promise not to shoo you out before then. As that comes up, we can evaluate whether to continue the arrangement or find you somewhere else to crash."

I nodded. I was having a hard time holding eye contact. The conversation couldn't end soon enough, probably because I didn't like talking about money. My eyes hung on her piercings and I forced myself to look back up.

"As far as payment goes --" Her eyes wandered down. "-- I wouldn't be opposed to you feeding me every once in a while."

"Alright, cool. I have a few favorite meals I like to make as well as a few ideas that I could make use of your air fryer for." I squinted and stared off into the distance. "I don't necessarily want to commit to making dinner every night, but I could definitely do three or four times a week. Does that sound good?"

"That sounds lovely, Addie. However, I was referring to sex."

"O-oh." My body flashed hot. "I-I mean, I doubt I would ever say no."

"I'm pretty sure you've said 'no' with your body language at least twice this morning."

"I just – I wouldn't want to --" I pulled my hands through my hair, and I heard the coffee maker beep behind me. I stepped out of the way to let her pull the carafe and dump the grounds.

So she'd noticed my hesitation, but she didn't seem offended by it? Still, she pretty explicitly wanted to know what was up with that.

"I feel like to a large extent I'm constantly interested in sex with you, but I'm kinda getting the sense you are all around a very physically affectionate person? I just want to be careful that I never like... draw conclusions and end up soliciting sex from you when all you were trying to do was express affection. Does that make sense?" It was almost true. I didn't want to solicit sex, but the reason had far more to do with me than her.

"That's very thoughtful. I don't think anyone has ever taken it that serious though." She pulled the red and blue mugs from last night out of the sink, rinsed them, and set about fixing us each a cup of coffee.

"In fact, I'm sure I've grown accustomed to seducing my friends involuntarily: so much so that I've developed this sort of subtlety? When I can wink and drop someone's pants, why bother going to greater lengths?" She considered me. "How about this? For you, since you are going to such lengths on my account, I will do my best to reciprocate. I promise to be both verbal and explicit when I am asking you to feed me."

I forced myself to ease my grip on the counter behind me. "So if you don't ask explicitly --"

"-- then I am most certainly either expressing platonic affection or trying to rile you up until I melt your little brain."

My stomach dropped. "T-that wouldn't be very nice."

"Maybe I'm not a very nice person," she cooed and pressed the blue mug into my hand. She didn't step back, though. I hesitantly took a sip as she drummed her fingers on the counter beside me.

"So now that you've fixed me coffee, do you have plans to make me breakfast in bed as well?"

I squinted at her. "Do you mean --"

Her smile turned sinister as she shook her head.

"Fuuuuuck," I breathed, and she giggled as she stepped back and made her way to the bedroom. I swear she was exaggerating the sway of her hips as she stepped out of sight. I should have felt relieved. I couldn't have asked for a better arrangement, but the feeling of unease had only grown. It must have been the caffeine on an empty stomach.

Smelling my coffee helped calm me down though. I had to admit, together, Mary and I made a mean cup of joe.

Minutes later, Mary had clothes on. She compromised some self-expression with the plain black slacks, and matching flats. Her white blouse however showed a peek of the pentagram tattoo over her heart. It was clear she was the sort to take any dress code to the limit.

I realized I had never asked what she did for work. I assumed it was something pretty nice given the upscale nature of her flat. She picked up my confusion.

"By day, I'm an accountant. But by night, --" she paused for dramatic effect and lowered her voice suggestively, "-- I'm an accountant."

"Is that a euphemism?"

"Yeah, you've got to download this meme app, 'In-Snare'. All the kids these days use it."

Seeing my confusion deepen, she elaborated, "Accountant is a euphemism for 'stripper'."

"That doesn't sound like a remotely kid-friendly meme, and that app sounds villainous as hell."

"It's fine, all you do is interact on content you like and the app will curate stuff to entertain you."

"Oh, so it doesn't just sound villainous, it's actually harvesting data for nefarious purposes."

Mary reached over the counter to grab her half empty mug. "Precisely. We'll work on getting you addicted. So the whole stripper thing doesn't bother you?"

"Nah. You probably have a natural talent for anything sexual, and if you enjoy it, all the better."

"I'll take that as a compliment."

"Please, please do."

She flashed me another smile and drained her coffee. I finished mine as she stepped past me to rinse hers in the sink.

"If you have the time, it would be a good idea to visit the front office and get you a guest key."

She led the way out of the apartment, and In minutes I was all set up. We parted ways at the elevator as she headed off to work.

# 9

⧼❊⧽

# Feed Me, Addie!

I almost went to the wrong home again after work. With all the hustle of the day, I forgot my house was rezoned to swamp land. To an extent, I didn't care anymore, and nobody had called me in the last couple days to follow up about it.

I stopped by a grocery store on a whim and picked up some supplies I remembered Mary didn't have. Altogether I arrived at her place right about the time it would be appropriate to put on dinner.

I saw her peek up from the couch as I stepped through the door and locked it behind me. She was still dressed and looked beyond exhausted. We exchanged pleasantries as I found room in the refrigerator for the food.

I half-turned to the living room. "Are you hungry?"

She had the most pitiful expression, and my heart melted a bit.

"Famished," she whined, "I ate so much over the weekend that I was bursting with energy but I overdid it today."

"I got some chicken I could fry up, but it would probably taste best if I brined it overnight. Maybe we could call something in?"

"No. Babe. I mean --" she dragged her hands down her face and gave me a sad smile. "Addie, would you please have sex with me?"

"O-oh. oh!" I stumbled as I rushed to get around the counter. At the very least, she smiled despite her exhaustion. I took her hand and pulled her to the bedroom. "How can I take care of you? What should I do?"

"It's fine, I'll take care of it. We can just go to bed --"

"Let me take care of you, silly!"

She relented, and I sat her down on her bed to work on getting her out of her clothes. I stripped as quickly and recklessly as possible as she looked on bemused.

I forgot myself as I crawled over her. I didn't even have a semblance of a plan as I held myself an inch from her face. Could I feed her by rolling around making out forever? I doubted that counted as sex. I saw her open her mouth to no doubt suggest something, but I cut her off with a kiss. I groaned as she started chewing on my bottom lip, and I lost my train of thought as her hands wandered.

I let out a squeak as her hands found my ass, and I jumped before settling down again.

She didn't bother attempting another interruption and raised an eyebrow as I thought.

"Should I try eating you out? I don't have much experience but I hope I can make up for that with enthusiasm."

She leaned to give me another quick kiss before shrugging and letting me crawl down.

Luckily her legs were still hanging off the bed, so I maneuvered my shoulders under her knees. I scooted forward till my nose just brushed her bush and looked up. "I feel like I've already fucked this up by skipping foreplay," I breathed, and she shook her head.

I sat back to check my nails and realized they had not grown much since I cut them a couple of days ago. That was lucky, not that they had the potential to grow much. I was in the habit of keeping them short for the sake of my nail-biting habit. She sighed as I worked my fingers around her outer lips as I would myself.

She urged me on. For some reason it was exciting to have someone eager for my attention.

"Will you give me feedback? On what's working for you and what isn't?"

"Do what feels right, you'll hear me when I'm vibing with it."

I decided there need not be further delay. I turned to kiss the inside of her thigh before leaning to kiss her sex directly. For her part, she stayed still and relaxed as I experimented. I spent a minute feeling around for all the familiar anatomy before looking up and sealing my lips over the hood of her clit. I heard the faintest sigh as I sucked and rubbed two fingers up and down.

Feeling bold, I used my upper lip to push back the hood, and flattened my tongue between her labia. I watched for her reaction as I pressed forward with my tongue and rocked my head to drag the middle over her clit. She closed her eyes. Her hips swung into the motion, and I pressed until my tongue ached.

I realized if I pressed harder, I'd likely be able to create a seal with my lips over her entire clit. So, I buried my face deeper. My chin dug in. Breathing through my nose grew difficult but I persisted. I nodded along as she rolled her hips. Her heavy breathing became gasps and whimpers. They were sounds I was causing.

"Addieeeee" she groaned. Her hand covered one of mine over her thigh and she held it tight in her own.

I couldn't place her tone between pleading and praising. Perhaps it was both.

"Addie!"

There was something special about how she shouted my name when I pushed my tongue into her. she switched her grip to holding my left wrist and I was nearly pulled off balance as she kicked weakly behind my back.

I only spared a moment to breathe and revel in her reaction. If that was how she felt about my tongue, I couldn't wait to see what came next. I used the index finger of my right hand to press into her vagina. Once I reached the first knuckle, I resumed my attention to the clit. I worked at alternately synchronizing and contrasting my hand movements with the rock of her hips. She was louder when things were in sync, So I followed along to whatever pace she set with her hips. I let her lead in that respect. She alternated faster and slower rhythms until I figured it was an excellent time to use two fingers. I switched to my middle and ring fingers, making a small show of licking them myself, before easing them into her. This time when I reached as far as I could, I found the spongy little pad I was looking for. I rested my cheek on the inside of her thigh, watching her chest rise and fall with her frantic breathing. her grip on my left wrist loosened so I shifted to hold her wrist in turn. I used that as leverage, pulling as I pressed my hand in deeper. I felt powerful. I had power over her. She tried to breathe and relax but she couldn't. I wasn't going to let her relax into these sensations. I didn't want her sighs anymore, I needed her screams.

I watched her breathing as I felt out what type of pressure worked her up. I experimented with pulling the pads of my fingers down and pushing them up before deciding the mystery would do her good. She flinched and gasped as I pressed and dragged harder than usual. Eventually, I was pushing and pulling on every thrust. She was breathing louder, and I hadn't done anything with my mouth for at least a minute.

I felt like I had a cramp coming on in my tongue of all places, but I was determined not to rush on my account. I took one last full breath before burying my face. Even as I kept my hand predictable, I kept her guessing with my lips. She wasn't rolling her hips anymore, in fact the way she arched her back was rather inconvenient, but I didn't let her pull away.

I continued her favorite pace for her as she crumbled under my attention and settled on a simple pattern. She hadn't told me to stop, so I focused on the repetition. Her ankles crossed on my back, her thighs clamped over my ears, and her hands pulled at my hair. I had to appreciate how she grabbed from the root. I committed to bringing her to a finish before I ran out of air, and sure enough, her moans turned sharp as she clamped down around my fingers.

As my vision clouded she relaxed. I took a couple of deep breaths as she released her thighs.

We stayed like that until she stopped spasming. My shoulder and neck ached as I struggled to sit up. I was out of breath, but still I glowed. If you had asked me a week ago if I was good at lesbian sex I would have said "What the fuck? That's private, don't be a creep!" But now... well yeah I would still say that, but I'd *know* that I'm not bad.

She crawled back on her elbows and I accepted the invitation to lay down. She rolled to her right as I lowered myself, and I was startled as she rolled me over entirely to sit on my hips and kiss me. She'd kissed me before, sure, but she was saying more with it now. She held my cheeks as she pressed her tongue to my lips. Apparently, that was how experienced kissers knocked on the door and I let her in as though it was my idea all along. I winced as our teeth bumped, but she wasn't perturbed. Soon, she let me take a breath. Her bright red hair was a halo around her face above me.

"Wow," she gasped.

I echoed the sentiment. She rolled to my right and tucked herself under my arm.

"Are you sure you haven't done that before?"

I rolled my eyes and wiped my mouth as she shook us both with her laughter.

"I think I'd know if I had."

"Well you did a good job. Wonderful intuition. Full marks. Grade A performance."

"You're silly."

"No, you're silly. Unbelievable even... Do you realize that I feed on *other's* sexual energy?"

I groaned and her amusement seemed to renew. "I'm such a doofus."

Her hair tickled my shoulder as she shook her head. "That's just it though. You totally got off on that. You might not have orgasmed but the sexual energy you were spitting while you did that was every bit as intense as it was when I went down on you."

"Oh," I shrugged but my face warmed. "Good that it wasn't a waste of time then," I had been excited by it. making her cum was somehow a perverse delight, as though even giving her an orgasm was actually taking something for myself. I caught her eye, but I didn't understand her expression. After a while, she shook her head but relented.

"How should I repay you?" she murmured, and I rolled my eyes. I tried to think as her hand wandered over my stomach.

"I thought I was paying my rent." She poked me and I swatted her hand away. "Pizza would be cool, a movie night might be even better."

When I turned to meet her eye, she wasn't remotely amused.

"Oh did you mean sexually?" I feigned ignorance and laughed as she shook her head. I genuinely hadn't thought she meant that but I realized that was more my fault than hers.

"Not anymore. Nope. Since you're a stinker you're getting pizza and a movie. Deal with it."

"Oh no." I exaggerated disappointment. "What a terrible fate."

"I could have blown your mind, but no. It's clear your desires are entirely material in nature."

"Hey... That's not true."

"Oh? Well for argument's sake, what would you have had me do to you?"

My face flushed as my imagination took off. The logistics were unimportant, the more places I could be touched, the better. No, the part that was important was that at my most vulnerable she would be there. I wanted it to be more than girls being friends. More than just helping out to be friendly. More than what I was certain this was supposed to be.

"What's up?"

My eyes stung. What was I playing at? Why did I want more? How was this flood of affection not enough? What could I possibly need to be different?

I managed not to flinch as she wiped away my tears. The last of my self-control vanished as she repositioned to pull me into her lap and held me to her chest.

"I'm so sorry. I had no idea it was a sensitive subject."

I let her rock me as she repeated her apologies. I was so upside down. I'd known her for less than a week for crying out loud! I calmed my breathing and I dragged my rational mind back from wherever my emotions had banished it. Romantic longing could go back where the sun didn't shine for all I cared. Everything was fine. Soon, I'd probably be strong enough to weather it, and I was sure it would be worthwhile.

I wiped my eyes. "Thanks, I don't know what came over me."

She clearly didn't believe it, but let it be anyways. I tried to will my mood to improve as I pulled on yesterday's pajamas and focused on what type of pizza I wanted.

My mind raced beyond my control though. She had asked me to have sex with her. She had needed something from me and I'd been able to provide it. I wanted it to mean everything and nothing all at once.

"What had you so worn out?" The question was given words

before I'd even had a chance to really think back on what she had said to start the whole event.

"Hmm?" Mary was still sprawled on her bed, and I felt a peculiar heat flash through my stomach as I looked back at her.

"It's just earlier you said you had overdone it after having so much 'food' over the weekend. I originally thought you meant human food but I'm assuming you meant sexual energy or something?"

"Oh! Right, well my dad taught me a few simple tricks to use mana in practical ways. It's embarrassing, but I actually mostly wiped myself out heating up water for tea a few times."

"You know they have kettles for that-"

"I know," she huffed and scooted to the edge of the bed. "Heating stuff is just one of my oldest tricks and I wanted to see if I could boil water. between you and Joshy I thought I had a lot more spare energy."

"Joshua?" My heart dropped. Me *and* him. Stupid, stupid Addie. It was so obvious, why had I assumed she hadn't had sex with him? Even when she arrived so disheveled when I first came to stay?

"Yeah that's what I call-" her voice trailed off and through blurry vision, I saw her stand. "Addie, what's wrong?"

I huffed a bitter laugh. *I* was wrong. I'd assumed a sex demon wouldn't sleep around. It didn't get much more wrong than that. It wasn't like I had any right to be mad. She wasn't cheating on me, hell, it was obvious Joshua didn't consider her sleeping with me as cheating on him. Sex with Mary was just something he and I had in common. Yet, it wasn't something I wanted to share. Not like that.

Mary had already pulled a shirt on and she rocked on her heels as I turned to look at her.

"Nothing is wrong." I managed not to stutter, but her doubtful expression indicated I'd detached my voice a bit too much from my feelings.

"You're jealous, aren't you." At least she softened the accusation with the semblance of a question.

"Who wouldn't be?" I waved my hands in exasperation. Something about the assertion boiled my blood and I could hardly rein my anger in.

"I wouldn't be, but that's irrelevant. Is... Is that going to be a deal-breaker for you?" she spoke calmly but there was something deadly cool about her tone. I couldn't help but think she was preparing to let go.

Fuck. If I was one-hundred percent honest, yeah. It was a deal-breaker. At least it *would* be if it wasn't Mary, if I wasn't in her apartment and relying on her hospitality. Still, the cool of her tone smothered all the heat of my anger into cold fear.

"No." I lied. It felt awful but necessary. I had too much invested in this to argue. I just had to pray she wouldn't press me. What was I going to do the next time she slept with someone else?

I met her eye for as long as I could manage, less than a second realistically. "It's not a deal-breaker. I was just surprised." A half-truth. My dishonesty was growing dangerously systemic tonight.

"Okay... I'm sorry for the unpleasant surprise." Mary reached past me and grabbed some underwear. "I'll try to be more delicate in the future?"

I felt upside down all over again. My stupid horny brain screamed that I was in the right and that she should do better, but I was far more sure that in truth she had done nothing wrong, and I was yet again causing drama by being immature and closed-minded. I had coached myself not to feel bad about this exact eventuality, yet all of that preparation had gone out the door when she said "Joshy".

"You don't... I-" I took a deep breath and pulled my fingers through my hair. "Thank you. I'm sorry that I'm so shit at surprises."

Mary gave me a half-smile. "I can relate to that."

She walked out of the room, leaving me alone with my racing

thoughts. It was both the kindest and cruelest thing I could imagine. I tried to focus on filing away the tidbit of her also not liking surprises, but many more unpleasant thoughts bobbed to the surface like poisoned apples in a twisted ren-fair game. Even the tasks of choosing pizza and a movie felt out of place and unachievable. I felt utterly wiped out.

Mary's voice floated in from the bedroom door. "What kind of pizza do you want?" I heard the boot-up sound of the TV from the other room.

"I don't know."

"Do you even know what movie you'd like to watch?"

I smirked despite myself. I imagined I saw the playful doubt in her expression to match her tone.

"Nope."

"Must I do everything?"

I leaned against the bedroom door frame and watched her melodramatic act.

"Yes."

"Fair enough." she pointed the remote at the TV and images began to flash across the screen. I recognized a few as movie covers and TV shows.

She made a show of releasing the button and the screen settled on a stand-up comedy act. "That solves that" she turned toward the kitchen. "Hey Wiretap!" She paused and the smart speaker on the counter blipped on. "Pick a random pizza for me."

I rolled my eyes as the lights blinked on the small device.

A smooth masculine voice replied a second later, "I recommend a thin crust pizza with Alfredo sauce, Canadian bacon, chicken, and pineapple."

I wrinkled my nose but Mary giggled with evil glee.

"Get wrecked Addie! Today you get pineapple on pizza!"

"Can't we just have it select another?"

"Nope!"

I sighed and fell onto the couch. immediately, I was followed by Mary, who sprawled across my lap, giving me a full view as she ordered the pizza. I tried to grab the phone but she held it out of my reach as she hit "confirm".

"I'm not going to eat it."

"Yeah you are."

"Fine, but I'm not going to like it."

Mary only stuck out her tongue in response as she grabbed the remote and started the comedy special. To my great displeasure, I did in fact like the pizza.

# 10

# He's Good With His Hands.

"Do you know how guest parking works here?"

I hadn't even heard the sleek black sedan roll up, all the more surprising given the echo chamber that Tristan tower's parking garage was. A startlingly attractive man was leaning out his window, and I realized he was talking to me after a quick look around. I gestured to the spots next to me.

"These unmarked ones are for guests, confusing I know."

He smiled and waved his thanks. When he got out, he surprised me with how tall he was. I wasn't used to being so much shorter than people, even with Mary having a couple of inches on me. This dude was an entire foot taller. Suddenly the "tall dark and handsome" cliche sounded reasonable, if a bit literal in this case.

"Need any help?"

I shook my head as I pulled the strap of my duffel bag over my head

"Nope. Thanks though!"

I nudged the trunk closed and led the way across the parking garage to the elevators.

He gestured for me to step in first.

"What floor?" I shifted my bags around so I could reach the button pad.

"Fifth. Thanks."

I got the right button on the second try and stood back to give him some space.

"Pretty nice place right?" He mused.

I nodded but I didn't trust myself to manage a more articulate response. If he minded, he didn't make it my problem. We stepped out, and I waved goodbye, but after a moment's pause I realized he was going the same way as me.

The paranoid part of me filled with dread as we passed door after door and I tried to be subtle about walking a little faster. Mercifully, he made no effort to keep up. I hoped he would find his destination before I did, but as I stood outside Mary's door, he continued to approach. I tried to keep my breathing calm as I set down my tote bag and reached for my mace. Naive as I may be, I knew pretty didn't mean innocent. He stopped about ten feet away.

"Are you Addison?"

I flicked the cap and held it out of his sight. After a long pause, he must have noticed my discomfort.

"I'm so sorry, hi, I'm Cyrus, Mary's friend."

I blinked a couple of times before forcing myself to relax.

"You're early," I murmured, and he held his hands up.

"Again, so sorry. Can I help you carry those in?"

"Yeah... Thanks."

I waved my card and held the bottom of the door with my foot as he picked up the tote and backpack I had set down.

"Hey, Addie- Cyrus!"

Mary threw her arms up and ran forward into Cyrus' embrace.

"You've gotten so tall!"

I looked from Mary, up to Cyrus. We were in our late twenties. His growth spurt had to have ended a full decade ago.

He placed the bags down, and I rolled my eyes as Mary hung off his shoulders. I busied myself dragging the lot to the bedroom as she asked him about his drive and I tried not to brood. I knew she would have other intimate friendships, but in my euphoria, I had entertained the idea I was special over the last week. I felt pretty stupid getting upset about being so wrong when I had no reason to believe I was different in the first place.

Finding out Mary and Joshua still slept together a couple of days ago softened the blow a bit, but it would be nice if I wasn't making it about me for a change. I took my time filling up the space Mary made for me in the closet, but I made the mistake of letting my thoughts wander. I caught myself breathing heavily through clenched teeth. I'd already leapt through half a dozen negative assumptions of both Cyrus and Mary and externalizing my frustration into my innocent (if inanimate) wardrobe was not helping in the slightest. I tried to rub some of the tension out of my brow and abandoned my half un-packed duffel bag. Clothes would be there later. I needed out of my own little world now. I still felt tense as I returned to the living room, but that was hardly unusual.

I forced myself to appraise Cyrus in a new light. Mary's skin looked like alabaster compared to his medium-dark skin tone. While Mary had wavy red hair, his was short, black, and tightly curled. His eyes were almost as dark as hers. Strange. I hadn't thought about how oddly dark her eyes were until now. Mary was only a little taller than me but I felt like he towered over both of us. I focused in on the conversation as Cyrus turned to me.

"Addison helped me find my way up. I'd forgotten how poorly laid out the place is since they apparently reorganize the parking garage every other month."

I managed a wane smile. I wanted to make small talk and get over myself, but I couldn't think of anything to ask that I didn't already know. Mary had told me he lived a few hours away in a big city, worked in graphic design for a basketball team, and was visiting to get away for a bit. I even knew the tentative agenda Mary had whipped up, but I was still on the fence about how much I wanted to participate.

My only nagging question was the one Mary thought was a non-issue. Were we all supposed to share one bed? Should I have been talking to Joshua about making other arrangements for the next few days? Who knows!

Even though Mary and I had bonded quickly, the scope and breadth of her established relationships intimidated me. She had to have known Cyrus and Joshua for years, but there was no way to tell how long. She acted just as familiar and cozy with me as she did with them. I felt like an imposter slipping into this intimate aspect of her life where they had each no doubt built more meaningful relationships.

This line of thought wasn't doing me any favors though. I had to focus on Cyrus out of the context of Mary. He was handsome, kind, already more self-aware than Joshua, and he had a more developed sense of style. I realized I was kinda interested in knowing more about him after all.

"Mary told me you do graphic design for the Tornados. Is it likely that I've seen your work?"

"Not really." He scratched the back of his head. "Even if you watch the games, none of my stuff appears on TV. I do the local billboards but mostly I'm like the little weirdo they keep on hand for when they want pretty name cards for their parties, or snappy tee-shirts to give out at events."

"Sounds like a handy gig. Do you do any art for recreation?"

"Yeah actually!" He became suddenly animated. "I did that

painting above the computer desk, and the pitchers Mary uses for her utensils are part of the dining set I made her."

My heart skipped a beat as he smiled. It was hard to believe someone so pretty was friendly and talented. I mean, of course, Mary was a sweetheart. She proved she had excellent taste. But if you told me Cyrus was a supermodel, the big surprise would be how his car was only worth five times as much as mine.

"So I've seen your work after all."

I glanced to the kitchen to re-appraise the pitcher he had mentioned. It was distinctly hand-made, but by no means amateur work. He shrugged good-naturedly when I turned back.

"If you're a fan, I've got a storage container full of it that you are so welcome to pilfer."

My eyes widened. "How? Why? Of course I want to look! What other media do you work in?"

Mary laughed. "You name it I'm sure he's done it. However, most of that space is spartan but *very* functional furniture."

Cyrus rolled his eyes. "I had a phase where I found ring plates and assorted rope tie-downs aesthetically pleasing. Mary found and voraciously commissioned me when the BDSM community ah... discovered me."

My eyes flicked to the dining room furniture. I'd asked about the strange handles on the sides of the chairs. Mary's invitation to familiarize me with them had caused me no small amount of anxiety.

Mary followed my gaze and grinned maniacally.

"I know what you're thinking." Mary pointed to the dining set. "But those aren't his."

"Then what --"

She nodded to the bedroom. I remembered the bed could fold up against the wall, and the decorative loops on the headboard and under the bed matched those on the footlocker, dresser, and nightstand. I rubbed my eyes and shook my head.

"I have to admire the construction I guess."

Mary laughed harder as Cyrus gestured helplessly.

"In my defense, I was very confused when she commissioned the bed. I merely worked off her specifications."

"How did you go from kink furniture to graphic design?"

Mary wheezed with laughter and slapped the counter as Cyrus put his forehead in his hands. Once she had calmed down, he spoke up. "One of my customers was the coach of a certain basketball team."

"Aaaah. Nice, nice."

"Mary told me you work in a test kitchen, but she didn't tell me how she met you. It wasn't one of those human dinner platter things was it?"

I rolled my eyes as he managed to prolong Mary's giggle fit.

"I met her through a mutual friend. She took me home from the birthday party."

He raised an eyebrow. "Well, that's not terribly wild."

"No," Mary gasped, "the wild part was that I was her first girl, and she came back the next day for more!"

I scowled and folded my arms but it was Cyrus's reproachful look that sobered her.

"Sorry, that wasn't very charitable of me. She would tell you I utterly seduced her, and then swiftly pulled her under my wing."

I rolled my eyes. "It's an oversimplification of events but essentially, yes."

"That's not so bad. Sorta sweet."

Mary looked like she wanted to argue but decided to relent instead.

"Subject change!" she announced, "Who's ready to go on a bar crawl bender?"

I weighed my options. I didn't want to spend the evening alone and watch them stumble in after midnight drunk.

I closed my eyes and nodded. "Should I drive? Or do y'all want to hoof it and hail cabs?"

Mary bounced in excitement. "We're all getting drunk, and that means we're hoofin it baybee!"

I rolled my eyes and went to collect my jacket

Mary led the way out, and I recognized a few of the names of the places she hoped to go. We had gone on one of these trips on a work night last week right after I started living with her, and we both ended up sick. For all our sakes, I hoped Cyrus was either a moderating factor, or that we'd find some other reason to show restraint.

The restaurant Mary led us into had a bar, but we were led to a table instead. I stared blankly at the menu as Mary ordered appetizers and Cyrus chose drinks.

"Are we eating dinner here or something?"

Mary patted my leg under the table, a little closer to the inside of my thigh than I would have liked given how many people were around. "Just some little munchies. I figured we would eat at one of Cyrus's favorite holes in the wall after this, but I wasn't about to let you drink on an empty stomach."

"It's not a hole in the wall," Cyrus grumbled, to which Mary raised an eyebrow.

"It's a kitchen. In a wall. With a bar to sit at on the street. How could it be any more literal?"

Cyrus rolled his eyes. "Physically it may be a hole in the wall, but emotionally it is a respectable establishment."

Mary turned to me. "He should be grateful I didn't call it the grease riddled junk it is."

"Oh. I thought you were talking about the sushi place."

"Nope, the burger joint."

Cyrus drummed his fingers on the table. "That would make more sense for drunk food I suppose. Does that sound good to you?" He turned to me and I stiffened, partly because of Mary's hand squeezing my thigh.

"Mhmm." I didn't trust myself with words, but that was probably more Mary's fault than his. Or was it mostly his? That would make more sense since I'm straight and all.

Mary extracted her hand and started pushing the condiments around the table. "So what were those drinks you ordered?"

Cyrus squinted and stared over our shoulders. "There were a bunch. Four different scotches, and the others were flavored whiskeys. Cinnamon, apple, vanilla, peanut butter." he grinned at my wide-eyed stare.

Mary recovered first. "Peanut butter?"

"Its surprisingly good, uncanny flavor." Cyrus beamed at us, he looked at the bar and right on cue I saw the waitress headed our way with a tray of small glasses. I tried to push down my dread as I surveyed the eight very similar small glasses of brown liquid.

"Those look... strong."

Cyrus lined them up across the table. "They are. It's just hard liquor, most are over eighty proof."

I blinked at him, waiting for him to elaborate before turning to Mary, luckily she seemed to know what I was silently asking.

"The drinks you like are effectively between ten and twenty proof."

"Is this going to kill me?"

"No!" Cyrus laughed and pushed one each toward us. "I mean, don't try to take it like a shot. Just a little sip, okay?"

"You didn't give me the peanut butter one, did you?" I swirled the liquid in the glass, it was one of the more translucent ones, but I wasn't sure that was a good thing.

"No, this is a lighter, caramel scotch. It's an easy spirit with a lot of sweet fruit scents like apples and peaches with honey. When you taste it you should get some sweet malty flavor as well as wet cardboard and a coppery metallic bite."

"I'm sorry, Cardboard? Metal?" I held the small glass further away from my face. "That sounds vile."

"More like it tastes like wet cardboard smells. Has the papery wood product vibe going. Give it a shot." He used that goddamn charming smile. I guess I would drink paper pulp for a pretty face.

I narrowed my eyes. "Is this a test? Is this like the zodiac thing that Mary does where she reads deeply into... stuff?"

I scowled as he declined to say more and copied Mary after she smelled hers and then took the tiniest sip. It didn't smell bad, it smelled really good actually but not like something that should be consumed. Like, you can appreciate the smell of fresh-cut wood without wanting to lick it.

I avoided Cyrus's gaze as I took a sip. I pursed my lips as I tried to calmly put it back. "It uh... that is a flavor."

"You hate it." He said it like a statement of fact, but the smile helped me feel there was no judgment. He took the small glass and drank half of what remained.

"Hate is a strong word."

"It's a strong drink." Mary nudged me and I rolled my eyes.

"I don't know. I like the wood flavor I guess. I don't know what you could have meant by light and caramel though. It made my tongue sting and now it's like it's numb but not."

Mary took her turn with it as I gave the other glasses a wary glance.

Cyrus prodded at the remaining glasses absently. "Did you get the apples? Or honey and vanilla?"

"Maybe apple wood." I searched for a more delicate description than the wood and pain I had tasted.

He slid me another. "This one is my favorite. It's aged a little longer and picks up a lot more complexity because of that. I like it because it smells like peat smoke, baked apples and vanilla along-side a briny smoked fish smell. It can also smell like burnt tobacco or rubber."

"Those don't sound like they mix well."

"They don't mix, they exist together. Anyways, that's just the nose. The flavor is more like the char from steak that evolves into a caramel ocean spray, varnish, and then finally orange and cherry."

"Did Willy Wonka make this? Am I gonna turn into a wooden barrel after a four course whiskey?"

"Har har. Let me know what you think."

I sipped and coughed, earning a sympathetic laugh from both of them. It was certainly different in that it wasn't remotely sweet. "That one goes straight to my nose." I swirled the glass and watched the liquor run back down.

"Any other thoughts?"

"Oh! Uh. I got the smoke, salt, and varnish. I'm not sure I would call the aftertaste fruity though."

He nodded and slid me yet another, I hesitated and stared at the table. I wanted him to like me, but It was hard to say how much more I could tolerate strong spirits tonight. I tried not to seem despondent as I picked up the latest glass.

There wasn't nearly as much character to the smell, but it tasted like someone made vanilla extract with slightly better alcohol than usual. "I tasted the vanilla on this one."

He glanced at Mary and sighed. "I should hope so, given its vanilla flavored whiskey."

"It's okay babe." Mary leaned in and breathed over my ear. She patted my back and turned to look at Cyrus. "I think he was just hoping someone would share his love of the finer things."

My cheeks burned. I wasn't sure if it was because of my performance, Mary's touch, or the buzz from drinking.

Cyrus rearranged the glasses. "I'm not disappointed, I swear. Scotch is an acquired taste, I wanted to see how you reacted."

I wanted to believe him. I *should* believe him because he wouldn't say that if he didn't mean it. Still, it was hard not to think he just read me and lied to make me feel better.

Mary was rubbing my back now causing me to reflexively lean toward her. Hardly a week with her and my tendency to flinch had been completely overwritten. It made no goddamn sense.

Out of the corner of my eye I saw Cyrus lean forward and rest his chin on his clasped hands. He was looking at me again. "So what did you think?"

I clenched my hands on my knees and glanced at the door. "They were interesting. I can tell why they're associated with luxury in the movies and stuff. I just feel like I failed a personality test because I don't taste what you described."

Cyrus chewed his lip. "It wasn't meant to be a test, but if it was it showed that you are brave and caring."

"He means that you're gullible and naive."

I covered my eyes as she had a laugh at my expense. I felt her flinch and looked over to her in time to see a straw wrapper fall on the floor.

"Bad Mary." Cyrus threw the straw at her too. "No putting words in my mouth."

Mary muttered something about mouths as she leaned away to pick up the debris.

Cyrus rolled his eyes and looked back at me. "I meant what I said, thanks for giving them a shot."

"Sure, anytime." I looked up as the waitress returned with a charcuterie board and deviled eggs. Luckily, neither Mary nor Cyrus seemed to mind polishing off the remaining glasses.

Mary picked up and looked over the drink menu. She pursed her lips. "I'll pick stuff out at the next place. They want just a bit too much for their cocktails."

I took a slice of cheese and watched idly as they discussed and sampled the remaining liquors. They seemed to be almost in a hurry to settle the tab, so less than an hour later we were back on the street.

When we arrived at the German pub we found seats at the bar. I sat next to Mary and felt a pang of disappointment when Cyrus sat on her other side. It made sense, he was here to visit her after all.

Mary spun back and forth on her bar-stool as the bartender approached. "Caaaaan we get a lemon drop, vodka cranberry, mojito, and an old fashioned?"

The bartender raised an eyebrow and glanced from Cyrus to me. "And what for your friends?"

Mary stuck out her tongue but Cyrus spoke up before she could mouth off. "I'd like a twelve ounce of the black and blue."

I imagined Mary was giving him a look as she turned to him, but I decided he shouldn't have all of the fun. "Can I have a pretzel and an order of sausages?"

"You just ate!" Mary threw her hands up.

"I haven't had them here." I looked past her to Cyrus. "I'll share if you will."

"If? I ordered-" Mary paused mid-rant to count on her fingers, "four drinks! Did you think I was going to drink them all by myself?"

Cyrus leaned against the counter and patted Mary's shoulder. "We're here to help you with your drinking problem when you are ready to tackle it."

"Fuck you!"

The bartender returned with a tray of small bowls and I zoned out as I watched him work. He pulled Cyrus's draft of beer first, but quickly began filling an assortment of glasses. He placed the red one in front of me, the tumbler in front of Cyrus, and the last two in front of Mary. I took a sip without thinking but Mary squinted at the bartender.

He grinned. "What? Did I give them to the wrong people?"

She continued to squint as she lifted the martini glass of yellow liquor to her lips. "I'm just not sure I appreciate the judgments you are making of me and my posse."

Mary was focused on her stare-down, but when I looked across to Cyrus I could see he was also lifting an eyebrow.

"Was I incorrect?" He held her gaze for a moment longer before rolling his eyes and walking away.

"What was that supposed to mean?" I tried to keep my tone light, but I was still terrified there was an edge to my voice. I wished I didn't need clarification.

"I was teasing." My heart sank as Mary glanced at me. "People joke about drinks and personality types all the time. He's joked with me in the past about what my drinks say about me and I was playing along."

"I think she was wondering about the posse bit." Cyrus turned on his bar-stool and tilted his head.

"Oh." Mary's eyes flicked to me and then pointedly away as she took a long drink of her mojito. "I just meant-- 'friends with benefits' is a bit of a mouthful and I worried that just saying 'friends' wouldn't communicate how important you are to me. Since I couldn't be plural with 'boyfriends', I improvised."

"Friends with benefits?" I raised an eyebrow but my cool demeanor evaporated as she turned to face me. "W-what are the benefits?"

Her knee brushed mine as she swiveled to face me. My leg clamped around hers as she slid her hand up the inside of my thigh and leaned forward. Her breath smelled like lemon and sugar as her hand cupped the back of my neck, was she going to kiss me? Here?"

"Affection and food of course."

I nearly fell forward as she retreated and turned to Cyrus. Fuck. I turned back to the bar and pressed my hands to my face, they felt cool. I leaned closer and found the straw of my drink, chewing it as I thought about everything and nothing all at once.

"Try this one." Mary placed her martini glass between my arms.

I leaned back and let her collect the vodka cranberry. I'd definitely taken more than my share, but she didn't even poke fun at the fact. I took a sip, wary of her doing something else to make me choke on my breath.

The cold drink warmed me. Ironic, I know. It wasn't even so much the alcohol, but the fact that it tasted exactly how she smelled.

"What do you think?"

"It reminds me of you."

And that, my friends, is why booze is dangerous. That wasn't just a failure to screen words, that was subtext with fucking intent. The confidence I had behind the teasing evaporated as her smile grew. Please don't ask me to elaborate. *Please* don't ask me to elaborate.

"How so?"

I took a shaky breath and took another sip. It didn't help.

"Just that you like lemons... and you're sweet."

"Mhmm." Mary leaned back as the bartender returned with my snacks and she snatched a mini sausage before the tray even hit the bar-top.

I ripped chunks off my pretzel as Mary turned her attention back to Cyrus, and for the moment, I didn't feel particularly jealous.

As we stumbled the impossibly long block home, it turned out that while Cyrus knew his limits, Mary and I did not. We hung off either of his shoulders, pausing occasionally to contemplate our life choices over the odd trash can. When he opened the door to the flat, Mary's condition had only worsened.

We made a joint effort to get Mary's shoes off and sprawl her on the bed. I found myself unopposed to the concept of sharing a bed with Cyrus. We had enough space, and he wasn't a stranger anymore. I leaned on the nightstand as he dragged his shirt off and crawled onto the middle of the bed. For some reason, watching him tuck Mary into his side filled me with yearning and that feeling sharpened as Cyrus looked to me.

"I'm... also a bit of a cuddler," I mumbled. I crawled in and accepted his unspoken invitation to his left side. The absurdity of the situation slapped me in the face. Once again I was laying with a man and experiencing skin contact as I had with exes before. He was fuzzier than Mary, of course, with a subtle roughness to his skin. But, at the same time, the long-overdue heterosexual experience encouraged me. No magic charms, just two normal humans trusting and consenting without any supernatural blood driving me wild.

## 11

# Play Nice

I chewed my lip as Mary closed the door behind her. She was going to work (the actual accounting job) and was leaving Cyrus and me alone. For hours. Long enough that we would have to figure out an activity or else die of boredom.

Part of me wanted to ask him what he wanted to do, but I could already see the same question on the tip of his tongue.

"You wanna go to the mall?"

He shrugged. Rather than say anything, he pulled on his shoes, so I went to the bedroom and grabbed mine. What would we even do there?

When I returned, he was ready to go. I knew I should offer to drive, but by the time I mustered the courage to ask, he had already caught my longing gaze at his car.

"I'll drive unless you really want to."

I wasn't usually big on sports cars, and I certainly wasn't in the camp of liking how they sounded or how fast they went. However, something about his made me painfully curious. It reminded me of a blocky silver sedan from an old movie I liked, but it was glossy black and seemed to have an identity crisis regarding its age. The boxy and flat panels seemed at odds with the modern tires and LED lamps.

The car doors lifted as we approached, solidifying the association with the famous time-machine car. How the ever-loving fuck could he afford this? He pulled his hands out of his pockets to reveal the key fob.

"That's a fun trick." I squinted as it made a futuristic humming whir. "Why does it sound like that?"

"It's a party trick. Electric cars are really quiet so they claim the sound is for safety at low speeds like parking lots. It lets people know you are there."

"It's like a spaceship."

"The other sound options just aren't as good."

I crawled in and sat down. I was about to reach up for the door when it closed on its own. The entire dash lit up in blues and reds.

He was still buckling his seat-belt as the car rolled backward.

"Is it self-driving too?" He shook his head and grabbed the steering wheel.

"Nah, I'm fucking with you. I put it in reverse when you weren't looking."

"I thought Tesla's were self-driving if you paid a subscription or something."

He huffed a laugh and looked at me sidelong. "This may be a novelty and an engineering disaster, but it isn't a musky one."

I rolled my eyes and turned my attention back to the interior.

On a whim, I texted Mary that we were going to the mall, and she texted back asking me to pick up some bath bombs for her. Truly she was an addict. She had even memorized the obscure names of each variety she liked and gave me a specific count of how many she wanted of each. The girl couldn't keep track of her phone and keys but apparently, managing bath bomb inventory was another matter.

Cyrus waited until we had traveled a block to turn on the radio, no doubt showing off how quiet the car was. I wondered if he intuited the aspects I would be most impressed with or had been lucky guessing. In particular, I had braced myself for him to show off its speed or power in some way, but his driving ideology was conspicuously conservative.

I almost wished he would gun it to meet my expectations for once rather than subverting them.

In no time, we got to the mall. As I expected (finally), he hunted out a sparse section of the garage and parked so nobody was likely to park next to him. If he had double-parked though, I would have told him to try again.

We strolled to the entrance and chatted about what type of window shopping we wanted to do. I wanted to go to the knick-knack and candy stores, but he was interested in coffee and hobby shops. I didn't want to carry around a bag of sweets for a couple of hours, so we went to the game store first.

"So dungeons and dragons is more like playing pretend than a board game?"

"In a way..."

He seemed half distracted as I followed him past the racks of tiny figurines. A few in a display case were painted but most were bare metal or plastic.

"The way I run games-- ooooh I've only seen pictures of this."

The subject was abandoned as he pulled down a particularly large creature and turned it over in his hands. I waited in vain for him to continue as he completely switched topics to explain why this particular one was special.

Still, for the first time I could remember, I found myself interested in engaging in a man's hobby. It was befuddling. Something about the childlike wonder he had for these two-inch figures inspired my attention and affection. What could I say? It was infectious. I even ended up buying some dice and a chunky little warrior dwarf. Just in case, you know? Besides, he offered to paint it, so refusing would be a waste. He assured me that if we played I could just borrow some of his stuff, but he wasn't very insistent on talking me down from buying my own.

I had an easier time restraining myself from impulse purchases until we reached the toy store. Most of the build-able sets were themed after one movie or another but to my surprise some familiar figures stood out. They were in boxes instead of cans now but the pictures were unmistakable. There were six different colored figures in total and my excitement grew as I recognized names and key characteristics.

The world narrowed as I grabbed the ice-themed box. Though it was clearly the same character I grew up with, it had been improved in every way, and rather than putting it back on the shelf, I pulled down box after box until I had all six toy figures stacked in my arms. White, black, blue, green, brown and even red.

"-- like a hand?"

I blinked and looked up to Cyrus as he delicately lifted three from my arms. I felt a parental instinct try to kick in before I realized he was holding them for me rather than taking, or worse, preventing me from buying them.

"Thanks," I murmured at last as I looked from shelf to shelf. On one hand I hoped for there to be as many of the familiar characters as possible, but I knew these six alone would sting my wallet enough. Any further sets would cause as much pain as joy.

"You're going to buy all of these?"

He didn't sound nearly as incredulous as I expected. Maybe he understood, given his own sort of figure collection.

"Probably."

I did rough math in my head and weighed my options. Picking one or two would be wise, but getting all six saved me a return trip for when the obsession inevitably escalated. Cyrus, ever the gentleman, stood patiently as I rationalized the purchases. Maybe it wasn't important that he knew the lore for me to buy them, but I couldn't bear to have a bad reputation with him. As long as he knew how important they were to me then he wouldn't be disappointed in me, right?

I cast a glance over the nearby shelves, hoping and fearing I would see the familiar evil counterparts, but luckily no other familiar faces jumped off the shelves. I contemplated trying to take back the boxes Cyrus was holding for me, but with my coordination I'd drop them all. The register then. The strongest thing I could do now was leave before I saw anything else. A tactical retreat.

I glared at the cashier as he remarked on the emotional journey I'd just taken and one surprisingly large yellow shopping bag later we were on our way out. The dopamine rush steadily gave way to spending anxiety.

"Don't judge me, I had to get them. It was imperative."

"No judgment here, it would be a bit of a pot-kettle situation after my trip through the last store."

"Hah, I suppose so. Maybe it's not so different? The whole point of these figures is their story." I pulled the white one out of the over-size shopping bag. "It's strange though, the names are the same, and their faces are mostly unchanged, but he's supposed to have a sword instead of a spear. And the shield is all wrong..."

Cyrus poked the edge of the bag and I let him pull out the red one. "All of them seem to have different weapons. I miss the flame sword, but the gold accents are nice."

"Oh my god, I was explaining as if you had no idea, I'm so sorry!"

"It's fine. It was cute. I didn't remember all the finer points anyways."

My face burned hotter for some reason. "Who's your favorite?"

"The one with light powers,"

I squinted. "I meant out of the original six but I'll let it slide on a technicality."

He shook his head and sighed. "Red then."

I exaggerated a gasp, and he held up his hands.

"Your least favorite I know. But I really vibed with the shield power. And, while his leadership skills weren't always the best, I admired his loyalty and self-sacrifice."

I grumbled. In truth, all the characters were pretty wholesome. Painting the fictional character, and by extension Cyrus, as an asshole was uncharitable of me. Besides, *my* favorite, white, was ice-themed in both aesthetic and personality. He was *actually* a bit of an asshole, possibly more so than the red one. Still, I satisfied myself with the fact we had common ground.

"But my next favorite is white, hands down."

I rolled my eyes.

"I'll try to believe you didn't say that just to get on my good side."

We were still talking about fantasy robot dolls while we waited for coffee, and I clung to the topic till we found the next store we wanted to browse. It had been so long since I had shared that aspect of my childhood. It was surreal to indulge in it again. Tolerating my info dumps about these toys was one of the few things my parents had done right, but I had become accustomed to keeping quiet about things I cared about.

We ended up skipping the candy store, (because oh my god, I had already spent way too much), and we chilled out at the food court. I asked him about his favorite tabletop games and characters while we ate. The diversity of characters he had played was fascinating. Interestingly, his oldest characters were female, but since college, he had defaulted back to male.

As the conversation stalled, he glanced at the theater.

"You wanna catch a movie?"

I glanced at my phone. Mary still had work for four more hours, so we had the time. Part of me felt like I would want to wait for her, but I figured if Cyrus wasn't concerned, maybe I shouldn't be either.

"Mmmaybe. What did you want to see?"

"I heard the new Animal Lord movie is awful but super gay."

I snorted.

"Well if it's gay I suppose we have to see it."

"See? You get it. Are you sure you're straight?"

I crossed my arms and leaned back from my tray. I'd gotten too comfortable– been too open. Now yet another person in my life would be arguing my identity. I sighed and frowned at my last few bites of orange chicken. Bye-bye appetite...

"Sorry, forget I asked."

I looked up and raised an eyebrow.

"You aren't looking very forgetful right now."

I struggled not to smile and rolled my eyes as he crossed his arms, mirroring my posture, but I didn't feel like I was being mocked.

"Forget about what?"

"Precisely." He beamed one of his infectious smiles and pulled out his phone. "I'll get us tickets."

\*~\*~\*

When we had finished eating, he led the way to the theater. I tried to follow along as he filled me in on how King and God made peace, but now they were being turned against each other by mind-controlling aliens.

As we settled down to watch, it ended up being even more ridiculous.

I laughed as Cyrus whispered anecdotes to me. He recontextualized their fights as BDSM and their intense stare-downs as loving gazes.

Our hands brushed over the popcorn bucket, and he jokingly

held my hand. But, when he let me go, I wished he hadn't. I spent a good third of the movie psyching myself up to hold hands with him until the film reached its climax.

I brushed my pinkie on his and looked at him out of the corner of my eye. I watched as he turned his hand over and let me place mine on it. My world became his thumb rubbing the base of my index finger before he went still and I relearned to experience my surroundings.

I wanted to shout when the movie ended like 5 minutes later, but he continued to hold my hand as we collected our bags and made our way out of the theater.

I wondered if this is how I caught feelings for Mary so quickly: holding hands as if it was no big deal. Surprisingly, Cyrus held my hand after we got in the car too, though he would drop it for a turn or gesture at something outside.

The drive back to Mary's went even faster, and when he forgot the garage code, I taught him the Christmas trick (seriously, why do people think 12-25 is secure?)

We were still holding hands as we stepped into the apartment, and I froze as Mary gave us an appraising look.

"Fuck! I forgot your bath bombs!"

Mary rolled her eyes but didn't complain as Cyrus and I dumped our haul on the kitchen table. We worked together assembling my new toy figures. It was silly, but I loved that he built the red one for me because it meant I had a positive memory to attach to the character. Maybe I wouldn't pose him getting pegged after all.

\*~\*~\*

My toy figurines were still sitting on the counter two days later as I prepared dinner. I smirked as I noticed the ways they had been posed while I wasn't looking. Blue was proposing to green(a terrible pairing, by the way), brown was giving black a piggyback ride, and white was stepping on red's groin.

I shook my head and cut off the noodle timer. I scooped out some of the starchy water before draining the pasta in the sink.

"Dinner's ready!" I called, and I felt a fond sort of amusement as Cyrus and Mary emerged half-dressed from the bedroom. The nightlife we had been living was catching up with us. For Mary, that manifested as naps she had no intention of taking alone. Cyrus and I had traded off on bedding duty as she got fussy. At first, she would tease me about finally coming on to her, but I never rose to the bait.

I mulled over my feelings about Cyrus and Mary being... intimate. How much did I care? I stopped folding the cheese and bacon into the pasta. Why did I care? I didn't have much time to think about it, so I busied myself taking their steaks out of the foil they had been resting in. I plated up the pasta as elegantly as I could.

Mary perked up as we ate. She always made a point to praise my cooking on the first bite, throughout the meal, and after. I had to admit I lived for the attention, and I glowed as Cyrus echoed and added his thoughts. I couldn't ask for a better audience. Sadly, the happy thoughts couldn't carry for the entire meal. As I stood to retrieve dessert, Mary brought up the subject of Cyrus's departure.

"What time do you intend to head out?"

"Pretty early to beat the morning rush hour."

I looked from Cyrus to Mary as I rapidly zoned out. I hated thinking about endings.

It was silly, but I'd gotten used to having him around. Since the mall trip, we had become physically affectionate: sorta like Mary and I had been early in our friendship. I hoped things would progress naturally toward affirming my sexuality, but I couldn't think of a worse reason to go to bed. At least I genuinely enjoyed talking to him.

I appraised Cyrus from across the table as we ate. In the light without his shirt on I had a wonderful view. He didn't have much body hair to speak of, which made it all the easier to see the thin scars running across his chest under his pecs.

"What are those scars from?"

Cyrus froze, and when I looked at Mary she was chewing her lip hard as she set down her fork.

An unspoken conversation took place between them in front of me. I could tell from the symmetry of the scars that it was a surgical procedure, but I was drawing blanks about what sort of surgery would be so sensitive. Men could get breast cancer too, right?

"You don't have to tell me, I don't want to pry." Neither of them seemed reassured. Cyrus rubbed his eyes, and when he steepled his hands under his chin, his composure seemed shaky. "I... Had a procedure a year or so ago."

I nodded. I didn't want to urge him on, but my curiosity only burned more. It really didn't help that both he and Mary were treating this as a delicate subject. I restrained the urge to start guessing as his eyes flicked to Mary. At the very least, her wane smile seemed to reassure him.

Cyrus sighed and looked around the room before letting his eyes fall on me. "It was a breast removal procedure. I'm transgender."

"Whoa." I breathed my shock before I could begin to plan my response. Immediately my mind raced over how that might have sounded. "I mean wow! That's really cool, I never would have guessed!"

Cyrus's smile seemed pained. Did I say something wrong? I looked at Mary but her expression was unreadable.

"Not that it's unbelievable." I backpedaled. "It totally makes sense given what you told me of your childhood and stuff."

Now Cyrus winced. Fuck. What had I said?

Part of me knew I should just shut the fuck up, but the idiot in control of my mouth decided I could fit another foot. "I don't mean

that you seem feminine to me either- you look and act like a man-"
Mary cleared her throat. Her expression was stern.

Damn it, this was *not* how this conversation was supposed to go.
I bit my lip and tried to be subtle about covering my mouth with
my napkin for good measure. This at least earned the smallest smile
from Cyrus.

Mary leaned forward, "What Addison means to say is that knowing that doesn't change her opinion of you in the slightest."

I nodded emphatically. I was completely out of my depth here.
Sure, plenty of things were special about Cyrus, but already I had to
worry if something about my opinion *did* change of him. Like, holy
fuck did this create a lot of questions, but my original estimation
of Cyrus's infinite patience had hard corrected to him being a very
sensitive and private individual. Even if this was a sensitive subject
that hardly seemed fair.

Cyrus rubbed his hands on his face. "I appreciate that you aren't
freaked out in a bad way."

Mary huffed a small laugh but my bottom lip was beginning to
hurt from how hard I was biting.

He stared at his plate and prodded his pasta with his fork. "I'm
sorry, but I don't think I have the energy to explain everything to
you right now. Is there any way we can just drop this?"

Fuck. "Yeah." I breathed and glanced at Mary. I suddenly had
my doubts that I could count on her to explain for him. Goddamn,
curiosity was going to kill me. "We don't have to talk about it."

If I was honest, that was a lie. *I* needed to talk about it. I didn't
have a handbook for this sort of thing. With Mary, the secret of her
demon dad seemed to be fun for her. With Cyrus though, even with
what little I knew, I was certain this subject had a lot of painful
memories attached. It wasn't as cool and fun of a secret for him as it
was to me.

I looked at my plate. I wouldn't be able to ask prying questions with my mouth full, so I rolled some noodles on my fork.

"So." Mary stabbed at the pasta on her plate. "Are we going to have time to get breakfast before you leave?"

"Probably not." Cyrus looked up at Mary. "Is that going to ruin your day?"

"Possibly." She glanced at me. "I get pretty grouchy when I'm hungry."

Cyrus raised an eyebrow. "Oh, were you talking about a morning quickie? If you don't think you'll be too tired..."

"No!" Mary rubbed her palms against her forehead. "I was talking about human food you fucking doofus."

"Fair enough, You probably couldn't handle Addie and I at the same time anyways."

My mouth fell open. Did he just say what I think he said? Literal seconds ago the conversation was too personal and now he was talking about threesomes?

Mary's face was flushed too, and I wasn't sure if it was embarrassment or excitement. "I could handle it, It's Addie you have to worry about."

"Hey!" I looked between the two of them. Something about the playful smile Cyrus turned toward me stopped my heart. "Don't put this on me!" I rapidly ran out of steam on this argument. Mary was right of course, I most certainly could not handle that, but that did not mean the prospect had no effect on me. Did Cyrus feel that way about me? Surely not. There was no way after everything I had just said. But why would he tease about it?

I found myself wishing he was actually interested in me. I wasn't sure what I would do with the interest if he expressed it, though. I didn't want to burn through a relationship with him like I had my exes, but I couldn't imagine how else it could go. Here I was, interested in a man for once, yet unwilling to risk my budding friendship with him.

"What do you two want to do with the rest of the evening?" Cyrus was looking at me now and I barely repressed the urge to say "what?" As my brain caught up to the subject change.

"Watch something? Maybe?" Typical. Even when I did decide something I sounded painfully unsure.

Mary and I frequently binged video apps to wind down. I had to admit I was interested in seeing Cyrus's interests in that form.

"Mkay." Mary picked up her plate and turned the TV on with a voice command while we followed her lead to clean up after dinner. Once I had the dishes soaking I joined them on the couch.

"What do you want to watch first?" Mary looked across Cyrus at me as I sat down and made myself comfortable. Cyrus already had his arm on the back of the couch so it was almost like he had his arm around me.

Fuck, Mary asked a question.

"Uh... maybe a stand-up routine?"

Mary nodded and searched up one of my favorite comedians. The guy was like a man out of time, simultaneously very relatable while sounding like a 70's radio talk show host.

I remembered this sketch word for word but it was worth it to hear Mary and Cyrus's reactions.

Cyrus chose a tabletop game scene, apparently voice actors played DnD online for audiences and I had to admit the result was entertaining even if I had no concept of who anyone was.

Feeling bold, I repositioned to lay my head in Cyrus's lap as Mary chose a cooking show. I wondered if she was interested because of me but when Cyrus ran his fingers through my hair I didn't wonder about anything at all.

The videos we chose must have been long because Cyrus cut in before I could choose the next video.

"I'd better get to bed soon. Morning is gonna come rudely early."

He didn't move to stand so I figured I had him pretty effectively trapped. Still, I released my hostage.

"G'night," I called as Mary followed him to the bedroom. I burned out my remaining restlessness on an episode of the twilight zone before following them.

\*~\*~\*

The creak of bed-springs roused me from my slumber. By the time I opened my eyes, Cyrus was getting dressed. Mary yawned and stretched on the other side of the bed, and I moved to sit beside her. I rested my head on her shoulder as he packed the last of his clothes and zipped up his bag. It was time for him to head back to Tristate and it wasn't even daylight yet.

As Mary stood and walked into his embrace, I had the peculiar urge to hold him in my eye to the last second. To follow him to his car and run to the street to wave as he drove away. The sepia-toned dream popped as I watched her drape her arms around his neck and pull him into a kiss. For the first time this week, I imagined being her. His hand on the small of my back, and my lips on his. Still, for as much as I romanticized it, the kiss was chaste.

She released him, and he turned to me.

"I'm sure I'll see you again before long, Addison."

I smiled and nodded, but he didn't turn away. I saw the slightest impression of nervousness as he opened his mouth to speak again.

"Can I kiss you goodbye?"

I couldn't hide my surprise, and my mind raced through implications and meanings.

"Yeah."

I stood as he stepped toward me. I didn't know what to do with my hands, so I let them fall on his sides as he leaned to kiss me. Again, it was chaste, but it still took my breath away as he cupped the back of my neck.

When I opened my eyes, he had stepped back. I sensed I was swaying, and it wasn't out of morning bleariness. Mary wished him safe travels and walked him out, but I only managed to lean against the bedroom doorway as he disappeared.

When Mary turned back to me, she seemed pleased with herself, as though this had revealed some secret of the universe and she was about to receive the Nobel prize for it.

I managed to unfreeze, and I turned to look out the bedroom window. I rested my forehead on the glass and scanned the street. The street lamps were still on but the sky was already glowing. After a few minutes, I watched his distinctive black car glide out and away.

# 12

# Doodle

I traced the star over Mary's breast with my fingertip. I wondered, not for the first time, what kind of tattoo I would get if I got one. I was always drawn to how inscrutable the meanings behind the drawings on her skin were.

Tattoos generally didn't inspire my curiosity. Joshua's sci-fi and anime tattoos told you what his favorite characters and monsters were. Other people would have quotes, symbols, or traditional shapes, but I didn't care about them much. With Mary though, the question of meaning burned its way forward in my mind again and again.

"What does the pentagram on your chest mean?"

"It's a protection rune."

She sighed and stretched before sitting up. "I loathe to be pedantic, but the five-pointed star within a circle is actually called a pentacle."

I hummed and sat up as well. As she reached for her toes, I

looked at the sprawling back piece. She leaned back on her elbows to catch my eye.

"I have washable markers if you want to color them in."

"Sounds like a pretty childish activity to me."

Mary shrugged and rolled out of bed.

"If the boot fits."

"Sure, sure. Will you tell me about the rest if I color them?"

She rubbed her chin. "I probably would have talked your ear off about them regardless, but now that you mention it, that sounds like a good activity."

I rolled my eyes and pushed the sheets down as she rummaged in her desk.

"Which one first?"

"Mmmmmm the tree."

She dropped a pack of markers next to me and got comfortable on the bed again, this time with her left arm facing me.

"Apple trees reference both knowledge and learning, as well as temptation and sin."

I colored in the red fruit. "Does it mean anything to have it on your left arm?"

"Not to me. It's just a good size place, especially since I like to be able to easily cover or show it off."

"And the fish below it?"

"The circling koi fish are like siblings to dragon tattoos. That, the pentacle, and the women with swords, are all sorta inspired by my dad. I'm not like-- Intrinsically religious or anything, but I guess I ascribe to a certain spirituality? Anyways, the koi fish are arranged in a yin and yang to symbolize duality and harmony. I put them under the tree to set a scene to communicate a duality between wisdom and temptation."

I took my time adding a sky, some grass, and a blue background for the koi pond as she carried on about her dad's apple tree tattoo and associated dragon.

Once I finished, she turned to show her other arm. She called it a card, but it looked like a stained glass window to me.

"This tattoo, and the one on my left thigh, are both the 'women with swords' aesthetic but this one in particular draws more from the 'Justice' tarot card. To me, the significance is fairness and an understanding of cause and effect: consequences for actions and so on."

She filled me in on some of the other well-known tarot card meanings, but the information slipped in one ear and out the other.

When I moved on to the thigh tattoo, I expected her to sit in front of me or move us to the edge of the bed. Instead, she crawled into my lap to straddle my hip. She held herself upright by my shoulder as I brushed in the watery background and her oddly sinister sword.

"This one is the 'lady of the lake' from Arthurian legend. Her name is Nimueh or Viviane and she lives in a mysterious castle beneath the lake surrounding Avalon. The sword she is holding is Excalibur which she gives to King Arthur."

"Didn't he pull Excalibur from a stone?"

"That's a different sword. It's not supposed to be called Excalibur but the stories get crossed frequently. Anyways. To me, it's sorta like a saint tattoo? Or a tattoo of a goddess? Maybe a mixture. It's a vague sort of reverence for history and communicates a loose adherence of my ideals to hers."

My brain overflowed with Arthurian legend as she launched into the "definitive" story of Excalibur.

When I finished, I looked at the stylized uterus tattoo she had over her womb.

"I'm a little too ticklish to color that one." She made sure not to smudge my scribbles as she crawled out of my lap. "That rune, typically associated with succubi, gives me intimate control over my fertility and sexual pleasure."

"Like... actual control?"

"Yeah."

She pulled up the skin on her belly to give me a better look.

"That sounds sick. Would it do the same for me if I got one?"

She shrugged and tilted her head from side to side.

"Maybe to a much lesser effect. It would for sure have a psychological effect on anyone you go to bed with. Succubus iconography tends to rile some folks up. Even the folks who don't understand the signs are not immune to its influence."

"Now that sounds goofy."

She shrugged.

"I'm just sharing my findings."

She turned her back to me and told me about the night sky on her back. She stretched to point out a few significant constellations before talking about the centerpiece. Two nebulae were colliding, one blue, one red, but their shape was of two lovers in a tight embrace. Where they met, the blues and reds mixed to purple. Toward her shoulders and sides, the deep black faded and bled out to rainbow watercolor splotches.

"Looks awful sapphic for someone who claims to be pansexual."

She snorted and shook her head. As I traced the hair of one of the figures with my fingertips she hunched her shoulders. A sinister part of me knew I could get pretty far with tickling before she stopped me, but instead I added pressure and switched to a gentle massage.

"What does the underlined omega constellation mean?"

"That's my zodiac sign. I'm a Libra and those are scales. Represent balance and all that."

She sounded less certain as I rubbed random patterns: as though the distraction made her doubt herself. I wondered if this was pressing her buttons.

"Is astrology important to you?"

She shrugged. "I guess? It's fun to think about and I get a little bit of dopamine from making connections and relating spirituality to the physical world."

"Didn't you ask me about my zodiac when we met?"

Her pause was telling, it hadn't come up in conversation since, but at the bar when we met we talked at length as she looked up my sun and moon signs after finding out I am a Gemini.

"Yeees."

"Did you decide whether to take me home based on my birth month?"

"I plead the fifth?"

"Uh uh. Too late for that." I leaned forward and pulled her into a hug from behind. "You are trapped and I will have my answer."

"All I'm saying is that if you were a Cancer the conversation would have stayed far less personal."

I snorted and shook my head. "Connections my ass. You are dictated by the stars."

"If you knew someone was a Cancer you would understand." She wiggled out of my grasp and crawled to the edge of the bed.

"Sure, sure. Anyways, why is this tattoo in color while all the others are black lines?"

"Just felt like it. I've thought about going back to color in a lot of the others, but then I wouldn't be able to be your coloring book on lazy Saturday mornings would I?"

I watched her walk to the bathroom and look over my work. "You're pretty good at this," she called, and I shrugged.

"It's just coloring in the lines." I rifled in my dresser and found some underwear to put on while she continued to admire herself in the mirror.

"Does this mean if I got you to learn to give tattoos you'd doodle on me for cheap?"

"Doubtful. My freehand is very unrefined. You've seen my hand-writing."

"Eh. The actual inking is just tracing anyways as far as I can tell. Fair enough though." She returned and set about getting dressed too. "If I learned to tattoo would you let me doodle on you?"

"Maybe. I don't think I'd want random scribbles, but I'd probably volunteer to help you practice or something."

"I hear they use pigskin to practice form, but I could use you to practice magical binding runes."

"W-what?"

"Simple stuff, binding you to my service forever, stifling your free will to make you oh so obedient."

She spoke in a low voice as she approached me, but as suddenly as the tone set on, she dissolved into giggles.

"Oh Addie, you are a riot! I would never use runes to enslave someone. Hell, I would argue heavily against you getting anything to even allude to surrendering ownership of yourself to me."

"I-it's not like I was thinking of doing that!"

"Uh-huh. Suuuure." She draped her arms around my neck.

I tried to suppress my reaction as she trailed her hands down my back and slipped her fingers past my waistband to cup my ass. My hands ended up on her shoulders as she pulled me to her sharply.

The movement was familiar and I flushed as I responded to the association.

I felt slighted by Mary's appetite, not for being voracious, but rather for being almost inconveniently easy to satisfy. I'd fed her last night and likely wouldn't be asked to again for two or three days.

"How often do you actually need to feed?"

Mary wore an exceptionally smug expression. If she was reading into the subject change, she wasn't outright teasing about it at least.

"Monthly."

"How many times a month?"

"Once."

Her smile grew as I tried to process the implications. She'd asked me to feed her several times now so she was surely bullshitting me with her diet one way or another.

She extricated her hands from my panties and clasped them behind my back. "If I'm keeping a low profile then I hardly need sex at all, but since it's ever so easy to get a snack whenever I want, I must confess I've been rather indulgent. Is that a problem?"

She batted her eyelashes, but I knew better than to speak my mind.

"No."

"I wouldn't want to put you out, you just seem *so* eager whenever I ask."

I rolled my eyes and squirmed out of her grasp. I took my time on a retort as I continued getting dressed.

"I'm not put out."

"You aren't even worried about being enthralled? Losing your free will as I suck out your soul little by little?"

"Is that a thing?"

Mary giggled and shook her head. "No, not at all. I mean maybe with vampires when *they* repeatedly feed on someone but you don't have to worry about it."

I was about to ask about vampires when she spoke again.

"Of course, if I could make you my thrall, why would I tell you the truth?"

She raised her arms, wiggling her fingers as though they were claws she would snatch me up with.

I shook my head and pushed my dresser drawers shut.

"You're too nice to do that. Manipulation just isn't your style."

"Or you're unbearably naive."

"Or both." I shrugged and pulled on a tee-shirt.

When I met her gaze again she seemed concerned, but she didn't push further.

# 13

## Accounting

When I got home, Mary looked like she was heading out to go to work. I never knew which job because she always made her accounting outfit a bit sexy and her stripping outfit a bit professional. It probably had something to do with catering to the market, but I had never been to a strip club and therefore had no idea.

"How would you like to make a quick thousand dollars?"

"No. Uh uh. I am not coming to work with you. Not for number crunching or otherwise."

She rolled her eyes and held up a camera.

"I meant holding this. We'll draw the curtains so there's not even a risk of catching your reflection."

"O-oh." I struggled to catch up. "You're working from home then?"

She only hummed her acknowledgment as she handed me the camera. I spied fresh batteries on the counter and wondered just how much work I would be signing up for.

"Can't you just use a tripod?"

"I usually do." She gestured to the camera bag on the bar stool.

"But if you operate the trigger I don't have to run back and forth as much."

She must have noticed my trepidation.

"It shouldn't take more than a couple hours. I really do mean that it will be an easy thousand dollars."

"You're serious about that figure?"

"Mhmm. Seems like a fair cut to me."

I begrudgingly fished the tripod out of the camera bag and let her show me how to attach everything together. In truth, the money was a draw, but the discomfort of accepting it washed that out to almost a non-impact. It was as much anxiety to take as it was comforting for my finances. The anticipation of watching through the lens, however, was another matter entirely.

Failing to decline, I let her direct me through the shots she wanted to take. Everything from her desk to her bed seemed to be fair game. It was bizarre watching her shed layers. Not because it was remotely new to see her naked, but because the event was usually paired with sex or at least snuggles.

"Okay, let me take a look at what you got."

I handed Mary the camera and watched over her shoulder as she flicked through the shots on the tiny screen. She snorted and shook her head at some of them before handing the camera back.

"I know you love my eyes, but I think most of my customers are more interested in my privates."

"Everything is in view, I don't see what the problem is."

"True, but as hard as you may find it to believe, some of my customers pay to see my feet and usually the subject of the photo is what goes in the center."

"What are you getting at?"

"I'm saying you're taking portraits of my face and I need portraits of my privates."

I wanted to continue grumbling, but I accepted the criticism and worked at adjusting my focus. The camera focused for me of course, I just needed to do a better job pointing, apparently.

The next time she checked in, she was far less dressed but much more pleased with the result. I tried to enjoy the praise, but the setting spoiled a lot. At least the end was in sight since she was done taking off clothes.

She handed back the camera and walked to the closet.

"Which outfit do you want to do next? The chef? Or the cat maid?"

"Cat maid?"

"Alright."

"I mean what are you talking about? Like a maid but also a cat?"

She nodded as if that was obvious, and I guess in a way it was.

"Sure. Whatever. This might as well happen."

"I agree, now help me into my tail plug."

*~*~*

"What do you think?"

I thought several things, many of them angry, as she returned from her next costume change with my uniform.

"I suppose I should be thankful you covered the company logo." I grit my teeth.

"Mhmm!" She spun in place before making her way to the kitchen. Of course it would be in the kitchen.

Fuck, that was the last place in the house we hadn't done it, and now I'd remember this any time I made meals.

"What should I cook for this bit?"

"You're actually going to cook?"

She nodded, and a sadistic part of me wanted to suggest bacon. But, I didn't want to remove grease stains from my dress uniform. Furthermore, either I'd feel bad if she got burning oil on her, or she'd enjoy it. The exercise would be pointless either way.

"Boxed mac and cheese I guess."

"That doesn't sound like a very sophisticated culinary activity."

"It's not supposed to. I figured you could lean into the ditsy pretend act."

"You think I'm ditsy?"

I groaned and dragged my hands down my face. A thousand dollars suddenly wasn't nearly enough money to photograph Mary taking off my clothes. Or rather- clothes that belong to me. Fuck, now I was imagining it. Goddamn it.

"You're fine, the character you seem to play for this is ditsy."

"I know, I'm just yanking your chain."

I shook my head and set up the tripod again. I had to put the camera above my head to see her ass over the bar, but I suppose that only made it a better point of view for the boys, tall and short alike.

I tried to stay detached as she worked and coached me through the angles she wanted. Despite everything, I was obedient. I couldn't bring myself to act on the spiteful impulse to ruin this part of the shoot.

Sure, I'd given her permission to borrow my clothes, but I didn't expect to see them used for this. I didn't even know she could make a plain white coat look sexy, but here she was, stripping down to nothing while joyfully stirring a pot of pasta.

I didn't conceal my groan as she tore the cheese packet with her teeth and dripped the sauce down her chin. She was naked at this point, and I'd already hung up my clothes, but watching her toy with the cheese sauce as a prop was cringe-worthy at best.

Distractions weren't a luxury I had now. I wondered if she had sensed that was my coping mechanism. Whenever she tried to rile me up I looked away, but now I had a task. Absolutely cruel.

She masturbated with a fucking turkey baster in various positions around the kitchen- I even had to talk her down from filling it with Mac and cheese. She didn't think there was a risk of the plunger moving, but I insisted on safety. Why did she have to defile a kitchen implement for her bit?

At last, she seemed satisfied, and I didn't envy her task of pouring through the photos or presumably performing touch-ups. I didn't see what there could be to change, honestly. The undertaking of covering tattoos would have been better done with makeup anyways.

I was still angry at hypothetical porn consumers when Mary fixed me a bowl of mac and cheese. Of course this was dinner. Why not? Why not just fucking eat the props after the shoot? I couldn't tell if I was irritable from being hungry or being teased for hours on end. Either way, I was unsure today was worth it.

"So how about it? Easy money right?"

I shook my head. I didn't feel like I could explain why I didn't enjoy the show without hurting her feelings. I mean, yeah, I enjoyed it at parts, but it wasn't for me. Making it both work and personal made it complicated. It felt like I was being asked to buy someone else a cake on my birthday. It was still a party, but it sure as hell wasn't my party.

As usual, my train of thought made for a long silence that Mary read into.

"Do you want to renegotiate higher pay?"

I sighed and pulled my hair out of my face.

"No, I don't know. I just have a bunch of difficult feelings I guess."

Even that felt like saying too much. Finding straight explanations for all this jealousy and arousal was going to be exhausting. Still, I managed to follow along as Mary suggested evening activities. She wasn't hungry in the sexual sense, so that was both a boon and a curse.

I reached forward to place my bowl next to the sink. I'd rinse it later.

"I'm gonna take a shower and then we can do whatever."

She gave me the look, and I rolled my eyes. Seeing my uniform hanging up on the closet door brought my arousal back to my mind, so I decided to forgo laying out clothes and just got to it. She waltzed around naked all the time. Why shouldn't I?

# 14

# The Usual

"Are you sure we couldn't just order carry out?" I walked with Mary up the short sidewalk to the now-familiar ramen shop.

"It wouldn't be the same, don't you want to see your favorite waitress? Besides, I wanna day-drink and you can't carry-out liquor anymore."

I felt my face heat up as I followed her in the door. The first time we came, it had been the dinner rush on a weekend. Today the weekday lunch rush had long passed. I was about to ask if Kimberly was even working today but I wasn't sure that was her name. Regardless, she was at the counter, already collecting napkin bundles.

"Hey Mary, Addison. The usual?"

"Usual?" I tried not to sound taken aback but I hardly felt a fourth visit made someone a regular.

She pointed to us in turn. "Spicy ramen with something lemony to drink, and miso butter corn ramen with a diet cola."

"I want to try something else to drink actually."

God I felt stupid. Why did I say that? Why would I open myself to choosing something? At the very least if Kimberly was put off she didn't show it.

"I'll grab a drink menu then." She smiled at me for some reason before turning to Mary. "I've been experimenting with making a bastardized lemon drop with sake, interested?"

"Always."

I slipped into the secluded booth as directed and to my surprise Mary sat across from me instead of beside me. I had approximately five seconds to mourn the lack of hand-holding before I felt her leg brushing mine.

Seconds or minutes later Kimberly returned with a tray of drinks and a menu tucked under her arm. Rather than passing everything out she slid the tray to the middle of the table and slipped gracefully into the booth next to Mary.

She peeked over her shoulder at the kitchen before pushing the menu to me and picking up the blue soda I now realized she had brought for herself.

"Joining us for lunch, Kim?" Mary draped an arm around her shoulder as I opened the drink menu. I tried to tune out their small talk, but I never fired on all cylinders around Mary.

I was partly relieved to have remembered her name correctly, but I was mostly distracted by the casual confidence with which she had joined us, almost as if this too was part of the usual.

Mary reached for the glass but stopped as Kimberly burst into a fit of giggles. The glass was brimming with neon yellow liquid.

"How the fuck did you not spill this?" She leaned across the table to take a sip.

"Very carefully."

Mary rolled her eyes as she sat back and looped her arm behind Kimberly again. I struggled not to squirm as she brushed the back of my calf under the table.

"Your skills are wasted here, you should be a doctor, a surgeon even."

It was Kimberly's turn to roll her eyes. "As if."

I failed to split my attention between the menu and conversation as Mary seemed to not-so-subtly bring up every possible interest Kimberly and I could share. If choosing wasn't hard enough, every time Kimberly spoke she looked to me. Like *I* was somehow the most interesting thing at the table when Mary was literally sitting right there.

Mary's legs around mine did not help. Is this what footsies was? Just fumbling blind under the table?

"Are there any drinks that *aren't* sake standing in for another liquor?"

Kimberly laughed and looked around the dimly lit restaurant. She glanced at the door to the kitchen a second time before leaning forward. "Nothing but sake and beer. It drives me crazy," She lowered her voice further, "I have some rum stashed away that I could mix into a cola for you though."

"Oh she'd love that." Mary piped up before I could even object.

I was still trying to compose a polite refusal as Kimberly took the drink menu. Her hand was warm.

I blinked and she was gone. Mary had a shit-eating grin and the tray had been taken away too. Intuitively I knew that time hadn't sped up. I'd probably even thanked her on autopilot but the last several seconds had been lost in fantasy.

Mary folded her hands under her chin.

"Still wish we had done take out?"

"Shut up." I meant to grumble but it came out as a panicked hiss. Kimberly was already returning with a full tray of food.

She once again invited herself into the booth, but next to me this time. Her shoulder nudged mine as she settled in.

It felt like everyone was looking at me as I fumbled with

chopsticks. I half expected someone to offer me a fork but I figured it out before I lost what dignity I had left. The taste of rum snapped me out of my thoughts as I took a sip.

"Did I put in too much?"

Thankfully, Kimberly didn't seem to notice Mary's smug grin. Mary stroked the back of my leg with her foot again but I managed not to squirm and resisted the urge to kick her feet away.

"N-no, it's good." I took another sip and managed not to sputter this time. Kimberly didn't seem convinced.

"I forgot you said you were adding rum."

I took a long drink. I don't know if it was good rum, but it wasn't bad. In stories, liquor seemed to fortify people and help them handle whatever they were struggling with, but I remembered far too late that it did no such thing for me. When *I* drank I made out with Mary.

I had only a few seconds of peace before Kimberly chimed in again. "Everything good? Or do I need to go harass the cooks?"

"No! I mean yes. It's fine. It's great. You don't need to harass them."

"I was kidding, I'm glad it's good though."

I expected Mary to weigh in as well but when I looked up she was still busy chewing. My relief proved short-lived as she finished and rested her hand on top of her drink.

"Of course, Addie is the sort who would sooner choke on dry noodles than report the slightest dissatisfaction."

"I would not!"

Kimberly giggled next to me. Of course Mary's word carried more weight than mine. There was no winning with her, at least not on my terms.

I bit back half a dozen different retorts with a scoop of noodles and turned to Kimberly instead.

"That doesn't look like anything I saw on the menu, is it just a loaded rice bowl?"

"Eh. Yes and no." She picked at it and nudged the bowl toward me. "It's a bit like the gyudon, just more beef, pickled ginger, and some truffle mayo thrown in. You want to try some?"

She was already scooting the bowl closer.

"Are you sure?" I asked before even thinking. Why did I have to ask? Nobody ever changed their mind just because someone asked for confirmation.

Kimberly nodded so I looked around for a fork. There was only hers. If I wiped it off that would mean I thought she was gross, but if i didn't it would be like an indirect kiss. Or maybe it would mean nothing at all. Chopsticks it was then.

I was proud I managed to scoop a small clump of rice and meat... then half of it dropped onto my shirt. The remaining shred of beef was delicious, but I could hardly appreciate it with the embarrassing mess.

"I got it."

Before I could even set my chopsticks down Kimberly had her napkin ready. She picked off the mayo covered scraps with surgical precision and managed to dust the grains of rice into her napkin without hardly touching me, not that I was breathing right now anyways.

I expected a lighthearted admonishment about my hubris but instead she wet the tip of another napkin.

Rather than hand it to me, she slipped her hand under the collar of my tank top to hold the fabric as she wiped the last of the mayo.

I knew I felt uncomfortable, that much was clear, but I couldn't tell if I felt weird because she intruded on my bubble, was overfamiliar, or if it was just irrational.

Irrational seemed right. That would be on brand and we were all girls here anyways, or at least that's the cliche I was supposed to believe. Still, it was hard to breathe with the back of her hand resting so gently on my chest.

Fuck I was in for teasing from Mary over this, no doubt something about having a girl's hand down my shirt.

"Thanks." Why was I out of breath? "--for the uh... bite... and napkin."

"Anytime. If you like it I can make it a secret menu item for the next time you come by."

Naturally, Mary chose this moment to rejoin the conversation. "I'll have to get it next time for sure. Is the clean up complimentary or will I have to conscript Addie for that part?"

"Oh hush you." Kimberly leaned away and stole another glance at the kitchen.

"It seems I am about twenty five minutes into my thirty minute lunch." She stacked her dishes and pushed them to the middle of the table before leaving the booth.

Somehow, I'd forgotten that she was still working even though she spent half her lunch break in the kitchen getting us food and drinks. I didn't want her to go. I must have done a shitty job of hiding my disappointment because she paused beside the table.

"I get off in a few hours and would suggest that we all hang out, but it's a pretty busy week for me-" She addressed me in particular now. "-but maybe we can hang out some other time?"

She didn't stick around for my response, much less for my thoughts to reboot. I tried to look anywhere but Mary as I took a drink.

"Pity, maybe we will catch her next week." She prodded the dregs of her ramen idly but I could tell when I was being scrutinized.

I grabbed Kimberly's abandoned bowl and took a proper bite with her fork, much to Mary's amusement.

"So you aren't scared of cooties?"

I squinted at her and took my time chewing before changing the subject. "If I didn't know better I'd accuse you of coordinating all of this." I gestured with the fork at the spread of dishes on the table, but the only detail that mattered wasn't here anymore.

"I did coordinate this. I literally told you we were coming to see Kimberly for lunch."

"What? Do you have her number or something?"

Mary cocked her head. "Yes?"

"Isn't it a bit weird to bother people at work?"

"Addie, she's my friend. Wouldn't you like to see a friendly face from time to time?"

"I wouldn't want to be their waitress." I grumbled and swirled the remainder of my drink in its glass.

"Fair enough." Mary rubbed her temple and shrugged. "Sorry it was unclear, but yes. Kimberly is a friend. Our schedules don't match the best but I *do* in fact hang out with her outside of her job."

"That's good..." Now I felt stupid. It still didn't make great sense, and for sure didn't pass the vibe check, but I could at least wrap my head around the idea that it was cool with them.

"Were you banking on her being available after work?"

"Not really. I certainly didn't commit to making plans." Mary fished out her wallet and pulled out a couple bills. "But since orgies are out of the picture today is there anything in particular you want to do while we are out?"

"Jesus Christ, Mary." I was more exasperated than appalled, and at this point I wasn't surprised. The topic had already been breached over both Joshua and Cyrus, in front of Joshua no less. It was lucky Kimberly wasn't in earshot.

Mercifully, she didn't tease that particular topic further and she instead focused on whatever shape she was folding a twenty-dollar bill into. In minutes a heart shape materialized. She turned the rest of the tip money into a display stand and hid the lot behind the napkin dispenser as Kimberly returned with the check.

"Sorry about being busy but it really was nice to visit on my lunch break."

Mary snagged the check before I could react and Kimberly caught my frustration. She held up her hands in a helpless but unrepentant shrug.

"You forgot to ask to split the check, and Mary does what she wants."

I could only squint at Mary as she clipped her card to the miniature clipboard. However, rather than objecting further, I moved the napkin dispenser so Kimberly could see the origami money.

"Mary, you little shit you *know* I hate unfolding that crap." She snatched the clipboard back and put her hands on her hips. "After all I've done for you... I'm keeping this, enjoy shopping without your credit card."

Mary remained distinctly smug as Kimberly walked back to the register. The threat proved predictably hollow when she returned with the receipt.

"Get out of my restaurant. Shoo. Git." Kimberly pushed Mary all the way to the door and made a show of dusting her hands as Mary pretended to have been handled roughly.

I wished I had videoed the event for posterity but I figured it was better for Kimberly's job that nobody else saw or misinterpreted the play. Kimberly held out her arms and after a tiny hesitation I accepted the hug.

"See ya later Addie."

She made a fart noise as I assumed she stuck her tongue out at Mary over my shoulder.

# 15

## Road Trip

"Do you want to go with me to visit Cyrus?" Mary looked up from her phone and put down her book

"Absolutely."

Even though it hadn't even been two weeks since I met him, I desperately wanted to see him again. It wasn't too soon, was it? Who was I to determine that anyway given I'd met Mary less than three weeks ago. Wait, weren't we supposed to check in at two? My chest felt tight. I didn't want to check-in. I didn't want to risk the end of this arrangement.

Mary was smirking. Apparently, my eagerness had been amusing. Lately, everything I did was either hilarious or frustrating, with little reason or medium in between.

"I didn't even say when, or for how long."

"Do you intend to schedule so I can't go?" I folded my arms and did my best to regain the semblance of a cool persona.

She squinted at me. "I'm not evil. What sort of monster would I be to come between you and your crush?"

"First off, that's a bit rich coming from a literal half-demon. Second... fuck you." I squinted back. She had me pegged. Saying he was secondary to her in my eyes would imply I had a crush on her as well, but denying my infatuation with Cyrus would be flat dishonest. I let the thought hang and looked away as she raised an eyebrow. Why was it so vital for her to both know and not know I cared about her?

"Whatever," I grumbled, "When did you want to go?"

"I was thinking we could leave Friday as soon as you get home, spend Saturday with Cyrus, and then visit my family on Sunday for a half-day."

"You're taking me to meet your family?"

"Sure! My dad is really chill, you've seen pictures of him right? His wives, Crystal and Mikah aren't much older than us."

I grimaced at her. "Your step moms are our age?"

"My dad is hundreds of years old. If you are going to be sensitive about age differences then that is the offending one."

I rolled my eyes. "Fine. Still, that's an awful lot of driving for such a short visit."

She shrugged. "They're worth it."

"I can take off one or two days to stretch the trip out if you want."

"If you're comfortable taking Friday and Monday off... we could stay Thursday night through Monday afternoon."

"Sounds good to me."

In truth, it sounded the tiniest bit dangerous. I'd be far from home, neither one of our cars was a spring chicken, and this would be my only vacation for the next two months. On top of all that I would be meeting her family. In-person. I wasn't sure I was ready to see a demon in the flesh.

She tapped away on her phone, and my pocket buzzed. She must have hit up the little three way "Cool Chat" she'd made when Cyrus had left. I supposed the name was two-thirds accurate. I couldn't even remember the last time I had traveled, and I realized today was Wednesday. I needed to give notice asap, and I had the remainder of this evening to pack because we would likely leave after work tomorrow.

"I better run to the convenience store," I mumbled, and Mary quirked an eyebrow.

"They sell condoms in Tristate too."

"Christ, Mary. For motion sickness pills!"

She made a show of nodding and winking.

"Well, would you mind picking up some tampons and condoms while you are at it?"

"Can't he buy his own? How would he get me pregnant anyways?"

Mary shrugged. "Dad is quite the artist with his transfigurations. Cyrus has a *very* functional dick." She wiggled her eyebrows. "Anyways, Cyrus and I don't use condoms, I control my fertility, remember? I just want to carry them in case you get caught up in the moment."

I rolled my eyes. "I'm sure I won't need them, but I deeply appreciate the concern."

"Spicy."

I shook my head and gave up. "I'll be back in a few minutes."

I managed to get my shoes on without further harassment, but I wasn't five steps down the hallway before my phone buzzed. Mary wanted tea, an ice cream sandwich, chocolate, and potato chips as well. Judging by that and the tampon request, I estimated Mary and I would sync up our cycles soon.

*~*~*

In the end, Mary ended up being so keen on hitting the road that she both dropped me off and picked me up from work. Even still, the drive was to be mostly in darkness. Despite Mary's attentive automobile care, our first stop ended up being at a hardware store to replace a headlamp bulb. I expected the motorized movement would complicate the replacement process, but Mary had us back In business and on the road in no time.

Now the right side was visibly brighter than the left. I wondered if I could convince her to change the other bulb too. It wasn't causing a problem necessarily, but it would be a dangerous distraction if I took a turn driving.

Instead, Mary had a marathon mindset. She had a basket of snacks and a preorganized book of CDs that she kept me busy feeding to her and the car respectively. Not once did she stop on her own account or show signs of fatigue.

I, on the other hand, was not so superhuman. I snacked far too indiscriminately to avoid a rest stop, but Mary was gracious in accommodating me. I loathed breaking her marathon, but I knew she had done nothing to inspire guilt. Still, it took all my willpower not to request a second stop. I sensed I was playing a dangerous game with my biological urges as we approached Tristate.

Blessedly, the only activity greeting us at Cyrus's apartment was sleep. The restful kind.

Once I finished in the bathroom, Cyrus gave me a tour of the apartment. Mary, having been there done that, helped herself to the shower.

It was kinda cute in a way to see a dungeon aesthetic now that I knew Cyrus- but if this had been a first-time meeting? Yikes.

Knowing his interests though, the figurine collections, custom game table, and general dark aesthetic felt more mystifying than unsettling. Rather than using the overhead lights, Cyrus installed strips under most of the tables and around the ceiling. The entire communal living space centered around entertaining guests for this particular atmosphere.

The bedroom was austere in comparison. It wasn't as large as Mary's, so the queen size bed dominated the space with little room for utility besides. Apparently, black-out curtains weren't enough, because a massive shelving unit covered both windows. I would have thought there were no windows at all were it not for the sills peeking out below.

"Is that a fire code violation?" I murmured.

"Shhhh."

I raised an eyebrow, and he relented. He popped hidden catches on the bottom of the shelving unit, and the middle swung open on a gentle gravity assist. The blinds behind were drawn shut, and I saw lights lining the backside of the shelf.

"This seems excessive. Do you seriously light up the window to pretend it isn't blocked?"

"The dark helps me sleep."

I shook my head and shrugged.

"If it works, it works...."

I looked up at the sound-dampening tiles covering the ceiling and remaining wall space. I could sense sound was a concern too, and I already felt self-conscious for not bringing my CPAP to prevent snoring.

"This feels a bit like you take the dungeon master aesthetic to an extreme in both senses of the word."

He laughed and shrugged. "In my defense, while I'm big on curating experiences in general, domination is more an expression of care I extend to Mary rather than a personal interest."

All I could do was nod. I had not prepared myself for him to casually talk about BDSM, but that was an "I should know better" thing.

More than ever, I didn't want to intrude on his room for the night, but I was at a loss on how to address it.

"Is my snoring going to be a problem?"

If the subject change surprised him, he didn't show it.

"Not at all."

"I can sleep on the couch or recliner if you want."

"You are absolutely welcome in the bedroom, but If you are more comfortable there, that's one hundred percent okay."

"Fuck," I breathed. I hated getting caught in politeness loops.

I was grateful for the distraction as Mary returned from the shower. "Please tell me you have a preference where I sleep."

He raised an eyebrow, and I kicked myself as I agonized over my wording. I meant to ask him to ease my burden of choice, but I couldn't help but feel like I asked him to take command of me instead.

Mary saved the day, whether knowingly or not. "I'd prefer to have as many snuggle buddies as possible."

Her tone tugged at my heart. At some point since we arrived, absolute exhaustion had caught up with her. The endurance spell she insisted on using had worn off and this was the cost. A switch had flipped and she was wiped out.

Cyrus nodded. "Sounds good to me."

I rocked on the balls of my feet before excusing myself to take a shower. It struck me how far I was from the comfort zone I lived in mere weeks ago. I was breathing weirdly heavily as I stepped in the shower but the hot water calmed me. I longed for routine to return, whether new or old, but dwelling on that desire paralyzed. me.

Mary was fast asleep when I got out, but Cyrus had waited up for me.

"Is everything okay, Addie?"

Fuck.

I rubbed my face. What did I even say to that?

"I think exhaustion is catching up with me." I couldn't meet his eye but he nodded as if this wholly and elegantly explained everything.

"It's been quite the month for you as I understand. Do you know of any ways I can help?"

Fuck. Fuck. Fuck. Goddamn emotionally intelligent people and their fucking mind-reading, subtext-catching tendencies.

I struggled to come up with an answer as my eyes watered, this conversation was barreling toward the "give up and break-down" zone.

"Would a hug help?"

It was worth a try. Whatever at this point, you know? I'm hundreds of miles from home, effectively homeless on top of that. Why not hug it out with a guy I was sporting a dangerously large crush for?

Fuck he was good at hugs. My emotional capacity doubled in an instant. What looked like a spillover point a second ago felt like a glass-half-full situation. I focused on dropping tension from my jaw and shoulders as he held me.

"I know we don't have the deepest relationship," his chest rumbled pleasantly as he talked, "but if you ever think there is something I can do to lighten your load, whether giving space or interceding for you, I hope I can help."

I felt stupid nodding. What should he care? For that matter, why did Mary care so much? Did people jump into emotional labor for near-strangers all the time? Who the fuck had the energy for that?

"I think... once I've slept, I'll be able to manage better for a while, --" I stood back and wiped my eyes. "-- but uh... I guess making decisions stresses me out, so I'll probably welcome efforts that allow me to give up the reins so to speak."

"I can for sure do that."

He looked like he would say more but he sighed and gave me a wry smile. He shook his head before pulling me close again. "I was going to ask if you were ready to go to bed, but how about I just decide it's bedtime for all of us."

"I'd like that."

# 16

## There Is No Ethical Consumption Under Capitalism

With the obligatory coffee fix out of the way, Cyrus, Mary, and I began our sightseeing adventures. We spent the morning at the local museum and got a private tour. I had pretty well internalized the fact Cyrus was a skilled artist, but I was still gobsmacked as the staff greeted him by name. They didn't let us in for free, but I found myself thinking that was the odd part as he pointed out not one but three of his pieces on exhibit. Maybe he had a vain streak, but he claimed he visited often because it was a quiet place with a lovely cafe.

As we moved on to shopping, I found my fundamental assumptions subverted. For instance, I knew Mary discovered Cyrus through his furniture, but I had assumed that was ancient history. And, while I thought road trips were monthly or bi-monthly at least, this was Mary's second visit, and Cyrus had only visited her a couple times apart from delivering her furniture.

I was still struggling to recontextualize my assumptions as we pulled into the biggest shopping center ever. I wanted to scream when Cyrus informed me this was the smaller of the three local malls because the others had either skate rinks or theme parks built-in.

Cyrus found parking and we met up with Mary at the entrance.

Her car could have seated four, but only if she had the back seat installed. Mine would've too but the poor old I-motto had stranded me before and likely would again. I didn't want to be six hours from home when that happened, even if I had company.

Mary beat us to the door, because unlike Cyrus, she didn't care where she parked.

"What sort of shopping are we going to get up to today?"

Cyrus and I both shrugged.

"No particular needs come to mind. I figure I'll find a way to spend money on shiny things I don't need regardless of where we go."

Mary cut in. "Now that I think about it, it wouldn't hurt to take you clothes shopping."

I raised an eyebrow at Mary but regretted it as she took this as her cue to shift from subtext to an all-out attack.

"Dear, you have been raiding my closet for every outing we have made over the last two weeks. Half the clothes you packed for this trip are mine."

I twisted my hands together as Cyrus looked at me, suddenly unbearably interested.

She pinched the fabric of my shirt- or rather *her* shirt- and patted my shoulder. "Now I don't want to imply that some sort of value shift is driving an evolution in your expression and style...." She exaggerated a contemplative expression. "Well actually, yeah. I do."

"I get it." I shrugged her off. "I could stand to shop outside your closet."

"We can see if the parlors or salons do walk-ins if that sounds easier."

"Parlors?"

"She means tattoo parlors, they tend to have people who specialize in body piercings." Cyrus was clearly enjoying seeing me put on the spot. Some ally he was.

I squinted at Mary. The thought had crossed my mind. I liked Mary's vibrant hair, and I noticed styles elsewhere now. Kimberly in particular continued to draw my eye with her neon blue hair, but I wasn't so naive to think that type of decoration wouldn't send mixed signals. Lately, Mary had made an event every time we visited the ramen shop. I had to wonder if she had ulterior motives.

"What? Scared you will look a little gay?"

I frowned at Mary. Over the last week, she had been getting confrontational. Doubts she used to express with looks and sighs were being given words.

"Actually, no. I'm not scared to dye my hair or pierce my septum, I just intend to think about those sorts of decisions for more than a couple of weeks before acting on them."

She looked like she would make a rebuttal, perhaps to point out she hadn't said anything about hair dye. Instead, she let the conversation lapse into silence and led the way to the map of the mall.

I stewed in my thoughts as they poured over the list of clothing shops we could choose between. She used to at least apologize for prodding, but today she didn't care that she struck a nerve. Given time I could let this ruin my day but I did not feel remotely inclined to do my part to fix it.

One moment she and Cyrus were muttering about the map, the next, her finger brushed the back of my hand. I hadn't even realized I was clenching my fists. I took a deep breath and forced myself to uncurl my fingers. When I met her eyes, she was confused. Given the option to let her take my hand or recoil, I elected not to react at all. She took my hand in both of hers and stepped between me and the map.

"I guess that wasn't very fun banter for you, after all, was it?"

I managed to shake my head "no", and I glanced past her to the map before meeting her eyes once more.

Cyrus took this as his cue to save the day.

"Are you two going to kiss and make up or something?"

Wooo give it up for super Cyrus.

"What? Like actually kissing? Here?" I looked from him to Mary. Naturally, being the snot she was, she only shrugged.

"Would that help? I also know some relaxation spells but that might make it hard for you to keep your balance, let alone consciousness."

I looked down past our clasped hands and kicked at the floor. She brought a hand up to cradle my cheek and nudged me to meet her eye.

"I'm sorry for picking a fight. I promise I only want to help and support you."

I stepped in to fold my hands on her lower back. I believed she meant well, but it was hard not to feel like everything she did lately was pushing an agenda on me.

"Thanks, I'm sorry I get upset about teasing so easily I guess."

"If I say 'no homo' will the kiss help more?"

"Just shut up," I grumbled. I waited for her to lean in, or perhaps even pull me in, but she seemed maddeningly content waiting. When I glanced at Cyrus he looked away, always the gentleman I suppose.

Even without the audience, I still felt rooted. If she wasn't going to kiss me- if I was supposed to initiate... Fuck. When she started it, reciprocating was only polite. I mean, it was so much more, but it wasn't like I was kissing her just because I wanted to.

Now I was hesitating. There was no getting out, I didn't want out. In a few seconds I would be kissing her and it would happen because of me.

I leaned in. I didn't have a reason yet. My lips brushed hers, and I didn't have an excuse. I drowned in the sensation of being invited in. Accepted. Wanted. As if I had never known the feeling of belonging before I found her arms.

I returned to reality when she pulled back. I'd been caught up in her responses and I'd begun pressing buttons out of habit. Maybe if I kissed her casually more often I wouldn't be so weird about it.

"Sorry." I murmured.

Her breath rushed across my cheek in a warm puff. "I'm not."

Cyrus coughed. "I said 'kiss and make up' not 'kiss and make out'."

I flipped him the bird and dropped my head to rest on her shoulder. "You said something about clothes shopping?"

"Yeah. If you want I can even try some of them on for you. That way you will know what it will look like when I borrow back, and you won't need to try on every single thing that catches your eye."

I shook my head against her shoulder before stepping back. "How could I refuse?"

Mary dropped her hands to mine and started out in a seemingly random direction.

"The first things you need are tops-- ironic, I know."

I shook my head again and let her lead.

"I could be a switch, you don't know."

"Honey, if I didn't know by now then I'm not sure who would."

I looked to Cyrus to back me up, but he held up his hands. Mary took this as her cue to continue.

"I guess if you really think about it, the first time I asked you to feed me you kinda topped --"

I was about to thank her before she barreled on.

"-- But every time since then it's been a whole lot less 'how can I feed you?' and a lot more 'take me, I'm yours'."

I dropped her hand and stepped over to Cyrus. He offered me his hand without missing a beat. When she looked over to me, I stuck out my tongue.

"Well maybe next time you ask, I won't be in the mood."

She snorted but didn't otherwise call my bluff.

She put her hands on her hips and looked across the first clothing shop she had picked out.

"This will be a good place to get you some patterned shirts. Unless you're feeling bougie, I recommend you limit yourself to two and we can thrift a few more besides that later."

"I'm sure I'll be able to show restraint."

I ignored the raised eyebrow she shot me. I hoped if I didn't acknowledge it, I wouldn't be held to my word later. Five new shirts later, she didn't indulge in more than a smug look, but she did insist that we move on.

"Now this is a tabletop shop." Cyrus tugged me through the door before my poor wallet could protest.

I tried to coach myself in self-restraint as I took in the scenery. A dozen or so pool tables filled the middle of the room, but they sat lower and without pockets. As I looked closer, I picked out the decor on each one. While Cyrus's game table was glossy wood with a video screen insert, these were all like poker tables.

Colored boxes filled the walls. I assumed those were board games, but to my dismay, a sizable section displayed mini-figures and dice of all sorts.

I expected Cyrus to browse, and let me follow him, but instead, he followed me as I approached the glittering display in a trance.

They had gemstone dice. Carved amethyst, fluorite, and who knew what else. My hand shook as I reached toward a stunning purple set, but Cyrus's hand covered mine. He wove our fingers together as he held me back. And I begrudgingly refrained from reaching with my other hand. If he wanted to restrain me he could. My mind briefly flew to a scenario where I reached out again and he caught both of my hands but I shook the fantasy from my head.

"But it's pretty!"

"You haven't even played a game yet. I would feel terrible if you ended up not liking DnD."

I pouted, but he continued to shake his head despite his amusement.

"That set costs over a hundred dollars, and they aren't even fair dice. I can't in good conscience allow you to buy them."

"How does being pretty make them unfair?"

"The shoddy tolerances they get by tumbling them make them unfair. I'll explain later."

"They look fine to me," I grumbled, but Cyrus didn't relent.

He continued to rein me back as I looked at Mini-figures and props. I had to watch him shop for half a dozen new figures and paints, but I wasn't allowed a single purchase.

Mary did not seem to share our compulsion. She drifted between the game tables, spectating the board and role-playing games at play.

At long last, my torture ended. Mary had gotten impatient, so Cyrus paid out and we moved on to the next clothing store. I managed to restrict myself to two pairs of jeans. Besides, now that I knew my size for this brand, I could buy them online. I didn't think too hard about the nonstandard sizing system until I had paid out.

My lack of curiosity must have been conspicuous, because Mary kindly informed me they were men's jeans.

"You seriously didn't look up to see that we were in the men's section?"

"Of course not! Why would I check? Why would you lead me to that section in the first place?"

"Pockets. Pockets and comfort."

"I've never been one for the boyfriend jeans thing...."

Mary rolled her eyes.

"They look great on you. They're part spandex and aren't even overly baggy in the crotch. There's literally nothing to complain about."

I scowled and looked at the two folded denim garments in my bag.

"Nobody's gonna know." I recognized Mary's tone and begrudgingly played along.

"They're gonna know."

"Nobody's gonna know. How would they know?"

Cyrus snorted at our antics.

I turned to him. "Did she get you into In-Snare too?"

"Yes. She probably sends me everything she sends you."

Mary cut in. "The memes are good for you. They nourish and stimulate. Anyways, the final thing we need is shoes."

I didn't see anything wrong with my modest collection, but I let her lead me to the skate-themed shoe store anyways. I found a pair with a rainbow checkered pattern and ignored Mary's looks as I paid out. I resolved to buy some insoles later because, as comfy as they were, I could tell I wanted arch support.

I supposed the shopping was fun, but I was glad to finish. The conversation moved to dinner plans, but I found my thoughts returning to the pseudo-argument with Mary. I wondered if this would be a theme of our relationship: her jabbing at my sexuality from time to time and me feeling chipped away at. I used to think I would get thicker skin or something, but I wasn't any less sensitive to her teasing.

I wasn't disturbed from my thoughts this time as we parted in the parking lot and I followed Cyrus to his car. It felt like a logical leap to expect all this erosion on my psyche to cause change, but I was at a loss of what to think about it. Was it going to make Mary and me a better fit as friends? Or was this what manipulation was? I sighed and tapped out a note on my phone to bring it up in my next therapy session. Maybe I'd bug Mary about it when I wasn't quite so far from home.

# 17

## D*ddy Issues

Mary's phone led us through a new-looking neighborhood on the outside of the city. All of the trees were saplings, the fences had hardly been weathered, and each home was essentially the same two-car garage, brick facade clone.

"You haven't been here before?" I helped Mary keep a look out for house numbers as we cruised the winding neighborhood roads.

"Nah, they just settled down. I mean, my step moms have lived here for a few years but Dad joined them pretty recently."

"I thought you said they had kids together?"

Mary chewed her lip "It's complicated."

I squinted at her. "Isn't that shorthand for 'it's not a good situation'?"

"Noooooormally, yeah." She tapped the steering wheel, not matching the beat of the music as she looked from house to house.

"Are you nervous?"

"No. Yeah. Kinda. I haven't spent all that much time with my dad since I got my own place. You know how it is going back to visit family for the first time after moving out?"

My heart sank. I knew it all too well. Parents could be so smothering. I already wasn't a very outgoing person but I felt like I had to hide and disguise my true self any time I visited my mom.

Mary pointed out the windshield and pulled to the curb of one of the houses. The only thing truly different about this house from the others is the flowers in the front had actual variety. In fact, there were all sorts of out of place decor. Plastic flamingos, upside-down pineapples, an actual rainbow flower bed with the wackiest looking gnomes I'd ever seen.

"I guess I'm mostly excited. It's weird to be homesick for a place I've never been."

"Homesick?"

"Mhmm." Mary cut the engine and opened her door. "When I was going to college, Dad lived nearby and I could visit him any time, but when I moved to the city he didn't really have much use for the house so he sold it and has spent most of his time off-plane as it were."

Is that what homesickness was? I could understand yearning for a familiar room and bed, but without that, what was there to miss? Family was always a phone call away.

The front door swung open before we even reached the porch, and a visibly pregnant woman in her early thirties stood in the doorway. She was about my height, wearing the same type of black lounge pants and tank top I liked to wear around the house. Her hair was even the same shade of brown as mine. It wasn't quite like looking in the mirror, but if I were pregnant I wouldn't look too different. That thought didn't sit well with me.

"Mary," she pointed to us in turn, "and Addison? Did I get that right?"

"Yep!" Mary chirped, "Nice to finally meet you, Mikah."

Mikah smiled and stepped back to hold the door open for us. I noticed the pile of shoes to the side and hurried to remove my new sneakers.

"Make yourselves at home, Crystal will be home from work any minute, and Mazer will be on his way once I let him know you're here." Mikah pulled out her phone as I wandered into the house. The entryway led into a lounge area with a dining room table near the far wall, but when I walked past that there was a more typical living room, this time with recliners and a TV rather than a piano.

A bookcase and fireplace dominated the far wall with room for a door to the back yard and entryway to the kitchen. To my amusement, there was also a window cut out of the wall separating the kitchen and living room, providing a view of the TV over the twin recliners.

The tell-tale whir of a garage door opening sounded from the kitchen.

"That must be Crystal!" Mikah stepped past me into the living room but seemed to jump out of her skin when a loud door slam shook the walls.

Thudding footsteps echoed from the kitchen and there was a racket of jingling keys. A moment later the other mom of the house, Crystal, stepped into the living room. She looked to be a few inches taller than Mary and her long blond hair was tied up in a ponytail. She had probably already hung up the jacket to go with her slacks on the way in. Wherever she worked, they seemed to have a really boring dress code.

I expected her to be in a sour mood, but she seemed to brighten noticeably when she noticed Mary and myself.

"Hey! Welcome y'all, I was wondering whose car that was in front of our mailbox." Crystal kicked off her shoes and disappeared back into the kitchen. I heard the fridge door open and close hard, I imagined I heard rattling glass.

Mary seemed unbothered as she fell into the couch across from the fireplace, but Mikah seemed to share my unease. Was Crystal angry about something?

"Do y'all want anything to drink?" Crystal called from the kitchen. Cries of small children answered from the opposite side of the house.

"Shit." Mikah grumbled under her breath. She rubbed her eyes and looked like she was going to say something but just excused herself from the room.

"Do you have ginger beer?" Mary seemed far more interested in the candles on the coffee table than anything.

"Hmm?" Crystal peeked back into the living room through the wall window.

"Ginger beer?" Mary repeated and a knowing smile broke out on Crystal's face.

"You are your father's daughter, where did Mikah go?" When Mary shrugged, Crystal looked at me.

"I think the kids woke up..."

Crystal's expression fell as she looked past me to the doorway Mikah had left through. She seemed to go on an emotional journey from frustration, to remorse in seconds.

"It's in the fridge, I'd better help with the kids."

She practically skipped across the living room, far quieter than she had walked before.

What was I supposed to do with myself now? Crystal and Mikah were probably going to have some sort of argument back there and I didn't want to intrude, but I also didn't want to just let people be unhappy either. Mary hadn't made a move to get up so I wandered to the kitchen. Glass clinked as the fridge door swung open and the green bottles were easy to spot. Why would they call it ginger beer rather than ale? I grabbed a couple and returned to sit next to Mary.

"Oh, thanks." She smiled and accepted the bottle. She produced a bottle opener from her key-chain and I let her open mine. I didn't intend to eavesdrop, but I couldn't help but listen for the tells of a whispered argument in the other room.

"You good?"

I focused back on Mary. "Me? Yeah. I'm fine," I lied. At this point Mary no longer took that personally though, she treated it as some sort of code for "I don't want to talk about it". Not that I ever wanted to talk about it.

She reached over and began to rub my back. When I took a sip she switched to patting as I coughed and choked. "Why is it spicy?" I coughed and set the bottle on a coaster. I could tell Mary was having a giggle at my misfortune but I refused to take offense to that.

"It has a real strong ginger flavor, a bit of an acquired taste I guess."

Mikah and Crystal returned to the living room, each carrying a three or so month old baby. I knew one of them was supposed to be Mazer's but I couldn't see anything demonic about either child.

"Sorry 'bout that." Crystal eased herself into the recliner nearest to me and put her feet up. "I'm working on noticing my noise levels better. I'm not used to sleeping kids-" she glanced at Mikah with an apologetic smile. "but I hope I didn't startle y'all either."

Mary shook her head and scratched lightly at my back. "You're fine, I don't pay attention to footsteps and doors like Addie does."

Crystal raised her eyebrow "Do you have super hearing or something?"

"Not that I know of" I took a much smaller sip of my beer. "I just learned to recognize people and their moods by their footsteps and such."

Mikah nodded but Crystal's brow furrowed. "Their moods?"

Mikah cut in, "Yeah, everyone has a sort of sound and cadence to how they walk. Variations can say a lot about mood."

Crystal's eyebrows rose "I guess, but you can distinguish different people's moods? accurately?"

"Sure," I cut in and glanced at Mary, "It's not like everyone's footsteps sound the same right? There's even a whole career centered around reproducing those sounds for films and such."

Mary shrugged and looked past me to Mikah. "But if you never have to sneak around for anything it's probably not a normal skill to pick up."

I crossed my arms and leaned away from Mary. "What's that supposed to mean?"

Mikah spoke up behind me. "I think she means that if you grew up without being allowed privacy or secrets, you'd have to be perceptive like that."

Mary shrugged and nodded. "Essentially, yeah. I just meant that if I wanted to stay up late reading I didn't have to hide under a blanket with a flashlight like they do in the movies. Mazer would catch me staying up late, sure, but I wasn't in trouble or something because of it."

"He didn't discipline you for that?" Mikah sounded incredulous, bordering on worried.

"What? like take away my books? No, he made sure I got up for school the next morning, and made it clear that I had time to read, but there had to be a limit or I'd be miserable and tired all the time." She laughed and looked out the window to the back yard. "One of my teachers got *really* pissed about me falling asleep in class and he just told them I was 'learning not to stay up all night'. That was embarrassing as hell."

"Wild" I mumbled.

Crystal chewed her lip and looked from me to Mikah. "Were your parents control freaks?"

Mary wiggled her fingers on my back, distracting me from Mikah's mumbled response. I turned back to Mary and scooted closer.

"Hey, sorry for accusing you of being a naughty child." there was a small smile in the corner of her mouth.

I rolled my eyes. "Sure, sure." I leaned into her shoulder as another door closed beyond the kitchen.

"Awwwww, you two are so cute," Crystal teased in a sing-song voice.

Mary looked past me and stuck out her tongue, "No, you."

This time I heard the signature click of dress shoes before a taller man with plum hued skin appeared in the kitchen doorway. He leaned over and kissed Mikah on the top of her head before doing the same for the baby in her arms. "Welcome girls, how was the drive up?"

Mary and I said "long" and "not bad" at the same time. Mary was already extricating her arm from behind me and she hopped up to hug him. She had shown me some pictures from when she was a kid, and I guess I should have expected him to not have aged a day. His jet black hair was styled differently now, combed back between his horns. He was even taller than Crystal, Maybe taller than Cyrus too, but not as thin as either of them. I expected him to have super broad shoulders or look like some sort of superhero, but he was much closer to a dad bod. Mary seemed to be practically swallowed in his embrace.

"It's good to see you again!" Mary seemed positively jubilant, side by side I could see some resemblance, same nose and ears, but Mary's hair was naturally blond under the bright red dye so her hair and physique was probably from her mom's side.

Mazer looked over Mary's head. "You didn't bring Cyrus? He's such a kind young man."

"It's Monday, dad, he had work."

"Well he's a good one. Hello Addison! Mary has told me so much about you!"

"She has?" I glanced from Mary up to him.

"Nope. She told me your name and that you were living with her now. How long have you been dating?"

My face heated up but Mary spoke first in a hushed tone "Daaad don't bully her."

"What? It's an innocent question!"

"We aren't... dating." I stared at the carpet under the coffee table. I could feel everyone's eyes boring into me. I guess it made sense that I would be expected to explain the nature of our friendship, but I hadn't expected it to come up.

"Married?" Mikah at least seemed unsure, much to Mary's amusement. I only flushed hotter.

Finally, Mary spoke up, "Addie is a dear friend, she's staying with me while some water damage gets sorted out at her place. It's become quite the legal mess."

I looked up in time to see Mazer turn his incredulous gaze to Mary. "Well as far as legal trouble, I can of course make some connections for her."

"Oh... Thanks." I pushed my socks into the carpet.

"My pleasure."

"Dad, you don't need to make contracts with all of my friends."

"I won't, I won't." he stepped out of Mary's embrace and collected a chair from the small table in the kitchen. He placed it next to Mikah's recliner and crossed one knee over the other as Mary returned to sit next to me. She placed her arm around me again but I couldn't help but feel like there was some sort of mixed message to it now.

"We can sort that out some other time though." Mazer glanced over his shoulder and I watched a green bottle float from the kitchen into his hand. "I'm just glad to know Mary is making friends."

"*Dad.*" Frustration was creeping into her tone.

"Fine, fine." He turned to me. "Is she eating her vegetables at least?"

"Dad!"

I shrugged. "She hasn't turned her nose up at anything I've fed her."

"Good, good. I guess she never was a picky eater."

Mary nudged me with her elbow and leaned closer, "That's not true, I have a *very* discerning palette."

I rolled my eyes and turned back to Mazer. "I'm not spoiling her or anything. I've just enjoyed cohabiting. I didn't realize how much I'd hate living alone until my roommates moved out a couple months ago."

Mary leaned back into the couch and put her hands behind her head. "I have that effect on people."

"Weren't you living alone before I came along?"

Mary bit her lip. "*technically*."

"What's that supposed to mean?"

"Just that I wasn't living alone when I moved to the area." Mary grabbed her ginger beer off the coffee table and took a sip.

"So did you just invite me over because you were lonely?"

Mary raised an eyebrow. "You shouldn't ask questions you don't want the answers to."

Something tightened in my chest. What was that supposed to mean? That the answer was yes? I did not, in fact, want that answer but I hadn't imagined it was on the table. Why would she be lonely? Everyone adored her!

I took a deep breath. Why the fuck did this conversation have to happen in front of her family? I grabbed my drink as well. The sting and burn of ginger could be distracting right?

Mary sighed next to me. "Dad was making a fatherly dig at the fact that Luke moved out over six months ago."

Mazer nodded. "It is my sacred duty to press her for marriage and kids, sometimes in that order."

Mary put her arm around me again. "Luke and I were engaged

for a couple years. I don't really believe in 'the spark' but whatever it was went out over time and we split as amicably as we could manage. I must not have been what he needed because it appears I am the last girl he'll ever date."

"Oh?" Mazer leaned forward. "Do tell."

Mary sighed "He's gay. I may be pretty queer, but I'm not that particular flavor." She rubbed her thumb on my shoulder. "It's been quiet since he left, I won't deny I jumped at the prospect of company, but I wasn't acting on impulse and I don't regret it in the slightest."

"That's good," I mumbled. I turned the cold glass in my hands. She'd been engaged, long term and everything. It created so many questions, many more than I was ready to ask.

Silence settled, broken only by the babbling of the baby in Crystal's arms.

"Really?" Crystal asked with animated interest. Mary huffed a laugh beside me as the half intelligible conversation carried on. Crystal would have us believe her daughter was very opinionated.

"Speaking of which," Mary stood and moved to my opposite side on the couch, closer to Crystal and Mikah. "Tell me about my half-sibs! I must say I'm pretty hyped not to be an only child anymore."

Mazer scoffed. "You have nearly a hundred older siblings."

Mary waved him off. "These ones are younger. It's different."

Crystal rocked in her chair. "This is Azrael," she nodded toward Mikah, "and that's Andy. Andy is a cambion, but Azrael is one hundred percent human."

"Mmmm." Mary hummed "Backwards from expectations. Sassy, I like it."

"I thought you'd appreciate that." Mazer reached to tickle Andy in Mikah's lap.

"Can I hold one of them?" Mary sat on the edge of her seat and drummed her fingers on her knees.

Mikah stood and transferred Andy into Mary's arms. I thought they might swap seats, but Mary sat down again beside me. Andy's tiny feet were in reach so I indulged in a little wiggle, much to her displeasure.

"Wow, she did *not* like that." Mary swayed, leaning into me as Andy's indignant babbling died down.

"Sorry." I wasn't sure if I was apologizing to the baby, or Mary. Neither responded.

"She's pretty heavy." Mary looked up, Mikah and Mazer had been looking on fondly.

"No more so than normal." Mazer scratched his chin and opened his mouth to say more but Mary shook her head.

"I know what's different about cambions, I was just remarking." Mary turned to me. "We can't leave. I'm trapped."

I rolled my eyes. "I'm not in a rush if you need some time to get to know your little sisters."

"*Fuck yeah*" Mary whispered under her breath.

Mikah jumped to her feet. "We can give them their bottles early, hold just a moment."

If possible, Mary became even more excited.

# 18

# I'm Always Trying to Get You Off- Like a Public Defender

A month ago, I couldn't get the rental agency to call me, but now it happened daily. Today wasn't even the first guilt trip. I would worry, but Mary had greased some contacts for me. Her dad had a bunch of legal connections, and we determined I wasn't liable for the water damage. It was fun to listen to the lawyers switch from good cop, to bad cop, to disenfranchised cop while they learned their client, the homeowner, had screwed the pooch.

For my part, the worst was behind me. The agency paid for my furniture to go in storage, and insurance replaced my ruined laptop. Who cared about the rest of the crap?

I must confess I'd gotten comfortable living with Mary. As I opened the door to her flat, she confronted me with just how comfortable she was as well.

"H-hey Addie." She stammered as I locked the door and hung up my keys.

There in the middle of the room, she was sitting on a barrel-shaped rideable fucking machine, dressed in nothing but ropes. As I watched, she rolled her hips and groaned. I couldn't lie; the display was having an effect on me.

I shed my jacket. "I didn't know you had one of those."

"It's a bit chunky so it stays in storage most of the time," she sighed, "you want a ride?"

Surprisingly, she had the presence of mind to wink, but I supposed she was a pretty good actor.

"Maybe some other time." I tore my eyes away. It was a trial of temptation then.

I busied myself in the kitchen while she got noisy, but when I made myself comfortable at the bar with a glass of orange juice, she dropped the act.

"Nothing?"

"Don't get me wrong, it's a very compelling display, but you aren't going to get me to beg that easily."

I was rather proud of how strong my resolve had gotten, but I knew she had me bluffing.

"Who said anything about begging?"

My eyes widened as she sat up off of a sizable flesh-toned dildo and brushed imaginary lint off her lap.

I bit my lip hard as she approached the bar next to me and took off her rings.

Jesus fucking Christ. I'd been conditioned.

The sound of her rings clattering on the counter triggered a Pavlovian response. If I wasn't already thoroughly in the mood from the show, this struck a deeper nerve.

I'd gotten used to her keeping me on my toes. Sometimes it was just a "wanna fuck?" out of the blue, and other times it was an elaborate tease. This time bordered on mean-spirited. She probably wasn't even hungry. Why couldn't she appreciate my insistence on not soliciting sex?

"I suppose I'll call Joshy over for some playtime then." She smirked as I failed to hide my scowl.

Try as I might, I still couldn't quite get past my jealousy when she pulled that card.

She shook her head and strolled over to her desk to dump her rings. She kept several bowls around the house, in the kitchen, bedroom, bathroom, and living room. She never traveled far when the moment struck. I winced at the clatter as once again she dropped her rings. Finally, she returned to the machine. She unplugged it and rolled up the cable. I suspected she was bluffing about calling Joshua, but she left me in suspense until she had the silicone cover off.

She put a hand on her hip, and I tore my eyes away from her rope work to meet her eye.

"Why are you still hung up on this? Most all my friends ask for it at some time or another, and I enjoy attending to them. What's so important about always waiting for me to ask?"

"I respect you too much --"

"Bullshit. You know full well by now I won't think any less of you. Hell, it would be flattering at this point." She looked me in the eye and shook her head. "Look, we're well past pretending you aren't interested, that ship sailed. What is this really about?"

Well *that* was confrontation if I'd ever heard it. Energy drained out my feet into the floor. Weeks of work for nothing. The argument had pulled into the station.

"I just shouldn't. I'm not supposed to." I regretted it as soon as I spoke. I shrank in on myself as she continued to stare at me, the fire in her eyes turning cold as I watched.

"Then you shouldn't."

"What?"

Mary turned and walked to the bedroom. Her voice floated back through the door as the light flicked on. "If you aren't supposed to, then don't."

Don't what? Did she want me to stop saying yes? Stop being with her at all? My stomach turned. I imagined I tasted bile and I walked around the bar into the kitchen on autopilot. I guess I was supposed to collect my things and go. That was how this worked right? How had things gone wrong so suddenly?

I turned on the cold tap and let it run over my hands. I coughed as I half shivered and realized how thin my breathing was. I couldn't do all of this at once. I couldn't breathe without moving, I couldn't move without puking, and If I made a mess I would only be making things worse.

I watched the water run over my hands and leaned my elbows on the sink. My hair would probably get wet but who cared? I rubbed my face and coughed a dry heave.

Minutes later I was still staring at the running water. I looked up when Mary returned to the living room, she was dressed in a t-shirt and sweatpants now. I pulled the tap a little harder than I should have and wiped my hands on a nearby dish cloth as the last of the wasted water trickled away.

I stepped back as she approached the sink but apparently it wasn't a matter of being in her way.

"Addie."

I managed a split second of eye contact before looking back to the sink. "I'm sorry." I swallowed hard. I couldn't put the words together and I didn't get the chance to before she stepped forward again, just a half step.

"It's okay, take a minute to calm down."

Tears filled my eyes, later than I would have expected. Even when I was ruining everything she was patient. Truly, I could ruin even the best things. I took as deep of a breath as I could muster, but even as my stomach stopped turning my throat closed up. "I'll call Joshua, I'm sorry."

"You don't-" Mary tilted her head and when I looked up her eyes were full of concern I didn't deserve. She sighed and pinched the bridge of her nose. "Please stay."

"What?"

"Please stay, I don't want you to leave."

"But if I can't-"

"Forget about the fucking sex, Addie," she spoke quickly, clearly exasperated, but she seemed to half-laugh the words out.

"I can't just expect you to house me for free, especially if I am being a burden or irritation."

She looked me in the eyes until I couldn't hold her gaze anymore. "You aren't just a warm body. You never had to feed me to stay, I never wanted to put that on you as an obligation, much less a term of our friendship."

"I didn't feel obligated."

She rolled her eyes and I saw a smile in the corner of her mouth. "Glad to hear it."

I wiped my eyes and leaned into the counter. "So I guess you're gonna go visit Joshua?" I felt proud of myself for screening bitterness out of my voice. In fact, I didn't feel bitter. It was peculiarly comforting to know someone could meet the needs for her that I couldn't.

"I was actually thinking of going out for Italian again."

"Oh." I managed a small smile. "Have fun."

"Do you want to come?"

I chewed my lip. I'd gone and manipulated her into pitying me again.

"No, thanks. I just got ho-... here, and I want to unwind a bit."

Mary frowned, but nodded and returned to the living room. "I'll bring you back some chicken fettuccine Alfredo then." She walked a lap around the couch before finding her phone and dropping it in the pocket of her sweatpants. "Do you want to use one of my bath bombs?"

"Why are you being nice to me?"

Wow. Not only did I fail to use one of my memorized polite refusals, I had been blunt in possibly the rudest way.

"I care. I want to dispense care." She sat down and started pulling on her boots. "Plus, it's hard to pack and disappear while enjoying a good soak."

"I'm not going to run away."

"And don't you forget it."

She walked to the bathroom and I heard the dull roar as she started filling the tub.

"Hey!" I heard no response so I followed her into the bedroom in time to see her drop a small toy plastic cauldron in the water. "I didn't say I wanted to take a bath!"

"Oops. My hand slipped." she smiled at me, and dusted her hands over the tub. "You aren't going to let it go to waste are you?"

I squinted at her. "Fine. I'll use it. Thank you."

"You're welcome!" she chirped and practically skipped to the bedroom.

I watched the soap-filled toy bounce and bubble around for a moment before sitting down to pull off my socks. I was in my underwear when Mary returned and I held my shirt to my chest.

I expected something crass about the nonsense of decency after what we had done together, but she averted her eyes and spoke more to the closet than me.

"So I was thinking," her eyes flicked to me and away again. "It might be... fun for you to spend some time with Kimberly."

"Spend time with her? I want to believe you mean 'hang out' but I can't help but think you want me to fuck her."

"What happens, happens."

I gave her my best unamused glare and stepped over the edge of the tub.

She folded her arms and leaned on the door frame. "I get that you won't proposition me because you have all your hangups--"

"They aren't--"

"Then what would you call them?" She raised an eyebrow and stared me down.

I squinted at her until I lost my nerve. I looked down and swished a foot through the bubbles around my ankles. "Hangup is as good a word as any." I grumbled and tossed my shirt down on top of the rest of my clothes. I braced a hand on the wall to try to maneuver out of my panties without getting them wet.

"I just think it would help if you socialized without me for a change."

I didn't bother forming a counter-argument. My social life before Mary had been work and Josh and I hadn't gone out on my own apart from work and errands since I moved in.

"So I should just ask her out to lunch or something?"

"She's more available for dinner, but yes. Would *you* like to ask her out?"

I lowered myself into the tub and winced at the feeling of cold ceramic on my back as I situated.

"I can do that I guess."

"You don't sound particularly enthused. Are you only going on my account?"

"Is that not a good enough reason?"

"I'm flattered, but I'd sure like for there to be more."

I nudged the fizzing cauldron with my knee, causing it to bob across the tub. "I would do many things out of respect for your advice and opinions, but yeah. Kimberly is pretty neat, I don't hate the idea of spending more time with her anyways."

"Mhmm."

"Are you going to give me her number?"

"You could find her on a dating app." Mary crossed her arms.

"Or you could give me her number."

"Or, rather than having me distribute her contact information without her permission, you could reach her through your own avenues."

"Or you can ask her if I can have her number."

Mary gave me a blank stare and then looked at the back of her hand. "Oh, would you look at my wrist!"

"You don't even have a watch!"

She ignored me and left the bathroom. A minute later she returned, placed my phone on the counter next to the tub, and then skipped out again. I heard the front door shut and when I turned off the faucet, silence settled over the apartment.

An hour later, I was sprawled across the love-seat. I had a date set with Kimberly, I had my favorite pajamas on, and just as my stomach rumbled I heard the front door open. I called a greeting to Mary as she dropped a bag on the counter and came to stand behind me. She watched over my shoulder as I flicked through the little video memes she had sent me for the day. Some of them were suggestive dances, but most of them were relatable skits about depression, ADHD, and the woman-loving-woman experience. I'd seen half of them already and I'd even considered sending many of them to her. Every day In-Snare tailored my feed more to Mary's interests. The algorithm was uncanny.

She massaged my scalp as I reached the end of the queue.

"I've done some thinking." I dropped my phone on my chest and looked up at her.

"Dangerous pastime," Mary muttered. "Are you coming out of the closet?"

I rolled my eyes but didn't rise to the bait. "I'm sorry for treating our relationship like a transaction. I shouldn't have written every-thing off as paying rent or feeding you."

"I know you never meant any harm. You're forgiven. Besides, it was my stupid idea to joke about you paying rent with sex." She pushed off the armrest and I heard paper rustle.

I accepted the waxed cardboard box of noodles and sat up to eat. I'd scarcely taken a bite before Mary was half in my lap and turning on the TV.

"I've also been thinking." She wiggled to situate with her legs draped over my lap. "If you're interested, I'd kinda like to make a more permanent living arrangement."

I nodded and took another bite. I didn't trust myself not to sabotage everything with the first thought to cross my mind.

"Do you just wanna add me to your lease when it renews?"

"I was thinking we could find a house to rent actually."

"You wouldn't prefer to live with Cyrus?"

"They make houses with three bedrooms."

I took a deep breath and rolled my eyes.

"Fine. I'll think about it."

"You aren't sure?"

"Are you sure? After today?"

"I think it's fine. I exercised a boundary and you respected it. We talked it out and we're going to be okay. Are things not okay for you?"

I picked at my noodles. Even thinking back to what she said caused my chest to tighten.

"I thought you were going to kick me out."

I picked at my food until the noodles turned blurry. Tension welled up in my chest but I directed my racing thoughts toward counting candles and listening for noise from the street below.

Mary shifted beside me and I tried to act casual stabbing at a piece of chicken. She'd already been clear that she didn't want me to leave, now I'd called her a liar and cruel to boot.

"Has that happened to you before?"

I shook my head. "I've never been the one who leaves. People leave me."

I always seemed to catch feelings at the wrong time. Too soon, too late... apparently I was always either overbearing or oblivious.

"You thought I would send you away? For not propositioning me?"

I huffed a bitter laugh. "It sounds foolish when you put it like that, but my mom sent my brother to boarding school for less."

"You haven't really told me about your brother."

I shook my head.

I hadn't stopped my tears from falling, but I'd missed my food and avoided ugly sobbing so that classified as mild in my book. I wiped my eyes and focused on taking another bite of food.

"Maybe some other time." I coughed and looked up at the TV and then to her. "But uh, if you have more patience where all that came from then things will probably be fine."

Mary gave me a half-smile and nodded.

"You know, living with me long term might turn you gay."

"You said it yourself, people don't turn gay, they just realize."

"Yep." She popped the 'p' and flopped backwards into the far armrest. "Polyamory is sexually transmitted too, you probably already have it."

"And I guess the tattoo's, piercings, and hair dye follow that?"

"I'm glad you understand the pipeline."

"I'm not in the pipeline."

"You can't honestly believe that."

"Why not? We already established that I'm straight."

"Goddamn it Addie, I am not an exception to your sexuality." She waved her hands in the air before dropping them back on her stomach.

"You don't think it's romantic to be the only exception?"

That earned me a few seconds of her feet kicking in my lap. "You can't use my playlist against me!"

"I'll do as I please. Anyways, I guess we'll see after I go out with Kim, won't we?"

"Oh, we will. I hope you like the taste of crow."

# 19

## Curiosity

I wished we had chosen a restaurant I'd been to before. Though trying new things was a good idea, I liked to have a soft cap on how many new things I tried at once. A date with a girl was already over that threshold.

I glanced around the dimly lit restaurant as I walked through the door. One of the perks of finding people with dyed hair was they stood out in a crowd. Well, at least if the crowd wasn't a convention of some sort. Sure enough, Kimberly had beat me here, and she waved from a strange table near the wall.

Unlike regular restaurant booths, raised floors surrounded the tables. The dining surface was a foot off the elevated floor, and it had a pocket underneath for our feet. I did not envy the job of cleaning food out of there.

After a bit of flailing, I managed to seat myself. I did my best to seem relaxed. Yep. First dates at new places were a no for me. Live and learn.

"Pretty cool right?" Kimberly was utterly at home here, and I tried to absorb that energy for myself.

"I've never seen anything like it for sure. Do you come here often?"

"All the time. This place has the best bento boxes."

I wanted to ask what those were, but I didn't want to sound more naive than I already did. Blessedly, I found them in the menu and had a surprisingly easy time determining which sort I was most likely to like.

"I must admit I was surprised when you reached out, are you polyamorous too? Or did you and Mary break up?"

"Break up? No."

She nodded and was about to speak again when I realized what I had implied.

"I mean- I'm not polyamorous either. She's uh... a close friend. I'm actually crashing at her apartment while my place is being repaired. We're just friends."

She nodded. "I see. You two seemed inseparable so I assumed. That's cool though."

I crumpled my napkin in my lap. I was making her drive the conversation, but what was I supposed to say?

"I was a little surprised you know Mary so well. Have you known her long?"

"Oh yeah. We go a little ways back." She laughed and shook her head. "She actually asked me out after a few weeks of the most awful flirting I've ever been subjected to. She's damn lucky she's cute... but yeah, I dated her and Luke back when they were engaged. When he split, She and I took a break too."

I struggled to mask my surprise. That sounded capital 's' serious, but they didn't act like exes to me. The skeptical part of me wondered if Mary was trying to use me to help Kim get over her or something, but all this development really told me is how incredibly little I actually knew about their dynamic.

Kimberly broke the spiral of thoughts. "How did you meet her?"

"About a month ago we met at a mutual friend's birthday party. Just kinda hit it off."

I needed to steer the conversation away from Mary, but I didn't know how. We paused to order drinks, and I put the menu down to focus on what I wanted to talk about. What did I even want to know about Kimberly?

"I've been curious about your piercings," I blurted, her eyebrow shot up, but I tried to press on, "Have you had them for a long time? Or uh... I don't really know what I'm curious about. I just really like them."

She laughed and smiled. "Thanks. Yeah, I've been sorta collecting them steadily since I came out. Of course, I had the normal ear piercings since middle school but the upper ear, septum, tongue, and various body piercings have been over the last few years."

"Body piercings?" I asked before I thought.

"Maybe I'll show you sometime," she giggled as I flushed red, and I buried my face in my hands. "Have you done any piercings or tattoos?"

"Not yet." I shook my head. I wanted to launch into a spiel about which of Mary's I liked, but I caught myself. "It's a bit of a new interest for me really. I'm not actually sure what sort of style I want to have you know?"

She nodded. "Did you realize pretty recently then?"

"Yeah, I mean... yeah...."

She leaned forward. "Oh my gosh, is this your first date?"

"Kinda." I winced and I braced myself.

"That's so cool! Congrats on coming out!"

I flushed. I didn't deserve her praise, but I couldn't bear to correct her.

"How did you realize?"

"Mary," I blurted and immediately regretted it.

If that put Kimberly off, she didn't show it. She urged me on and put her chin in her hands. I decided to go for broke. I had never talked with any LGBT people about my experiences with attraction. Maybe Kimberly could help me figure things out a bit.

"So we kinda clicked at first you know? I think she somehow read my interest, and with the help of a few drinks, things escalated pretty wildly. I woke up the morning after in her bed in quite the panic."

Kimberly giggled. "That sounds like her alright. So you just decided to be friends?"

"Pretty much. She still doesn't strike me as the settling down type, but she's been pushing me to be more outgoing and stuff. She's a real wing-woman I guess."

"I'll be sure to thank her for nudging you toward me."

"I didn't- she-..."

Kimberly laughed as I gestured helplessly.

"In my defense, I noticed you by myself."

"Oh, I know." She winked, and flushed further.

We paused again to take orders and receive our drinks, so I had the chance to steady myself. I had the vaguest sense of what I wanted to learn.

"What was coming out like for you?"

Kimberly drummed her fingers on the table. "I was kinda the last one to come out in my friend group." She shrugged and took a sip of her water. "I had subconsciously surrounded myself with queer folk, and as they discovered themselves I vibed with their experiences."

"I don't think I have many LGBT friends..."

"That's okay too. It's been a long time, but I have a vague sense of my feelings back then, you know?" She squinted past me before looking me in the eye again. "So I guess part of my gay awakening was comparing my experiences with girls and guys? Like I grew up surrounding myself with guy friends, and I even would sleep with a few of them, but to some degree, I felt like I was maybe acting? I did what I was supposed to because I knew my role, and I prided myself on being the very best at getting boys' attention like I was supposed to. My friendships with girls were different though. I understood them, but I also sorta misunderstood them too? Maybe the best way I could describe it is I had an almost adversarial relationship with other girls. Not like I was competing for boys' attention, but there was this 'me vs them' sentiment where I looked for and emphasized what set me apart from them. I'd pick things I didn't like about them like gossip, vanity, backstabbing, and so on. After a while, my relationships with men turned adversarial too. I developed my group of gay friends and defined myself by how I was different from all the other people I knew. From there I tended to gravitate to the people who were like me, whether they were out or not. The gay folks were cooler and nicer. They understood."

I didn't relate much at all. I kinda got the vibe with guys, but I didn't have many female friends before Mary.

Well... that wasn't true, was it? There were the mentor figures I built up in high school. The social outcasts who graduated before I did. I found them cool. I liked their style and idolized the things I found rebellious about them.

Kimberly was rearranging the condiments when I returned to the present.

"Sorry for zoning out there." I managed the small victory of taking a drink of water without spilling.

"S'okay," she smiled and looked back at me, "how was figuring out that jazz for you?"

I thought back, and the words tumbled out as I reflected on the last month. "I felt drawn in. I felt engaged and interested for the first time. Rather than feeling like the connection was something to build and call finished, it felt like I was always finding something I wanted to work at. With men before, I would win them and move on but... it's not like that with anyone anymore." I trailed off as I realized I was about to say too much.

When I met her eyes, she had that same appraising look Mary tended to give me.

"Can I ask what draws you to me?"

"O-oh," I stammered, and she smirked as I shifted in my seat. "Besides your aesthetic I was... well part of me tried to write it off as me misinterpreting the whole customer service act but, I was really smitten by how you smiled when you saw me, and would make a point to sit down with us if it wasn't busy so we could just... chat about stuff. You're just so cool you know? I'm really interested in getting to know you, and I was kinda eager to do that in a setting where it didn't feel like you were paid to be nice."

"Awww. That's sweet." She leaned back as the waiter came by with our bento boxes. "For the record, I never sit down with other folks. I'm sorry the kindness and professionalism wires were getting crossed for you."

"That's... good to know." I wanted to feel relieved, but I'd written off her genuine efforts at friendship. Still, I didn't feel safe adjusting my expectations for others. Just because Kimberly wanted friendship didn't mean anyone else did.

While we ate, our conversation drifted away from Mary and sexuality toward hobbies and dreams. She had this grand plan to make a living as a writer, and, in turn, I shared my goals of starting a mail-order bakery.

We chatted and laughed well after our boxes were empty, and as we made our way out of the restaurant, I let her take my hand. The short stroll down the street to the parking lot lasted forever, but in a good way. When we got to her car, she turned to me.

"So --" she released my hand, leaned back against the door, and folded her arms across her chest. "-- Are you still curious about my piercings?"

My eyes flew wide, and her grin broadened as I stammered, "a-a little."

"Regrettably, they aren't appropriate for polite company. Would you like to carpool? Or should I text you my address?"

"D-do you mean --" I blinked and shook my head. Of course, I knew what she meant. "-- what's your address?"

She winked and turned to get in her car. "I sent it to you when we left the restaurant."

I was still standing there stunned when she pulled away, but as soon as she was out of sight, I practically ran to my car.

# 20

# Ganic (Gay Panic)

I was still dazed when I got back to Mary's. The lights were on, but I didn't see her anywhere. While Mary had been gentle thus far, Kimberly had left marks. She had asked, of course, and I had tentatively agreed, but as the night went on, I had developed an interest. I wasn't sure how I would wear a bra tomorrow with how many bite marks there were along my shoulders.

I must not have been as quiet as I thought I was because Mary appeared in the bedroom doorway before I could get my shoes off. She crossed her arms and looked unbearably smug.

"Did you have a nice night?"

Her smile was turning into a shit-eating grin as she focused on my neck and arms.

I rolled my eyes. "Yes. Kimberly and I had a lovely time."

"Soooooo?"

I was too tired for games.

"So what?"

She rolled her eyes and shook her head.

"Whatever. Come to bed, doofus."

"With pleasure," I grumbled as I finished getting my shoes off. I searched my dresser for a sleep shirt that wouldn't rub my shoulders too much and settled on a tank top. I grabbed some boy-shorts as well and went to the bathroom to change.

As I redressed in front of the mirror, I got a better sense of the damage. I'd had rough sex before, but I had never liked it. In that sense alone, this was new. If I thought about it, I could remember the order I had gotten most of the marks in. I knew which ones she had asked permission for, as well as the darker ones I had asked for after them.

I hoped showing off the extent of the biting could trigger some jealous, or at least protective, instinct in Mary, but I put the thought out of my mind. The part of me that cared about that was irrational, after all.

As I pulled on my shorts, I reflected on the date as a whole. We'd talked about a bunch of stuff we had in common, as well as all the coming-out stuff.

I wondered if I had blocked out or repressed some critical memory that would fit all the puzzle pieces together. As though some detail could coalesce my experience into something that made sense.

I was halfway through brushing my teeth when an idea popped into my head.

Given the general sentiment I had toward Kimberly, wasn't it fair to compare that to how I felt about Mary? I wondered if I would be able to see the exact way in which Mary was different.

What about Mary being a cambion was making me attracted to girls?

Well, that didn't make sense. Her being a cambion was only supposed to make me attracted to her. My attraction to Kimberly had to be-.

It would mean-.

I dropped my toothbrush in the sink and spat.

"Fuck" I whispered to my reflection.

I liked Kimberly, and it wasn't Mary's fault.

I rinsed my mouth and returned to the bedroom. Mary made no comment as I lay down and I let her pull me back into her arms. I sighed as she kissed one of the sore spots on my shoulder.

"Hey, Mary?" She didn't say anything, but I knew she was listening. "You said a while back you would never use magic on me without my permission..."

"Mmhm," she hummed, "as far as I remember I've been upfront every time since the intervention."

I huffed a sigh. She wouldn't see me roll my eyes but that was fine by me.

"So there's no chance you could do any magic accidentally?"

I felt her move behind me as she presumably shook her head. "Nope. I'm leak-proof. No scrap gets out. Why?"

"Just thinkin. Thanks."

I was close to falling asleep when she spoke up, "Don't forget, Cyrus is coming over tomorrow."

I hummed. "Do you need me to do anything? I can probably cook dinner for all of us if you'd like."

She shrugged. "If you're up for it."

I nodded and shifted to get comfortable. I reached up and tangled my fingers in hers on the pillow next to me. I smiled as she brushed her thumb across the bite mark there, and I fell asleep wondering if Mary would ever play rough with me.

*~*~*

I was alone in bed when I woke up. Mary had set out some pain relievers and a glass of water for me.

I sat up and straightened my shirt before grabbing my phone. I wanted to stretch, but I sensed my aches wouldn't appreciate it in the slightest.

I flicked through my contacts until I found Joshua, and my finger hovered over the call button. He might be able to help, but he was historically indelicate. If the cards were going to fall where I thought they would, the past few weeks would be awfully embarrassing.

I scrolled back up and found my therapist.

"Green Therapy, how can I help you?"

"Hey, my name is Addison Luli." I cleared my throat to get rid of some of the sleepy sound. "I have an appointment for next week, but I was hoping I could get that moved forward."

"How soon would you like?"

"As soon as possible."

I heard the secretary type.

"We've had a cancellation, can you be here at ten?"

I glanced at the clock; it would be close. I screwed my eyes shut and held my breath.

"Yeah. Yeah, I'll be there."

"Excellent, we'll see you soon."

I debated standing up but Mary's return interrupted me from my thoughts. She leaned in the doorway with two cups of coffee.

"Those bruises look like they hurt," she mumbled.

"It's a good hurt," I made a weak beckoning gesture. "Or at least that's what I'll tell myself."

She nodded. "I couldn't help but hear your phone call."

"Yeah. I gotta go talk some stuff out. I'll fill you in when I get back." I mustered a smile, but I knew it didn't meet my eyes.

She handed me the blue mug and sat next to me on the edge of the bed.

"Is there any way I can help?"

I snorted despite myself. "You wanna pick me out an outfit that's likely to get me admitted?"

Her smile turned devious. Rather than reply, she strolled over to her closet. I realized I hadn't specified it had to be my clothes, and she fully understood that.

A minute later she returned and I had to admit I didn't hate it. Above all, it looked comfortable, if out of fashion. Cargo pants, a crop top, a bomber jacket, and a studded belt to round it out.

"That will just make me look cooler than I am but I'll allow it."

I felt sure if she had her hands free, she would have done little claps, but she settled for a small hop as I took the cargo pants and started getting dressed. I had to hope therapy would help.

\*~\*~\*

I dragged the blanket off the back of Mrs. Green's couch, sat, kicked my shoes off, and tucked my feet under me. She raised an eyebrow at the behavior, but it wasn't the first time and wouldn't be the last.

We sat in silence as she glanced through her journal and jotted at points, but after a few seconds she sighed and addressed me.

"Tell me about the crisis."

"I didn't say there was a crisis," I countered, but all she did in response was lazily look at my shoes, the blanket, and back to my eyes.

"It's Mary," I mumbled.

I stared at the patterned rug between us, afraid to meet her eye. I expected to hear some "aha" moment or understanding response, but apparently two words wasn't enough of an explanation.

"I'm supposed to be straight but I'm developing feelings for girls."

"Is that causing you anxiety?"

I wanted to get sarcastic. I was suddenly feeling vindictive and irritated at the obvious questions, but I stopped myself. This was part of the process. I loathed the labor, but I needed the catharsis.

"Yes." I picked at the blanket and avoided her gaze as she waited for me to elaborate. "I'm confused and stressed because this has never happened, and I feel like it's already gotten away from me. Like I'm in too deep, out of my depth."

"What about your attraction to Mary makes you anxious?"

That... was a good fucking question. Irritatingly good in fact.

"I think... that's what I need to figure out."

"Well. Tell me what's new since we last talked. I seem to remember you hit it off at Joshua's birthday, hung out the day after, and then she offered to let you crash on her couch when your water heater exploded."

I winced. "So I might have left out key elements." I pushed my fingers through the holes in the crocheted blanket until I figured she wasn't going to ask.

"I slept with her the night of Joshua's party... and then, I went on a date with her and we slept together again. For the last month I have been sharing a bed with her and *going* to bed with her any time she asks."

Her eyebrows could scarcely go higher as she bit her lip and nodded. She looked at her notes and blinked several times as if seeing them for the first time.

Seeing she wasn't going to interrupt, I barreled on. "And since then, our friendship has been pretty good. We hang out a lot, share hobbies and go out together. She's been kinda prodding me to open up, and I guess admit I'm not straight or something but the latest event was she uh..." I rubbed my hands on my face. "Okay, so this is gonna sound stupid, but she effectively told me to stop sleeping with her if I'm going to keep insisting I am straight."

"Please don't take this as condescending or patronizing, but what I'm hearing is you have been living with and sleeping with Mary for about a month now. You seem concerned you are developing feelings for her?"

"When you put it like that, I think it's actually the implications about my sexuality that give me the most anxiety."

She folded her hands under her chin.

"We'll touch on that in a bit then. What about loving her gives you anxiety?"

"I know she doesn't feel the same way."

"And you know because...."

"She doesn't say she loves me. I mean, she does, but she doesn't mean it like that."

She beckoned, so I dug deeper.

"She's romantically and sexually involved with other people. Like Joshua for instance. Our relationship isn't as special to her as it is to me."

"I don't believe her relationship to others indicates anything about her relationship to you."

"How could it not?"

"Because from what you're telling me, Mary is polyamorous. She likely doesn't have or want one primary relationship, and I find it highly likely she reciprocates your sentiments very closely. Else, your relationship would not be as strong as it seems to be."

I rubbed my temples. It made a kind of sense. Demanding exclusivity of her wouldn't be fair. I shouldn't feel slighted since she didn't offer.

I was still deep in thought when she spoke again.

"What do you think your anxiety has to do with your sexuality? Or more specifically, why would it be distressing to be something other than straight?"

"I don't identify with lesbians, I mean I do, they're very relatable, but I'm nervous about being seen as one."

"What about being perceived to love women scares you? I presume your date was in public. Were you scared then?"

"Not really, but nobody who knew me saw that, I don't care about the opinions of people I don't have to interact with. I mean, I was a little worried someone would make a scene, but I was already in too deep to do anything about that."

"Would it be bad for Joshua to know you like women?"

"No."

"What about your family?"

"Not really?"

"Co-workers?"

"Kinda."

"How would any of them know if you don't tell them?"

I opened and closed my mouth a few times. I wanted to say they would just know.

"They wouldn't, I guess."

Mrs. Green sat back in her chair. She took her reading glasses off and let them hang around her neck.

I laughed as she made another impatient gesture.

"Okay, I guess I'm not straight."

# 21

# Say It, Out Loud.

"It's so prettyyyyy!" I cooed as I inspected my D&D miniature.

"I'm glad you like it." Cyrus looked amused by my wonder, but in my opinion, he should be proud. My little dwarf barbarian was immaculately detailed. There was wear and tear on the armor in addition to a very expressive face given it was the size of a pinhead. You could tell he was ready to fight.

I put my little warrior back into his display case (another gift from Cyrus), but I couldn't stop staring. For god's sake, he even painted cloth texture on the cloak!

Mary broke me from my trance, asking to see it as well, so I let her look it over while I greeted Cyrus properly. I'd missed him. Something about distance and growing fonder. I dunno. We'd stayed in touch, but it wasn't the same.

Once I'd latched to his midsection long enough, I stepped back and picked up my routine. I had forgotten to take off my shoes, and I had a celebratory dinner to put on!

I busied myself on the other side of the bar, portioning the frighteningly expensive steak and preheating the oven. This meal would be as indulgent as it was easy. Steak and potatoes. Tale as old as time. I got out some butter, crushed a couple of cloves of garlic, and set about seasoning all sides of our steak portions. Mary and Cyrus made themselves comfy at the bar. It felt good to have the gang all here. I mean, I guess I could consider Joshua part of the gang too. Maybe even Kimberly... Still, I didn't want to make Joshua and Cyrus get along while I worked on my friction with Mary's relationship ideology.

Don't get me wrong, I didn't want to control Mary, but I still struggled with the feeling of being lesser when she slept with others. Even after the therapy today, I still had a long way ahead of me to internalize the values I wanted to adopt.

I pulled my thoughts back to what I wanted to talk about. I knew I'd get sass for confessing now, after all this time, but it was still worth facing the music.

"Hey, Mary..."

Her attention was both encouraging and intimidating as she folded her hands under her chin. I took a shaky breath. I could do this.

"So I uh... I had that epiphany I was supposed to have a month ago... or maybe earlier. I dunno. God, I wasted so much time with my head up my ass."

Before I had time to sink into despair about her inevitable disappointment, she shook her head. She reached across the bar and held out her hand, and I took it.

"Please stop beating yourself up. I want to know what you discovered."

I struggled to decide whether to say I'm attracted to women or that I'm a lesbian or bisexual, but all I said was, "I love you."

Cyrus and Mary both looked at me wide-eyed.

Whoops.

I tried to act casual as I chewed my lip. That was not right. I mean, it was true. But not what I should say. And in front of Cyrus...

I was about to elaborate with "like a friend", but Mary had unfrozen.

"I love you too."

Oh.

OH.

Well then. It wasn't unbelievable exactly? She had said she loved me before. We both had. But now It meant something changed, and she knew it. I was speaking of unambiguous romantic love, and she was as well.

"N-not that I should have said I love you a month ago! I meant I should have admitted my attraction then. And not that I didn't mean it I just --"

I trailed off as she shook her head. She released my hand and walked around the bar.

"It's okay." She pulled me into a hug.

"I know you think you wasted time but I want to assure you that you didn't. You took the time you needed to be sure. You moved at your pace, and that was what was important to me above all."

"So you knew..."

"I suspected. Besides, the bright side of all that panic and stress, is it gave me time to suss out my feelings in turn. If you had realized and confessed your love that first week, this conversation would have been quite awkward."

She smiled, and I tried to feel reassured. Still, I wondered if my slip had rushed her. Hell, I'd barely known her for a month. I still couldn't even tell what the difference between friend and lover was for her. Every tool I had for analyzing context and intuiting feelings was useless.

I realized I was panicking. How could I even ask her to reaffirm that she wasn't coerced to reciprocate my confession? Asking for clarification would result in hurt feelings and push her to restate a lie or even reconsider. What if asking her to say it again made her decide it wasn't true?

She sighed and pulled me into another hug. Maybe this is how it would always have to be. I'd have to take a leap and trust her with my heart.

The oven's beep broke the moment, and she stepped back again. I let her return to her bar-stool, and I tried to pick up where I left off. Steak. Potatoes. Dinner.

I wasn't hungry anymore.

I stared at the ingredients before me. On a whim, I stuffed the washed potatoes back in their bag and grabbed a bag of tater tots from the freezer.

Neither of them commented as I dumped them on a sheet and put them in the oven. I flicked on the burner and preheated the pan. I'd say I knew how they liked their steaks, but it shouldn't matter this time. Neither had a hangup to the point where they needed meat well done, so for this grade of beef, medium rare was pretty much the most I could cook it.

Focusing on dinner calmed me. Sure it was like work, and to a degree, it disconnected me from my feelings, but right now, my emotions were running away in every direction.

When I looked up, I saw my audience was watching me work like this was a dinner show and I couldn't even make it entertaining. Still, their attention didn't intimidate me as much, at least not in this context. Two of the most important people in my life, both here and each of them I had met in the last month. That was an upside-down way to live, and yet, nothing could turn me away.

Blessedly, conversation resumed as the steaks hit the pan.

Cyrus told us about some of the crazy drivers he had encountered on his drive. Mary gave a cryptic innuendo story about hard jobs in accounting. Something about crunching numbers and achieving customer satisfaction. Cyrus laughed, but I didn't have the presence of mind to figure out half the code. I supposed that was okay, though.

The tots and steaks finished right on cue, and I took my time resting and plating them. I let them carry their plates to the table while I wrestled the cork off the wine I had bought. On a whim, I tried out the hack I'd seen on that godforsaken meme app and blended the lot for about thirty seconds. If Cyrus and Mary cared, they didn't comment.

My appetite had almost returned when I sat, but that went out the window too as Mary spoke up.

"So I had a big idea of sorts I wanted to discuss as well."

Fuck, I wish I'd taken my anxiety medication.

"I was thinking maybe when we move next month... we could move closer to Cyrus."

I blinked. I stole a glance at Cyrus, he didn't see this coming either. It was encouraging to know she had waited to bring this up with both of us at once. I guess. Still, it might have been nice to warn me first...

I didn't have a chance to consider the implications as she barreled on.

"I know it would be a big move, a new job, stress of all sorts, but I think it would be a really positive move. It would put us closer to my dad and his family as well as all of us closer together."

When I expressed interest in living with Mary, it hadn't felt groundbreaking. I'd had roommates before, and the fact we were having sex still felt transactional at the time. Now the idea of relocating to live together felt huge. Enormous even.

This should be encouraging. This was very affirming as far as backing up a confession of love. It was a pretty clear move toward "I want to build a life together", and yet wasn't it being roommates somewhere else with extra steps?

Fuck my appetite, I guess.

Of course, Mary noticed my anxiety, and I could tell she wanted to soothe it, but what was there to do? She wanted more. She had family and other romance there and wanted to work toward it. I always dreamed of someone with a plan sweeping me away, but I never imagined that requiring I break routine. God, I was a hypocrite.

I forced myself to take a bite. I supposed I should be glad I wasn't nauseous. That would be a lousy gut reaction. Not that gut reactions were reliable in the first place. Fuck my gut. That motherfucker was merely prepared to act on random specific shit.

I realized I was not making a good look as far as responses go. Neither Cyrus nor myself had spoken, so at least he saw this as seriously as I did. I swallowed and mustered my thoughts.

"I feel like... if I say no... you might pick up and move without me, but now that I say that, if you decide not to go it means I held you back." Tears clouded my vision as I stared at my now blurry plate.

"Oh my goodness no! Addie, it's not like that!"

I pushed my palms into my eyes. I needed space, but if I took space, I'd be pushing them away. A roaring sound filled my ears as I tensed and curled in on myself. I couldn't breathe, but just when I thought I'd break out into full-blown sobs I managed a shaky breath.

It helped that Mary kept talking.

"Please take some time to think about it, it's not something we should rush into."

Cyrus mumbled his agreement, but I was at a loss. How would time make me less self-absorbed? The logic was simple; I wanted what was best for Mary, love took commitment. If I loved her enough, I would leap, and if I didn't, I wouldn't. Did I love her enough? Probably. Living with her, near or with Cyrus as well, was a dream. My literal goal. It was what I wanted! Why wasn't I sure?

Maybe I was sure after all. I'd have to be strong, but what was

I risking? It's not like I was at risk of falling out of love with Mary or of becoming unemployable. With the choice between heartbreak and happiness, I could make a decision, and I'd risk having a choice made for me later. What was the difference between breaking my own heart now or later anyway?

I wiped my face on my sleeve. I was burning up and my eyes already ached from the few tears that had made it out. I got a handle on my breathing and found my voice.

"I'll do it."

"I said to take time, Addie. You don't sound remotely enthusiastic."

"Because I'm scared. Terrified even. I've never had to acknowledge that there's an actual path to travel between where I am and where I want to be."

"That... What? What are you talking about?"

I rubbed at the sides of my head and met her eye at last.

"I don't know that I need to take time at all. What you're talking about doing is literally exactly what I want. I just can't grasp why it terrifies me."

Cyrus was still silent, his hands clasped under his chin.

I needed him to draw heat off me, maybe he sensed that, or he had just collected his thoughts.

"For my part I am interested. It's hard not to be really, you're asking nothing of me, and I only stand to gain. As the smaller party should I not be the one moving here instead?"

"But your career...." I don't know why I was arguing. I wanted him to move instead and make this easy for me. How easy it would be...

He shrugged, and we fell silent. It was intimidating how serious this conversation had turned. Mary rubbed her face.

"It's not fair. It's rotten that I'm asking Addie to uproot her life, but my reasoning is that you moving here doesn't bring me closer to my dad. His family lives in the suburbs like half an hour from your workplace."

"Then I veto it," Cyrus said at last, and Mary and I both looked at him in surprise.

"Addie is clearly distressed, and she won't be comforted by you withdrawing the suggestion."

It felt like a solution. I was so close to relief until I realized they had both chosen my comfort over their happiness. I had become a drain. A dead weight.

I shook my head. "Fine. I'll take some time. I'm distressed and I should stop making fatalistic ultimatums for myself. Or something."

"Okay." Mary gave Cyrus a look, and he relented as well.

"Let's just try to enjoy our weekend, and we can check in later."

I nodded and wiped my eyes. I forced myself to take another bite, and though my appetite didn't miraculously return, I had the momentum to take care of myself despite it.

"The steak is delicious." Mary sounded so composed you'd think she didn't just witness a near breakdown.

I smiled and resisted the urge to roll my eyes. Right on cue as always.

"Thanks."

# 22

# Eye To Eye

Though I could put the moving stress out of my mind, I kept remembering the plan I made this morning. Even as I busied myself with errands for the day, I had planned every way I could ask Mary to make love to me. Yet, not one of those theoreticals had considered how Cyrus factored in.

Did I love him? Sure.

As more than a friend? Maybe.

Should I say that?

Uh. No.

Was it a good time to become sexually involved with him?

Fuck.

On the one hand, the risk of compromising my relationship with him or Mary by having sex with him was so low. I had every reason to believe it would be a thoroughly comforting and enjoyable time. However, I had been through the ringer today, and the fact was I wanted to get physical with Mary. Today wasn't the time to expand scope.

So how the fuck did I do that without excluding Cyrus? I wasn't very well going to wait till he was gone, and I dreaded the effort of communicating all of that. Like what would I do if he offered to step out for coffee while we did something? It's not like I wanted to have a secret time with Mary behind his back!

I wasn't making progress. The way out was communication or patience, and I already knew which one I was capable of.

I let myself into the bathroom while Mary was showering and sat on the toilet seat.

"Hey Mary?"

"Yeah babe?"

"I need a bit of advice. Or help. Or both. I don't know."

"Sure, lay it on me."

I could see through the door she had turned to look at me, and I smirked to myself as she peeked over the top.

Pressed against the frosted glass, she was giving me quite the view.

"I want to make love with you. All day long, I've wanted to ask you to make love to me for the first time, and I'm not sure how."

"Well, you kinda just did."

I snorted as she returned to her activities.

"Yeah, and that wasn't quite as romantic as I hoped, but that's life."

"Well, I'd be happy to accommodate you. What's the issue?"

"It's Cyrus." I sensed I was treading on thin ice, so I made sure I spoke as I had rehearsed. "I care deeply for him, and in a real sense I'm interested in a sexual relationship with him. But tonight I wanted to express myself to you alone. The problem is I can't bear to exclude him either. I figured it would be better to have this conversation, rather than just wait until he went home."

She hummed her acknowledgment, and I watched as she worked her fingers through her hair. It took a lot of willpower, but I managed not to agonize over her silence.

"Well, he's a big boy, so I'll ask him to give us some privacy tonight."

"Simple as that?"

"Simple as that," she agreed.

"You don't think I'd be hurting his feelings? Or offending him in some way?"

"Hmmm. I mean, I'm sure he would be very enthusiastic to comfort you himself, but as you said before, I have good taste in men. I guarantee he will respect your boundaries first every time."

I wiggled my toes on the bathmat.

"I guess I kinda assumed privacy was kinda... not a thing in poly relationships."

"Sometimes it is, sometimes it isn't." She shut off the water, and I hopped up to fetch her towel. "In some relationships, every connection is discrete and private. In others, every aspect is kept painstakingly public and open. The balance between the two ideologies is something that each person must determine."

She stepped out of the shower, and took the towel as she stepped into the tub to catch the drips.

"How should we balance?"

"I don't know yet, and it might change over time. There's a chance you and Cyrus won't connect perfectly. While Cyrus and I are both very open individuals, if you find you are more closed then we will likely endeavor to accommodate that in any way we can. If I had to guess, at this moment, we lean toward a 'no secrets' relationship model. I think you picked up on that or you wouldn't have been so concerned about making sure sex you wanted to share with me alone wasn't treated as a secret from him."

My mind drifted to the first time we had spent time with Cyrus. He and Mary had frequently gone off in private just as she and I had a couple of times. While it wasn't a secret, it wasn't announced either. I wondered if this was a sign our relationship had evolved.

She ran her fingers through her hair a few times and shook water off her hands. "The first time, while you and Cyrus got to know each other we treated my relationships with the two of you as discrete. Though you might not classify your relationship with Cyrus as romantic, you have an established relationship now. That is another reason we are having this conversation."

I rubbed my eyes and nodded.

"Do you want to use my hairdryer?"

"No thanks, I have my own thing for when I'm in a hurry."

She continued to run her fingers through her hair, frequently shaking them dry or wiping them on the towel.

"Are you heating your fingers or something?"

"No, no, no. That wouldn't be much better than ironing wet hair, I'm drawing off the water." Already her hair had taken on a lighter color and matte texture. Loose curls and waves bounced as she straightened up. "Have I never shown you this? A while back I figured out how to siphon excess water without stripping the oils."

I shook my head. "That's cheating."

"I'll do it for you if you ask."

"That's ingenious and resourceful," I amended, earning a chuckle.

She disregarded her clothes and walked out to talk to Cyrus. I didn't pick up most of the conversation, but I heard him call "have fun" before the front door shut. I didn't think he needed to leave the apartment, but I guessed I shouldn't complain.

I was still sitting on the edge of the tub when Mary returned. God, I was weak for her. It was like a switch flipped. Innocent adoration became lust.

I took a deep breath and stood. I prepared to be led to the bedroom but she continued to approach me. She pushed me against the shower door. Her lips were on mine. Her hand was cradling my neck, and my shirt rode up as she reached for more skin to touch. I was holding onto her for life itself, and it still wasn't close enough.

Part of me expected her to ask how I wanted it. Instead, I felt like she was trying to set my head spinning and keep it that way.

"Do you care much for these pajamas?" She murmured. I shook my head.

"Me neither."

A dozen knives traced down my skin. Fabric fluttered as all of my clothes fell off in ribbons. All at once the sensation of soft cotton gave way to her warm skin and the cold glass behind me. She brushed a strip off my arm before dragging me by the wrist to the bed.

"I'm going to mess with your sense of touch now." She wasn't asking, but I nodded anyway. Already, this was far more magic than she usually brought to bed. I watched with idle amusement as she put a generous dollop of lube on her fingers and crawled over me.

I expected her to make me sensitive or make everything feel erotic, but instead, she smothered my sense of touch. Even as she laid down on me, worked her leg between mine, and eased her middle finger between my labia, an imaginary heavy blanket separated us. Still, I acclimated to the sensation. The small movements of her hand were firm and soothing rather than frenzied and sharp.

Since I was unable to determine how her skin felt against mine, as far as I was concerned she might as well be everywhere. Even though I knew her hand was holding the back of my neck, I felt like I was floating. I could hear just fine, my breathing was even, and I felt at peace even as my heart hammered in my chest. Still, even as dull as it was, I felt the pressure on my sex like a heavy pillow.

I relaxed my back and submitted myself to her weight. I focused on breathing in time with her movements. The simple act of having my expectations met wound a tension that spanned my entire body. Without any distraction, I was able to give that my full attention.

As I thought I might let go, she paused. I groaned and propped myself up on my elbows as she crawled off the bed to collect rope, clamps, a spreader bar, and cuffs. She put the spreader bar on my ankles first and tied each end of the bar to the bottom of the bed. She attached my cuffs and clicked them into a carabiner above my head. Then, she clamped my nipples and laid the chain across my lips.

"I bet you'll have fun with that," she whispered as she trailed her hand down.

I wrinkled my nose at the smear of lube on my stomach, but I cared far less when she reached her destination. She wasted little time rubbing before easing her middle and ring fingers in. Occasionally she pushed at my clit with her thumb, but her main focus was on being firm, and goddamn was she holding my hips down now.

I lifted my chin to tug the chain, and sure enough, the sensation came through pleasantly. Rather than sharp pain, it felt like dozens of rounded points were being pressed into my skin. Pairing that sensation with her attention below took my breath away. I tested my restraints and found the confinement enriched the tension. It was like having my ankles and wrists grounded made it so I couldn't release it if I tried.

As she kissed me over the chain, I began to acclimate. The strain in my body was unbreakable. Conceptualizing my limits gained me nothing. She deftly took the reins from my mouth and undid the clamps with her teeth.

I scarcely had time to miss that sensation before she gave me back my sense of touch. The carabiner above my head made a sharp crack, and that was the last thing I heard for a long time. If I had been floating before, now I felt like my tether was cut. Like thunder, I experienced sound like a dull rumble as the tension broke and ripped through me. I wanted to wrap myself around Mary but I couldn't move. Mercifully, she was holding me close anyways. The only movement I had left was my back, and I found the residual waves felt better when I rolled my hips in time with them. They faded, and I grew tired.

The burning pain remained on my chest. I realized that just because I didn't feel it before didn't mean I wasn't leaving bruises. At some point, Mary undid my restraints. She held me as I realized I was breathing, and I calmed my ragged gasps.

"Wow." I stretched and arched my back into her. Fresh chills radiated from my lower back, sweeping over my skin and making her touch feel new all over again.

She giggled, and I turned to receive a kiss.

"I still have a few tricks I haven't shown you," she murmured as I relaxed my shoulders and hips.

"So when do I see the other tricks?"

She paused and put a hand on her chin.

"I'll pace them out, save some treats for when you've been an extra good girl."

"I'm sensing a descent into erotic pain."

"Is that okay?"

I rolled over to get my hands under me and sit up. I was stable here, but I knew if I tried to stand on my knees I'd embarrass myself.

"A little pain is probably okay. I haven't really experimented with it."

"Your litany of bruises say otherwise."

"I... Kimberly has a thing for biting I think. And I kinda like doing things other people like."

"Do you know what you like?"

"Uh... doing what other people like?"

"Wrong answer, doofus."

She sat up across from me and crossed her arms.

"Well... I kinda remember a while back. Do you remember the first time you asked me what I wanted to do? I think you said something about payback... anyways. I had a itty bitty meltdown because

I wanted just... really romantic care stuff. Sex was great but I got twisted up about how you felt about me in that process."

"Mhmm." Mary picked at the blanket for a second before looking up. "So I've kinda sussed out that your love languages are giving service, giving gifts, and receiving... well... you're pretty starved for everything so it's hard to tell what you want most, I just know that words of affirmation can sometimes mean less to you."

My mouth hung open a bit as I tried to catch up. Was I supposed to know all of that about her? She was right about me of course but while I could see how she knew those things about me I had no idea how I would be sure about those things for her.

"What are... your love languages?"

If she was disappointed I had to ask, she didn't show it.

"Quality time is a big one. I like when you are mindful of me- which you have been. I like words of affirmation. Gifts are really easy to not go well so... that's a risky one. I love a good gift, but when people give me junk I feel more bitter about being misunderstood and having to act thankful. Touch is good. I like touch. Quality touch time is the fun stuff I think. Service, like gifts, is kinda meh."

I nodded. It made sense. I'm not sure I could have outlined it as elegantly as she did for me but there wasn't anything I'd been misunderstanding up to this point. I just hadn't thought it all out.

She scooted forward and nudged my knee.

"Sooooo what do you want?"

"Do you have any tricks that are particularly good for you?"

"What? like spells I can cast on myself?"

"Or if there's one you can teach me that would work too."

"If only." She gave me a wry smile and laid face down beside me. Her voice came muffled through the blankets. "I don't know that you would be interested in them."

"I dunno..." I trailed my fingers along her back and she rolled into my touch. "I am pretty crazy about you."

She only grumbled in response.

I walked my fingers up over her shoulders and scratched lightly across her back. "You know, I've heard some pretty loud slapping sounds through the door when you've played with Cyrus."

"You didn't seem interested in pain play." She lifted herself enough to turn her head.

"Mhmm, but it occurs to me that it wasn't Cyrus crying out after each hit."

She rolled onto her side and gave me a look between boredom and amusement. "Tell me you wouldn't freak out if you hit me."

"I wouldn- I might not freak out? I do in fact have the capacity to inflict pain."

"Mhmmm."

"Okay so I probably can't do a good job pretending but that doesn't mean I can't play rough!"

"I don't know, you pretended to be straight for an awful long time."

"Fuck you!" my voice sounded like a squeak and she laughed as I pushed her shoulder.

"That's certainly the idea." She rolled on her back and looked up. I watched her eyes flick between several places far off in space.

"Have we done anything you've liked? Or have we just been doing stuff for me all this time?"

"Maybe I like doing what other people like as well." She gave me a wry smile and reached up to cup my cheek as I crawled closer.

I propped myself up on my elbows and tried not to shiver as she brushed her fingertips over the back of my neck.

"How about we break out the swing again." I leaned in to steal a kiss.

"What do you plan to do with that?"

"Maybe I can surprise you for a change."

Her eyebrows rose but she wasted no time skipping to the closet.

I thought back to all the things she had suggested in the past that I hadn't tried. There was the TENS unit, candles, spike wheel, whips, paddles... Why did she have so many goddamn toys?

I struggled to contain my nerves as she clipped the swing to the ceiling near the foot of the bed. I wanted to have her as a captive audience before I showed my hand this time.

"You first." I struggled to keep my tone level as she raised an eyebrow at me.

"You don't want to climb up with me?"

"Very funny. No, I have other plans."

She sat down and kicked the bed to start swinging as though it were a tire swing.

"Will you tell me your plans now?"

Rather than answer, I grabbed a candle out of the drawer.

"Not that one, I prefer the red, the purple ones are for you."

"For me?"

"Yeah. You know, just in case. The red ones burn way hotter so they aren't as friendly to delicate little flowers like you."

I gave her my most indignant scowl and tossed a red candle and lighter on the bed. Next, I grabbed the plug-in massage wand and the smaller TENS unit.

Mary shook her head and sighed. "Bless your heart Addie."

"What?" I sounded a bit sharper than I intended and I frowned as Mary climbed out of the swing.

"Let me help with the preparation."

"I can do it."

Mary chewed her lip. Her look very much said "no, you can't", but even if she wouldn't say that I knew she wouldn't let it go. "*Please* let me help?"

I sighed and waved my hands. "Fine."

By the time I found an extension cord for the wand she had

laid out small bowls with ice and water respectively as well as the waterproof blanket.

Right. Safety. The impulse to be bitter at Mary for correcting me turned inward. Stupid goddamn safety and its phenomenal ability to squash spontaneity.

She kicked at the edge of the blanket with her toe as I finished plugging in the wand. She didn't make a move to get back in the swing.

"Am I forgetting something else?"

"The TENS unit and wax both benefit from lotion." she trailed off and smoothed out the blanket with her foot idly. "I'm sorry for hijacking your plans."

"You aren't doing anything wrong, I am." I dropped the wand on the bed. "Which lotion should I get?"

"Addieeeee," Mary groaned and reached out to pull me into a hug. I stumbled back and we ended up doing a half-controlled crash onto the bed.

"Whaaaaat?" I exaggerated playful ignorance. I knew what she was picking at, and I didn't even really want her to say it out loud.

"You're usually pretty good about accepting advice and stuff. What's different right now?" She kissed my cheek, neck, and collar before resting her head over my heart.

"Help and advice feel different." I felt her nod and her hair tickled my chin. "I've gotten used to being wrong all the time, but I feel bad when I mess up with stuff I care about."

"So you weren't just mad at me because you thought the stuff I was fixating on didn't matter?"

"I'm not mad, I just didn't want to be reminded that I don't know anything." I managed a huff of a laugh, but I doubted I really managed to sound sarcastic.

She hummed and let me sit up. "So when you're done with me do I get to do everything back? For education of course. And science."

I chewed my lip. The fantasy instantly pivoted from what it would be like to hear her in the throes of ecstasy, to what it would feel like being at her mercy again.

"I don't know if I can handle what I plan to do to you." I retreated to the bathroom and found one of the larger bottles of lotion. I held it in the doorway so Mary could see. "Will this work?"

"Yeah. Haven't you heard of the golden rule?"

I rolled my eyes. "I don't want to bore you with the lack of intensity I can handle."

"I can enjoy low intensity, there are multitudes within me."

"So you don't want to hang in my arms while I shock, burn, and buzz your nerves away?" I crawled onto her lap and popped the cap of the lotion bottle.

"I'll just assume you mean that in moderation." her hands trailed over the outsides of my thighs and towards my belly.

"Bad idea, communication will be key."

"That's rich coming from you." she slipped her hand quickly between my thighs and cupped my sex. I caught her wrist, but I didn't try to push her away.

I struggled not to jump out of her lap, I couldn't untense with that sort of touch, but I would endeavor not to give her the satisfaction of compromising me.

I released her wrist but my nonchalant act was shattered as she applied pressure and began easing her ring and middle fingers in.

"You'll get carpal tunnel contorting your wrist like that." My voice sounded like a gasp as I rested my forehead on her shoulder

"Worse yet, I could get injured if you made any sudden moves."

"God, you're a bitch sometimes." My laugh was cut off as she moved and I rolled my hips instinctively.

"Oooh, I like that sound. Do it again."

"Damn it Mary." I growled and pushed her hand away.

She exaggerated a sigh and fell back into the bed.

Feeling particularly uncharitable, I poured lotion directly on her chest and stomach.

She squirmed and reached to take the bottle from me, but I held it above my head. She narrowed her eyes. "They have a term for people like you."

"Adorable?"

"I appreciate the self love there, but I was thinking 'brat'."

I set the bottle down behind me and started rubbing the lotion in. "Takes one to know one."

"It really doesn't."

I felt her rumble beneath my fingers as she hummed tunelessly. She seemed to be exaggerating delight in the attention, positively melting beneath me. I saw her lips quirk up as I worked around her chest. I couldn't help but feel jealous, she didn't make the slightest twitch of discomfort no matter where I touched her. Whether I scratched or brushed lightly, she was maddeningly proficient at remaining relaxed.

"What if I don't want to use the swing anymore?" She sighed and shifted beneath me.

"We don't have to."

"Will you be happy if you just massage me like this for the rest of eternity?"

"I don't have that sort of stamina."

She waved her hand dismissively. "I can help with that bit."

I sat up and stretched, my back was already tensing up from bending over so long. What would I say to that? I always seemed to get my way with her, and I couldn't live with myself if I denied her the one time she expressed an interest in me doing something for her.

"Okay. Should I continue to just use the lotion or do you have massage oil somewhere?"

She made a sound like a groan crossed with a whine. "Don't

threaten me with a good time." She sat up far enough to prop her hands behind her and sag sleepily. "We can get oil some other time. I wanna know more about this nerve frying you have in mind."

"Oh." I crawled off her lap and busied myself collecting up the various instruments we had laid out. "I mean, it wasn't anything crazy. I just thought I would get you set up in the swing and then just... I dunno. See how things go?"

"Cool, cool." She took the TENS unit and climbed back into the swing. She stuck the pads on either side of her clit, and then cranked the dial. I heard her suck a breath through her teeth before she turned it back off and handed the controller to me.

"Jesus Christ, Mary."

"What? I can take it. Were you planning to put the pads somewhere else?"

"Yes? I don't know where but I'm not trying to cause nerve damage here."

"It won't damage anything."

"I'll take your word for it." I couldn't keep the skepticism out of my tone, but I busied myself adjusting the swing. I got her situated so she could rest her ankles on the bed while the swing cradled her in the net spanning between the three loops. Seat-belt style latches allowed the loops under each thigh to be disconnected easily, but the loop behind her head was much shorter and just held all the netting to make the triangle shaped sling. She'd been proud to tell me she'd woven it herself. It was comfortable, and it would even make a nice reading chair if it didn't hold my knees so far apart when I sat in it.

I pushed the swing and Mary made a quiet "wheee" as she swung side to side. With a little turning, I settled down on the edge of the bed between her knees.

"May I ask, were you intending to fuck me with a side of pain? Or just fuck around with pain to see what's fun for you?" Mary folded her hands behind her head. She certainly didn't seem worried about pain.

"I, uh- I don't know. Honestly, I kinda just want to do whatever I want but somehow be doing exactly what you enjoy."

"Don't we all? But if you want, I can act like I'm enjoying it no matter what."

"Harsh."

"It means I care about your feelings!"

"It would mean you would rather suffer in silence than communicate."

Mary raised an eyebrow.

"Shut up. I don't fake orgasms for you."

"I didn't say anything!" Mary held her hands up.

I had the peculiar urge to spike the TENS unit.

"Regardless. Genuine feedback please." I scooted forward and threaded the wand through Mary's left leg loop.

"Can do."

I hooked the TENS unit by its belt clip to the sling above her shoulder. It had a "dog collar" setting and when Mary didn't react to me turning the power limit up, a devious idea formed in my mind. I held the wand like a pen, looping the cord around my wrist so that I could draw imaginary patterns over her thigh and stomach.

I kept the intensity low and lingered occasionally near the pads. I leaned forward to place a chaste kiss over her heart where the pentacle tattoo lay.

This close, her hum sounded like a warm roar of a rumble and I leaned into it on some sort of instinct. She combed her fingers through my hair and I felt her breath rush past my face when I eased the wand down between her thighs. She twitched and pulled herself closer, crossing her ankles behind my back.

Her breath was heavier, warmer as I maintained the lightest

pressure below. She made a particularly loud sigh that cut off sharply as she flinched.

"Did you seriously do that?" she whispered.

"Do what?" In contrast, I spoke at a normal volume. She kicked in my arms and dug her fingers into my shoulders.

"Bit of a mixed message here babe. Do you want me to talk or not?"

I pressed the head of the wand in and wiggled it until she moaned and kicked again.

I whispered this time, "On the contrary, this ensures that you will either communicate out of great personal sacrifice or for your own benefit. I find both scenarios desirable."

"Can you turn it down a bit then?"

I reached up and turned it down to the lowest setting. "Sure, if you'll put your hands behind your back."

"Are you going to tie them?"

"No, and I meant inside the sling. Really tangle them in there."

I felt perverse glee as she leaned forward to comply. With a few seconds of shifting around, she had settled in again. I had to lean further forward now to take her left nipple in my mouth, and I amused myself toying with the simple barbell.

I heard her scoff, a huff more of amusement than anything. "Having fun?"

I let the wand hang between us and pulled her toward me. I pinched the ends of the barbells between my lips and pulled just enough to look up at her. She was biting her lip hard, but she leaned back, pulling free of my lips.

"Yes." I whispered. "I am."

"That makes two of us."

"Oh yeah?" I picked up the wand and straightened up so I could get a full view of her.

I slid my left hand up under her other breast and squeezed, matching the pressure with the wand below.

"Addieeee."

I released her and reached up to turn the TENS unit up a hair. "Yes dear?"

She pulled herself to me and I pushed back with the head of the wand, enjoying the way she started rolling her hips against me. I suspected she lost her train of thought as her head fell back into the swing and she seemed to lose herself in that movement.

Part of me wanted to deny her, to make that frustration another part of the experience, but I decided there was more value in rewarding her. I held the wand in both hands, bracing my elbows over her thighs to take over her rhythm.

If she was feeling the sting of electricity, she wasn't letting it stop her. She moaned freely as she thrashed what little she could. Her grasp on my waist slipped and her movements became shakier and less coordinated.

After a few seconds of erratic tensing with poorly smothered moans, I felt her pull back from the wand. I turned it off and reached up to switch off the TENS unit as well. I slipped my hands behind her back and held the netting of the swing out of the way so that she could free her arms.

"Did I do it right?"

"Probably." She peeled the pads of the TENS unit and tossed them over her shoulder.

"I guess we're done with that?"

"For now. I'm not reusing those pads."

"Are we done with the swing too?"

"Afraid so." Her voice sounded strained.

I hurried to loop an arm under her right knee and unclipped that corner of the swing. Before I could help her with the other she got her leg under her and stood up.

She used my shoulders for leverage and flopped on the bed beside me. The move was made less graceful by the leg strap catching on her left ankle, but she kicked it free and dropped her leg across my lap.

"Did I hurt you?"

"Wasn't that the point?"

She rolled on her back, sassy as ever but her expression fell when she met my eye.

"I'm not injured, I just didn't think through the pad placement very well and the TENS unit ended up overstimulating some muscles. Who would have thought that the muscles for closing my legs would be so weak?" She arched her back and pulled the lighter and candle out from under her before relaxing again. "It's a joke, Addie. I'm saying that I don't close my legs."

"I got the joke."

"You didn't laugh."

"I'm sorry, you're very funny." I don't know why I decided to deadpan that. It was funny, I just couldn't laugh when she was in pain and it was my fault.

"Damn straight skippy."

I shook my head and crawled backward to sit next to her. "May I help work out soreness?"

"May?"

"Touching your skin is of course a privilege."

"You're full of it." She stretched and dropped her hands above her head. "I don't want to fuck around with deep tissue massage, but touch would be soothing, yes."

"How about wax?"

"Oh hell yes."

"That's soothing?"

"Maybe? Probably not." she pressed the candle and lighter into my hands. "Grab the ice too, fuck me up."

"Sometimes you scare me."

"Sometimes? I'd better step it up." Once I was out of the way she rolled over and made a nest of pillows to lay over.

I tossed the waterproof blanket at her and crawled back onto the bed with the bowl of ice. It had melted a bit, but wasn't likely to spill. I set it on the small of her back while I laid out the blanket next to her.

"You're so fucking rude." She grumbled and contorted to grab the bowl off her back. She almost spilled it but I caught it and placed it near her elbow.

"I am the model of politeness." I rubbed the patch of cooled skin and grabbed the lotion.

Despite my eagerness to play with fire, I took my time rubbing her down. The last thing I would want would be for her skin to dry out- if that was even a thing that happened with wax.

"Are there any guidelines I don't know? I'm not planning to hold the flame to your skin unless you ask."

"Oh thanks. I'm glad that even if you think I am absolutely insane you will still check in."

I smacked her butt, hard enough to make a sound, but not a mark.

"Fine!" Mary propped herself up on her elbows and took the candle to demonstrate. "Try to hold it a good foot or so above my skin. You can tilt the candle pretty hard to make it drip faster but I'm not in a hurry if you aren't.

"Got it." I flicked the lighter and lit the candle.

*~*~*

An hour or so later, I stumbled from the bedroom to the living room. Mary had taken the time to find and one-up every mark Kimberly had made and the result was my pleased and pampered self. Clothes sounded like too much sensation, so I gave Cyrus a show as I got a glass of water in nothing but my boy-shorts.

Did I intend to show off? Hell no. I assumed he was still out and about. Was I going to scurry back to the bedroom? Oh. I guess that was an option. Fuck. At the very least I figured I could trust Cyrus. I wouldn't get a disgusted look, hell he'd probably do the careful eye contact thing. He was a nerd like that.

Once I had my orange juice I mustered the courage to look at Cyrus.

He was watching the TV.

For a moment I was offended and disappointed at his ambivalence but then I saw that the show he had on was paused. Yep. Nerd.

Mary for her part looked as smug as ever. She kissed Cyrus on the cheek and stopped at the dining room table. I watched as she looked into the white box that hadn't been there before and snorted. She shook her head and beckoned me over.

Through the plastic window, I saw a round cake decorated with frosting flowers. Elegant red script filled the space in the middle.

"Congratulations! You had sex!"

# 23

## Good News?

"Finally coming around to that threesome suggestion?"

Joshua looked from me to Mary, and I rolled my eyes.

"In your dreams."

I let myself into his apartment and set the beer on the coffee table. I brushed aside debris to make room for the pizza Mary was carrying.

I wondered if Mary should bring the bad news since I was already snubbing him. At this point, it was a bit late to replan.

"Those look fancy." He eyed the beer carrier but hardly spared a glance at the bottle before popping the top on the edge of the table. "Must be big news."

I sighed as he flopped in his favorite chair. Mary took my hand, and I was about to explain when Joshua cut in again.

"Is it marriage? Are you pregnant?"

I rubbed my eyes as Mary laughed. At least it was funny to her. Once I had some faith he had gotten the guessing out of his system, I met his eye.

"Mary and I are moving away."

It did not take long for Joshua's grin to disappear. He looked between us.

"Shit..."

I took a beer and fussed with my key-chain to get it open before sagging back on the couch.

"How far? Where to?"

Mary picked up a bottle and popped the cap off in one smooth motion. "Tristate, so about a six-hour drive. It'll be closer to my family."

Joshua nodded.

"Damn."

I tapped my feet on the carpet. I wanted to grab a slice of pizza, but I didn't want to be the first one this time.

When he didn't say anything, I spoke up, "We're gonna have a moving party and drinks at Sean's Pub."

"I'll be there for sure."

I relaxed as he took a piece, and I waited about five seconds before the following suit.

"I didn't think your dad... lived here you know? Or are you re-connecting with your mom?"

Mary snorted. "Nah fuck that bitch... She's super dead by the way."

Joshua and I both stared at her cavalier attitude.

Unperturbed, she continued, "Dad settled down for a while actually. He sorta formed a polycule and has two kids with another on the way. Might be cool to hang out with my half-sibs and moms, and if not, it's a big city."

I wasn't particularly worried about her family. On our Tristate visit, Mikah, Crystal, and Mazer had been delightful. It was kinda cool to have babies in the extended family to fawn over.

"I guess polyamory runs in the family," Joshua mumbled and took a sip of his beer.

"It's sexually transmitted, actually."

Joshua coughed and covered his mouth.

I rolled my eyes. Mary never was one to let go of a bad joke.

We lapsed to silence until Joshua became impatient. "How are we gonna dig the evening out of this weird hole?"

"Threesome?" Mary offered.

"No!" I spoke a little louder than intended and I felt my face heat up as Mary laughed.

Joshua snorted. "Eventually these jokes are going to stop being funny, and I fully endorse investigating exactly when we reach that point."

"I'd rather have a threesome, actually," I muttered, much to their amusement.

Joshua shook his head, "So what else is new?"

"I'm not straight."

Joshua blinked at me twice and glanced at Mary.

"Please tell me that's not new."

"As of Monday." Mary enjoyed dragging me under the bus. The fact I enjoyed teasing didn't mean she should have that much fun with it.

Joshua shook his head. "Congratulations on determining you like girls, Addison. It only took a month of --" he gestured at Mary, "-- that."

"For your information, I've determined I also like boys."

I regretted the outburst and braced myself for another threesome jab, but it never came.

"That's progress. I still remember when I figured that out."

He clarified before I could articulate my surprise.

"I'm bi. Don't beat yourself up for not realizing. If you thought you and I were both straight all this time, you probably thought Mary was too."

He took a sip as if he hadn't roasted me, and Mary turned to me with a smirk.

"For the record, how long did you think I was straight?"

I didn't appreciate her wording, but I relented anyway.

"I probably first entertained the idea you weren't straight when I woke up in your bed for the second time."

"Didn't I tell you about my sexuality before that?"

"Probably. Time isn't real. The point is I didn't realize until well after you took me home."

She nodded as if that was reasonable, or at least expected, and Joshua shook his head.

"Well. Like it or not we reached that point. It's not that funny anymore... wanna play a game?" Before we even agreed, he handed out controllers. The mood lightened as we moved past looming goodbyes.

*~*~*

Kimberly had been enthusiastic as ever when I reached out to her about meeting for lunch. Even though we had only gone on one date, I still felt it would be appropriate to tell her in person. I wasn't sure I would maintain the relationship physically, or even online. Still, I always found myself caring far too much about what people thought of me.

Mary, as lovely as she was with advice, supported my decision either way- but not enough to come with me. It was so much easier when people told me what to do. I just did what I was told and then, If I did my best, it wasn't my fault or problem.

I over-thought everything. The coffee bar was convenient for her to get to, she'd have her car if she wished to leave, and the booths were reasonably private. Still, I worried I'd offend her if she felt I wasted her time on something that could have been a text.

A month ago, sex was something that happened with someone

you were dear to. It spoke of a lasting relationship. Kimberly and I had sex before I knew her favorite color.

I waved to her as she came through the door. She was happy to see me. Even though I continued to dread this regardless of her mood, it still felt like that was important.

"Hey, Kimberly." I stood to greet her and hugged her. She kissed my cheek, and it took me a bit longer to stop reading into that.

"Hey, Addie! It's good to see you."

We sat, and she picked up a menu as I twisted my fingers together.

"Do you know what's good here?"

I shook my head, "I've never been."

That was enough for her to pause and recognize my anxiety. I could tell she wanted to ask, but she gave me her full attention instead.

"I'm moving next month. I wasn't sure how to tell you so I'm so sorry if I wasted your time coming out here and you definitely don't have to stay."

"It's alright, that sounds exciting. Tell me more."

Fuck. I think I planned for everything but this.

"Since my place isn't getting fixed, Mary invited me to move in with her. The more she thought about it, the more she wanted to move to the Tristate area to be closer to friends and family. She invited me along and I said yes."

"That's fucking sweet!" She held up her hand for a high five, and I tentatively clapped it.

I watched as she picked up the menu again and glanced over the options.

Is this what lesbians did? They just- cheered when the people they went on dates with settled down with other girls?

She set down her menu and folded her hands under her chin.

"So, is it getting pretty serious with Mary after all?" She smiled conspiratorially.

"Y-yeah."

"Hell yeah girl!"

I was curious about why she was so cool with this, but my energies were better spent appreciating the positive response rather than looking a gift horse in the mouth.

"We're gonna have a going away party that you are super invited to."

"I'm psyched. I'll be there."

The waiter came by to take our orders, and I was too slow to say I wasn't ready. Kimberly ordered both a drink and food, so I panic-chose an oat milk latte and the Belgian waffles.

"Soooooooo." She folded her hands in front of her. "Tell me mooooore."

"I mean, I don't know how much you already know."

"There's what you told me verbally of course, what you've broadcasted with your body language, and what Mary divulged when I prodded her after our date."

"Oh."

Fuck.

"I'd tell you what she told me, but I think it's funnier if that part is a mystery."

I pulled my hands through my hair. "So yeah... uh... I guess first off I'm sorry for using our date to feel out my sexuality without your knowledge. You didn't sign up for that. I mean, I did my very best not to lie, and I think at the time I was being honest to an extent, but I was also misleading."

She blinked and nodded. "Aaaand now I feel bad for lying about talking to Mary."

I dropped my forehead on the counter.

"Fuuuuuck."

I expected her to leave. Like, she might or might not say good-bye, but I was sure that was unrecoverable. Instead, when I looked up, she was still there, giving me a sad smile.

"So what all did you feel out? Aside from my hot bod of course."

I groaned despite myself. She was both kinder and crueler than I deserved.

"I learned that I'm a dumbass, that I've been attracted to girls in a very gay way for a while, and that Mary was not somehow an anomaly amongst my perfectly straight sexuality."

"Yeah... yeah." She nodded as though this was simultaneously a disappointing surprise but also completely expected. "So did you confess to her?"

"Yeah. We used the L-word. It's officially a romantic relation-ship now.

"So now it's U-Haul time. Saucy. Do you plan to adopt cats or dogs? Or both?"

"If it's inevitable, I guess we haven't chosen. She has a bunch of plants. Does that count?"

"Kinda. I'll let it slide for now."

She bullied me into sharing my actual gay awakening story now that I had one. Most of it she knew because it was her point of pride to have rocked my world so hard I got my head out of my ass. We continued to chat after our food arrived, and, in general, she was genuinely happy for me. I couldn't fathom that ride-or-die solidarity for other women.

I insisted on paying the whole bill. I'd like to think she relented, even though I had to race her to the register and wrestle her while the cashier gave us concerned looks. I figured she wasn't upset be-cause she could have restrained me into an absolute puddle if she had tried. The girl was strong.

I caught my breath as she shook her head outside the coffee bar.

"So. You have my address. Your girlfriend is polyamorous. You wanna put two and two together to see if our legs still make four?"

"What the hell does that mean?"

"No fukken clue. Made it up. I mean you definitely know what it means but I don't know what I'm half-heartedly pretending it means beyond the innuendo."

"I get it, I get it," I sighed. "Last time I came home from your place, she took every mark you left as a challenge. Some of those bruises still haven't faded and it's been nearly a week."

"See, and if you didn't want *me* to take that as a challenge, you should have told me that in a text once you were a six-hour drive away." She winked at me and twirled her keys as she walked to her car. "I'll see you at my place in fifteen."

In truth, I was there inside five minutes. I'd like to think that was because I was a daring speed demon, but she probably gave me time to stare after her car as she drove away. Apparently that's a thing I do now.

# 24

# Heck You, I Quit.

"I know we're gonna get away pretty permanently in a couple weeks, but I was thinking maybe this weekend we could get away."

Mary came up behind me and wrapped her arms around my stomach. I let out an involuntary sigh as she kissed the base of my neck.

In turn, formulating a response took extra time. "Did you want to go to Tristate again?"

I braced my hands on the counter and leaned forward as one kiss on my neck became several. With the way her hands slipped up my shirt, I thought Mary might have her way with me against the counter-top.

"Eh. We'll have plenty of time there. I suppose we could invite Cyrus, but I was thinking we should go somewhere else, just the two of us."

I wasn't sure what she was playing at, pairing this innocuous conversation with her physical attention. I only managed a nod. Turning around was a herculean task.

"I don't know where I'd want to go, I don't even know when I could go. I'm out of vacation days."

"Then quit. Let's go to the beach."

I don't even know what undignified sound I made as she lifted and pushed me to sit on the counter. The toaster dug into my back as it was forced out of the way, but I had difficulty caring as she leaned in.

"I get the feeling you are trying to influence my decision making process."

"Hm? No. Never. Have I been riling you up? It must be my subconscious telling me I'm hungry."

"You're so full of shit."

I admit I pretty readily submitted myself to her attention. If she wanted me here on the counter, I'd endeavor to accommodate.

I leaned back against the cabinet as she hugged me close. If she planned to escalate further, she wasn't making much of a move in that direction. Maybe I'd simply be trapped here until I relented.

"Fine, let's go to the beach. But we will have to get a swimsuit because it's been years since I've gone swimming."

"Or we could go to a nude beach."

"Or we could not do that. That sounds good, let's not go to a nude beach and never say we would."

"Oooh such a visceral reaction. Are you scared of being seen? Or does the thought of other people staring at me set off your jealousy?"

"What day is it?" I made a show of holding up her wrist, though she wasn't wearing a watch. "Is there a national 'be a stinker' day that nobody told me about?"

"Fine, fine. We can get you some boring clothes for the boring beach."

She released me from my counter-top. prison and took over washing the dishes I had already forgotten about. I half-listened and dried dishes beside her as she laid out plans and details for our little getaway.

*~*~*

While I didn't dislike my job at the test kitchen, it was fun to show up in vacation clothes with Mary to finalize my termination. Mary, in particular, had drawn a lot of attention. She had elected to wear her sea-foam green crocheted swimsuit with an open blouse and denim shorts. She even wore her sunglasses indoors as if it was important everyone knew we were going somewhere fun after this.

"To Beach-town?" Mary already had her car running when I climbed in. She was so eager to depart that she waited neither for my response nor my seat buckle.

"That was the plan, yeah."

"You don't need to drop stuff off at home or anything?"

"I ought to drop it in the garbage."

"Not the tequila!"

"It's not even good."

I smiled as she became animated.

"It's booze! It's not supposed to be good!"

I decided not to argue the point. I thought some alcohol tasted alright, but I guessed Mary's blanket sentiment explained her taste in drinks.

I fished blindly behind Mary's seat for a snack as we hit the highway. My hope was rewarded as I retrieved a Mocha Munchie.

"You imported candy for our vacation?"

I broke the wafer bar in half and held the bigger half out for her to take a bite. I rolled my eyes as she chewed with exaggerated ecstasy.

"Quality snacks are the hallmark of a good road trip. Mocha Munchies are the best candy bars ever invented so the decision was automatic."

"Objectively of course. Couldn't be that the inclusion of coffee, maple syrup, and chocolate simply touches all the bases for your favorite things. It must be an undisputed fact that it's the best candy bar."

"I'm glad you see it my way."

I shook my head as she took another bite and squirmed to shake wafer crumbs out of her bathing suit.

"Did you wear that just to flaunt it in front of my former co-workers or is that how you want to drive?"

"¿Por qué no los dos?"

"Why... no the two?"

She snorted and switched back to English.

"Why not both? It's a meme from an advertisement a few years back. I'll show you later."

"Right... Were you satisfied with the result?"

She hummed and took the stub of the candy bar from me. "Jesse, Hanzo, and Angela all gave me their numbers so I'd say so."

"I'll save you some time, Jesse reeks of tobacco, and Hanzo hasn't gone a day without sake in fifteen years."

"What about Angela?"

I grumbled and looked out the window. Angela was intimidating. She was the very image of refined but not even remotely bitchy about it. The fact that she gave Mary her number befuddled me. Her interest in women wasn't exactly a surprise, but her interest in Mary felt threatening nonetheless.

I must have been silent for a while because Mary spoke up again. "I'm just kidding, Jesse and Hanzo are clearly banging each other and I actually gave Angela my number rather than the reverse."

"Not better," I grumbled.

"Why do you act like they are competition?"

I wanted to say "because they are," but I bit my tongue. This whole song and dance was tiresome. First Cyrus and Joshua, then Kimberly, and who knows who else. Every time I dealt with a slightly smaller pang of jealousy, but this time it didn't feel smaller for some reason. I cared entirely too much about what Mary thought of others. Some narcissistic part of me still thought everything she did or thought was about me somehow.

Again, Mary was the first to move the conversation forward.

"I love you."

"What?"

"I love you." She repeated and made a quick glance to meet my eye before returning her attention to the road.

"I love you too?"

I heard Mary sigh as she drummed her fingers on the steering wheel.

"Maybe that's not the right thing to say right now. I mean it of course, but what I really want to communicate is that I can tell you are jealous and I worry that you are placing fault or blame somewhere because of it."

"I'm not--" I didn't need to see the look she gave me to give up and drop the lie. Yeah. I was. "I don't know what I'm supposed to do about it."

My heart dropped to my stomach as she took the next exit.

"Let's workshop a bit." Mary turned to me once she parked. "Your jealousy shouldn't be something you have to do every bit of changing alone to overcome. Our relationship is about us fitting together, not just you fitting to me."

"I don't see how me being narcissistic is your fault."

"Who said you were narcissistic?"

"I did. I'm jealous because I'm making your private decisions about me."

"That isn't necessarily narcissistic..." Mary unbuckled and twisted to grab her water jug from behind the seat. "For one, narcissistic people don't care about their self centered attitude and feel no incentive to amend their behavior or philosophy."

I shrugged. "So maybe I wasn't being charitable. What do we do about it?"

She took a sip from her jug and pulled her fingers through her hair. "My intent was to tease as a way to help you acclimate, but I'm starting to think this isn't helping. Specifically, since you know that my interactions with others aren't about you then maybe you don't need acclimation so much as reinforcement. Prodding your jealousy isn't helping you process at this point, it's causing a crisis."

"I wouldn't say it's a crisis."

"Babe, you would sooner believe that you are a narcissist than accept that your feelings don't define you."

"But my feelings do define me."

"No they don't. Your actions define you. If my feelings defined me then I would be a murderer for every time I saw Kits-News."

"Still, what do you want to do about it?"

"I'm not sure. For starters, there's nothing to gain from me being so outwardly polyamorous and making a show of flirting. It sounds like rather than exposure, I should be giving you time and affirmation."

"I like affirmation."

I smiled despite myself as she rolled her eyes and capped her water bottle.

"Then we can work at checking in when jealousy crops up. Meanwhile we can make my flirtation something to bond over rather than something for you to spectate. For instance, do *you* have any feelings about Angela?"

I shrugged and shook my head.

"What about your work wife?"

"Stephanie isn't my work wife."

"Oh yeah? How did you know who I was talking about?"

I squinted at Mary. She wiggled her eyebrows but didn't press further. She turned back to the steering wheel.

I thought she would restart the car, but instead, she flipped a lever on the steering column, pushed the wheel up, and leaned over the center console.

I let her pull me into a kiss. As suddenly as she had pulled me forward, she switched her grip and pressed me by the neck into the seat. She followed again, half climbing into my lap as she kissed me forcefully.

This was foreplay. Nothing casual about it.

Just as I was mustering the wherewithal to consciously submit to her, she retreated.

"What was that?"

"A distraction." Mary patted the inside of my thigh, and I squirmed as the touch sent heat up my back.

"Cruel but effective."

I calmed my breathing as she readjusted the steering wheel and rebuckled her seat-belt. Feeling spiteful and bold, I put my hand on the inside of her thigh. She shook her head as she re-merged onto the highway.

"Have fun but don't cause an accident."

I trailed my hand up, and she pushed me back toward her knee.

# 25

It's Coarse, Rough, and
Irritating... and it Gets
Everywhere

"Can't say I'm a fan of the smell."

"Of the beach? Or the sunscreen?" I rubbed in the pseudo-lotion as she had for me. She fidgeted as I attempted to work a bit under the straps of her new black two-piece suit. It looked just like my one piece suit, but without the middle. Of course, I also had one of her button up shirts and a swim skirt, so altogether our outfits didn't match nearly as much as she'd hoped.

"The sunscreen. I don't think I've ever used it."

"What? Do you just get sunburns willingly? Are you not concerned about cancer?"

She shook her head.

"I don't need it. I don't burn or tan."

"Then what am I doing this for?" I put my hands on my hips

as she turned around. I wanted to be indignant about the wasted effort, but I suspected the reason already.

"Because I'm pale as a ghost and if folks see me give you sunscreen but not the reverse they will be either concerned or suspicious."

"I think you overestimate the amount of attention you draw." It wasn't the reason I expected, but I guess it made sense.

"You're right, I just wanted you to rub me down."

Ah. There it was.

"Well joke's on you, now you have to wait half an hour to get in the water."

Mary grabbed her tote bag out of the trunk and surveyed the beach.

"Indeed, what a terrible fate I've met."

I rolled my eyes at the sarcasm and followed her down the weathered steps to the sand. I thought we would set up a camp of some sort first, but she made a beeline for the nearest cabana.

Minutes later, we were crowded under an umbrella.

"What now?" I hated sitting around when it was too hot to cuddle.

"Well. The loose checklist is play volleyball, eat watermelon, flirt, barbecue, argue over boob sizes, and light sparklers."

"What the fuck?"

"We don't have to do all of it, that's just what Joshua said we should do."

"Joshua watches too much anime," I grumbled. Mary only shrugged.

We watched the waves for a few more minutes before my restlessness won out.

"I wanna doooo something."

Rather than answering, Mary stood and held out her hand. She pulled me up and dragged me down the beach until we were wading in the ocean.

"Better?"

I didn't dignify her tone with a response and fought the urge to start a splashing fight.

"How do you even expect to do a barbecue out here?"

"Probably a restaurant, you definitely aren't the party crashing sort."

I picked up a glob of sand and shook it underwater to see if there were any shells or pretty rocks. One of them was a really strange shade of green and when I held it up I could see light through it.

I held it out to Mary and she inspected it too.

"Seaglass, neato."

"Is that a volcanic rock? I've never heard of it."

"Nope. Literally just glass that got fucked up by the ocean. I think this type is radioactive too."

"So it's garbage?"

Mary gave me a scandalized look. "It's treasure!"

I rolled my eyes as she searched her two-piece suit for pockets and when she tried stuffing it in one of the cups of her top I held out my hand.

"You're not going to throw it away?" She held it like it was some sort of delicate sea creature.

"No, I'll keep your stupid piece of glass for you."

She squinted at me but surrendered it nevertheless. I refrained from pretending to chuck it. "Anyways. What were we talking about? Activities? Food? Fishing weird rocks out of the ocean?"

"Or..." Mary's tone turned mischievous. "We could trace the words 'will you marry me' in the beach in front of a resort to fuck with people."

"And then what? You pull a ring out of nowhere and put me on the spot?"

"Only if you want, I'm sure there is a jewelry store we could browse nearby."

"Jesus Christ." I turned and waded back up the beach.

"All I'm saying is if you're gonna collect rings you have to start somewhere."

I shook my head. I wished I had spent more time thinking of what I wanted to do rather than just counting on agreeing with all of Mary's plans. For all I knew, this was a test.

I dumped our briefly unattended drinks and returned the cocktail glasses. When I got back to our umbrella, Mary had two bowls of fruit, probably pineapple and watermelon from the nearby vendor.

I made myself comfortable at the foot of her chair and traded the sea glass for the snack. My first impression was that the pineapple had spoiled, then I realized it was gushing alcohol rather than juice.

"So you're gonna get me drunk? And then what?"

"Propose of course."

"Don't you dare."

"You don't want the drama of saying no in front of strangers?"

I squinted at her but her expression only grew more smug. It took me a few seconds to form my rebuttal.

"We wouldn't have a photographer so all our scrapbook photos would have to be staged."

"So you would say yes?"

"I would cry and probably puke."

"From happiness?"

I shook my head and stole a piece of her watermelon. At the very least she seemed to take the hint.

Later, my expectations were thwarted as she led the way to an antique store. I felt under-dressed, but apparently we were not yet far enough away from the beachfront to be indecent.

It rapidly became clear Mary wanted to buy me rings and she wasn't satisfied till we had chosen five. At least she let me wear them out rather than retaining one for a secret proposal. Frankly, I don't know what I would do if she wanted to make our commitment explicit. I wasn't sure it would ever need to be nailed down more than it already was, but I could see a romantic appeal to it.

I watched bemused as Mary spotted and bought sparklers. What I thought would be a quick photo for Joshua's amusement turned into an entire event as she set up time-lapse photos and other effects on her phone.

"All that remains is barbecue and boob envy." I sat heavily on a bench and tried to shake the sand out of my sandals.

"You forgot volleyball and flirting."

I shook my head as she sat down next to me. The sun was about to set on the ocean, and somehow nothing obstructed our view.

"I don't know that I have the energy for more activities."

I slumped into her shoulder and watched as the sun crawled under the waves.

By now, I knew- unlike previous partners -she wouldn't beg, bargain, or guilt me into doing more than I wanted. I had to wonder if part of me was pretending I was worn out. Was I acting like I didn't want to do anything to limit further activity? Did I have the energy after all?

"Tomorrow is another day." Mary murmured and pulled me close.

I was about to offer to do maybe one more thing before she stood. My feet protested, but the walk to her car wasn't terribly long. I managed to help square stuff away in the trunk before sinking into the passenger seat.

"It will be another hour or two before the decorators are done setting up the proposal scene in our hotel room. What do you want to do before then?"

I was about to say "food" as a knee-jerk response before her words sunk in.

"What?"

She looked at me for a few seconds, probably expecting my brain to catch up on its own, so I clarified, "I heard what you said, I'd like an explanation."

"It's nothing crazy. Just champagne, flower petals and stuff like that." She spared me a glance,

I slumped in my seat and stared out the window. I didn't have the energy to drag motives and details out of her. "Let's just hang out at the hot tub or something I guess."

She nodded and started the engine.

I laid my head against the window as we cruised along the beach. The crowd hadn't thinned so much as changed. I found myself comparing the demographic shift from family fun to adult nightlife to my own mood shift.

Mary's phone buzzed a few times during the drive, but she ignored it, and I didn't offer to check it for her. I took my time getting moving after she parked and cut the engine.

"They actually finished early so we can just go straight up and you can soak in the terrace pool."

"Our room doesn't have a terrace pool."

"It does now."

She must have been trying to work me up and tease me, but I was determined not to play along this time.

She collected our new room cards, and I let her lead me by the hand to the elevator and then our room.

"What's the proposal?" I looked from the flower petal path to the edible arrangement on the table. Despite being a honeymoon suite, the room was hardly any larger than the previous one.

"Will you marry me?" She had a cocky smirk and was holding out my favorite of her rings on her palm. She hadn't even taken a knee.

I kicked my sandals off and took the ring.

"If I say 'maybe later' can I still have the ring?"

"How do you know I'm not serious?"

I dropped it back in her hand and turned to the terrace pool.

"*Are* you serious?"

A worm of worry formed in my stomach as I avoided her eyes and dipped my feet in the pool. She sat down beside me and I watched as she toyed with the ring in her hands. She was less than a year past a broken engagement, why was she so eager to get engaged again?

"Did you have a good day?" she pushed off the edge and dropped into the shallow pool.

I bit back a complaint about the subject change. When she reached the underwater bench she turned back to me and I managed a nod.

"Was the proposal upsetting?"

I rolled my eyes. I was upset alright, but not in a completely articulate way.

Luckily, she didn't demand articulation. "Was it bad because you wish I'd been more serious? Or would you rather not think that far ahead?"

I turned to meet her eye. She was sprawled on the other edge of the basin. I looked to find another ledge before resigning myself to sharing hers and made my way over.

"I didn't think our commitment needed symbols or trinkets yet."

"Are you willing to give words to it though?"

I hung my arms around her neck and draped my legs over hers, but she made no movement to reciprocate the embrace.

"What did you have in mind?"

She looked past me for a while but relaxed and brought her arms around to hold me.

"Will you marry me for a month?"

"Just a month?"

"For now."

"Seems like a short goal."

"Traditionally I might ask for a year and a day, but I feared that would be a larger commitment then you are ready for."

I freed a hand to rub my eyes and fought the urge to rest my head on her shoulder.

I wanted to complain that proposals should be a formality that you only go through when everyone is sure the answer is yes. But, in this case, she did seem to know me better than I knew myself.

"Yes. I'll marry you for a month."

I rolled my eyes as she took my left hand. I expected her to make a show of giving me a ring, but she kissed my palm and wove our fingers together.

"Thank you."

I was struck by the reverence of her tone. And for a second, I almost doubted if I'd said the right thing.

"I-... Did I not seem committed before?"

She shook her head and looked at our fingers wrapped together.

"At times, early in our relationship, I felt that you were look-ing for a way to run and only stayed because you were unable to escape. As though the condition of our partnership was you trapped with me."

She pulled her fingers through her hair and looked out to the ocean. She spoke more to the horizon than me when she continued.

"It means something that you choose to stay. Even if there is still a sense of there being no escape."

I wanted to pull her into a kiss or perform my love for her some-how, but all I could do was sit as the silence dragged. I wished I had my phone to make a literal note to do better, but a different idea took shape in my head.

"You know that second wind spell you used for the road-trip to Tristate?"

Mary nodded and turned back to me.

"Can you do that on me?"

She squinted but didn't ask for clarification. She nodded and exhaustion faded away, almost like an instant hit of caffeine.

"You aren't going to like the side effects." She warned, but I was already climbing off her lap and dragging her up out of the pool.

"That's future Addison's problem." I grabbed her a towel. Luckily neither of us had gotten our hair wet, so drying off was a short affair. She unzipped her top but paused as I held out a robe.

"I'm officially confused." She discarded the top, trading it for the robe as I raided the edible arrangement.

I stepped into slippers and made sure I had my key card.

"I'm going to grab paper and a pen from the lobby so we can make a marriage contract."

Part of me expected Mary to roll her eyes but she seemed paralyzed with surprise.

As I turned the handle she caught my hand.

"Are you sure?"

I let the door click shut. She still seemed dazed as I pulled her into a kiss.

"Mhmm."

I loved having Mary in this rare form. So uncharacteristically unguarded. Throwing her off balance was a selfish pleasure, but I made sure I didn't indulge often.

"I love you." She whispered as I stepped back toward the door.

"Love you too." I refrained from rolling my eyes at her love-sick tone.

# 26

# Idyllic

The beach was dark and completely quiet. Water glided over the sand before me, creating waves that rolled under me. I was here for a reason though. Mary had asked me to find her something, a seashell.

I pushed my hand through the loose sand. I dug up shell after shell, but each one was broken. Every time I found another there was the telltale sharp edge.

Mary sat behind me, the sand beneath us gave and then conformed again, perfectly cradling us as I continued my task. She was impatient. Not upset, just frustrated with me as I searched and searched.

It was a simple task, or it would be with light, or if the beach hadn't been picked over so completely. Mary was pulling insistently now, it wasn't fair. Sand poured into the hole. I had to start over, but I couldn't very well search with her arms around me.

"Addie."

The silence shattered. Light peeked through the curtains. I took a deep breath, stretching as the rest of the details fell into place. Mary let me turn to face her, even in such low light she was perfectly clear.

"Good morning." I pushed sheets out of the way and flipped my pillow. We must have forgotten to set the AC.

"Were you having a bad dream?"

"No?"

"You were so tense. What were you dreaming about?"

"The beach I think. I was digging in the sand."

She worked her arm under me and pulled me closer. "What were you digging for?"

I tried to abide the heat. Sometimes she was an absolute furnace. "Sand stuff. Maybe I was going to find you some more seaglass."

"Mhmmm. That would be sweet. I don't know why that was stressful though."

"The best part of those dreams is forgetting them."

"What?"

"The dream world is purgatory. When it gets to the point I am half-lucid, I just fall into loops: redoing the same thing until it's right, forgetting where I was going with that, and drifting to the next thing."

"Do you ever have good dreams?"

"I've steered lucid dreams to nice places before, but those usually just happen when I've woken up and immediately go back to sleep."

"Hmm."

I took the opportunity to roll away and get on my hands and knees. I'd swear this mattress was goose down all the way through. It was remarkable I didn't have the falling dreams.

I heard Mary rustle around as I found the AC and cranked it down.

"Where would you go with a dream... if you could go anywhere?"

"Somewhere comfortable." I crawled back into bed and flopped next to her. "If I'm imagining a conversation, then things might hold together better. It helps when the concept is intangible to start I think."

"So you don't dream of rolling meadows? No action or thrills?"

"I mean I probably could, but conversation holds more detail and feeling than the concept of some setting would. Your ideas sound more interesting on paper maybe, but in practice a dream is only a series of feelings, facts, and emotions."

When I looked over she was staring into space, but she focused back in when I turned and faced her properly.

"What are wet dreams like then?"

I snorted. "Not terribly dissimilar from blindfolded sex i guess."

"You dream of being blindfolded?" Mary propped herself up on an elbow.

"What? No?"

"How do you know you aren't dreaming now?"

"I can see you?" I spoke slowly, but she narrowed her eyes further. "Okay, so it's not that simple. I can't tell what reality is when I'm sleeping, but right now I'm pretty sure I'm not dreaming because... I don't know. Why does it matter?"

"I guess it doesn't."

She pushed away the sheets and made a show of sitting up. She arched her back like a cat before standing on her knees and throwing her arms wide.

I didn't have much warning as she crawled over me and lay down. She worked her leg between mine and my cradle turned into a crater as she found her spot and settled.

It was fine, I didn't really need to breathe anyways. After a moment though, she had most of her weight on my hips instead.

"Can I help you?" I knew where this was going, but the urge to sass was overpowering.

"Yes. You see I've fallen, and I can't get up."

"Quite the pickle."

The unexpected jab in my side caused me to thrash, but luckily I managed not to hit her. Sometimes, I felt like the danger of bodily harm thrilled her.

All bets were off. She'd started the tickle, and now any and every touch could prolong it. I pushed her hands away and curled in on myself, but she was resourceful. She was lucky not to crack her skull against mine when she went for my neck.

I was on the defensive, but no defense would work against her. My left hand was captured, my right-handed counter attack on her side was completely ineffective. Checkmate. Game, set, match.

She rolled her hips before I could catch my breath. I had let her effectively immobilize me, yet I didn't feel like I was learning my lesson.

"Comfy?" I heard her, muffled against my shoulder as she nipped at my collar bone through my shirt.

"A little warm." I waited for her to release me but she only stilled for a moment.

"Jesus Christ!" my thrashing renewed as her touch turned to ice.

If I'd been even slightly sleepy before I wasn't anymore. My breath shuddered as every flinch brought freezing cold to my skin somewhere new. She wasn't focusing under my arms but that was only a small mercy. Her leg between mine burned and I struggled to both pull away from her and pull in on myself.

Soon the torture ended, her touch turned from ice to fresh water and finally to an almost human cool. Her kiss on my neck might have been soothing if everything didn't sting. Still, I was surprised I didn't see my breath as she continued to sap heat from me.

"Better?"

"You know d-damn well it's not."

My back ached but Mary was making it very hard to relax.

"You seem tense. It must have been a *very* scary dream."

I gave up and let my free arm fall across her back. She could get away with anything. Absolutely anything. If she decided she wanted to try a hemoglobin diet, I'd pull my collar down for her.

"That tracks. I obsessed over disappointing you and right on cue I've received punishment."

I regretted the remark as soon as I finished saying it. At the very least, she gave me a bit of breathing room as she pushed herself up. Now she was upset, and it was my fault.

I hugged my stomach and searched for excuses to avoid her gaze.

The bed sheets rasped as she moved to straddle my waist, but I was no less trapped.

"Did I hurt you?"

"No. It was just a bad joke. I'm sorry."

"What would make it better?" She cupped my cheek and then brushed my hair back. My eyes watered as I met her gaze at last.

I dreaded the pain of my impending breakdown so rather than fight it I made a conscious effort to just let tears out. What did I want? Why did my pea brain immediately think I could just pave over my problems with sex?

Luckily I didn't have to answer. I guess she remembered who she was talking to: indecisive bitch extraordinaire.

She sat up and put her hands on her knees.

"Well at the very least I can work out some soreness."

"You never know, muscle cramps could be my kink."

She didn't dignify that with an answer. I let her pull me upright, and I didn't resist as she pulled my shirt over my head. Now that the AC had caught up, I was feeling chilled and rather foolish.

In short order she had me on my stomach, I hoped she would just smoosh me for a while but instead she pressed knuckles into my back.

Right. Working out soreness.

"I'm not really into the whole 'deep tissue' thing either."

"Hmmm, thanks for letting me know."

She rubbed instead, occasionally using her nails as she made mirrored patterns with both hands. I still tightened up when she drifted toward my sides or lower back, but she wasn't teasing anymore.

"Are you doing this because I liked the hurt and comfort story you gave me?"

I heard her laugh and then felt as she switched to straddle my thighs. "If the boot fits."

"It's 'if the shoe fits'."

"Not where I'm from."

About the time my skin had acclimated I felt a second set of hands. The pattern she had been rubbing on my shoulders continued, but now there was a new touch near the middle of my back. I was only surprised for a moment before I gave up. Whatever. Magic.

"Are you familiar with how delay guitar pedals work?"

"Electrically? No."

"Well there's one on your nervous system right now."

"Nerd."

She moved to another place and the sensation of the first pattern faded. I originally thought she had to repeat every action a few times for it to continue, but she steadily added new patterns faster and faster.

Gentle tracing became trails of nails and eventually unbroken snaking movement.

I focused on breathing deeply as she wrapped her hands around each of my arms in turn, twisting so it felt like ropes were coiling around me. I imagined I was immobilized, and the fantasy became easier as she invented new restraints.

Patterns no longer faded away, they slowed to feel like constant pressure instead of friction.

I sighed as she pushed her fingers through my hair, and soon every breath was practically panting. God, I hoped this was foreplay.

Satisfied with her work on my back, she pulled my bottoms off and worked on my legs. I tried to move to get her hands toward the insides of my thighs, but she seemed content to work down my calves first.

"How're you doing down there?"

"Haaa-h -m. I'm doing good. It's good, this is good."

"I thought you'd like it."

She stopped long enough for me to catch my breath, and I wondered if she would just leave me to cool off like this.

She coaxed me to roll over. The sensation repeated a few times so I had to stare at the ceiling until the vertigo ended. I let my arms fall above my head as she trailed her hands across my rib cage. If she slipped toward my sides I might actually die, but she neither tickled me or touched my most sensitive places.

Just as she got down to my waist she moved back up to my shoulders, up my arms and finally to my wrists. She wove our fingers together momentarily before dragging down.

Finally, she attended to my breasts. Trailing touches turned to kneading and squeezing and light pinching. Fucking hell, I was nearly undone and there was so much more she could touch.

She paid little attention to my hips before returning to my legs. I was not prepared. I held myself together while she worked on my right leg: but when she got to my left I broke. My leg shook in her hands as my orgasm echoed through my spine. I kicked weakly at the sheets and clamped my hands over my ears as energy erupted through my pores. I collapsed into the bed as the last dregs disappeared. Touch was still everywhere but softer, comforting like a blanket. Still, I didn't even catch my breath before she resumed.

At some point she had lost patience. She lay half on top of me and I felt her lips again and again, from my neck, to my heart, and then my breasts. Kisses became hickeys as the circles she rubbed on my stomach drifted lower.

I nearly lost my mind as her leg dragged between mine on her way down. I didn't have the presence of mind to marvel as she slipped her hand between us. I needed to move, not to escape, just to vent a bit of energy. Even as delirious as I was, I feared I would squeeze too hard if I held her. When I arched my back into her she slipped her arm under me. It felt like she had all her weight on me.

I forgot about showing restraint when she eased her fingers into me. I was already losing it as she made her way in. There was no reprieve and she covered all the bases. G-spot, clit, she could probably bruise my cervix and I'd still praise her.

Waves of electricity crashed and ricocheted through me as the buzzing all over my body turned almost cruel.

This time, as the onslaught faded it did so entirely, I felt like I had new skin. Everything felt more than it should. Especially her skin on mine.

Stars faded from my vision as I unclenched my eyes. The more I focused on relaxing, the easier it became. Exhaustion overwhelmed tension until I felt nothing in my body but Mary, my heart, my breathing, and gravity affixing me to the bed.

"Hehe." I huffed a breathless laugh. "You played me like an instrument. Did I sing the right notes?"

"It was lovely music, a symphony." She gave me a chaste kiss, but there was sadness in her eyes.

My plan to call her a nerd again died in my throat. I held eye contact, hoping she would lay the issue out for me, but she wasn't forthcoming. I wrapped my arms around her as she rested her head over my heart.

"You're worried." I meant to ask, but it sounded like a statement of fact.

"I'm worried." She squeezed me to her before relaxing again.

"Is it because of my dream?"

"Why don't you call it what it is? A nightmare."

THE FOOL, THE LOVERS, THE DEVIL  -  249

I sighed and traced idle circles on her back. Why did I want to argue when I knew she was right?

"My nightmare then. Does it worry you when my insecurities haunt me?"

"Is that all it is? Haunting?" She lifted her head to look me in the eye again.

"You can't tell me I've never disappointed you. I've driven you to and past the point of exasperation countless times."

She squinted and pursed her lips. "I'm not disappointed *now*."

"But it's bound to happen again."

"So?"

"So, I'm not good enough."

I felt a puff of air across my chest as she huffed and shook her head.

"You talk mad shit about my wife for someone in tickling range."

I groaned and preemptively pushed her hand down. Luckily, she didn't fight me this time. I gave her my full attention as she pulled her arm out from under me and propped herself up on her elbow.

"I'm serious though, I really wish you didn't think I was so shallow. You know me, and it's not fair for you to act like I'm a perfection obsessed jerk."

I felt my face flush at the accusation, so I bit back a reckless retort. Here I was venting my insecurity and she just fired back with another way I'd let her down.

I took a deep breath and rubbed my eyes. Fine. I wasn't a complete fuck up, I could probably talk myself down when I started imagining her as cruel.

She squeezed my arm and reached to pull my hand into hers. "Do you understand what I'm getting at?"

I looked at her sidelong and then back to the ceiling. "I'll do my best."

"I'm not like your mom, I don't need your very best every waking moment."

"Are you going to pick apart every unintentional insinuation I make?" I didn't check to see if I'd upset her with the outburst. It was safest to just assume I had.

I heard her sigh and I shifted to let her work her arm back under me.

"I don't blame you for your nightmares, and you didn't do anything wrong by feeling your feelings. I'm just trying to build up framework against it."

She released my hand and held my cheek until I looked down to meet her eye.

"I'm only telling you, in no uncertain terms, that you are enough. You always have been."

I hummed and let my head fall back into the bed. I tried imagining my mind like a room and I searched for the perfect place to put this assurance so I'd have it when I needed it.

Nope, mind palaces were still bullshit to me.

I looked over to the bedside table and grabbed one of my new rings. That would work. I amused myself trying to put it on with one hand until she spoke again.

"I think I fucked up the after care."

I shook us both with a laugh. "I feel sufficiently cared for."

"Okay good, because I want waffles before we head home."

I tried weakly to keep her in my arms but she escaped and set about getting dressed. I looked at my ring for a while longer as she laid out clothes for me across my legs.

# 27

## How Do You Want To Do This?

The hallway Mary led us down was much longer than I expected. Even with our torches we couldn't see the end of it.

Joshua and Mary had insisted heavily that we needed to stop by this old crypt-like cellar and, having lost the vote one to two, I'd elected to come along despite my trepidation.

"What are we looking for?" I tried not to sound bored as they scrutinized the map. Apparently old blind men were reputable sources for maps now. Who knew?

"There should be a door ahead."

The way they talked about it you'd think it was some sort of speakeasy: as though a password would get us VIP access to a hidden bar. I had no delusions about there being drinks though. Knowing Mary, she was probably hoping for whips and chains anyways.

"And after the door?"

"I don't know. That's the exciting part isn't it?"

Ah. Blind leading the blind. I followed on nevertheless. Joshua in particular was on high alert, constantly inspecting and prodding at every rock as though we were looking for a magic door.

Judging by the racks of barrels, this was a cellar for a local winery, but Mary was certain this was the right path.

Two forks and a turn later we arrived at the door that Mary and Joshua were in such a tizzy about.

I made it a good five seconds into their inspection before I grew impatient.

"Just open the door."

"Wait-" Mary looked up but Cyrus cut her off.

"Are you opening the door?" His tone was hard to read. I couldn't tell if he was excited or just as impatient as I was.

I cut off Mary's objection. "Yes."

Cyrus folded his hands under his chin as Mary and Joshua groaned.

"Roll initiative."

Cyrus organized his sheets and plucked a twenty sided die from his collection. He always chose that die, and I suspected it rolled high despite his insistence on it being fair.

I tossed my d20 and searched my character sheet for the modifier as Mary and Joshua reported their numbers to Cyrus.

"Seven" I'd beaten Joshua in a surprising turn of events.

I knew I wasn't going first, I hadn't even once tonight.

Cyrus reached out and placed a new miniature on the table. "The cat is surprised. Mary, what do you want to do?"

"I'll shoot it."

"What?" I leaned forward to peer at the figurine. The enemy monsters we had fought before always looked openly malicious but this seemed like a normal cat. Small and gray, seated on a short pillar.

"You're close quarters and it's a small creature so you definitely have disadvantage."

"Fuck." Mary mumbled as she grabbed another die and rolled them on her mat. "8?"

"Your arrow ricochets off the flagstones and flies off into the dark. Addison?" Cyrus turned to me, fingers still steepled under his chin.

"I grab a piece of dried fish from my satchel and drop it in front of the cat."

Mary and Joshua both stared at me incredulously as Cyrus rubbed his chin. He didn't seem concerned.

"Joshua? What do you do?"

"Uhhh. I think I have to do a double move to get past everyone into the room."

He counted out spaces while Cyrus rolled the largest, roundest die I'd ever seen.

"The cat was startled by the arrow but snatches up the fish. Back to you Mary."

Mary looked at me. "I ready my throwing knife in case there's any funny business."

I waited for her to continue but Cyrus gestured to me instead.

"Uh... I kneel in front of it and hold out another piece of fish."

Cyrus pursed his lips but failed to hide a smile.

"I guess I'll ready an axe..." Joshua shook his head and leaned back in his chair as Cyrus rolled another die.

"The cat snatches the fish from your hand but you don't see its head move. It seems like the cat is pulling the food into an opening in its chest. Mary?"

"I ready my knife again."

"So... is this a weird kind of cat?"

"Nope."

"Am I in trouble?"

Cyrus shrugged and rested his chin back on his hands.

"I... give it another piece of fish?"

"Hmmm." Cyrus rolled another large die and drummed his fingers on the book beside him. "Well. I think we can conclude combat. The 'cat' is not hostile."

Before Mary or Joshua could object, he continued on, "The mimic shambles up to you, It tries to climb your leg but it sticks to you more like a gecko than a cat."

"Mimic?"

Mary snorted. "It's a monster. I think you've adopted a pet."

"Oh. Uh. I pick them up and give them more fish. I think I'll call them Peety."

Mary rolled her eyes and I heard Joshua grumble about "another mouth to feed."

"How do pets work?"

Cyrus shrugged again. I was getting tired of that deflection. "We'll burn that bridge when we get to it. Peety feels like a stone gargoyle in your hands. It's warm as though it's been in the sun, and it's not terribly heavy, but otherwise it feels and looks like stone."

"Well... I guess we can continue on." Mary moved her figure the rest of the way through the doorway and Cyrus revealed a larger section of the map.

I expected a lecture about traps and patience but nobody seemed upset about how the encounter started or ended. At the next door, Joshua made a joke about waiting for a check but that was it.

Occasionally, Cyrus would describe Peety hopping down to inspect random stones or choose the direction if we went a way they didn't agree with.

"They are definitely leading us somewhere." Mary drummed her fingers on the table. "I just can't tell if they are helping us or serving us up to their master."

"Peety is a good mimic!"

Joshua rolled his eyes but nobody made further arguments.

Cyrus revealed another section of the map. "As you approach a wrought iron door, Peety jumps out of your arms again and paws at the middle. It appears to be unbarred and you hear footsteps approaching on the other side."

"Is there somewhere to hide?" I scoured my character sheet to see if there was anything about stealth or invisibility.

Mary ended up being decisive. "I drag Addie and Josh to hide against the wall as quietly as possible. Do I need to make a stealth check?"

Cyrus waved dismissively. "The door swings outward and light pours into the room. You see the flickering shadow of a humanoid on the far wall, but you don't hear anyone moving from the doorway."

Cyrus cleared his throat and contorted his face to squint around at everyone.

"What are you doing here, Goliath? You were to watch for intruders."

Mary made an amused snort as Cyrus pretended to look around.

"What was that? Who goes there? Goliath you blasted mimic what have you done?"

Cyrus looked around the table as if waiting for one of us to do something before pulling another figure from his bag and continuing in a normal voice. "You hear a thunk and see Goliath or 'Peety' skitter across the floor as though kicked. A cloaked figure steps into view but they can't seem to see you."

"That motherfucker." I pounded the table in only half-joking anger. "I run over to punch him."

Mary looked at the ceiling and shook her head as Joshua looked around for his dice.

"As you step toward the stranger, Peety latches onto their ankle. The cloaked figure flails, slips, and falls hard. They appear to be unconscious."

"Serves them right."

Mary nodded her agreement as Cyrus revealed more of the map.

"Inside the well-lit room you see a desk, a large glass tube of glowing green gel, and scattered books and papers laid carefully on the floor and pinned to the wall. As you watch, the glow fades on the tube and gel begins to seep out the seams. With a pop and a crack the entire apparatus falls over and the gel forms into a cube on the floor next to the desk." Cyrus looked around the table and chuckled to himself. "And that's where we will start next time."

The table groaned in chorus as Cyrus stacked papers and folded up his divider. I retrieved my miniature.

"That's so mean! It's a total cliffhanger!"

"I think it's a ploy to get me to Tristate for the next session." Joshua squinted at Cyrus. "It's working but I'm not happy about it."

"Oooooh sneaky! I like it." Mary tugged at Cyrus's sleeve before helping roll up the play mat.

"We aren't going to play again until we move?" I didn't know whether I should whine at Mary or Cyrus. Neither one was moved to sympathy.

Mary spoke first in her 'Santa isn't real' voice. "Cyrus won't be back until moving day and I guarantee we won't have time then. Besides, a lot of the apartment will be packed away."

Cyrus continued to pack despite my objections. "I'm glad you were invested. If it's any consolation, gelatinous cubes aren't very serious enemies to fight."

Mary cut in. "And I am very sure you will not be able to make the cube a pet."

"Well now I *have* to try."

"I know, dear. I know." Mary patted my leg under the table before standing up and stretching. "Man, all this role-play has made me thirsty!"

She yawned and I stood to slip under her arm as she stretched.

She rested her hand on my shoulder as Cyrus and Joshua both yawned as well.

I stumbled after her as she practically dragged me by the neck to the kitchen. I finally slipped out of her grasp as she opened the fridge.

"Well now what?" Joshua zipped up his backpack and lifted it over his shoulder.

Mary scratched my back for a second as she walked back past me to the living room area. "I can pull out the couch if you wanna crash here, it's pretty late and all."

"So it *is* a pull out?" I put my hands on my hips. "I thought you were a firm believer in condoms, Mary."

Not long ago I was sure that would earn a snort if not full-on laughter but she just shrugged. "You would have known if you even once resisted the temptation to crawl into bed with me."

Joshua coughed and rubbed the back of his neck.

"For the record, I was teasing Addie, not you." She walked up to Joshua and draped her arms around his neck. "In fact, since she's being a snot I think *she* should take the pull-out."

My face was suddenly burning. She'd never kicked me out of the bedroom before and to do it so casually while flirting with Joshua felt mean-spirited.

Mary looked over to me, probably expecting to see how well the joke landed but her smile fell as she understood my mood. She dropped her hands from Joshua's neck and took a step back but Cyrus was already on his way over to me.

"I guess we get a bed to ourselves." He leaned on his elbows across the counter from me as Joshua seemed to realize for the first time that there was some tension in the room.

Seeing Cyrus's goofy grin caused the corners of my mouth to turn up. I had a momentary impulse to try and turn it back on Mary, but

I knew jealousy was just my issue. She'd probably be happy for me even. I took a deep breath and looked at Mary.

"It seems we do." I was proud of myself for keeping my tone neutral but Mary was still giving me a concerned look.

I rolled my eyes and waved her to the bedroom. "I accept my punishment."

Still, she didn't move so I let the humor facade fall. "It's fine. Sleep well you two, Cyrus and I will be good on the couch."

She didn't seem entirely comforted but when Cyrus looked back to her she made up her mind. If Joshua was concerned, he was far too distracted to act on it.

"You good?" Cyrus reached across the bar to touch the back of my hand.

"Yeah." Even though I still felt a little sour, I decided I'd fake it till I made it.

We worked together relocating the coffee table and shared a look as familiar muffled sounds came through the wall. Cyrus turned on the TV and I stepped out of the way as he unfolded the bed in one smooth motion. The sheets were already made so he just tossed his travel quilt over it and crawled over the covers.

"You forgot the pillows." I teased but before he could get up I went and pulled a few down from the linen closet.

He caught the first one I threw to him and exaggerated a wounded groan as the second one smacked his face soon after.

"Man down! Man down!" He cried and pretended to faint. He held the pose for a second and then resituated to put a pillow behind his head before posing again.

"Do you need me to kiss it better?" I walked on my knees across the bed until I was kneeling next to him.

"I wouldn't object."

I tucked my hair behind my ear and leaned down to kiss his forehead.

"My nose still hurts." He half whimpered and I rolled my eyes before kissing that too.

"And my lips..." I hardly heard his whisper over the TV.

Feeling bold, I resituated to lay down half on top of him and let him catch me as my lips met his.

I couldn't even count how many times I'd kissed him now but there was something different about doing so in bed alone. Or at least some part of me needed it to be different.

"Better?" I tried to sit up to see his face but he was still holding me tightly.

"Mhmm much better." He pulled me even closer and my efforts to hold myself above him failed.

Before I could regain my bearings he rolled toward me. One of his legs slipped between mine and I struggled to relax into the bed as he held himself above me.

"How do you see the night going?"

I was confused for a moment as I folded my hands on his lower back. Sometimes I forgot I was in a communication and consent relationship.

I knew he was interested in sex, I could feel as much on my thigh. But knowing I had a say in the matter helped me reframe sex as something that *could* happen with me, rather than as something that was about to happen to me.

"Just kisses and cuddles, if that's alright with you."

Even after all this time I worried I would hurt his feelings somehow but he didn't make the slightest indication of disappointment. He lay down a little less on top of me and helped me situate the pillows as I snuggled up closer.

"I'm not sure of the best way to frame this question--" He trailed off as I gave him my full attention. "--but do you know how you are feeling in regards to our relationship having a sexual aspect? In the future?"

The formal wording amused me but I managed to keep my composure as I thought.

"Certainly for the future. You'll be the first to know when I get over my hang ups."

"Anything I can do to help that?"

I chuckled and shook my head. "I don't want to talk about it."

"Fair, fair."

We lay in comfortable silence for nearly a minute until I leaned back suddenly.

"Fuck, I was supposed to ask. Are you interested in sex?"

The bed shook as his surprise turned to mirth. Despite his amusement though, he appeared to consider the question. "Yes, Addison. I'm interested."

"You aren't sure?"

He rolled his eyes and looked at the ceiling. "I'm interested in our relationship having a sexual aspect, I wouldn't hesitate to say yes about that. My interest in sex itself is... inconsistent. I don't want to imply that I'm impatiently awaiting sex." He turned to meet my eye. "But I also don't want you to think I don't find you attractive."

"C-cool" I stammered as I relaxed in his arms again. I was unsure why that had to be explicit, nobody just wanted sex all the time right?

He hummed and kissed my forehead.

Just as I was about to fall asleep he shifted to turn the TV off and get under the covers. I felt like I moved in a daze as he pulled me back to his side and I calmed my breathing again.

"I love you." I sighed and hugged him tighter for a second.

I didn't even realize what I'd said until a few seconds after he said "I love you too" back. Even in the resulting mini panic I knew I still meant it, and so did he.

# 28

# Bust a Move

I couldn't decide if having a moving party was Mary's best or worst idea. The flat was a buzz of activity. Joshua and Cyrus were occupied unmounting the bed from the wall and the rest of us worked at loading up a cart to take to the freight elevator.

Crystal looked just like she had when I met her on the first Tri-state field trip. She had her long blonde hair tied up, and her crop top with her painter jeans said business.

Mary's dad, Mazer, was using a human glamour today and he looked uncomfortably like Cyrus. Same height, similar black curly hair, and skin that could as easily be sun-kissed as mixed race. I guess he preferred three-piece suits for every occasion.

I assumed he had intimate control of his glamoured appearance, so I wondered whether he always used this look or if he chose it as a fatherly dig at Mary.

Mikah, Mary's other stepmom, had stayed home to care for the kids.

Supposedly, family and friends were cheaper than movers, but if

Crystal and Mazer drank anything like Mary and Joshua, we were in trouble.

I decided literal demons make things weird. Crystal and Mazer were lovely, though. Like as far as... uh... fuck... in-laws? Mary and my marriage wasn't exactly a matter of law but it might as well be given my full intention to resubscribe as it were. Mary called all of them except Mazer by their names, so I probably would too. Whatever.

By the time the boys had the bed off the wall, the rest of us had moved pretty much everything. Luckily, the bed had no shortage of handholds. With seven sets of hands, it only weighed a goddamn fuckton per person. Holy shit. I swear the cart flexed when we set it down, but with that, our obligations were complete. Mary had already said "fuck the deposit", and left everything she didn't want to clean or take. Goodbye ottoman. You were a real one.

Joshua exaggerated a stretch and dusted his hands off as Mary and Cyrus rolled the cart away.

"Whew. That was thirsty work!"

I looked him up and down. None of us had broken a sweat.

"Uh huh." I deadpanned and rolled my eyes as Kimberly hopped on board.

"I know I could use a drink."

"Yeah yeah, I know. We're going to the pub. That was always part of the plan."

I shook my head as she and Joshua shared a devious look before locking up and following Mary and Cyrus. Thank God I wasn't picking up the tab tonight.

Soon we were back where it all began. A couple months ago I was single and terrified to mingle and now I was married. Fuck. That was not my favorite perspective.

I stressed over how festivities would proceed with such mixed company, but I'd misplaced my concern. Kimberly and Crystal really hit it off. While my gaydar still wasn't tuned in, I expected some shenanigans when they came to deciding who would top.

Meanwhile, I saw a new side of Joshua as he fawned over Mazer. I first suspected it was an act at Mary's expense. Like "to hell with you, I'll fuck your dad", but he was legitimately infatuated. It amused Mary to no end.

In the end, our goodbye party was more like watching our friends hook up with Mary's family. Just... what the fuck? I was so distracted I forgot to even get buzzed. This was cruising rapidly toward being an orgy, and I couldn't imagine a better or worse send-off.

Cyrus and Mary were not as surprised or interested in the goings-on. They did not stop drinking and did not shy away from making themselves a spectacle as well.

Nothing made sense. I got to watch as Mary, the femme fatale herself, turned to putty in Cyrus's hands. The bear-like Joshua hung off of Mazer like drapes, and Kimberly was power bottoming. The girl who tried to break me was climbing into the lap of a girl she just met. The more I thought about it all, the less it surprised me.

"Having fun?" I had to practically climb into Crystal's lap as well to be noticed by the couple. Kimberly was getting handsy.

"So mush fun." Kimberly was flushed but Crystal seemed composed. If anything, the attention compromised her more than the drink.

"How about you?" Crystal didn't miss a beat turning her charm from her to me.

"M-me?"

"I noticed you only packed three air mattresses for tonight's ah-activities."

"W-what?"

She made a meaningful glance to where Mazer and Joshua huddled in a booth nearby, and then to Mary and Cyrus who were watching us with interest.

I felt like a wayward sailor nearly overboard for a siren as she clearly implied something and I struggled to understand.

"Have you decided which bed you're taking for tonight?"

"I just assumed-"

Kimberly cut in, clearly struggling not to slur. "You should know you have your pick."

I flushed further as Kimberly, intentionally or not, grazed my chest before tugging me closer. Her effort to whisper conspiratorially came across far more brazen as she made her invitation explicit.

"Just think about it." Kimberly patted my cheek before falling back toward Crystal.

"I doubt she will be able to think of much else." Crystal spoke in a low voice as she toyed with Kimberly's hair.

I mumbled excuses before stepping away and blessedly they took no offense to my retreat as I fled back to Mary. Suddenly I was reluctant to socialize with Joshua and Mazer. The prospect of another proposition was mildly flattering but far more embarrassing.

\*~\*~\*

It was nearing midnight when Kimberly's hands wandered a little too far. Being the only remaining adult, I made the executive decision to pack it in early. I made sure Mary settled the tab then I wished the bemused bartender a good night and herded my cats homeward.

Luckily for me, Mazer could hold his liquor, so we carried on a civil conversation as we linked up the party like kindergartners. I tried not to read into the stares we received as our chain held hands along the sidewalk. I lead, followed by Cyrus, Mary, Joshua, Mazer, Crystal, and Kimberly.

One interesting elevator ride later, we stumbled into the apartment. I set about inflating everyone's mattresses. I wondered if Mary was clairvoyant or something because it turned out three queens were plenty after all.

Selfishly, I plugged in the automatic one for Mary, Cyrus, and me. Then I rolled out the other two up in the living room for Mazer and Crystal. Through Mazer and my combined efforts, we kept everyone off them during the set up.

Well. Mostly. Kimberly didn't quite make it to the "lay out the sleeping bag" phase, so she ended up bent over a pair of bedrolls as Crystal had her way. I didn't see Crystal put on a strap-on, but I was not looking close enough to find out the how or why of that particular situation.

I felt terrible for Joshua as he passed out immediately, but Mazer didn't look put out as he made the bed. I found myself staring as Mazer pulled his shirt off his shoulders. I wasn't surprised he had a full back tattoo, but I was bewildered that it appeared to be a stained glass portrait of a woman holding a sword. In fact, it bore quite the resemblance to one of Mary's tattoos. I snorted when I saw the devil tattoo on his upper arm. I'd definitely ask him about them when I knew him better.

Back in my room, the sight of Cyrus and Mary sprawled on the mattress greeted me. This time apparently, Cyrus had not respected his limits. The result was the loves of my life half-dressed while their bedrolls lay forgotten.

If I was honest, I wasn't terrifically ready for a threesome anyway. It had been thrilling to let myself be pushed toward it, but only in theory. Ironically, It wasn't that I had any remaining trepidation about sexual intimacy with Cyrus. I just felt anxious at the thought of managing so much attention and focus.

I transformed one of the sleeping bags into a blanket and tossed it over them. Then I kicked on the fan and started some soothing music on my phone before taking off everyone's shoes.

"Gotcha," Cyrus whispered drunkenly. I muffled a squeal as he pulled me forward into his arms and rolled me over toward Mary. The sprung trap completed as Mary snuggled up behind me, and I managed to relax as they sandwiched me. I could still hear Crystal and Kimberly If I focused, but I absorbed myself with my little cuddle pile. Sleep came with minimal groping.

*~*~*

The sun on my face woke me but the remarkable warmth surrounding me was due to Mary and Cyrus. The Addie sandwich had come apart overnight, our makeshift blanket was gone, but all was not lost. I extricated Mary's arm from my shirt before crawling across the deflated mattress and retrieving my phone. It was dead, of course, but I didn't sweat it. I could charge it during the drive.

I found Mazer and Joshua lounging on their Mattress against the wall, nursing coffees in the living room. Mazer had resumed his demonic appearance, and with his shirt off I had a good view of his Plum-hued skin. I was surprised to recognize another tattoo, a pentacle like Mary's, but pointed down. I'd have to ask her about that sometime if I remembered. While most of Mary's tattoos were in ordinary black ink, his were white as chalk. I realized I was staring, so I turned to the other bed.

Crystal snored with a naked but content Kimberly in her grasp. She'd had the foresight to put her hair up again, but Kimberly wasn't so lucky. Sleep, or other activities had disheveled her bright blue hair, but she waved as I helped myself to the box of coffee on the counter. Mazer or Joshua must have gone out or had it and the donuts delivered.

I grabbed a donut and leaned against the counter. The same windowless government building filled the view out the window, and the sounds of the traffic below penetrated the glass.

I tried not to look or laugh as Joshua toyed with Mazer's horns affectionately. When I could no longer bear it, I excused myself back to the bedroom. More-so for my sanity than their privacy. Mary stirred as I shut the door. When she spied the cup in my hand, she bolted out of bed to stumble to the living room: this, in turn, woke Cyrus, and he sat up.

While I'd made no comment on the spectacle behind me, I heard Mary's amused snort as well as a thunk as Joshua no doubt knocked his elbow on the wall trying to save face. I shook my head as Cyrus raised an eyebrow.

"You ready for the big trip?" He sighed as he stretched, and I shrugged. I watched as his shirt rode up a bit, and I had the perverse thought of how much fun it could be to give him road head on the way to Tristate. It would be so easy, I'd whine about needing him to drive my car for me, Crystal or Mazer would drive the moving van, and I'd be home free.

His rumbling chuckle brought me from my thoughts as well as my eyes up from his waistline.

"T-there's coffee in the kitchen," I stammered before shutting myself in the bathroom.

When I returned, the bedroom was empty, so I busied myself packing. I heard rustling in the living room, indicating the same was happening there. The party dressed and mingled around the donuts as I joined them a few minutes later.

Kimberly and Joshua each hugged me goodbye before departing. Before long, all that remained was the caravan. We discussed seating arrangements. Mazer was going to drive the van, so while Crystal wanted to keep him company, Cyrus elected to ride with Mary. I burned with jealousy, but I didn't dare speak up. Still, they should know by now how much attention and affection I needed all the time.

My fuming turned to embarrassment and shame as Cyrus recognized my mood. He promised to switch over after the first stop. I supposed I could at least look forward to some quality time with him, but I felt stupid for putting so much thought into something so vain and selfish.

I watched with mild interest as Mazer recast his glamour, but this time when he finished, he looked like a supermodel version of *my* dad. I blinked and stared. Same hair, eyes, nose, ears... he had turned himself into a hybrid of myself and his demonic form. The fact was not missed by Mary. She rolled her eyes, and Cyrus snorted his amusement.

Mary left to take care of the admin stuff while Mazer and Crystal raided the convenience store for snacks. I had Cyrus to myself as we finished packing and found a cart to take the remaining bags downstairs.

"You have quite the jealous streak don't you?"

I managed a shaky, noncommittal shrug. His tone wasn't unkind, but the situation was still embarrassing.

"I'll grow out of it," I mumbled, and I nearly fell over when he nudged my shoulder.

"It's okay."

I furrowed my brow as he met my eye.

"I mean obviously don't let it turn into drama and hurt feelings, but I promise it's okay to feel your feelings. It's cool if you grow out of jealousy but it's also okay if you grow strong enough to communicate desires and manage in other healthy ways."

"I'll... keep that in mind."

"For now, do you want to talk about it?"

I sighed. "I was jealous that you chose Mary over me. I was looking forward to more quality time with you, and had been obsessing for a good part of the morning about how I'd... manipulate my way into getting it."

I feared a reprimand but instead, he pulled me under his arm and kissed the top of my head.

"It's not manipulative to ask. It's not even manipulative to broadcast feelings until someone notices to attend to you. The latter is just risky if the signals are missed and things go crazy. Thank you for talking about it. I look forward to our quality time."

I rolled my eyes and tried to keep step as we approached the apartment, possibly for the last time.

# 29

## So Not The Trauma

Even though I toured this house and a few others with Mary, Cyrus, and Mazer, the size didn't sink in till we tried to fill it with our things. My storage container arrived ahead of me. But, even with the best of both Mary and my furniture, the place was sparsely decorated.

We suffered a massive overlap on cooking and baking supplies. Neither of our kitchen tables was a good fit for the dining room, and this living room dwarfed Mary's lounge set. We didn't even speak of the couch I had.

Since we didn't shell out for the four-bedroom house we wouldn't have a shared bedroom beyond our private spaces, but it wasn't a horrible arrangement.

"Why did we even pay to deliver my container here?" I rested my hands on my hips as I looked at the furniture scattered on the drive-way. This was the junk that didn't make the cut, and the majority was mine.

Mary put her arm around my shoulder. "It's okay babe. The

shipping fee was literally less than the value of what we kept. It's still a better deal than junking the lot."

I pouted but accepted the point regardless. Besides, I had a feeling used furniture would be in higher demand in this larger city. Or something. I was reaching.

It was true my machines and bedroom set were worth more than the delivery fee, but I still didn't feel jazzed about how much was no good or not good enough.

Besides that, though, it kinda sucked for Mary that her bedroom would become the de facto common room. She deserved her space and privacy, but I was afraid she wouldn't get it. On the one hand, this motivated me to tailor my space to accommodate guests, but the roadblock to success was funding. My gigantic bedroom held my lonely little twin-size bed, the dresser I got off my neighbors curb five years ago, and a nightstand.

God, I wanted to decorate.

Mazer joined us in the garage and handed us each a key.

"Thanks" I tried to smile but I felt a pang in my heart as Mary practically tackled Mazer in a hug. Rather than burning, I ached with jealousy. I felt robbed by the clusterfuck my parents had made of my childhood and I never had warning when the old wounds opened. Mary didn't have a charmed life either, but she had a good dad.

My heart skipped as Mazer held out an arm for me as well and somehow I didn't hesitate to join the hug. I felt like I was being greedy or presumptuous to think he would consider me family, but I held onto hope even still.

I heard Cyrus step into the garage and we broke up our little huddle so he could receive his key as well. If he was sad to miss the hug, he didn't show it.

"You girls ready to mount the bed?"

For a moment I thought he was making an innuendo. Mary's

groan asserted the truth. The bed. Mary's bed. Ugh. I followed to the master bedroom, where the frame lay in pieces. Blessedly Cyrus had already found and prepared the studs, but now we had to do the lifting.

For how much I dreaded mounting the bed, the actual process wasn't terrible. Cyrus was pretty good at making furniture, even if he made it a bit heavy. The frame bolted in, and lifting the platform into place was remarkably manageable, even with the four of us.

Mazer clapped his hands. "You kids ready for dinner?"

The guy was such a stereotypical dad sometimes. Mary made a whole ceremony out of locking up with video and everything. It struck me as goofy but I played along anyways.

Rejected furniture still littered the driveway but it wouldn't be a problem if some of it walked off. We left it and piled into Mazer's minivan. I wasn't dressed to go out, so it was lucky that the five-minute trip ended up at Mazer's house. We lived *close*.

I could smell the pizza as we walked in. Some traditions transcended planes. I hugged my greeting to Mikah and Crystal in turn before visiting the babies, Azrael and Andy.

Twin half-siblings... I had originally assumed Crystal and Mikah each carried one, but it turned out Mikah had both of them together. I didn't even want to know the kinky demonic shit led to that particular logistical outcome. At least the parentage of the child Mikah was currently carrying, while baffling in its own right, had a scientific basis. Mazer was particularly excited to explain that trick to me. From the looks Mikah and Crystal had, it had been one of his favorite stories for the last few months. Long story short, this next child would be all three of theirs at once. Pretty wacky shit.

It was cozy crowding around the dinner table. It felt like having a family again, and it was the weirdest goddamn family I could have imagined. I wondered idly if Mazer would be a new father figure for me. I could certainly use one of those. I made a mental note to work at shelving my paternal issues so I didn't find myself calling Cyrus and Mazer both "Daddy".

"They are just too cute." I bottle-fed Andy after dinner. Mikah and I lounged in the matching recliners as the twins had their meals. I heard a cacophony of overlapping groaned arguments; the gist of them was, "you don't know them as we do."

Of course, I, in my infinite foresight and wisdom, ran my mouth. "I'd like to."

Mikah's eyes widened so much I couldn't see the bags under her eyes.

"I will pay you so much money. Please please *please.*"

She noticed my alarm and took a quick breather.

"So. Andy is a cambion like Mary. As you know that doesn't change too much, she doesn't go like 'Zach-Zach attack' or anything. But at the same time we can't trust her with just anyone in case she does something... special. You know?"

"I really don't."

Luckily, Mazer jumped in to explain. "For starters, cambions have neither a pulse nor a need to breathe until they are about seven years old. The pulse isn't a big deal, but good babysitters will investigate if a child doesn't appear to be breathing. Beyond this, when I was raising Mary I lost several sitters because, -- they quit, by the way, they didn't die. --but Mary tended to express herself in interesting ways humans generally can't. Her favorite trick was raising her body temperature by about forty degrees. One day she ran a fever, and before her mother could intervene a very enthusiastic doctor was drafting their medical journal submission."

I suddenly felt overly conscious about what might be out of the ordinary about the baby cambion in my arms. I should have realized she hadn't been breathing this whole time.

I tried to be subtle about checking for a pulse, and sure enough, nothing.

Mazer sat on the couch nearby.

"Demons such as myself are also known as nephilim, hybrid offspring of 'angels' and humans. Genealogy would indicate I am half spiritual and half-human. But the reality of how supernatural offspring work is far more complicated. The best way I can describe it is, while my parentage makes me in a sense wholly human and wholly supernatural simultaneously, cambions are wholly human and far less supernatural."

"And that means...."

Mazer scratched his head. "Since before recorded history, all humans have been supernatural to some extent. The impact of angelic ancestors will never disappear or wash out of humans. Mary and Andy have a little something extra."

"So they are like a quarter angel rather than less than a percent?"

Mazer shrugged. "Relatively speaking as far as supernatural powers go it's more like angels are one hundred percent, I am thirty percent, Mary and Andy are ten percent, and everyone else is between one and three percent."

"I hate math," I grumbled and adjusted the towel on my shoulder to burp Andy.

A small part of me expected Andy to belch fire, but all that happened was the tiniest spit-up and one particularly impressive burp.

I saw Mikah put down Azrael's bottle. "So does knowing that dissuade you from wanting to get to know our kids?"

I was already shaking my head. "Nah. It's clear you need a break, and I'm willing and available to help that happen."

I looked away as Mikah teared up. I was not prepared for such a strong reaction.

Mary returned and flopped on the couch beside Mazer. I realized this was balanced. Three of our names started with "A", and three started with "M". Funny how that happens.

Mary spoke up, interrupting me from my musings of all the ways Her, Cyrus, and My initials could spell words.

"Motherhood suits you."

"Uh uh. No. Nope." I shook my head. Cyrus snorted as he leaned on the doorway to the kitchen, so I elaborated.

"I neither want nor am capable of having children."

Mazer raised an eyebrow. "I am quite proficient in fertility treatments, should that ever interest you."

Andy kicked their disapproval of my animated response, so I made an effort to calm down.

"That is a very kind offer, but even if caring for Andy and Azrael awakened some maternal instinct in me I would rather be a weird aunt than a mother myself. Please for the love of god, talk me down if I start to express interest in pregnancy."

Perhaps I imagined it, but I thought I heard Mikah mumble, "Amen sister."

Mary was still concerned, so I elaborated.

"I had a pretty cool doctor so I got my tubes tied a few years ago. I was lucky I didn't need to shop around."

"Oh. You're really serious about it."

"Yeah. One of my exes was a little difficult. Getting him in a condom was like pulling teeth, and I was having so many negative side effects from birth control so I gave up. Invitro is always an option so why not you know?"

Everyone was staring at me.

"You got a tubal ligation because your boyfriend wouldn't use a condom?"

"More because of the birth control," I murmured, but even I didn't believe the lie.

I couldn't bear to meet Mary's eyes, and when I looked at Mikah, she was profoundly sad.

The room was silent except for the squeak of my rocking chair.

When Crystal joined us, I took the opportunity to hand Andy off to her. I mumbled about going to the bathroom and made my best guess as to where to go.

I ended up letting myself into the master bedroom and using the private bathroom. That was probably why it took so long for Mary to find me.

"I'm worried about you."

Great. Flat out fucking confrontation.

"Yeah?" I didn't feel like moving the conversation along, so I shrugged and waited for her to elaborate.

"Did he abuse you in other ways?"

"He didn't abuse me. He was just a bit of a dick." I folded my arms but refrained from making an effort to step past her out of the bathroom.

"Addison. This is serious. Have you gone to therapy?"

Full name treatment. Awesome.

"You know I was seeing a therapist."

She rolled her eyes. "Did you talk about this with them?"

"Probably. I don't remember. Why are you making such a big deal about it?"

"Because I hadn't realized you had a history of being abused by partners and I'm very seriously worried about a repeat of that situation."

"I'm not going to abuse you."

"I'm worried you will take extreme action, instead of communicating with Cyrus or me."

"That won't --"

"Promise you will communicate." Her tone offered no room for debate.

"I'll try."

"Promise." She stepped forward.

I waved my hands ineffectually. "What am I promising? How am I supposed to know what you would consider extreme?"

She didn't answer. I looked away as she put her hands on her hips.

I found myself focusing on coming up with what she would want to hear and debating what I could commit to. I knew she'd hold me to my word.

"I promise I will communicate on issues prior to taking extreme action."

She looked me in the eye for an uncomfortably long time before finally pulling me into a hug. I reciprocated the hug and focused on dropping my defenses. I was about to speak up when she pulled back.

"I love you, Addie. I want to do everything I can to support you."

"I love you too, I just wish I could do for you what you do for me."

I scowled as she gave me a pitying look.

"You're minimizing your contributions."

"I'm being realistic."

She pulled me into another hug.

"We'll work on that."

I bunched up her shirt in my hands. I'd have to work on contributing more for sure.

# 30

## Fur Babies

I let Mary pull me from the car to the shelter. I worried about how much more interested she was than me, especially since I would be the primary caretaker for whatever animal we might adopt.

I sensed that this was another of those conditioning things. If I thought about it, Mary had frequently talked about how cool having a pet would be, but she didn't make any actual moves until I said something about it half an hour ago.

Now here we were.

"So I've been researching and I'm thinking a cat would be a really good fit."

"Of course you have. You aren't worried that your costume ears and tail might send a cat mixed signals?"

"What? Ew. No."

"If you're sure...." I let the question hang as she rambled about how that photo series wasn't even popular. I struggled to believe that wasn't due to my camera work.

I saw a sign outside the shelter saying visitations were by

appointment only, but mysteriously we were let in without a fuss. Mary explained they had a cancellation, but she did so when the staff weren't in earshot.

Mary knew most of the cats by name and when she asked about some that were no longer here, I spoke up.

"Do you come here regularly or something?"

Alex, the person guiding the tour, nodded but switched to shaking their head when Mary made a face.

"I wouldn't say regularly..."

I pinched the bridge of my nose. "Which one are we getting?"

"I wanted you to choose-"

"Which ones do you want me to choose between then?"

She sighed heavily and then pointed in turn to various glass-walled cubicles.

"Ellen has always been sweet and affectionate, Lina is a clingy brat but lovable, Derby is a bit zoomy, more so than typical, and Ghost is just so pretty."

"What about Sonia?"

"I mean, she's cute I guess. She's been shy and hasn't come to say hi to me before."

Alex spoke up, "She has an interesting personality, I've never seen so much separation anxiety and codependency in a cat before."

My heart melted. Unlike Mary's favorites, Sonia was smaller if the size of her lump in the blankets indicated anything.

"I wanna say hello to her." I tried to contain my excitement as Alex opened the door for me.

"Separation anxiety sounds like a problematic personality trait if you want to get a day job."

I just shook my head and leaned into the box. Sonia retreated into her blanket when the door opened, but when I drummed my fingertips next to her bed, her paw shot out to bat at me. We played a brief game of 'whose hand gets to be on top' before Sonia seemed to give up and just stare at me from under her blanket. She let me hold her paw for a few seconds before retreating completely. I expected a sound or something, but she turned motionless and silent underneath the blanket.

"I'll come back to you," I whispered and stepped back to let the glass door close.

Sure enough, when I went to the other cubes, Ellen snuggled up immediately, going so far as to crawl onto my shoulders. Derby rocketed out of containment, and we spent a good minute catching her to put her back up. Lina used a bit more claw in her cuddles, and I found a few stray threads poking from my shirt when she was done making biscuits. Ghost played aloof, shying away from pets in favor of strolling around her cubicle and bathing.

"Tell me about Beth and Jessica since you've apparently socialized with them all."

Mary rolled her eyes as Beth's box opened.

"Beth likes to --" She didn't even get to finish before a bed and blanket tumbled from the door. "Well... she likes to do that. She seems to hate when things sit on top of other things. Could prove disastrous for Cyrus's figurine collection."

I nodded and scratched behind Beth's ears before returning her bedding and letting the box shut.

"Jessica is vocal." Even as we spoke, Jessica pawed at her door while screaming.

"We have to be careful what toys we give her." The employee opened the cage and dropped a treat. "That might buy us a minute of quiet if we are lucky. Given attention, Jessica is generally lovely but she has an endless appetite. She finds anything that makes noise and abuses it to get her way."

Done with her treat, Jessica expressed affection, and I picked her up as the employee continued.

"You'll notice we had to pad the box she stays in pretty thoroughly.

That's because she is unbearably smart. She's learned how to open every latch we have tried and we can't use padlocks because she will just rattle them. Sure, she wants to escape, but mostly she wants to break into the food cabinet or bang her cage door repeatedly until she gets attention."

I practically had to peel Jessica off of me to get her back in her cage, and I stepped back to ponder our options.

"Let me guess, your favorites are the ones I didn't mention at first."

"Mmmaybe."

Mary rolled her eyes, but I was unapologetic.

"Sonia seems really sweet and I think she's at the top of my list. Beth and Jessica are really interesting too though. Ellen seems like a really easy cat to care for and so does Ghost. Derby and Lina have pretty unobtrusive quirks."

"So what I'm hearing is you want a problem child."

"I wouldn't put it that way."

"Mhmm I'm sure you would frame it as some sort of advocacy for the disadvantaged."

I squinted at her but made no reply. The point of discussion was becoming useless.

"Maybe we should just both pick one. I bet Sonia would get along with any of your favorites and possibly even be a moderating factor if her codependency manifests as social attentiveness."

"We came here for a pet. Not for multiple pets. We haven't even looked at the dogs yet."

"I don't like going on walks."

Mary sighed and looked between the different boxes. She turned to the employee.

"Do any of them get along particularly well or poorly with Sonia?"

The employee shrugged. "Sonia doesn't interact much in group settings. We haven't exactly been doing any compatibility tests but

I can at least assure you that we haven't had fighting issues with any of this lot."

"That's good." Mary murmured absently. "I'm most interested in seeing how Sonia and Ghost get on together. It seems the most fitting to me."

"So you decided... just randomly... that the standoffish beauty and the codependent shy cats should live together."

Mary beamed at me. "Yep! It just seems the most logical given my personal experiences."

Great. Suspicions confirmed. I could press further, but I knew that would only play into her hand. I, for one, didn't want to be exposed as the codependent anxious one in front of a stranger.

Since I hadn't taken the bait, Mary either switched tactics or changed the subject.

"Are you sure you want to pick Sonia? You haven't even seen her."

"Looks aren't everything." I squinted at Mary.

"Whatever. They're all adorable. I guess we can get two cats."

Alex pulled paperwork out of pockets on Sonia and Ghost's doors. "If you do have trouble with fighting or any personality friction you can bring them back."

I turned my attention back to Sonia as Mary and Alex discussed the adoption procedure. As if she sensed being chosen, Sonia emerged from her blanket fort and approached the door. While Ghost had long hair and was the lightest possible shade of gray, Sonia was about half her size with short hair and a tortoiseshell pattern. I wiggled my finger in one of the holes of her box, and she nuzzled it before biting softly. I snorted. If that was her idea of misbehaving, we would get along well indeed.

\*~\*~\*

I was crashed on the couch with Sonia when Mary returned from the store. Alex had recommended we pick up two extra litter boxes, bringing the total to three since apparently, the rule of thumb was to have one more litter-box than you had cats. In addition to this, though, Mary had a huge box with a picture of a complex cat tower.

This one looked like a castle explicitly designed for multiple cats, and I could already imagine Sonia and Ghost staking out their respective cubbies.

"Need any help?" I called as Mary set down the box with a huff and moved out of sight, presumably for another load.

"Nah. How are the girls getting along?"

"It was the funniest thing." I tried to sit up, but Sonia remained glued to my chest as I struggled to reposition. "I had Sonia in my room while Ghost got acclimated, and it looked like there would be a problem because Ghost was hissing and reaching under the door. But, when I let Sonia out, Ghost calmed down pretty quickly. Sonia just kinda rolled over and let Ghost push at her and rub on her for a minute."

"Sounds like Sonia is a total sub." I could hear amusement in Mary's voice, but I managed not to take the bait.

"You probably would think that, but I think they have been sharing and cooperating very equitably for the last hour."

"So you're telling me --" Mary peeked around the corner from the garage door, "-- that Ghost asserted dominance, Sonia turned into a puddle, and you think a total transfer of power looks equitable?"

Mary held my gaze as I squinted at her, but I refused to rise to the bait. Eventually, she returned to the garage for another trip.

"It's okay if you're a bottom," I whispered to Sonia as she purred. I nearly jumped as Ghost hopped onto my lap as well. I hadn't seen her approach. I wondered if there would be some sort of jealousy thing going on, but Ghost just lay down on Sonia and groomed the top of her head.

When Mary returned, she took a picture of all of us and shook her head as she flicked through her phone.

"Says here that dominants groom submissives."

I rolled my eyes. "I think it just means they are getting along."

"We'll see..." Mary seemed smug as she set about filling the new litter boxes and fitting their covers.

Mary was still in another room when the grooming session turned violent. I was startled as they fell out of my lap. I'd never seen a cat-fight before exactly, and that paralyzed me more than anything. It was quieter than I expected, and I wasn't sure where to intervene.

Sonia moved erratically and attempted multiple tackles, but Ghost would brush her off or pin her down briefly before sitting up and watching again. Despite the relative quiet of the Fight, Mary soon appeared and watched from the doorway as they rolled around.

"Should I separate them?"

"Nah," Mary shook her head and leaned against the door frame.

As suddenly as it began, though, Sonia calmed down, and Ghost sat on top of her to resume grooming.

"Were they playing?"

Mary nodded as if this was obvious.

"Yeah. If I had to guess, Sonia or Ghost just wanted to work out some of their aggression. It's much more likely that Sonia was playing while being submissive than actually rebelling against the established dynamic."

When I gave Mary a doubtful expression, she pressed on, "Sorta like how you --"

"Fine! I get it! You think there's a pecking order. If you are sure it's just play, that's enough for me."

"Oh, I'm sure. No hissing? Blood? Pissing? It's fine."

She looked like she was about to continue, so I cut in. "Great. Perfect. Do you want any help with the cat tower?"

Mary rolled her eyes. "Mhmm. Might as well deliver the queen and princess their tower."

I wrinkled my nose. "Doesn't that imply family relations?"

"So you admit they have a dynamic."

"Oh hush."

"Fine. Queen, and queen consort. Better?"

I didn't dignify her with a response as I helped her with the box.

# 31

## Packing

My thoughts got away from me as I stuffed and closed up the twentieth tiny paper box of the night. The fact that Mary had bailed out on Cyrus and me was both a blessing and a curse. *Originally* the plan had been to help him pack, primarily for the sake of his mini-figure collection. In her absence, the event had progressed more like a dinner date. Somewhere along the way my hang ups over intimacy with Cyrus had faded away leaving all the tension, but precious little restraint.

Mary was decidedly not helping from afar. She claimed she had an early day tomorrow but she was clearly still awake and had nothing better to do than meddle. Her first trick was sending me packing innuendos. So many fucking innuendos escalating to "dick in a box" gags and full-on cringe-worthy porn clips. Next, she switched to the group message and renamed it from *Cool Chat* to *'Cule Chat*.

"Very clever." I grumbled and I saw the corners of Cyrus's lips turn up as he checked his phone. The packing innuendos resumed in earnest until Cyrus went in and edited her nickname to brat, kicking off the great nickname war of 2023. I had hoped he would somehow reveal his level of interest through her teasing, but I couldn't read him for the life of me. God damn it, being an adult that communicated with words sucked so much.

I was running out of reasons not to ask to see his bed, but I also was also doing an absolutely lousy job of initiating. I did want to make serious progress on the packing, but I knew I couldn't count on him really starting anything. Not after I asked him to wait. I was truly in a hell of my own making.

I watched as he took my latest packed figure and added it to the dense pattern he had puzzled together in the bottom of the moving box. We had made pretty quick progress, but I wasn't sure I was up for packing dishware after this.

Cyrus looked up as I reached to pop up a new figure box. "Are you getting tired?"

"Of this?" I looked at the ragtag group of characters that remained. "I can do a few more..."

I saw Cyrus shake his head out of the corner of my eye.

"We don't have to do it all tonight."

"But there's so much to do."

I didn't know why I was making excuses. I didn't want him to think I was reluctant to be intimate, but if all I managed to do tonight was eat and fuck, I'd feel a bit shitty for taking advantage of the night.

I wrapped foam around some sort of fire person and stuffed it into the smallest box I could manage.

When I handed it to Cyrus he unfroze and blindly tossed it on top of the others. "Maybe we could take a break."

I dropped the roll of packing material.

"Sure! We didn't do dessert. Do you still have that pint of ice cream?"

"Yeah, it's still there."

He followed me to the kitchen space. It had been hell to try to cook here when I visited last, and I was glad to never need to again.

He pulled down bowls as I tried to warm his ice cream scoop under the tap. Even with that, I struggled to dig even half an inch into the brick of cream. Either his freezer wasn't working the best, or it had been there too long.

"Here, let me."

I handed him the scoop and stifled a laugh as he had similar difficulty.

"Fuck." he muttered under his breath.

"Good idea." I took the pint and dumped it.

"What?" Cyrus raised an eyebrow.

"You said 'fuck', I said good idea." I didn't know where I was manifesting my confidence from, but I'd be damned if I let my rational mind backpedal "Do you have any cheesy innuendos you want to use? I'm drawing blanks."

He turned and leaned back against the sink. "Mary texted me a few packing innuendos earlier."

Damn you, Mary. I shook my head. "I'm strictly vetoing those. Any backups?"

He exaggerated seriously pondering the question, quirking an eyebrow and stroking his chin for effect. "I could suggest a movie, or talk about body piercings."

"Mmmmmm vetoed again, but points for sass."

"DnD references?"

"Not sure I'd get them." I stepped in and hugged him, resting my chin on his chest as I looked up.

"But you aren't vetoing that one?"

"I mean... good luck turning 'cast fireball' into an innuendo."

"I'll have you know there is a wealth of dirty humor to be had in tabletop games."

"You can table top me."

"See *that* works. Context is everything." He walked me backwards toward his room, faking me out with a turn toward his table before pulling me through the door.

A part of me wanted him to actually top the hell out of me but the moment he sat on the edge of the bed I was climbing into his lap. I wanted to push him back onto the bed too, but I knew that would just make clothes a different sort of obstacle. I held his face to mine as he slipped his arms behind the small of my back.

I had a moment of panic as he leaned me back.

Now I felt like a captive audience in his lap. I had to hold onto his shoulders to keep from busting my ass on the floor.

Cyrus however was far more content with this arrangement. He laid a trail of kisses from my cheek to my collar as I tried not to squirm. Unfortunately for me, riling me up seemed to be his intent. When I made the mistake of leaning my head back, he went for the proverbial and literal jugular.

"Cyruuuus." I couldn't wiggle or loosen my grip on his shoulders, but begging proved effective at least.

"Yes Addison?" He pulled me upright and leaned back on his elbows.

I didn't feel like being articulate with my response so I shifted off his lap so that I could kneel on the bed next to him.

"This is going to be pretty difficult if we start out on the bed." Eye contact was difficult right now.

"You aren't up for the challenge?"

"I didn't say *that*."

"I have safety shears. We could role-play trauma team."

"Is that your kink? I never was the 'play nurse' type."

"First time for everything."

"I'm not sacrificing these clothes to your snipping kink."

"It's not my kink."

"Is stalling your kink? Or would you call it delayed gratification?"

"It's called 'edging' my dear, it's where you-"

"-fine! Keep your clothes on!" I pulled off my shirt and stepped off the bed. His sassy remark died as I dragged my socks off and undid my pants.

He was still staring as I piled my clothes and tied my hair in a short ponytail. I'd wait on the underwear until he got moving again. I'd chosen a matching set specifically for this eventuality and I wasn't going to breeze past that detail, especially if Cyrus could appreciate the significance.

I crawled back onto the edge of the bed and waited for him to unfreeze.

Even if he wasn't moving, his eyes were roaming, "If I didn't know better, I'd say this is premeditated."

I cheered inside. "I'm sure I have no idea what you are talking about."

He sighed and shook his head.

"What?" I titled my head to the side. "Did you have your heart set on unwrapping me? I can put it all back on."

That got him moving.

"I'm sure I'll have plenty of chances to divest you of your clothes personally."

I rolled my eyes but thankfully he wasn't stalling anymore. His shirt made a graceful arc into his hamper.

I inched closer as he lay back to work on his pants. I *wanted* to help him but he proved to be very capable on his own. I didn't even get kicked in the face when his jeans came off.

"You tied your hair up pretty quick. Do you do this often?"

"This is our first time babe, but I don't mind making it a regular thing."

He raised an eyebrow but he knew a deflection when he saw it. I wasn't going to let one thoughtless question ruin my night.

He brought his hand up to cup my cheek. "Is everything okay so far?"

"Yeah. All good."

"You'll tell me if anything changes?"

"Mhmm." I crawled the rest of the way forward and straddled his lap. I felt his dick poke me through his boxers but he didn't seem perturbed.

I gave him a quick kiss and squished my fingers in his hair. I considered doing a little hop in his lap for good measure.

"I love how we have such an articulate plan of what to do. Very iconic of us."

He huffed a laugh and rested his forehead against mine.

"I have to get up to get a condom."

I clapped my hands. "Okay. Game plan then. You get your willy wrap and I pose like one of your french girls until you know how you want me."

I let him up and flopped on his bed as he went to rustle around in the bathroom.

"You know you get a say in this too."

I waved apathetically. "I don't have to know what I like, I have a medical exemption."

"You knew you liked Italian food."

"Irrelevant."

"Do you want to be on top? Bottom? Otherwise?"

"I'd really like you to uh... hold me down. That's for sure."

"Doggy? Prone? Missionary?"

I wrinkled my nose at him as he returned.

"I hate that you said those words, but face to face, yes."

I remembered that I was supposed to get my underwear out of the way and I was still flailing with my panties when he returned.

I nearly fell backward before I got my bra off but he helped me untangle before settling above me.

"What about you?" I reveled in the feeling of his skin on mine. "Any high notes you want to hit?"

"Your g-spot?"

"Hush."

He rolled his eyes but, unlike me, he didn't take long thinking about it.

"Hand holding is fun. Always love to hear you say my name-- Oh! If you want to cross your ankles behind me that would be okay too."

"Well I'm not one to kink-shame."

"As if that doesn't align with your interests."

He eased a bit of weight onto me. I could tell he was watching me, but I couldn't keep eye contact.

I let out a huff of air as he relaxed his hips, the weight was exquisite, certainly making breathing a bit harder but not remotely uncomfortable.

"How you doin down there?"

I nodded. I didn't know what else to do. Was he asking something? It wasn't rhetorical was it? Fuck, was it even a yes or no question?

I rested a hand on his back. As much as it pained me, I could see this was one of those verbal check in points.

"I'm still okay." the words felt forced though, not because i didn't mean them, but because this was a bit of a diaphragm exercise already.

So now I sound constipated. Excellent.

He shifted to hold himself up on one elbow. I didn't need to look to know what his other hand was doing.

"Cyrus-"

He didn't stop, I didn't want him to.

"Fuck me."

He only hummed his response as he pressed in. acclimating at first was my least favorite part, but he seemed to know how to make it easier. He brought his hand back to take mine, pressing it into the pillow above my head.

He looked ready. I felt ready. I mustered the strength to cross my ankles behind him.

I saw him huff a small laugh before he pressed the rest of the way in, even with this small weight on me, he pushed me across and into the bed, practically curling me up under him as he pressed deeper.

My ankles slipped but I recovered. The size was familiar... conspicuously reminiscent of Mary's newest strap-on.

He reached up and grabbed a pillow from the head of the bed.

"Let me put this under your hips."

I obeyed and I felt a little rush at the feeling of having my hips higher than my head. I only had a moment to wonder why he had such a firm pillow on hand before he pressed in again. This time I wasn't so curled and I also didn't feel the ache in my hips that i thought was required for missionary sex.

There was no fumbling from Cyrus. No slips, shakes, nothing. He pulled out part way and pressed close again. Strong as he was, he couldn't balance as well when I pulled him to me. The resulting thrust was sharper, and Cyrus played at being disgruntled as he released my hand to prop himself up on both elbows.

"My, My, so impatient."

He punctuated the statement with a roll of his hips. I made a show of gasping as I dug my fingers into his shoulders.

When I didn't sass further, he worked his hands under me.

I wasn't sure why I thought I would need to act. I mean, of course I would have given a Broadway performance out of care for Cyrus, but I'd performed enjoyment for men I liked far less. It wasn't that Cyrus magically knew what I liked either -he didn't even do a perfect job of reading my reactions- but goddamn did he have focus. I thought sex with men was "lie back, make sounds, and let them get their little happy feelings on their dick." but Cyrus had a subtly different ideology.

It was almost like he didn't even want the friction. When I cupped his face he stopped to kiss me and *I* moved into him. It was a pathetic movement, just the slightest roll of my hips as I tried to pull myself onto him. It was clumsy, but even as amused as he was by the effort he didn't take that as his cue to resume. I braced myself against the bed and made a slightly better thrust and this time he moved against me.

Holy fuck.

I managed to contribute to maybe a dozen thrusts before I lost my focus and he was doing all the work again. I feared he would do the traditional sudden jack-hammering but even as the pace quickened it stayed firm and even.

I could do nothing but breathe in time, if I lost focus on that, I had to gasp and stumble to find my breath again. When I threw my head back he took the opportunity to attack my neck. His hand tightened on mine, but his pace never faltered.

"Cyrus!" I gasped as I reached the brink. I hardly had the breath to groan in exasperation when he stopped.

I wanted to beat my fists on his chest. The little shit knew exactly what he was doing and his loving gaze all but confirmed it. I had nothing to do but catch my breath as he pulled out and sat up on his knees.

"You seem displeased."

God he was cocky.

"You know damn well how close I was."

"But won't the final release be all the sweeter?"

My glare didn't affect him in the slightest.

"Now that you know I'm going to edge you a couple more times, what would you like to do?"

"What if I don't like edging?"

Aaaand that was the pouty face. Damn it.

"Would you try it for meeee?"

"You can have a little edging. As a treat." I squinted up at him. "
I want a turn on top."

"As you wish."

He laughed as I pulled him down onto the bed next to me. I
wasted no time swinging a leg over and situating myself. Unlike
him, I made no fanfare. I could only hope my knees held out longer
than him.

My delusion of control evaporated as he mirrored my movements. I wasn't surprised, but I was certainly chagrined at the
development. At first his hands only rested on my hips, but now he
was pulling me down, gradually increasing pressure until he could
seize complete control of the pace. I was only allowed to lift myself
now, and only when he permitted.

The most absurd part was that I apparently wanted to go faster
and harder than him. His thrusts just barely held back, as though he
was pulling the punch. Even as my breathing became frenzied, we
could agree on a pace but not the pressure. When I fell harder he
caught me softer.

The game wasn't lost though, he was getting worked up. There
were little sounds, gasps and sighs just audible over our movements.
I leaned forward, intending to work him up further but my plan
immediately backfired.

"Cyrus!"

I grabbed his arms as he changed the pattern.

"Getting close, Addie?"

I hung my head, goddamn right I was.

"Not yet."

"Mhmm."

He squeezed my hips and made a particularly violent thrust,

causing me to fall forward toward him. Damn him he knew exactly what I wanted now.

"Liar."

I shook my head. I still had a chance. He hadn't stopped yet and he had to be close now.

My breathing got heavy. I struggled to work with his rhythm. He wasn't pressing as hard now, if I could just keep control a moment longer--

God fucking damn it.

I practically lifted him off the bed as he suddenly had a vice-like grip on my hips. He was deep inside me, but he wasn't moving a goddamn inch.

He eased his grip after a second. I leaned forward off his dick to smoosh him to the bed. He was a big boy. He could deal.

He was definitely a bit out of breath, but I'd lost round two as well. I never had been good at poker.

"How're you doing Babygirl?" He rubbed his thumb across my cheek as I held myself up above him.

"I won't lie, I'm a little frustrated."

"Not used to losing?"

"Oh no. I *never* win when Mary feels competitive, but I hoped I had a chance with you."

"Would it help if I said you nearly got your way?"

"No."

He leaned up and I let him meet me in a kiss. I couldn't even stay fake-mad at him for long.

I sat back on his lap as he got his arms under him. I took a quick glance to make sure the condom had stayed in place.

"Is this going to be a 'rematch until I win' thing or are we going best three out of five?"

He laughed and shook his head.

"It was indulging my interest in edging."

I felt my face heat up. Not in anger, but shame. Fuck.

"Sorry." I mumbled.

"It's all okay. It would have been okay if you had 'won' so to speak."

"No, it wouldn't."

"Addie..."

"I want to try again. I'll make it up to you."

He snorted, not in disbelief, but amusement.

"There's nothing to make up for."

"Oh just shut up and take the olive branch. One more edge and then I want to see about this payoff you promised."

"Okay, okay. I accept the olive branch." He seemed deeply amused by the whole thing, but that was a better result than being hurt. He was always more gracious than I deserved.

He sat up as I crawled the rest of the way off his lap.

"Would you like to do prone?"

"Never tried it. I'm guessing it works like it sounds?"

"Yeah. Doggy, but a little flatter."

"I hate that word."

"Mhmm." He pulled a pillow from behind him to the middle of the bed. "If you put this under your hips it should be a bit more comfortable."

As I laid down, the logistics made sense. It was a bit of contorting but not much.

I pushed sheets and pillows out from under my head. I hoped he didn't want to hold my arms behind my back.

The bed shifted as he moved to sit on my thighs and I struggled to relax as he rubbed my back. I hadn't expected the brief massage but it wasn't unwelcome.

"Is this comfortable enough?"

"My chest is kinda crushed."

He reached over me to grab another pillow and I put it under my stomach.

"How about now?"

I stretched my hands out over my head. "Better."

"It shouldn't hurt, so stop me if you have any pain, okay?"

My response came out as a gasp as he leaned forward. He got far deeper than I bargained for.

I grabbed fistfuls of the sheets. He started slow as he had before, pushing me down into the bed as he worked. Occasionally he would brace a hand on my back, and I wished he would more often. I had no range of movement. I didn't have the strength in my back to even reciprocate and it hardly felt useful to be able to kick my feet when I couldn't lift my arms more than a few inches off the sheets.

I didn't have a way of knowing how close he was getting, and I was powerless to do anything about it.

I lifted my shoulders off the bed, bracing my elbows under me with great effort. Cyrus didn't push me down. Now that I was resisting his forward pressure, the friction was overwhelming.

I knew any second he would stop, but I'd tempered my expectations in that respect. I fought the urge to seek out that crest of pleasure and instead distracted myself by focusing on breathing.

Still, the sensation was inescapable. I was about to be made to cum, and for the first time in my life I didn't want to.

"Cyrus!"

His pace barely slowed.

"Cyrus, please!"

"Please what?"

Why the fuck wasn't he stopping?

"Stop! I'm going to cum!"

I flinched as he pulled out. I couldn't remember ever needing this much willpower. Even a few seconds later I was still consciously struggling to keep my orgasm at bay. Finally, the sensation faded, replaced by the now familiar tension. God was I horny.

"Jesus Christ, Cyrus." I groaned as he sat up off of me and let me roll over. "I hope you appreciate the willpower that took."

"I do."

"Were you fucking with me? Was that a test?"

"I didn't intend for it to be."

"Why didn't you stop on your own?"

He shrugged. "I didn't know you were close."

"What about when I said please?"

"If you had been asking me to bring you to orgasm, I would have obliged."

I rubbed my face. "Dear lord."

"I'm proud of you."

I waved him off. "You're welcome. We did the edging, now please oblige me."

"Are you going to make that an innuendo?"

"*Fuck me, Cyrus.*" I growled through clenched teeth.

"Ooooh spicy Addie." I bristled at his teasing but at least he was moving.

In mere seconds he was on top of me. He lifted my right leg by the ankle and easily aligned himself and slipped in. I could only scramble to grab sheets as he thrust, and I had no way to sit up as he worked above me.

"Fuck! Cyrus!"

"Yes dear?" He rested my leg on my shoulder and leaned forward.

I had nothing. No response for that. I couldn't move my leg off his shoulder but I wanted him closer. I held out my arms to him and he got the message. He only took a moment to drop my leg before he was down against me, just as when we had started.

"You better cum-- as fast as you can." I wove my right hand into his. I'd kiss him, but we'd knock teeth at this point.

He huffed a laugh, and I had to admit it was an absurd request.

He seemed almost as affected as I had been all this time. His pace wasn't as consistent. The closeness I felt now made everything else seem distant. He was *here*. He wasn't showing off anymore. No more theatrics. No vanity.

This time when I pulled him down he didn't resist. It didn't have to be the right pace anymore. I didn't need to focus or have my expectations met. The end was inevitable, and it didn't seem like either of us had control of that.

I was dizzy now. I couldn't breathe deep enough. I couldn't even form his name as I cried out. He stopped as my orgasm broke over me. He was spent and so was I. I tensed involuntarily as he thrust one last time, and then his weight was off of me. I wished he would just crush me. I heard him fall onto the bed beside me as I went limp and I tried to roll toward him but my legs spasmed in protest.

Fuck.

"So-" Cyrus managed to sound smug, even when out of breath. "-have you accepted the gospel of edging into your heart?"

It took me a moment to process. Gospel? What? I searched through my memory. It meant "good news" but I didn't consider the term remotely interchangeable.

"Fuck no."

The bed shook with his laughter.

# 32

## Why Don't We All Go Fishing?

I stretched as I climbed out of Mary's car. It was barely daylight on a weekend but even though this was a normal time to wake up, I bemoaned the loss of sleep. Mazer had packed the minivan pretty completely, and I wondered how many cars this would take. Hell, I wasn't even sure Mazer's crew would all fit in their van.

I latched onto Mary's back as Cyrus got out of his car.

"Can we take one of their cars?" I murmured in Mary's ear.

"Stealing is wrong."

"It's borrowing, snot."

I looked longingly at Crystal's silver sedan. It wasn't as new as Cyrus's car, but it looked damn comfy compared to Mary's

"We probably won't take my car, so yeah. We can arrange to give you a bit more space."

She swayed side to side a couple times and I had the most peculiar sense of foreboding.

"Kinda funny." She covered my hands over her waist. "Usually you seem to crave small spaces, but when it comes to my car you are downright claustrophobic."

"Blankies, cuddles, and cubbies are comforting. Your beloved Phoenix is a roaring and rattling demon."

"Fine, fine." She extricated herself from my grasp and practically skipped over to help Mazer.

Fucking morning people.

Cyrus draped an arm around my shoulders and yawned. I hoped that I would get to lean on him, but it was my turn to be supportive.

I looked up at him. "Have you ever been fishing?"

He squinted and went on a conflicted face journey. "Kinda. There was one camping trip, but the other girls all wanted to hurry on to canoeing. I didn't catch anything."

"I bet we'll have better luck with all their fuckey magic stuff."

Cyrus squeezed my shoulder, and tugged me toward the gathering group. "Hold on to that hope, babe."

I was kinda surprised Mazer wasn't using his glamour, given he was out in the open on his driveway. Still, if he didn't see a problem he probably knew better than me.

Mikah was in the same boat as me. We were the sleepy bitches surrounded by morning people.

Mary returned from the house with a cooler and I rolled my eyes as Mazer did a little clap to kick off his pep talk.

"So, it's an hour and a half to the river access, we have lunches packed." He gestured at Mary. "Is everyone ready to load up? Nobody needs the bathroom?"

I pursed my lips as I remembered my last family road trip. Grandpa took bathroom stops so personally.

I begrudgingly excused myself as Mazer and Mikah worked on getting the kids into car seats. By the time I was back I was the only one not ready. On the bright side, I didn't have to pick where I sat.

I might be a bit lonely up in the front with Crystal, but Mary had decided half of the backseat was for storage too.

Oh well. It was best that I could see out the windshield since I forgot my motion sickness pills.

"Are you ready to be the navigator?" Crystal handed me a walkie talkie after I'd buckled up.

"Sure."

I flinched as something cold touched my elbow. It was just Mary passing me a drink. I held it and the walkie talkie as I tried to will the morning fog out of my mind. Failing that, I popped open the can of tea.

"Am I going to have to do the paper map and stuff?"

"Nah." Crystal tapped the screen on the dash. "I can handle the GPS and tunes with voice commands."

She pulled out of the garage as Mazer set out. Like Cyrus's car, it was quiet. Her music taste sounded aggressive and dated, but she played it so soft that it might as well have been silent as she drove through town and got on the highway.

"So." Crystal drummed her fingers on the steering wheel. "How has your plunge into the supernatural been?"

I looked over my shoulder at Mary and she was already asleep, or at least pretending. So much for that explosive energy she seemed to have before.

"Pretty exciting I guess. It's easy to forget about it though. I guess it helps that Mary doesn't turn purple when she's around the house."

"Pity, purple is the best color. Still, Mary seems like the red type."

"Because of her hair?"

"Maybe." Crystal shrugged.

I tried to imagine Mary with a demonic appearance, strolling around the house with bright red skin, horns, and a tail. I couldn't exactly picture it but i knew it would suit her.

"Has it been weird for you?"

"Oh for sure." Crystal laughed. "Even after a year and some change, it strikes me how much everything is different."

"How so?"

"Well... Mikah met Mazer a bit like you met Mary. She got in pretty deep before she knew what was going on, and there were some growing pains with settling out afterwards."

"How did you meet him?"

"Through Mikah. She tangled herself up in a contract and... Well, now we have kids."

My eyes widened. "Is the whole situation just a contract? Mazer seems so nice!"

"No no no. Not anymore. I mean there is a contract, but it's marriage. We are past the 'bear him children and feed his appetite' stuff."

I looked out the window as my face heated up.

"How did it change?"

"We sat down and communicated, and it wasn't even terribly long ago. Hell, I think we wrote our vows about the time you met Mary."

"Oh."

Crystal laughed nervously. "Yeah. If you thought Mary wasn't the settling down type I think the ordeal of landing an incubus might have you beat."

"So what happened?"

"The situationship caught feelings. We had kids to raise together. Mazer usually feels like he has to be distant and hands off, like he was with Mary at first, but we convinced him to be a little more present." Crystal frowned at the radio and tapped the skip button on the console until it registered and started playing a new song.

"Where would he go if he didn't stay here?"

"Hell."

She said it so casually. I wondered if she meant it the way I'd been told about it as a kid.

"So he was just going to, I don't know, send child support checks?" I looked back at Mary, still asleep in the back. Nobody I knew made it out of childhood without baggage, but I'd still held the idea that she'd always had the perfect dad.

"Essentially."

"His relationship with Mary seems idyllic though. Are you saying he was an absentee father?"

"Pretty much. He liked Mary's mom, much like he was drawn to Mikah. But she wasn't ready to be a mother. That resentment and regret just... ruined everything."

I chewed my lip as Crystal let silence hang. What could I say to that?

"We insisted that our kids know their dad. Maybe the defining difference is that our children were never a cost."

"Does Mazer just... go around having kids? For the hell of it? I look at him and see a family man but the way you explain it he seems tied down."

"His children give him meaning. We are trying to cure him of that pressure but at the end of the day it's a rather human drive. He's had dozens of kids and he has loved all of them. It's what his life is about, really."

Mary yawned behind us. She pawed at my shoulder until I gave her my hand to hold.

I hoped Crystal would take another turn asking about something I could share, but I got the feeling neither of us was the best conversationalist.

"What was your contract?-if it's not too personal."

Crystal chewed her lip. "I don't know how much I should share." She glanced at me. "There have been four. The first, Mazer... helped Mikah's self image in exchange for a child."

It seemed like an odd thing to want help with, but I guess in a way that's what he did for Cyrus. Crystal shrugged at me as I put the pieces together.

"The second was just attention in exchange for communication. Mikah needed to learn boundaries and that was the device he used to help her. Third, he enabled me to give Mikah a child in exchange for 7 years of uh... food."

"That sounds steep. What was the last?"

"Marriage. A commitment to be re-examined in a year and a day." She looked at me sideways and smiled. "And as far as food goes, I think you'd agree that cambions and incubi alike are delightful to cook for."

I rolled my eyes.

"And Addie is a wonderful cook." Mary murmured from the back. I wasn't sure if she had just missed the subtext in her sleepiness, or if she really just went and said that. My face burned, but Crystal only chuckled under her breath.

"How about you and Mary? A little birdie told me you got married recently."

I sighed and glanced at the back seat. It would be rude to deflect, but it was weird talking about this in front of her.

"It's been wild. These have been the longest months of my life, mostly in awesome ways. It's fast. Blindingly and terrifyingly fast, but I still think it's the best thing to ever happen to me."

"It is a pretty huge leap to go from the closet to proposing that fast."

"She proposed."

"Oh? Interesting."

I fidgeted with the tab of my tea can until it snapped off in my fingers.

"I dunno. I wouldn't have asked her but that's just me. I've always been critical of hasty relationships. It seems like half the people

I know have broken families, I'm not sure I won't fuck this up spectacularly before long, and I'm not sure I'll ever grow out of that fear either."

"Heavy."

"What?" I looked at Crystal.

"Do people seriously not say that anymore? Ugh. I don't know what you'd say... I guess the vibe is I sympathize with your burden."

"Oh, thanks."

"I think you've put the hardest stuff behind you though. Coming to terms with sexuality, embracing polyamory... not to toot my own horn, but I think you've joined the coolest and most excellent support group around."

"Hah. Yeah, you guys are pretty cool and excellent."

Crystal flashed me a smile before refocusing on the road. "Not to give you a license to break my step daughter's heart, but even if it doesn't work out you won't be cutting off everything and everyone. You have a relationship with all of us, and while nobody wants to be in the middle of a divorce, it's also not like every connection you have rests on Mary."

"You don't think Mazer would kill me?"

Crystal barked a laugh. "Give him a few months and he will consider you his own. Inexorably."

I had my doubts, but I don't think Crystal expected me to believe her either. It was a strange thing to reassure me of, but it was kind in a way.

I looked out the window. The city had given way to forest while I'd been distracted. Soon we would be winding our way into the mountains.

"Do you all go on these fishing trips often?"

"Nope." She popped the P. "This is a first for most everyone."

"Who's idea was this?"

"You don't remember? *You* suggested this."

I stared at her wide-eyed until the corner of her mouth turned up.

"Kidding, kidding. No, I'm not sure between Mikah and Mazer. I think the concept of a big grand outing bounced around between both of them until it was inevitable. The sneaky bastards spent a couple weeks making sure nobody would be busy before they sprung their trap."

"Mary seemed suspiciously on board, perhaps there is a spy in our midst."

She still looked asleep when I checked, but her hand twitched in mine.

"They also got all the supplies right?"

"Probably. If all else fails we will have a riverside picnic." She shrugged and looked at me. "With Mikah, I've learned to just roll with it. It's more fun that way."

The walkie talkie blipped and I heard Cyrus.

"Come in alpha delta India, this is Charlie Yankee Romeo. Over."

I groaned. I'd already forgotten what silly code names he'd just used. Something about this song and dance felt stupid, but I still felt I had to give my best effort.

"Uh... this is alpha... deli Yankee?. I read you? Over?"

I heard him chuckle. "Good effort, good effort. I just wanted to check that you are gonna take exit forty two as well."

"That's what the GPS says..."

"Good, good. So how are you?"

I sighed and shook my head. Walkie talkies had to be my least favorite venue for small talk.

"We're doing fine. How about you?"

"We-" a faint wail interrupted him. "Mikah has her hands full. Some of the crew doubt the efficacy of this venture."

"Do you expect mutiny?"

"Depends on which side you take."

"I'm just along for the ride."

I heard Cyrus sigh. "We have... one more hour to go."

"I'll ride with the kids on the way back."

"Oh thank god."

I was about to reply when his radio blipped through again. "What would it take to get you to switch early?"

I rolled my eyes. "Name the stop, love."

"The next rest area?"

I looked at Crystal, she seemed sympathetic but amused.

"We'll follow where you pull off."

The line stayed silent. I wasn't sure what I could do for the kids from the passenger seat, but I figured soon it would be my task to find out.

Why couldn't Andy and Azrael be like Mary? Mary could sleep anywhere, any time, but I supposed the twins either didn't have that skill or didn't want to use it.

# 33

## Let Sit, and Allow To Bond

To my surprise, the twins calmed down soon after we switched. They even remained relatively peaceful for the rest of the drive.

I held Andy against my shoulder as everyone but Mikah unpacked and set up. I was honestly afraid we were going to be wading frigid water to get far enough out, but this site had a proper dock. There was a picnic table, fire pit, and even a sandy section of beach. It was all seeming a little too good to be true until I spotted the trail up to a half obscured cabin. I had written it off as a park administration office but now I wagered it was someone's house.

"We aren't trespassing are we?"

Mazer followed my gaze to the log cabin nestled in the trees.

"Not at all."

I expected him to explain beyond that but I ended up turning to Mikah instead.

"It's a timeshare of a sort."

I raised an eyebrow. "Like, demonic shadow organization? Or is it the evil kind?"

She smiled. "Mazer has connections older than all of us. He barters in favors and this is a perk I guess."

"So the middle class life is an act? Why?"

"Not an act. He operates under a different sort of currency than we do. He does his work, and he liquidates assets to support his presence on our plane."

I stared at her blankly. This sounded a lot like "please don't ask what illegal things Mazer is involved in."

"So there's an exchange rate between human money and demon-" I waved my free hand. "-stuff?"

"He can explain it better if it's important."

On one hand it wasn't important, but now I was curious and it would be best if I settled that early in the obsession. Still, there wasn't much I could do if Mazer was a serial killer. I'd bend my morals alarmingly far for Mary.

I looked from the cabin to the dock and out over the water. "God I hope I don't get used to this."

"So that it's always a treat?"

"So that I never feel like I'm owed all of this..."

"How far does that go?"

"What do you mean?" I waved at the picturesque scene before us. "This. All of it."

"You don't think you should get used to receiving love?"

Shit.

Just once, one single time, I'd like to encounter someone on my level of emotional maturity. Just so I didn't feel like an infant for a change.

I sighed. I found myself swaying with Andy.

"Honestly? No. I don't think I should."

I braced myself for a speech, or perhaps even a lecture about self worth or something but she just looked sad.

Cyrus waved from the dock, he'd set up a rainbow of folding

chairs for us. I waited for Mikah to move, but she was looking far away.

"Keep having these conversations."

I had to admit, that was not the advice I expected.

"And that will help?"

"I mean, you could always fuck around and find out. I did. I just think you will save yourself a bit of grief by soliciting some affirmation every once in a while. Affirmation is like other forms of self care. Everybody ought to know how to feed, water, and bathe themselves. If you can't, having someone else do it is better than nothing."

I hardly had time to process before she shook her head. "I take that back. That sentiment had some ableism. Fuck."

I half smiled as she screwed up her face in concentration.

"Never mind. I won't pretend I'm ready for this mentoring stuff. I'm a decade behind on emotional intelligence and I'm hardly out of the woods on my shit too- I mean look at them!" She gestured with her free hand down the beach. "Pardon my crudeness but how the fuck did I pull *that*? Crystal is just... the best, and then an incubus? A paragon of sex? With this?"

She gestured at herself and then waved her hand. "You don't know what I looked like before. Anyways. Not to say I understand what you're going through but I think you're picking up what I'm putting down right?"

"Yeah." I looked at Mary and Cyrus. It felt like a simple perspective issue. *I* looked at Mikah, Crystal, and Mazer and saw a family unit. Equals. Meanwhile Mikah seemed to have the same insecurities I did.

Maybe she saw the same in me, and maybe her perspective was truer than mine.

"So I'm a hypocrite, but I'm working on it." She set out toward the dock. "Still, I think we're all in good hands."

I reached into the van and popped out one of the baby seats. I didn't feel like unpacking a stroller too, but it would be good for shade or as a little rocking chair in a pinch.

Mazer was already passing out rods and tins of bait when I arrived. For all the planning that had been done, a remarkable amount of the specifics were a mystery to me.

Obviously the point was bonding and relaxing but were we keeping the fish? And cooking them? Did our success in that vein determine how well lunch would go? Was I going to have to touch slimy fish? Very mysterious all around.

I took the green chair. It was the only choice. First, it was the best color, but it was also located next to the cooler.

Mikah had her priorities straight too, we would get to snack as the other four fumbled through baiting hooks.

"So now what?" I watched as Mary and Cyrus struggled with their rods. It didn't seem complicated at face value, but I guess it would be easier with three hands.

Mary dragged a chair closer to the edge and tried to balance the rod in the cup-holder. "Fishing I guess." She looked over to Mazer. "Do we have to be quiet and stuff?"

"Talking is no big deal but we shouldn't stomp." He had already dropped his line in the water. I watched as he hooked a chair with his toe and pulled it under him as he sat.

I resisted the urge to tap my feet impatiently. Sunlight was already crawling across the river toward us, and I didn't see any umbrellas packed away. Even if it was cloudy today, I found it hard to believe that I wouldn't get a little toasted.

"What are we fishing for?"

Cyrus pulled out his phone and flicked across the screen. "Uh... fish." He put his phone away and saw my unamused expression. "I have no service. I'm not sure what is around here."

"Coooooool."

Mikah reached over and patted my knee.

"You should try it. Who knows, it might give you focus. Could be a zen thing."

I squinted at her.

Mary figured out her bait and turned her chair toward me as she sat down. She looked like she was going to drop her line downstream of Crystal and Cyrus, but she turned toward the other edge of the dock instead.

"It's worth a try. Fire is a particularly potent amusement for us ADHD types. Maybe running water is too?"

"I don't have ADHD."

It was Cyrus's turn to chuckle.

"I mean it! I'm not on Adderall, I just have antidepressants!"

Mary raised an eyebrow

"I think my therapist would have told me if I had ADHD."

"That's a psychiatrist's job. Did you ask?"

"No?"

Mary shrugged and looked back to the water.

"Why are you so convinced I have ADHD?"

Mary chewed her lip. I could tell by her eyes she was about to tease.

"All I'm saying is In-Snare is pretty quick and accurate about pointing out that sort of thing."

"Sure I'm depressed, but I highly doubt I'm ADHD or autistic. Everyone sees those memes."

Cyrus was shaking his head but Mary waved him off. "Fair enough, I do see them as well. Regardless, you might enjoy fishing."

"Fine. I'll give it a shot in a bit."

I half expected Mazer to cut in and say 'you have such and such' but he remained intently focused on the little plastic ball on his fishing line.

I didn't know what to think about Mary's casual group diagnosis.

It made sense for her, sure. She had half a dozen abandoned hobbies crammed in her closet, but I wasn't nearly so creative when I had difficulty focusing.

I shifted Andy to my other arm so I could dig in the cooler. The options seemed to be burritos and sandwiches.

I pulled out a burrito and Mary made grabby hands at me. "Hand me a couple, I'll warm them up."

Mazer looked on with undisguised interest as she wrapped both hands around one. I might have imagined it, but I thought I saw steam escape the foil wrapping.

"You've been practicing." Mazer looked distinctly proud as Mary warmed the second one.

"I've always been able to manipulate heat."

"True, but there's a difference between raising your core temperature and targeted radiation."

Mary looked like she'd just received a gold star. She partially unwrapped one and reached to hand it to me.

And she said *I* had a praise kink.

"I didn't think you were interested in practical magic." Mazer leaned back in his chair and crossed his legs.

"Mana used to be scarce."

I felt my face heat up as she winked at me.

"What else have you been practicing?"

My face burned as she launched into an explanation of all the experiments she had been doing, and every goddamn one was something she had tried on *me*. My mortification only grew as Mazer peppered in his suggestions in turn. I coughed and choked when he brought up summoning and recommended contacts.

"All good over there?" Mary's eyes sparkled as I wiped my mouth and looked pointedly away.

"I'm fine."

"You can tell me more later, Dad. That way it can be a surprise."

"Jesus Christ." I muttered and grabbed a beer from the cooler.

Before I had even popped the tab, Crystal jerked her rod up and started reeling. I thought the rod was bending alarmingly far, but nobody else seemed concerned.

Mazer put his rod down to lean over the edge of the dock.

He snagged the line and pulled as he got on his knees and then to his feet.

I wasn't sure if I expected more or less. For how much the rod strained, I expected a shark, but then again Crystal hadn't been struggling so the rod could have been pretty flexible. Still, I thought we would be getting fish in the one foot range at most and this was at least twice that.

Cyrus snapped a pic as Mazer grabbed the fish by the mouth. It instantly went peculiarly still.

"Did you kill it?"

Mazer shook his head. "Sedated." He pulled pliers out of his pocket and Crystal took up the slack in the line as he pried the hook out.

I waited for him to throw it back or something but he walked over to the larger ice chest and laid it across the lid.

"Sixteen inches is long enough for trout. We can keep it if we want."

I guess I didn't have a good sense of scale after all. Nobody was saying anything so I spoke up. "I don't think I've ever had trout."

Mazer looked around and nobody objected so he carried it up the dock. I wasn't surprised when he washed it off but I was not at all ready for what he did after that. Mikah and Mary seemed to share my aversion but Cyrus actually went over to get a closer look! What the fuck?

A few minutes later Mazer returned to the dock, blessedly free of viscera. He packed a few plastic bags in the large cooler, and then sat back down.

"Per our license, we are allowed to catch seventeen more, since Andy and Azrael didn't get fishing licenses."

"We aren't going to, are we?"

"No, I don't think so."

The breeze picked up and I watched as ripples raced across the water. The sun had rapidly traversed the river but the gigantic willows behind us still blocked most of the sun. Still, I suspected they wouldn't for much longer.

I wondered what conversation there was to carry. Crystal was the only one I knew to be remotely interested in sports, though Cyrus was fairly knowledgeable by proxy. I wasn't sure I was up for more talk about sex magic.

Otherwise, magic was an interesting topic. Apparently I was the only one Mazer hadn't done business with... Well Mary was more the product of a contract than a participant but still. Cyrus, Mikah, and Crystal had all worked with Mazer for some pretty intense stuff.

I had to wonder what I wanted bad enough to make a deal with the proverbial devil over. They each had problems they couldn't solve themselves, and they had presumably done so before getting close to him. Contracts didn't seem like the sort of thing one writes up with their father in law.

At the same time, Mazer had already stepped in to provide legal counsel on my renting bullshit. It seemed unfair that I got everything handed to me for free when they had all made sacrifices.

I felt detached as I watched Crystal catch yet another fish. Cyrus asked what her secret was and they laughed and joked about techniques.

Mary walked over so I opened the cooler for her but she was holding out her hand to me.

"I'm happy holding Andy, I don't need a turn."

"I forgot something in the car, come with me." Her tone was light but her eyes, while still kind, were concerned.

I wondered what I had fucked up this time. Crystal hopped up to take Andy off my hands so I didn't even have that as a distraction or excuse.

Predictably, Mary spoke up once we were out of earshot. "Did I upset you with the talk about magic? Or did the fish stuff gross you out?"

"No."

She raised an eyebrow and gave me the "I smell bullshit" look.

"Fine, I was a little uncomfortable but I'm over it."

"I'm sorry." She pulled me closer and put an arm around my shoulder as we crunched up the gravel path. "I feel like I'm not getting better at respecting your privacy. I want to, it's very important to me, but I never seem to notice in time when I'm crossing a line."

"You aren't crossing a line. You don't need to worry about me."

I felt like we'd had this conversation before. There was always some deeper thing she wanted to pick at so I tried to head her off.

"This isn't a self respect thing. They're family and I should be okay with bonding and sharing with them. You shouldn't have to change how you act just because I haven't adjusted yet."

"Bedroom activities are not a normal thing to talk to your father in law about."

"So? This is a different sort of family. It's my job to come to terms with that."

Mary sighed and released my shoulder as we reached the car.

"You seem to think everything has been going on for ages before you met me."

"I don't see how that's relevant."

"I mean you're acting like there are ancient rules and customs you have to adopt when there are none."

She leaned against the car, and when I didn't have anything to say to that she pushed on.

"Mazer, Mikah, and Crystal are really just now settling down. When we met, everything was technically just contracts for them."

"That's not *that* recent."

Mary rolled her eyes and stared over my head at the trees.

"You met Cyrus less than a month after he and Mazer made his contract."

"What?"

"The day you met him was the first time I had seen him in person since the procedure."

I bit back my retort. While surprising, none of this seemed particularly relevant. Mary didn't wait for me to ask for details.

"I hadn't actually gotten intimate with Cyrus before I met you."

Okay *that* surprised me.

"Then how come- you always seemed..."

Mary shrugged and folded her arms.

"Falling in love with him was a pretty recent thing. Dysphoria can be a pretty big barrier to intimacy, and besides, you don't have a monopoly on moving fast in this family."

She smirked but I was still dumbfounded.

"I... don't know what I'm supposed to do with all of this."

"I just want you to cut yourself some slack."

I gestured helplessly. How was I supposed to give slack where there was no tension? More than anything, the sudden knowledge that there wasn't much foundation anywhere just made me fear instability.

"You aren't relaxing."

She smirked as I met her eyes. I made a show of taking a deep breath.

"It would be rather out of character if I did, wouldn't it?"

"Fair, fair." She nodded and turned to rustle in the car. To my surprise, she pulled out chocolate, marshmallows, graham crackers, and toasting skewers.

"Pity that your impending sugar high won't help."

# 34

## Subs and Subterfuge

Our house was a home now. Cyrus had brought all his art, including new works from storage I hadn't seen before. Every wall had something hanging on it, and even the empty spaces had a plan in store for them. A new sectional couch would be here next Monday, a colossal TV arrived tomorrow, and the farthest quarter of the four-car garage was already laid out into an impressive wood shop.

My room was the straggler in that sense. Sure, Cyrus and I had an appointment of sorts to build my new bed frame, but I was somewhat at a loss on most of my furnishings. I had jokingly suggested a floating bed and had steadily warmed up to the idea as Cyrus explained how he could hang the foot of the bed from the ceiling. I reasoned I could make monthly plans of this sort until my bedroom was fully furnished, so I made no rush toward immediate renovations.

Our house was really so cool. Cyrus had merged and expanded his and Mary's smart light system to the point where the whole home felt automated. The kitchen had lights under all the cabinets, and the living room had pretty extensive modifications planned to black out the windows on command. Our "movie nights" would be awesome.

"Pity your room doesn't have sick ass glow-in-the-dark stars like mine." I sprawled on Cyrus's bed as he tossed clothes from boxes to drawers.

"Pity." He agreed, but I could sense he had no envy.

His insistence on dark and quiet at bedtime was one of his cute quirks. He could sleep without it, he'd made do with my snoring after all, but I felt disruptive both of the times Mary and I had visited.

"Are you going to do the sound foam pad thingies again?"

He hummed and straightened to look around the room.

"This time I was thinking I'd do a checkerboard pattern with red and black."

I tried to visualize it. "Would that make the room soundproof?"

He shrugged. "It means when you lay in my bed nobody will hear your screams."

I flushed hot. I never expected it from him. Mary had a tone she used for innuendo. You saw it coming with her. Cyrus, however, delighted in using random tones regardless of the content of his statements. He would deadpan the most erotic things, and it always hit different because of it. He said it was unintentional and inconvenient for him, but it kept things interesting for better or worse.

Now though, I didn't know how to respond to that. Did I joke about that sounding a tad murdery? Did I ask him to take me? Right here, right now? Each option seemed equally valid.

"I'm kidding of course, Mary would still be able to hear, being one wall away and all. The neighbors though? Unlikely."

"That's... good."

Cyrus smiled and resumed his unpacking.

"Why would Mary be in the other room?" I spoke without thinking, and I half expected him to give me a sassy look.

"I guess she wouldn't necessarily," He mused as if considering a lunch menu. "As far as I know that would all be up to you."

"That's a lot of pressure."

Mary chose that moment to walk in. "I heard my name, and something about screams or pressure, so I'm here to lend aid. Who needs some punishment?" She crawled on top of me on the bed and flopped to sandwich me.

"See, she hears all," Cyrus laughed as I wiggled to get comfortable under her.

"Maryyyyy, Cyrus is teasing meeeee."

She sat up on my hips and considered him.

"How should we remedy this? Teasing him back seems only fair."

"What?" Cyrus and I echoed, just out of sync as Mary did a small hop on my hips.

"What if I fucked you on his bed, and made him watch?"

Similar to Cyrus's deadpan she chirped about sex as though it would be a casual walk in the park. Even Cyrus blinked surprise as the statement landed.

"W-what if he's into that sort of thing?"

Mary pushed her hands up under my shirt to rub against my belly.

"We won't know until we find out."

"That wouldn't be very nice of us."

"Maybe we aren't very nice girls," she cooed as she pushed my shirt up.

"Waaaait," I whined, and she stopped. I flushed red under their combined attention.

"I don't want to make him watch."

I pouted, and Mary smirked above me.

"Then invite him to join, silly."

I kicked my feet helplessly, and Cyrus chuckled. For all the tension I felt, he appeared relaxed, leaning against his dresser.

Mary was still waiting above me.

"But what if I can't give both of you enough attention at the same time?"

Mary roared with laughter and sat back. She shook her head and looked back at me. I forced a cough and tried to look anywhere else.

"Oh, you're serious. Is that what you've been worrying about all this time?"

I shrugged. She climbed off my lap, and I sat up to lean on my elbows.

"How about this? Addie, you are cordially invited to a threesome after dinner this evening." She turned to Cyrus. "Would you like to fuck me senseless?"

Cyrus shrugged and nodded. That seemed weirdly apathetic to me but Mary wasn't perturbed.

"Cyrus will be fucking me senseless and you are invited to participate at the capacity and extent you wish, --" She paused and winked. "-- and if nothing else I know you will enjoy the show."

"Why after dinner?" Cyrus asked, and Mary turned to me.

"Because I'm very mean. I fully intend to tease our little Addison to the brink of insanity in the intervening hours. If you want to help, she will probably get wet at the sight of you shirtless."

He raised an eyebrow, but when he saw my blush deepen, he turned smug.

I fixated on his right hand as he grabbed the bottom of his left sleeve. In one unbearably smooth motion, he pulled the garment over his head in a graceful arc.

"Y-you said you were going to tease Cyrus," I whined, and I covered my eyes as Mary reached for the bottom of her shirt. A moment later, soft fabric dropped over my face.

She crawled the rest of the way off the bed, and when I pulled her shirt off my face, she was holding Cyrus's hand to her chest. She pulled him in for a kiss and whispered in his ear before collecting her top and departing.

I watched her go, but, like gravity, my eyes fell back to him. I watched his eyes trail to my waistline before I pulled my shirt down, and he smirked. After a minute of watching him work without a shirt, I managed to excuse myself.

As the house chef, I was about to make the executive decision to have dinner early.

*~*~*

I was feeling particularly smug as I announced dinner was ready less than half an hour later. The air fryer had made quick work of frozen dinosaur-shaped chicken nuggets. I used the kettle to boil water for instant mashed potatoes, and meanwhile I microwaved broccoli as a healthy side. Let it not be said I was not thorough in my greedy laziness.

Mary was the first to report for dinner. She had still not put on a shirt. Likewise, Cyrus appeared half-dressed. Mary looked over her plate with a bemused expression.

"I feel like I should internalize some lessons from this result but honestly I'm so okay with dino nuggies."

"If nobody dawdles, I could be convinced to break out the ice cream."

Cyrus raised his eyebrows. "Truly you have become a powerful negotiator."

To my delight, they made quick work of their food for my sake, or for their own if I was optimistic. I doled out the ice cream, and since I was feeling charitable, I dispensed toppings as well.

Mary shook her head and folded her hands under her chin as I drummed my fingers on the table.

"Wolfing down nuggies is one thing, but brain freezes are another matter entirely."

I sensed I was being teased again as she took a leisurely bite. I swear to god she intentionally dripped on her chest. The first time, she wiped it up with a finger, but the second time, Cyrus said, "I got it" and leaned over to lick it up.

"I'm starting to wonder if I've learned something after all," Mary mused between bites. "Less than an hour ago, you were completely hung up on threesomes. Now, by merely taking off my shirt, you have moved mountains to speed up the clock."

"You are a skilled negotiator." I grumbled and picked at the edge of my place-mat.

"Or maybe, it's just the fact that hang-ups resolve themselves quickly when you communicate."

I pouted and shrugged. She laughed and lifted her bowl to drink the last of her ice cream soup. Soon, Cyrus did the same.

"So now what? Mary stacked her and Cyrus's bowls and carried them to the sink.

I pretended to think. "I know I've been waiting for Cyrus to fuck you senseless, so we could start with that."

"Well for truly senseless fucking I ought to be tied up. I really just don't think you would be patient enough for that."

Keeping with the theme of the night, I acted the child and took the bait. Hook, line, and fucking sinker.

"I can wait."

"Oh good!" she cooed. She led the way to her bedroom and pulled out bundles of ropes.

She took her time considering the assortment, so I piped up, "purple."

She met my eye, and I half expected a sassy remark about patience, but she handed the purple ropes to me. I saw her ponder briefly and look at Cyrus.

"In the interest of time, it might be faster if we first arrange the ropes on Addie, and then I'll slip into them after."

I tilted my head. "How so?"

"Well Cyrus and I are both pretty efficient at tying each other up. Working together we could probably fashion a harness on you remarkably quickly, but you and Cyrus working on me would be slower."

"You can just do that?"

Mary nodded, and, after a pause, Cyrus did as well.

"Essentially."

"Okay, I'm game."

Mary had an oddly predatory smile as she stepped up to me. "Let's get you undressed."

"Why do my clothes need to be taken off for this?"

"To prevent tangles of course."

I shrugged and let myself be undressed.

Cyrus made quick work of my shirt as Mary worked her fingers under my belt. In mere seconds I was naked, and they set about finding the center of the long rope. They spoke in some sort of code to discuss what type of harness to do.

They had me sit on my knees on Mary's bed and lined out an inverted pentagram across the center of my chest. They followed that with a series of knots off the star's bottom point. I watched as they created an elaborate snakeskin pattern by weaving into the loops between the knots.

When they ran out of rope, Mary grabbed red, and Cyrus grabbed blue. They had me lie on my stomach as they coaxed me to bend my knees and cross my arms behind my back. I could no longer see what they were doing, but I could tell how the actual immobilization would be done. They worked off the existing harness to anchor my arms behind my back, and once Cyrus was satisfied with his work on my legs, they helped me sit up on my knees.

I craned my neck to inspect their work, overall it wasn't tight, but it was restrictive. I was impressed to find my breathing wasn't impaired by all the wrapping across my chest.

"So how do we get me out of it?"

Mary hummed as she poked and prodded around to check tightness. "Same way it went on."

"How was this faster then?"

"Oh, I assure you, it is much faster for us to tie you up than for you two to tie up me. I'm sure with practice you will get pretty fast as well though"

Heat rushed from my face to my shoulders as I realized. God, I was gullible.

"What are you going to do to me?"

"Absolutely nothing --" Cyrus smiled predatorially. "-- that you don't want."

Fuck fuck *fuck*.

What had felt like pretty innocent checking before devolved into intentional groping.

I gasped as Cyrus worked his fingers under the ropes across my thighs. He gave them a couple of firm tugs while Mary weighed my breasts in her hands.

"Would you like to wear the clamps?"

"Maybe."

She smirked and hopped off the bed to retrieve them. Blessedly, she chose the rubber-tipped ones, but they still hurt when she attached them. She played with the chain between them before tucking it into the star on my chest and trailing her fingers lower. She stopped at my belly button and skipped to drum her fingers on my thigh.

"Almost forgot," she mumbled and crawled off the bed. A moment later, I heard it. She dropped her rings one at a time into the bowl on her nightstand. Finished, she returned to me and scooted forward on her knees till one of her legs was between mine. She kissed me on the neck and ran her hands down from my shoulders.

"Well, she hasn't really expressed her approval verbally, but -- " I cried out as she pushed her middle finger into me. "-- yeah. She's wet."

She caught me as I nearly fell over from squirming. "We can get started now I guess."

I watched as she crawled over to Cyrus and unbuttoned his pants. I had the sense they were making out in front of me, but my gaze glued to Cyrus's dick.

An eternity later, Mary stopped and crawled toward me. She lifted my chin to meet her eye, and I realized they were both thoroughly amused.

"I said... is there anything you would like us to do for you?"

# 35

## I Confess, You Have Me At A Disadvantage.

I struggled to process Mary's question. Was there something I wanted them to do to me? The answer was, of course, yes. I wanted to be double-teamed mercilessly, but that desire came from a selfish place.

Cyrus sat back on his heels as I fought to come up with an idea. I could do better than saying, "have your way with me", but I didn't know how I would excuse myself for asking for their attention.

"I guess we will play twenty questions."

I tried to shrug but, while the ropes permitted some movement, they constricted in a very distracting way.

"Do you want to be untied?"

"No."

"Do you want us to fuck you?"

"Yes." Obviously.

"Do you want Cyrus to dick you down?"

I leaned forward as I felt a stab of arousal bloom in my gut. "Yeah."

"Are you interested in being suspended from the ceiling?"

I looked up and wondered what they would even hang me from. Regardless, it wasn't a particular interest of mine.

"No."

I struggled not to flail as she helped me lean to the side and then fully on my back. She'd made a small stack of pillows for me to lean back on so that my head could rest across her lap.

"Do you like this position?"

I shifted to put less strain on my shoulders and nodded. She brushed my hair out of my face, but when I looked up her eyes were trailing down.

I tried to imagine what she saw. Me, bound and helpless in her lap gazing up at her. I bet that was a pretty tempting spectacle for her dominant side.

She twirled my chain around her fingers as Cyrus walked on his knees to line himself up.

He rubbed his hands over my belly before slipping his hand under a knot and wrapping it in his fist. I gasped as he lifted me, and Mary helped him stuff pillows under my hips. I struggled to breathe as he pulled my knees to his chest. I could feel his dick, hot and slick between my thighs as he leaned close, I didn't even see him get out the lube but I definitely appreciated the gesture. I was distracted by his hands on my thighs when he rolled his hips back and because of that, his first thrust was a surprise. I couldn't believe he had managed to line up hands free until I realized Mary had leaned over to help.

"Hoooooo my god." I sighed. If I had my hands free or even a bit of leverage to move I would have pulled him down to me. By now though, I knew this was one of those "wait for verbal confirmation" moments. Or maybe he wanted me to beg.

I tried a little wiggle to communicate my impatience but he only raised an eyebrow.

Damn it.

"Fuck me, Cyrus." The request sounded like a whimper, but for all I knew he might prefer it that way.

I strained against my ropes as he pressed the rest of the way in. My efforts to arch my back failed as he lay down. He paused to brace his hands and adjust his position before laying flush against my thighs.

Flattened up under him like this, I could barely breathe. Perhaps he could sense that because he lifted himself before I had time to worry. My gasp of relief was cut off as I was made intimately aware of the associated movement inside me.

I was afraid he would torture me like this, thrusting as I struggled to breathe. Luckily, he didn't wait for me to beg. The pace he set up wasn't fast but it was gloriously consistent.

He must have thought I was hyperventilating because he paused to let me catch my breath before he had done even a dozen thrusts.

"Should we make this a race?" Mary waved a toy in front of my nose.

Before I could respond she clicked it on and held it to the chain on my chest. Yep. Felt that alright. Cyrus was still deep inside me when she moved the wand to my clit instead. I jumped as it kicked past the highest setting to the wave pattern. I scarcely had a chance to breathe in before Cyrus thrust.

This time I came violently undone.

Cyrus stilled as I attempted to bring my knees together and I tensed involuntarily as the vibrator continued to buzz. Finally, Cyrus pulled Mary's hand away and he leaned back. He caught my knees as I melted into a puddle.

As my breathing calmed, I managed to tune back into what Mary and Cyrus were saying.

"I know racing was my idea but If I had known she was close I would have offered to turn down some sensations for her."

"You underestimated my power."

At least Cyrus seemed pleased with himself. I rolled my eyes as Mary waved him off. She looked down at me and put the wand away.

"Sorry about that, do you need to be untied, Babygirl?"

I mumbled "no" as she pulled her fingers through my hair.

"If you'd like I could turn down your sensations so we can edge you a bit longer next time."

"That would be okay."

She hummed and the now-familiar blanketing sensation fell over me.

"How are you feeling?"

I rocked side to side a couple times. I tried to shrug but again the ropes did not permit. "I'm okay." I felt embarrassed. I probably disappointed Cyrus by getting overwhelmed so fast and I imagined Mary had to be bored of this. More than anything though, I wanted to make sure everyone had a good time.

Mary sighed. "We want to take care of you. What kind of care do you want right now?"

I avoided looking her in the eye as I agonized over what to say. "I want to go again with Cyrus but I don't know what you would do in the meantime."

"I have some ideas then."

I recognized her devious look, I frowned as she leaned over to conspire with Cyrus but I wasn't made to wonder for long.

Mary grabbed more rope and made a peculiar loop behind my back. I figured she could just use a spreader bar to keep my knees apart- my ankles were already tied to my thighs after all -but she and Cyrus seemed to agree this was the best option.

Still, the ability to close my legs had been the last real mobility I had.

Mary went off to peruse her toys as Cyrus held my knees. Even with my senses muted, I felt him teasing me.

"I'm sorry to ask forgiveness rather than permission... but I forgot to put a condom on earlier. Would you like me to?"

I felt my face burn. With Rich, I'd plead for a condom because of how gross I felt after lying with him. But with Cyrus, particularly with such low risk of infection or pregnancy, the mess felt exciting.

"Y-you can cum wherever you p-please."

"Oh? You don't mind a creampie? Or a string of pearls? Perhaps you even want a taste." His smile was perfectly kind, as though he were asking me about my thoughts on lunch.

"Cyrussss that's gross!"

"True, true. Let me think, what would be most exciting?" He pressed into me unexpectedly. "I think I'll paint your womb. If it's all the same to you."

I couldn't meet his eyes. I was making a thoroughly undignified moan and I swear to God, between his cringe-worthy bedroom talk and the overload of physical sensation, I wasn't so sure Mary's spell was working.

Mary returned with a bullet vibrator and tape. I feared she'd stick it up my ass, but she sat by as she put it on herself.

"Everyone ready?"

I didn't have a chance to ask what for before she was crawling over me. I worried she would sit on my hips, but she instead lowered herself over my face.

"I've been wondering how well you will perform under pressure." She wove her fingers into my hair. "Seeing as you're so easy to distract."

Cyrus took this as his cue to provide a diversion and Mary smirked at my reaction.

"I-I'll do my best."

"Good girl." She leaned forward and grabbed a couple loops on the wall behind me, but she maintained eye contact as she gave me access.

It was peculiar working alongside the vibrating wire. Ordinarily I would have directed my oral attention at the surface level, but on a whim I decided to test how far I could stick my tongue into her.

"Shit!" Mary gasped and jumped up slightly out of my reach.

Cyrus took this as his cue to get to work and that was nearly the end of me.

Mary seemed a little out of breath as she settled down again. "You seem to have this handled, but in an effort to simplify your focus I have uh, liberated you of your ability to orgasm."

Cyrus scoffed behind her and Mary jumped again as I heard a smack.

Mary shot a look over her shoulder before looking back at me. "All of that to say, you need not worry about Cyrus's attention causing any unwanted interruptions. We will see that you are relieved at the opportune time."

I gave her my best unamused glare as I worked my tongue into her again. If I couldn't cum then there wouldn't be a limit to how much Cyrus could compromise me.

And, speaking of the devil, I felt him avail himself of my breasts as he pushed in again. If they wanted to play games, I would endeavor to compete.

If Mary had any other taunts to throw down to me, they seemed to slip her mind. She grabbed my hair when I caught the wire of her bullet with my teeth and yelped as I tugged on it.

Though Cyrus hadn't stopped, I sensed he was more on my side than hers. He delivered less weight and depth in his thrusts, which was still fun, but less mind-melting.

"Cyrusss." Mary spoke through clenched teeth and I raised an eyebrow.

"Yes dear? Do you need me to stop?"

Mary shook her head and leaned further forward. She was hanging by the loops now and when she jumped forward unexpectedly I got a view of what had her distracted. Cyrus had produced a dildo out of thin air and he'd buried it quite deep. Mary rocked forward as he pressed in sharply and I felt the matching movement between my legs. The spectacle went out of view as Mary corrected her position.

It seemed that Mary's bid to double team me had backfired on her spectacularly. She did most of the moving for me as I attended to her clit instead. I could tell she was losing herself in the sensation as she pressed harder and harder.

Just as I thought I was getting the better of Mary though, Cyrus resumed his attention to me. I moaned into Mary as he pressed in all the way, and I scarcely had a chance to breathe in before he did it again.

I heard Mary mutter "hah" above me, but there was a sense that we were both at his mercy now. I grasped weakly for some sense of composure. I couldn't control my vocal reactions but I managed to suppress them to hums. This precluded some tongue attention but Mary was getting her friction in other ways.

Cyrus proved to be the most composed of us. "Is everything going as you expected? Mary?"

"Keep testing me and you'll get yours."

"Oh? What are you going to do?"

She winked at me as I felt Cyrus spasm between my legs.

"Fuck!"

Mary tossed her hair, and I felt Cyrus brace himself on the bed.

"Where's your precious control now Cyrus?" She taunted as she paused above me. She sat up and now that everyone was somewhat still I could feel Cyrus's small spasms.

"What did you do to him?"

I heard Cyrus groan as she looked down to address me.

"I gave him a prostate orgasm." Seeing me frown, she continued. "He isn't spent though. I give it maybe fifteen seconds before he's recovered. You'll get your precious creampie yet."

"So he didn't cum?"

"He didn't ejaculate, no."

I heard another gasp from Cyrus as he pulled out.

"You really just can't stand to lose can you?" Cyrus sighed as Mary shook her head.

"Nope."

She had approximately two seconds to be smug before Cyrus's arms wrapped around her. She flailed as he effortlessly lifted her and we both gasped as he pressed her down between my legs. She tried to push herself off but he grabbed her wrists and I didn't hide my smirk as she fell into me again.

Cyrus sounded irritated. "Are you ready for your punishment?"

Mary's face was scarlet, but to my utter amazement, rather than sass, I heard her whimper, "yes sir."

She jumped as I heard a smack, and then gasped. I was made to feel every flinch as she was overpowered above me.

Cyrus tossed the bullet vibrator on the bed next to me and then he got to work. Mary and I rocked together as he thrust and I heard occasional smacks. She wasn't shuddering anymore, and I could swear I felt her drooling on my chest as she melted into me. Her shoulders relaxed and I felt her arms wrap around me. I half expected her to make her bid for freedom but she held on to me for life itself as he unmade her.

I smirked as I recognized the sounds. Her breath got throaty and her grip loosened and tightened erratically. She locked up and her moan cut off before she groaned and relaxed into me.

Cyrus was breathing heavily and I felt him pull back. He patted my knee.

"Sorry about that, Addie. I couldn't let her behavior slide."

"All good, all good."

Mary groaned as she got her arms beneath her. She was still flushed as she crawled to collapse on the bed to my right.

"Now, where were we?"

Cyrus crawled over me and brushed my hair out of my face.

"You didn't finish in her?"

He shook his head. "Bad girls don't get treats."

Mary whimpered beside me but he ignored her. "How about you though?"

"Everything's fine for me. Peachy keen."

"As long as you don't feel slighted."

"No sir."

He rolled his eyes as Mary huffed a small laugh.

"You're both such brats."

He took a moment to sit up and finish catching his breath before scooting up between my legs again.

I debated whether I wanted to act out too, but I remembered his remark about treats and opted to restrain myself.

I felt him push in again, and while I didn't need any delay to acclimate, I did notice that the sensation wasn't remotely muted. I looked at Mary and she wiggled her eyebrows.

I didn't have a chance to warn Cyrus before he lay down against me. I gasped as he made a few slow thrusts and cried out as he pressed down hard. He paused as I struggled to catch my breath. I didn't have the chance to talk before he made another single thrust.

He raised an eyebrow and looked at Mary.

"Are you meddling?"

"Maaaybe."

He shook his head.

"Please try not to make her hyperventilate."

I didn't have the chance to protest.

Realistically, there wasn't anything particularly remarkable about the way he was fucking me. He'd driven me wild this way a couple of times before, but I had never been so compromised. I was in no mood to savor the moment and luckily, neither was Cyrus. Something about the way he lost his composure was exciting to me. The little sounds and his focused expression were cute.

I tried to let go but I found I couldn't. Goddamn it Mary. I could only hope Cyrus wasn't waiting for me.

At last, he groaned and pressed in deep. He shook slightly as he pulled at the ropes under my arms.

I had hardly a second to bask before Mary belatedly sent me over the edge. That bitch.

I yelped, more from pain than pleasure as I spasmed in surprise. By the time I realized my restraints weren't giving, I had already put all my strength into testing them. Tears filled my eyes as I struggled to breathe and process so many conflicting sensations.

I felt like I regained consciousness crying, I was dizzy and I felt detached from my own screams as I struggled to breathe.

"Shhhh shh relax, don't strain, I'll get them off. Cyrus, hand me the shears."

The tension holding my knees apart loosened and I fell on my left side as I struggled to curl in on myself. I could only cough and sob as she struggled to get through the coils of ropes on my legs.

"Y-you don't have to cut them." I practically croaked as she finished releasing my legs.

"I'm cutting them. Ropes are replaceable, you are not."

I did my best to lay still despite the intensifying cramps, and I found the release of restraints didn't magically return strength to my limbs.

"How are you feeling?" Mary asked behind me.

I made a half-hearted effort to turn to her before giving up.

"Loved."

"I meant physically."

"Ouchie."

"What hurts?" Mary reached over to hold my hand as Cyrus massaged one of my legs. At least *that* felt nice.

"Hips... shoulders... neck."

I felt her run her hands over my shoulders and hips.

"I don't think anything is dislocated but I sure did a number on you. I'm so sorry."

I let her hold my hand and as I gained some control over my shuddering breaths. The sharpest of the pains faded. Still, I was afraid to move and set them off again.

"How would you like us to care for you?"

"Mmmmmm. Bathing, kisses, and cuddles I think. I need a moment though."

"Are you sore?"

I huffed a laugh and rolled on my back to look at Mary.

"Right. Right. Sorry."

I shook my head and took a deep breath.

"No harm done." I groaned as I sat up. But I overcame my body's protests. When I looked back I caught her staring.

"The bath! Right, I'll go start that. I'll be right back."

Cyrus took his time on the remaining set of ropes comprising the harness. He helped me up as I tried to stand and I looped my arms around his neck to pull him into a kiss. Instead, he took the opportunity to pick me up and carry me to the bathroom. They worked together to situate me in the tub and before long I was partially floating, or at least the weight was off my hips.

A minute later, Mary did some gymnastics to squeeze into the tub as well. The water level rose, and I heard a trickling sound as the spillover drain did its job. I worried about her jabbing her back with the faucet, but she was content leaning against my knees.

It felt kinda silly being washed as though I was an invalid. Mary busied herself with my left side as Cyrus rubbed down my right, and

I had to admit it was a pretty pleasant sensation altogether. I knew I'd hate myself later, but that thought was drowned out by laziness and a thirst for touch.

Cyrus said something about changing the sheets, and I let Mary stand to maneuver to sit behind me to work on my back.

"You're going to be kicking yourself about this later aren't you?"

I groaned. "How could you tell?"

"Because getting you to ask for care is like pulling teeth. Do you realize we literally had to tie you up to get you to stop obsessing?"

"Sorry."

She poked me under my ribs, startling me more than anything before dropping the washcloth on the edge of the tub.

"Don't be sorry... I appreciate that you always leap to help out and do whatever needs doing. I just want you to be comfortable asking for care when you need it too. You shouldn't have to be literally physically trapped before you start communicating."

"I'll talk to my new therapist about it next week."

Mary hugged me to lay against her. I snorted as she reached to squeeze my breasts before settling back again.

"Until then, I guess I'll just ask you what you need relentlessly."

"Mmmm, I don't like that much."

I felt her breath against my neck as she sighed again. I must have winced as she nudged my shoulder because she loosened her grip and rubbed my back.

"Then we'll just smother you with affection until something clicks."

# 36

## The Grooooove

There was a pattern to life once more. A nice little routine. I had a day I shopped on, a schedule for demon-sitting, and Cyrus and I stayed up watching TV on Sundays.

I'd migrated to sit practically on top of him tonight. Laying my head in his lap hadn't worked, but draping my legs across him left us too far apart. I'd settled on curling up under his arm, at least for now.

I hadn't heard a word of this documentary for at least five minutes now, his hand on my back was simply far too important. I sighed as he switched between using the pads of his fingers and his nails. I was spoiled absolutely rotten.

I mustered the energy to open my eyes. The TV was still showing factory machinery. I squinted as the narrator described the process. It looked like they were making phone cables, but the voice over was talking about kink resistant weaves and insertion ratings: and not in a very professional way.

I sat up and focused in as Cyrus chuckled beside me. Currently it looked like they were checking tensile strength, but apparently I was to believe this was the punishment for "dirty little slut cables that kink too much."

"What the fuck?" I whispered, causing Cyrus to erupt into laughter.

"I wondered how long it would take you to notice. Someone re-did the voice-over for this documentary."

"Has the narrator ever touched a woman? Or grass perhaps?"

"Oh come on, you know satire when you see it."

I shrugged but devoted a little more attention to the show. I bit back a smirk as the packaging process was described in bondage terms. I didn't expect to envy a goddamn charging cable but here we were.

"Twist ties are not a safe restraint method."

"True, true. Now if those poor cords struggle they might get nerve damage."

"Yet another harmful depiction of BDSM in the media." I ex-aggerated a sigh, playing up the melodrama, but I didn't know how I'd make a segue off of that.

Cyrus pointed the remote at the TV and started another, this time about cherries. Now the narrator was overly insistent that there was nothing sexual going on.

"The one about birth control is so much worse." Cyrus glanced at me.

I waited a few seconds so my subject change would be less rude before putting my hand on his knee. "Can you put your feet up? I wanna lay down to snuggle."

"Sure, sure."

He adjusted pillows and made a small cushion against the arm rest. Now when I was situated under his arm, I was between him and the back of the couch.

I made a half-hearted attempt to pay attention as the next video started and I traced my fingers idly over his chest. He seemed entirely focused on the TV, but when I trailed my hand lower he took my hand and held it over his stomach.

I chewed my lip. That was my only free hand, but necessity was the mother of invention. Still, my attempt at a game of footsie was met with avoidance.

Well fuck. I guess I had to ask nicely if I wanted to get anywhere.

As was tradition with me, I spent a full minute psyching myself up and agonizing over wording.

"Cyrus?"

"Hmm?" He looked at me and his hand stilled on my back.

"Would you like to have sex?" I hated being direct. I always felt so out of place when it wasn't innuendo.

"Not tonight." He resumed rubbing my back and looked back to the TV as if that settled the issue. I was left stunned.

Damn it.

I stared through the TV as my thoughts dove toward obsession. Why not? I had asked nicely and everything! But I wasn't owed anything either. If he didn't want to then he didn't have to. Still, was it because he was repulsed by me? Was the only difference that he didn't have the energy to pity me right now? That couldn't be right, he'd never been anything but genuine with me.

I felt like I was burning. My back turned numb where he touched it and I struggled not to shake with the effort of not moving. When he took his hand back to scratch his ear, I tried to be subtle about retreating a little further. It helped at first but I was still trapped under his arm.

Was he mad at me? Or not feeling well? Why didn't he explain why he didn't want to have sex? Was he afraid his reason would hurt my feelings? Maybe he just assumed I didn't really want it enough. Mary had a practically biological need for sex but I just liked it. I guess it was only fitting that he said no to me.

The TV turned blurry and a rolling thunder filled my ears as everything got away from me. I was falling apart for no fucking reason and if he didn't want to make love then I'm sure he didn't want to deal with my crying fit either.

His hand had stopped on my back and I couldn't hear the TV anymore. Fuck. I was leaking tears all over his shirt now. I couldn't hold it together and the first cough of a sob hurt all the more because of it. I was stuck here. I was making him guilty with this huge crying fit over being told "no". I was being a goddamn toddler. Why was I such a manipulative bitch? I wasn't raised to be that way, my mom had always taught from the beginning to control myself but now I was incapable. Or maybe I was just too lazy to do it right.

I felt dizzy as I continued to choke on my own breath. I couldn't get air in, but I still needed to hold back at least something. I couldn't just let everything out. I didn't deserve that. Catharsis was for people with actual pain.

At some point he had helped me sit up. He was close but he wasn't touching me anymore. I should be grateful, but it only really meant he was disgusted with me. I rubbed at my face ineffectually as he got up and walked away. At least I didn't have to be the one to leave. Too bad I was too much of an asshole to appreciate it.

I had just gotten control over my noise levels when I felt a heavy blanket fall over my back. The coffee table made a screeching sound as he moved it and I saw his legs where he knelt in front of me.

I guess we'd have to talk about it now.

I pulled the blanket over my head and closed it in front of me. Shadow would be my friend.

He didn't say anything. I guess it was my job to apologize after all. "I'm sorry."

I don't know if he'd even be able to hear that with my abused vocal cords and smothering blanket.

"It's okay, Addie. You're okay. I'm still here, just breathe, okay?"

It was a simple enough command. I owed that much. I took a couple shallow breaths and then remembered the exercises Mary would put me through. It took a few tries, but I managed to breathe in for three seconds and out for two.

Cyrus was probably still waiting for something. I peeked out and he had a box of tissues. I suppressed bitterness about his pity long enough to pull one out. I don't know why crying made my nose run but it was disgusting and inconvenient right now.

Once I had wiped my eyes I pulled the blanket off my head. Time to face the music.

He held out a hand and I stared at it for a good second before reluctantly taking it. He wasn't pulling, just holding.

"How can I make it better?"

I gave myself some time. The first two answers of "have sex with me" and "you don't have to" were either wrong or unproductive. I'd have to either firmly refuse his comfort, or submit myself to it. Even if I didn't know which would give me more guilt, I knew which would be kinder to him.

"We can just talk. I don't know."

He took a deep breath and repositioned his knees.

"I think I'll circle back to explaining myself, because first I want to affirm I care. I'm doing my best to create space while staying close and I want you to have the power to find where you want to be in that zone."

I nodded and reached down to grab another tissue. I wondered how much he had to deal with meltdowns like this, because the whole blanket-tissue combo seemed practiced. Luckily he was okay with one-sided conversation.

"I *do* love you. You are a comforting presence, your touch, voice, spirit, all of it. The fact I care for you is unchanging even if the ways I express that are."

I shrugged and cleared my throat. "I love you too." Still sounded like a toad. Cool.

"A while back I told you about how I wanted to affirm that I am attracted to you even if I wasn't overzealous about it all the time. I don't think you've experienced one of those luls before."

"I don't think you used those words." I met his eye and he smiled back.

"Perhaps not." He took a deep breath and sighed. "Everyone has moods, you know? I feel like the conventional thought is that everyone either actively wants sex, would be okay with sex, would never want sex, or has a specific temporary reason they don't want it."

I nodded and shrugged.

"For some people there are other moods. One of mine is not wanting sex for no reason in particular, and I feel that way more often than you might think."

"And that can't become an 'okay with sex' mood because-?"

"It's not a matter of just needing to get in the mood. When I don't want it, I can't really be made to want it."

"So it's just inexplicable?"

"I don't know about that. Asexuality, demisexuality, grey asexuality... the labels are kinda treated like the explanation sometimes."

I rubbed my forehead.

"I keep thinking 'oh! Yeah, I know what that feels like' but I guess I don't. If I care enough about someone, there has to be a pretty clear and understood reason not to be okay with sex."

"Is that going to be okay?"

"What?" I looked up to him, dumbfounded. "Yeah, of course! God, I'd have to be a special sort of monster to call that a deal breaker."

He raised an eyebrow.

"I mean- ugh. Now that I *know*, I won't obsess over finding a reason you aren't interested."

I picked at the blanket while I tried to gather the rest of my thoughts. He rubbed his thumb over the back of my hand while I swayed in place.

"So. I have a couple questions."

"Shoot."

"Do you know how much time you spend between those moods?"

He sucked in a breath through his teeth and scratched the back of his head. I immediately wondered if I was going to hate the answer.

"I would say... I spend a good half of the time completely disinterested, and half of the time okay with it."

I waited for him to continue but he seemed reluctant to finish the thought.

"I'm almost never actively interested in sex."

"Fuck!"

He laughed as I threw my hands up.

"I mean, that's so fucking valid of you but god*damn* it! Now that I know it's such a rare event I'm gonna have to like... pop champagne or something." I gestured inarticulately before pulling up my blanket and taking his hand again.

He shook his head and sat back as he rolled his eyes.

"What was your other question?"

"Well I don't know if I wanna ask."

"No, no. I want to hear it. What were you going to ask?"

"Oh all right." I mimed shooing a fly away. "Well I *was* going to ask that you come find me the next time you were in the mood, but now I don't know if I want to wait that long!"

He sighed and pulled my other hand into his.

"As a personal favor to you, since I love you *so* dearly: the very next time I realize I'm open to the possibility, I'll let you know."

"Well that's mighty charitable of you."

"I'm a charitable man." He climbed to his feet and rubbed his knees. "So. How's the temperature? More social time? With or without snuggles?"

"Snuggles please. I promise I'll behave."

"Mhmm suuuuure."

I held out the corner of the blanket and with a bit of maneuvering we were settled in, comfortable as ever.

# 37

## Just Enough Cooks

"Safety glasses!"

Cyrus pointed at the cubby next to the door as I stepped into the garage. Part of me wanted to complain about noise, or suggest sound dampening but I figured I was being oversensitive.

I donned the glasses and made my way around the cars to the furthest garage section. Sawdust was getting everywhere.

I went back and dug in my car for one of my cloth masks and then approached a safe distance from Cyrus.

"Good idea!" He shouted and then turned off the table saw. He put the panels he had just cut behind him, dusted off his arms and turned back to me.

"Welcome to the shop! What brings you in today?"

"I was hoping you would make me a full chess set with hand carved mahogany pieces." I did my best to sound posh and entitled.

"Expensive tastes I see."

"It's just a status thing, I don't remember how to play chess."

"What would you offer in trade?"

"Hmm." I pretended to think. "My first born?"

"Clever, but I don't think I'd ever collect."

"A diamond the size of my fist?"

"No good to me."

"My hand in marriage?"

Cyrus coughed and covered his mouth. As intended, he was suddenly a little flustered.

"That is far more valuable than a mere board game."

"Awww you're sweet. So what are you making?"

He rolled his eyes and beckoned me over to his work bench. The drawing was simple, I wasn't even sure it needed to be drawn since it was just a box with some holes in it.

"This is going to be part of the dust extraction system."

I looked around at the now brown floor. "I can see that being nice."

"I'll sweep up." He waved his hand and then pointed around the ceiling. "I'm going to run tubes around the edge into boxes like this, and connect all of that to a vacuum behind the garage."

"Seems elaborate. How much have you done?"

He looked from the drawing to the panel of wood. "I need to make a few more pieces to start on the boxes, and then it will just be tubing and installation."

"So you've barely started?"

He grinned. "Yep."

"So, through hours of work, you will save minutes by not having to sweep up anymore?"

"I'll still have to sweep, just a little less."

I laughed and shook my head.

"All I can say is I hope you're having fun."

"Loads of fun. Just the most."

"What's next?"

He counted out the stacks of wooden plates on the table to himself. "Three more cuts and then I can start gluing."

I nodded and looked around the shop. I guess the boxes were vacuum terminals to go on each of the power tool stations he had set up, with a couple extra for expansion.

"The boxes will let me block off the suction on tools I'm not using so the vacuum directs all its power to the right place."

"That's pretty genius."

"It's not my idea, or even design."

"Still, that's cool. Can I help?"

"Sure!"

He picked up the largest remaining board and placed it back on the table saw. I tried to pay attention as he talked about fences and depths but most everything went in one ear and out the other.

"I should probably do this bit myself."

I stepped back as he flipped a power switch and the blade spun. He picked up a long stick and seemed to use excessive care pushing the wood through.

Before I knew it, the saw was off and the wood plates made a clap as they joined their stacks.

"So why the sudden interest in woodworking?" He pulled his glasses down for a second to wipe them before grabbing a gun-shaped hand tool and a white bottle.

"I don't know about *sudden*."

I was going to say sappy stuff about being interested in everything he did, but I changed my mind on a whim. "I just figured if I volunteered on something easy here, I could guilt you into cooking with me."

"Interesting choice of words."

"Oh? How would you say it?"

He stopped and squinted at me. "I probably just wouldn't say 'guilt'. Besides, Mary and I have offered to help cook but you've always seemed to want the kitchen to yourself."

Ah. Yeah. That. I'd set myself up for that one.

"Well. On *occasion* I would be amenable to sharing control of my realm."

"It's politeness bullshit isn't it?"

"Yeah. It's politeness bullshit. But it's no big deal, I genuinely am happy to do the cooking solo so it's not like I'm telling you not to help and then resenting you for not insisting or something."

"That's good. Is there anything that you cook that we can't help with?"

Ah shit.

"There miiiight be?"

"No examples come to mind?"

"I mean sometimes there isn't enough to do to need any help."

"Uh huh." He grabbed two different plastic funnels and laid them out along with some of the various sizes of panels.

I watched him measure and re-measure for a minute before looking back at the drawing.

"I'm surprised that there isn't a commercial solution for this. Isn't it just a valve?"

"There is one. Several actually."

"Are they expensive?"

He shook his head.

"Do they not work well?"

He shook his head again.

"So why bother making them?"

He looked at the drawing for a moment before giving me a sly smile.

"Why do you make scones from scratch when they sell them at bakeries?"

"Oooh touché, touché."

"This set looks ready for assembly." He stacked the walls of the box in an approximation of the final assembly.

I tied up my hair as he grabbed a cup and poured glue into it.

"Good idea, things are about to get sticky."

*~*~*

The table shook with Cyrus's pounding. Everything rattled as he worked, but I wasn't particularly concerned about anything falling over.

"You like that, slut? You like being flattened on the counter and pounded?"

"Cyrus *please*." I dragged a hand down my face.

Inviting him to the kitchen wasn't a mistake- I was in fact having a wonderful time -but I could still do without the commentary.

"Too much?"

"Just a bit."

"Would you rather I choke the chicken?"

"I said *please*." I set down my whisk and pulled back the top layer of parchment paper. I was afraid he would beat holes in the chicken breast in his exuberance, but the thickness was remarkably even.

"Now what?" He twirled the tenderizing hammer as I flipped the chicken onto a cutting board.

"Now we cut the strips."

He picked up a knife but hesitated.

I handed Mary the mozzarella cheese sticks to unwrap and grabbed the paper to throw away.

"One to two centimeters wide should be perfect."

He nodded. "I was thinking though, what if we wrapped the chicken around the cheese and breaded that?"

"*That* would be far more prone to inedible failure."

"Or excitement?"

"I don't know that I would call chicken stuffed with cheese *exciting*."

"Pleeeeease."

"I'm not choosing the pizza if this goes tits up."

I rolled my eyes as he fist pumped.

"I guess if you will split five or so sticks in half down their length then we can make it work." I turned to Cyrus. "On the bright side, we might not need to freeze them if we do it this way."

"What would happen if we didn't freeze the cheese sticks?"

"They would disintegrate, and you would cry."

"I would."

Before I could recommend how he did the next step, he grabbed a slice of mozzarella and rolled the chicken over it till it was covered. He sliced it cleanly, but couldn't seem to get the chicken to stay closed around it.

"We can try toothpicks and prayer."

He nodded. "Kinda sounds like you've done this before."

"Not this exactly, but the same premise applies for stuffed jalapenos or taquitos."

Mary chewed threads off of a cheese stick.

I turned to her and crossed my arms. "You didn't touch raw chicken did you?"

"Have you ever seen me get sick?"

I rolled my eyes. "Yes. You have drunk yourself sick multiple times."

"Aside from that."

"You threw up at the theme park too."

"Stop giving examples!"

I laughed and shook my head. "Please just wash up. Us mortals have to take cross contamination seriously."

"I'll remember this. One day I'll make you rue the day you policed my fun."

"I'm soooo scared."

My sass earned me a poke in the ribs, but luckily I wasn't holding a knife.

"Oh no!" Mary gasped. "Your shirt is contaminated!"

I didn't have a chance to escape before she had a hold on the hem of my shirt.

Cyrus, rather than saving me, reached across the sink to close the blinds.

As usual, Mary had her way. In no time I was relieved of my shirt.

"Now will you wash your hands?" I put my hands on my hips.

"You contaminated your pants!"

I danced out of her reach and hid on the other side of the counter.

This time Cyrus did come to my rescue, he caught Mary around the waist as she tried to dash around the island to me.

"You're going to get us exiled from the kitchen."

"Fiiiine."

She exaggerated a pout as she washed her hands and returned to peeling cheese.

She fidgeted as I pulled down the toothpicks and pinned the chicken cocoons shut.

"Is something wrong, Mary?"

"Won't you need a shirt for the frying part?"

"Hmm? No, I don't think so."

Her face reddened as Cyrus took over pinning and I dredged the sticks in egg and bread crumbs.

"I think Mary is getting hungry." Cyrus nudged me with his elbow.

"Well it won't be terribly long till dinner."

"Can we do something before then?"

Ah. *That* hungry.

I'd assumed Cyrus had fed her recently but it occurred to me that wasn't necessarily the case. Hell, it had been a few days since my meltdown and he hadn't visited me so that would put Mary at a nearly week long dry spell.

I laid out the last of the sticks and spritzed them with oil. I had expected to freeze them, so I hadn't heated the oil. The air fryer didn't need to preheat though, and that practically eliminated the risk of leaks.

I washed my hands and looked around the kitchen. Mary was still flushed and Cyrus seemed deeply amused.

Both were attentive, perhaps for different reasons, as I turned on the air fryer and set a timer.

"They should be done in a little over ten minutes." I reached for one of the bowls but Cyrus was faster.

"I can clean up if you are okay with fixing Mary a snack."

"Okay. Stick one with a thermometer when the timer goes off. If it doesn't read one sixty-five, pop them back in for a bit longer."

Mary was bouncing in place now. How had we not realized she was hungry before?

"Thanks Cyrus, okay Mary, let's see what we can find you in the pantry to tide you over."

It was hard not to play at being inconvenienced as she skipped to the bedroom, it felt like it would be so fun to tease, but ever since I confessed, Mary had been reluctant to initiate verbally. The agreement on specificity seemed to have expired as soon as we became formally romantically involved and she had swung hard back to nonverbal cues. This was the closest she had come to asking explicitly in weeks.

"I'm sorry I didn't ask."

She was already shaking her head. "You don't have to."

"But I ought to- I want to care for you but I completely dropped the ball this week. I should never have made you be the only one to initiate. Besides, I'm not any sort of asexual like Cyrus, it would take a lot for me to be unavailable to you."

I worried that she thought I wasn't interested in her, but her reassurance set off a dark thought in the back of my head. Maybe she was beyond desperate and I was just the coffee tent in the lobby to her right now.

"Addie, it's not that deep. Sometimes you forget to eat all day when you fixate on a task. That is essentially what I did. I forgot."

"It's not that you just don't want me?"

"No, I love you, that's your insecurity talking, but thank you for checking in. Where are you going?"

"I should have showered before starting dinner, it was hot in the garage and I only really washed my arms to prepare for cooking."

"I'd fuck you on the garage floor if you let me."

"Well that's a you thing. I'll be out in like five minutes."

"I doubt that."

"I'll hurry, I promise."

"Oh I'm sure you will, but I might not."

And she wondered why dinner got cold.

# 38

## Dig a Little Deeper

I compulsively rechecked my agenda. I had precious little free time to job hunt before I needed to grocery shop, babysit, and start dinner. I'd try to work in a lunch snack while babysitting.

So far, every job I found had pretty prohibitive hours. Not that it would be easy to keep up with babysitting and cooking with a typical job anyways. Let alone cleaning. God, it was demoralizing to try so hard and accomplish so little. I mean, sure, Mazer was paying me a generous wage for babysitting. Still, it felt like I would be wasting all the efforts if I didn't find employment in the culinary field.

I shut my laptop and buried my face in my hands. It had been weeks, I hadn't paid a rent check yet, but I still found myself spending so much to cope. It wasn't money I didn't have by any stretch. Everything was conceivably a necessity, but still.

Before you ask, yes. Cat toys are a necessity. Speaking of cat toys, Sonia, Ghost's toy cat, was currently pinning me down as she lounged across my lap.

I lifted her into a bridal style carry over to the lower tier of the kitty castle. The penthouse was Ghost's of course. My concerns melted as I dispensed attention onto my fur baby but reality crept in as it does.

I took one last glance through the fridge and pantry and headed out the door. I'd left enough time to grocery shop this time. As long as I didn't sidetrack into the home decor, I would be fine.

I dropped my insulated grocery bag in the back seat and climbed into my car. It started on the second try like usual, but it lurched weakly and stalled when I pressed the gas. I put it in park and waited.

Shortly after the big drive up, everything about the way it drove turned sluggish. A couple of days ago, the stalling began.

I started the car again, and it caught on the first try, but when I put it in drive, it immediately stopped the engine. Not in a stalling and slowly dying way either, but a lurch, crack, and then unsettling silence.

Fuck.

I spent a couple of minutes trying to get it to start, but all I got was "check engine". No click. No sign of life outside the light-show of warning lights.

Ooookay. I checked my phone. I had plenty of time to walk to Mazer's. As long as I was quick, I could shop for groceries online and bite the bullet on the delivery fee. All wasn't completely lost.

I reset the parking brake and climbed out. I could call a repairman in my free time tomorrow or something.

I pulled a hand through my hair. This was okay. I still had time. Nobody would be mad at me, and I could still get a bit done.

I mean, I'd miss my therapy appointment tomorrow, but I could reschedule. Hell, Mazer might let me borrow the minivan if I offered to pay him or something.

With nothing better to do, I started walking. I could fill out the grocery list, I supposed, but I should call the therapist first. Of course, that all required that my phone didn't choose this moment to die.

Goddamn my obsession with that god-forsaken meme app. I rued the day Mary introduced me because, though I appreciated the amusement, the battery drain was prohibitive.

I'd charge my phone when I got to Mazer's. Everything was still okay.

The walk itself was less than interesting. I had time to look at the houses, but all I could see is that they were all the same. All the trees were young or recently planted. Nothing in this neighborhood was established, least of all me. Naturally, this was a particularly warm spring day, but at least it wasn't raining. That was supposed to be a positive.

My feet ached by the time I got to Mazer's, and to my surprise, the house was empty. After checking all the rooms, I resigned myself to waiting and hunted down a phone charger.

It took several minutes for the poor thing to have enough power to boot up. My heart sank as I watched the notifications roll in. Three voicemails. Twenty-one notifications. Fuck.

I listened to the first voicemail.

"Hey, it's Mazer. I wanted to let you know you don't have to babysit today, Mikah and Crystal are taking the twins to the park so you can relax. Sorry to cancel at the last minute, I'll still pay you for your time today though."

The next message was from Mary.

"Hey Addie, I saw your car, but you aren't home. Please get back to me soon. I'm worried."

She sounded frenzied in the next message.

"Addison. Call me as soon as you get service or charge your phone or whatever. I'm about to call the police."

I sighed. Fucking perfect. I dialed Mary, and she picked up immediately.

"Addie? Where are you? Are you okay?"

"Yes, yes. I'm fine. I'm at Mazer's house."

"Why didn't you take your car?"

"It didn't start."

"Why didn't you tell someone?"

"My phone died."

I rubbed my forehead as her voice grew shrill.

"So you walked to Mazer's?"

"I'm sorry, okay? I didn't want to let them down. I guess I messed up. I'll fix it."

"I'm coming to get you."

"You don't have --"

"Oh my god just --" I heard her take a few steadying breaths. Her tone was far calmer when she spoke again.

"I'm going to come pick you up. We're going to go get something to drink, and walk in the park or something."

"Okay. I guess we might see Crystal, Mikah, and the twins there then." I tried my best to sound upbeat, but I could tell what this was. Apparently, walking around with a dead phone was one of those extreme things Mary made me promise not to do. I was officially in the dog house.

Mary didn't talk for a moment and I heard jingling keys in the background. "I'll see you real soon. I love you."

"Love you too," I mumbled, and I let her hang up.

I flicked through my messages. Mazer, Mikah, Cyrus, and Mary had all been texting me with varying degrees of concern.

I responded to all of them with apologies and assurances before unplugging my phone and heading outside to wait for Mary. I triple-checked that I locked up behind me because the last thing I needed was to piss off anyone else today.

I didn't have to wait long. Mary rolled up the street and halfway into the driveway. Before I could even take a step, she was out of the car and crashing into me.

"I'm sorry I worried you," I mumbled into her shoulder, and she nodded. I eased my grip on her but she only held on tighter. "Coffee would be nice."

I expected her to say something, anything, while she drove, but she was disconcertingly quiet for the entire drive.

She ordered my favorite, and we sipped in silence as she made her way to the park and found a space. I took my seat-belt off, but she didn't move after shutting off the car.

"I'm not mad."

I couldn't suppress my snort of disbelief.

"I... can see how you might have thought taking a short walk without your phone was not a big deal, and in a real sense it wasn't. I'm sorry for reacting so strongly."

"I'm sorry I put you in that situation."

She looked me in the eye before slumping in her seat.

She dropped her drink in the cup holder, and I let her take my hand.

"I want to reassure you in a way that will take... We haven't been communicating as we should, and I'm having a lot of trouble understanding what I can do to help that."

I shrugged, and she rubbed her thumb on the back of my hand.

"Tell me what has you strung out like this."

I sighed. "I don't want to whine."

"You won't be whining. I am sincerely and desperately asking what is going on."

I looked her in the eye before relenting.

"I'm not happy with myself. I'm not doing enough, but I don't know how I will be able to do more. For example, all I'm really doing right now is cooking, a bit of basic cleaning, and babysitting, but even that tiny amount of responsibility exhausts me. I'm struggling to search for a job that will allow me to continue my other duties. I'm just not functioning high enough, and I'm scared I won't be able to afford rent when you start asking for it."

Mary stared at me wide-eyed. She opened and closed her mouth a couple of times before muttering, "Holy shit."

"Pathetic I know," I grumbled and looked out the window.

"I don't even know where to start." Mary's tone had so much bewilderment and frustration I didn't feel like I could look her in the eye.

"To clarify, why do you think I am going to ask for rent?"

"It's your house, you bought it. I should pay my way."

"Honey. Mazer bought it. As a gift. For all of us. I will eagerly and enthusiastically pay for all the utilities until you insist on contributing to that how you want."

"Oh." I mulled over the implications. It was a relief, I guess.

Mary dropped my hand and ran her fingers through her hair. "Do you enjoy babysitting for my parents?"

"It's nice in its own way. It gives me plenty of money, it's feel-good work, and I am praised and appreciated heavily for it. I just feel like I'm wasting my education by not cooking professionally."

"Then don't babysit so much. If you want to have a career and help them on the side, then adjust childcare to fit your career."

She stated it so simply, but that seemed too easy. What was even the point of it all? It was like no amount of work I could do would be enough. Why would it make a difference if cooking was my primary job rather than homemaking?

I was still working at expressing this despair when she continued.

"What do you think 'doing enough' would look like for you? What would make you happy?"

"I don't know. Maybe I just want to feel like an adult that makes adult money as you and Cyrus do? Cyrus has his fancy car and a nice job, and you already have a new job you seem to be thriving in. I feel like I'm less because I don't have that."

She looked around before focusing back in and taking a sip of her drink.

"Can I give you my perspective real quick?" When I nodded, she pressed on, "For the last few weeks I have worked a low-stress part-time job and come home to delicious home-cooked meals. You even prepare meals I can take with me at my leisure. I am completely cared for emotionally and physically, and have quickly become comfortable."

I shrugged. "That's good?"

She sighed. "That's what I want for you. I want you to feel like you make low stress, low time engagement contributions, in exchange for an outpouring of care and comfort."

"I have that."

"No, you don't. You babysit for at least five hours a day, six days a week, pile grocery shopping and cooking on top of that, and it occurs to me not once have you asked for us to help with your expenses. You have obligated yourself to an objectively large effort and time-intensive share of work, and decided it is not enough."

I was still forming my counterargument when Mary grabbed her drink and opened her door.

"We came here to go for a walk, let's walk."

I let her take my hand and toyed with the idea of arguing back as we stepped into the shade of the trees. She led me down the meandering walking path.

"I don't know what I should do differently."

"Communicate. Relax."

I rolled my eyes, and she squeezed my hand.

"Take your time searching out your wants and needs, and then talk with Cyrus and me so we can help meet them. Right now you have this goal of being superwoman. You do it all and save the day every day. I just want you to have a more human-level goal to work toward."

When I made no response, she bumped her shoulder into mine. "We'll get through it."

I waved to Mikah and Crystal where they pushed the twins on the swing-set.

# 39

## Lonesome Bliss

Ugh. Horny.

I looked at the clock Mary had gotten me. One AM. Fuck you In-Snare. Thou art fickle with how you give life and take sleep.

I considered using my hands like some type of self-sufficient person, but I couldn't be bothered when we had a literal bookshelf of sex toys in Mary's room.

I clung to a feeble hope sleep would bonk me on the head, but ten wasted minutes later, I was still staring at the stars projected on the ceiling.

I rolled out of bed and shuffled to Mary's bedroom. I frowned as I noticed two distinct bumps under the sheets. Cyrus was in here, and he was a light sleeper. At this point, it was too late. He would notice me leaving if I gave up, so I flicked on my phone's flashlight and searched for a wand.

Right on cue, the sheets rustled. I heard Cyrus shuffle up behind me. He squatted and I spared him a glance.

"Can't sleep?" He mumbled.

"Something like that."

I unplugged the smallest wand and buzzed it to make sure it had juice. I saw him rub his face out of the corner of my eye.

"Would you like me to take care of you?"

"I don't want to trouble you."

"It's no trouble."

When I stood back up he was a little closer, I nearly stumbled when he reached to rub my back and pull me into a hug.

I wanted to say "it's okay", but I also really didn't want to. I only wanted to be thought of as self-sufficient, or at least polite, but at some point there wasn't anything especially polite about refusing care.

"Okay," I whispered. I hoped he didn't need me to repeat myself.

I expected him to lead me to his, or maybe my bedroom. Instead he tugged me toward Mary's bed. I tried to shush him as he used a voice command to turn the lights on, and I folded my arms as the room glowed to life. Mary stirred, sat up, and stretched. She looked around, taking in the sight of the lights, the still dark windows, the time on her clock, and me: caught red-handed with a vibrator.

"Trouble sleeping?"

Well, now I wasn't feeling terribly horny.

I shrugged, and Cyrus nodded.

Mary held out her arms and beckoned me forward. Cyrus, however, held out a hand, and I surrendered the wand.

Mary scooted back. She pulled me to her and Cyrus followed me in. Now I was sandwiched. Mary on my right, and Cyrus on my left.

"Did you have a nightmare, Babygirl?"

I rolled my eyes. "Are we role-playing me being the child sneaking into mom and dad's bed now?"

"Depends," Cyrus drawled as he held up the wand, "do you have a thing for incest scenarios?"

"Jesus Christ," I mumbled.

Mary rubbed small circles on my stomach as her tone turned to baby talk. "Tell me all about your bad dream so mommy and daddy can make it all better."

"Oh my god, please stop."

"Belligerent isn't she?" Cyrus mumbled as he resituated a little closer.

"Fine! I stayed up too late looking at memes, and I was horny, so I came to borrow a toy to take care of myself. I'm sorry I woke you up."

"I'm not sorry." Mary's hand slipped under my shirt. "To think! That in the deepest calm of the night, with naught but your own company, you would indulge in such lonesome personal bliss! All while I lay mere steps away, waiting for your call to bring me from slumber to your express aid."

I took a deep breath as her hand trailed up, just inches from my chest. I leaned into the touch but when I looked at her she only raised an eyebrow.

"What would it take for you to behave?"

I shrugged as Mary leaned closer to kiss my cheek.

When I didn't say anything for a few seconds, she switched tactics.

"May I attend to you?"

I scoffed and rolled my eyes. "You don't need permission to touch me anymore."

"Nuh-uh babe. You know better."

"Can't I just give some sort of blanket consent?"

"Would you be able to enforce your boundaries if we cross a line?"

I squinted at her. "Point taken. Yes, you may."

"Any particular preferences tonight?"

It was hard to focus with her hand up my shirt.

"I was just going to crawl under a bunch of blankets and lay on the wand."

"We can be your blanket." She leaned closer and lay half on top of me.

I didn't know what to say to that. I wasn't even sure what that entailed but realistically I'd probably enjoy it if she literally just laid on top of me.

"Yeah... okay."

Mary sat up on her knees. "Don't laugh, I have an idea. Cyrus, can you grab your phone and pair up the wand?" She crawled off the bed and in seconds she returned with a couple straps.

I rolled my eyes as she fumbled while attaching the wand to her right thigh. She spent an eternity fussing over the exact positioning before cinching it down.

Once everything was on, Mary crawled over to me. I laughed as she wormed her arms under me and wiggled to situate. It was harder to breathe, but still comfortable. I glanced at Cyrus as he fiddled with his phone, he seemed to be struggling to control it left handed with his right arm behind my head.

Still, Mary's leg started buzzing between mine before long and hot damn was there pressure behind that.

Everything started as casual as I imagined it would. Cyrus experimented with intensity, and Mary held me as I shifted to see what felt best. After a minute Cyrus got his arm out from behind my head and I felt him running his fingers through my hair. Normally, I might worry about getting overstimulated, but it seemed to help that I kept my clothes on. I already imagined what this would be like with the feel of her skin on mine, but I put that out of my mind when Mary began to move her hips. I hugged her tighter and she answered with her fingertips pressing into my back and a gentle bite on my shoulder.

"Try to relax." I heard her whisper into my neck.

I forced myself to let go of her. Releasing tension in my hips, back, and neck was difficult, but even the small progress felt exciting.

"Good girl."

I whimpered as she pressed her teeth to my shoulder again. I had to wonder if relaxing was for my enjoyment, or if she just wanted me to submit to her. That frame of mind somehow made it easier. Mary was safe for me. Submission was safe. I let my head fall back as the sensations washed over me. I thought relaxing would soften the orgasm, or at least calm things down, but the dopamine hit was the same. Always stronger than I remembered.

I couldn't bring myself to feel sad when Cyrus cut off the vibrator a bit sooner than I would have liked. This was perfection. I got to be on bottom, everyone was giving me attention, and there were cuddles throughout. Everything was soft.

I giggled drunkenly as Mary sat up off of me. I was practically in a crater now. Still, I needed something to hug. I groaned as I sat up just enough to latch on to Cyrus, and ever the gentleman, he held me as I finished calming my breathing.

"We might have to make midnight snacks a thing." Mary mused as she returned to the bed.

"It's all fun and games until I sleep through lunch the day after."

"I'll make you a really nice cup of coffee tomorrow."

"With ice cream?"

"Sure. With ice cream."

I tried not to hold Cyrus back as he sat up to plug in his phone.

I debated how I wanted to be arranged within the cuddle pile, but my mind was made up for me as Cyrus rolled me and pulled me back to his chest. Mary scooted backwards to trap me to him. I reached up to hold Cyrus's right hand as I draped my left arm over Mary. She wove our fingers together over her heart, and, as I got comfortable, Cyrus commanded the lights off. I slipped rapidly toward deep sleep.

\*_\*_\*

This time when the lights came on, it was morning. When Mary and Cyrus stirred to get up, I heard them grumble their amusement as I refused to let go. Mary pried her hand from mine, but Cyrus lifted me into his arms. Once he had settled me on his hips, he carried me against his chest as he got out of bed. I wondered how long he could go about his morning like this.

I didn't have to wait long before I was deposited on the bathroom counter-top. He kissed me good morning until Mary came by to tickle my feet, and he turned to kiss her too.

The day asserted itself to my mind, and my mood did a skydive as I remembered every detail. My car was broken. I didn't know how I'd get to therapy. I scared Mary yesterday. It wouldn't surprise me if they were secretly irritated that I woke them up last night.

Even as they expressed affection to me, I was eroding our relationship out from under us. No amount of effort was helping.

Mary apparently noticed my subdued mood because she worked her way between my legs. She put her hands on my hips. I could tell she was looking me in the eye, but I couldn't bear to meet her gaze.

"What's on your mind, babe?"

I sighed. For once, I knew what I was thinking. The whole list had just asserted itself to my tortured brain, so I begrudgingly relayed the bad news.

"Thank you for communicating. What time is therapy?"

"One thirty."

"Excellent. We can all work together instead of dividing to conquer."

I met her gaze. "Work on what? What about your job?

"I'm calling in." She turned to Cyrus. "What are your plans?"

He shrugged. "Sleep all day."

I snorted, but Mary was far less amused.

Cyrus rolled his eyes and pretended to think. "If I don't get to sleep I'd probably like to spend the day with my darling girls, have a fancy brunch, do some recreational shopping, and splurge on some comfort food for dinner."

Mary rolled her eyes. "Those plans seem compatible." She turned to me. "How do you feel about working in some shopping and junk food --"

"Comfort food," Cyrus interrupted.

Mary rolled her eyes.

"I saw that."

She turned to look at his reflection and stuck her tongue out.

"It's the same thing. Anyways. Shopping and *comfort* food. Interested?"

"How could I say no?"

Mary smirked. "Well first, when asked If you were interested, you would reply 'no'."

"Thank you for coaching me on how to give consent."

"You're welcome. Now, hop in the shower, we need to conserve water."

"Myth Testers did that one, showering together doesn't save water."

"They didn't test with three people. Besides, I don't actually care. Would you kindly accompany me in getting wet?"

I rolled my eyes as she grabbed the silicon-based lube and herded Cyrus in. I spitefully took my time collecting towels and feeding the cats before joining. I wasn't surprised they washed Cyrus's dick before all else.

# 40

# Tender Loving Care

"So what exactly was wrong with your car?"

Cyrus turned to look back at me as Mary drove us toward our brunch outing.

"Ever since the long drive up, it's been sluggish and weak. A week or so ago it started stalling at random times, but yesterday it stalled immediately and wouldn't start again no matter how I tried."

Cyrus hummed his acknowledgment and flicked through his phone. "It's an I-motto right?"

"Yeah. I-motto Minima. I've had it for like seven years. Do you think it's time to change the battery or something?"

I heard Cyrus suck air through his teeth.

"Mmm what you are describing sounds very much like a transmission or engine problem. Luckily, for a car as old as yours there is a rather simple solution for that."

"Oh, that's good. I definitely want to get just a little more mileage out of this car before buying a new one."

Cyrus and Mary shared a look, but before I could ask, we pulled into the brunch place Cyrus had requested.

Getting seated and ordering was a pretty straightforward affair, mainly because Mary wanted to try multiple things and I always went halfsies with her for that. Cyrus explained what a transmission was and how his car differed from that.

"I've actually been thinking about what kind of car I should get next. Back when I was searching up all things gay, I saw a lot of talk about Sobaros. I kinda dig the utility aspect, and I heard about some sort of hybrid thing they could do where it would be a half electric car like Cyrus's."

Cyrus tapped away on his phone, probably looking it up. Soon, Mary picked up her phone to check as well.

"There's a store that sells Sobaros right next to the shop your car got towed to. We could probably look at them for fun while your car is getting checked out."

I shrugged. "Could be fun."

*~*~*

I slumped into the couch in the therapy waiting room. Mary and Cyrus were like rabbits. They could go and go forever, and as charming as it was, it had made the morning incredibly busy. I was exhausted, and all this coaching and oversight piled on an emotional toll. I was under a magnifying glass, and though I didn't feel like I deserved better. I longed for the time when I could convince myself I was independent.

I waved goodbye to Mary and Cyrus when I got called back, and I tried not to zone out as Mrs. Hendrix led the way to her office. Our first session had gone well, but I was having a hard time feeling optimistic about our sessions turning productive any time soon.

"Were those your partners waiting with you?"

I blinked. Apparently, I had zoned out after all.

"Yeah. Mary and Cyrus. They've been uh... hanging out with me today since it's been a rough week."

"How has it been rough?"

I pulled out my phone and brought up the list Mary had coached me through on talking points. It was good that they were written down because it was a long list, and I had forgotten about many of them.

"Well, the first thing I have is I'm struggling with communicating."

"What sort of communication issues have you been struggling with?"

"There's been a lot, the theme of the issues though is they want me to open up about my problems and struggles, but that continues to be very difficult. I'm never in a position where I would sooner reach out for help than try to solve issues myself. So it ends up that nobody knows what's going on with me unless they pry and dig into me. Then, that sucks because that's painful for everyone."

"What are some of the problems you are trying to solve by yourself right now?"

"Pretty basic stuff, just balancing responsibilities like homemaking, babysitting, and job searching. In the past, I had difficulty working through my sexuality and romantic identity or whatever that is called. Meanwhile, I'm tackling little things that pop up like car trouble."

"You are responsible for housework and childcare, while also obligated to get a job?"

"I mean, I do the housework and babysitting to make myself useful. Having a job is just a personal goal of mine."

She took a moment to catch up on her notes. "Are your partners concerned you aren't listening to them?"

The subject change confused me. "Not that I know of. They've mostly communicated love and affection, and any concern has been more an expression of pity and maybe frustration, rather than anger."

"So what I'm hearing is your partners are trying to get you to stop isolating yourself."

"Not in those words exactly... I mean I wouldn't call it isolating, I still spend time with them physically and emotionally, I just try to keep my problems to myself for independence's sake."

"Do you feel lonely?"

"I-. I mean objectively I am not lonely at all. I'm scarcely ever alone lately."

"But do you *feel* lonely?"

"That's just one of the irrational feelings I deal with, like jealousy, and-- I dunno. Mary kinda implies my insistence on complete independence is irrational too."

We sat in silence, and I defaulted to browsing my list of topics. Most of them stemmed from a drive to be strong enough to do things myself, if I thought about it. The biggest issues would also resolve themselves if I was mindful of other people's concerns for me.

"How do you feel today with Mary and Cyrus spending time with you?"

"Not the greatest honestly. Like I love the company, but I miss feeling like I was a low maintenance presence. With my car breaking down and needing a ride today, they have kinda taken it a step forward to manage my car issues for me, and actively coach me on what to talk about here and stuff. I don't like being babied so much."

"Have you expressed your discomfort?"

"Not verbally. I dunno. Do I have the right to be uncomfortable with the help I'm getting? It's helpful and effective even if it's uncomfortable."

"You certainly have the right, and you can communicate discomfort without shunning their help. It seems to me you have a pretty decent support network, and it wouldn't surprise me if Mary and Cyrus want to help you in a way that is more comfortable for you."

I didn't feel convinced, but throughout the therapy session I regained a sense of agency in how I could get my life back on track. I'd be working with help rather than it being a "my way or highway" situation.

*~*~*

Mary and Cyrus weren't in the waiting room when I returned from therapy, but I had a message waiting on my phone saying they were on their way back. Apparently, they had decided to run a quick errand while I was in therapy, no doubt some effort to manage my car issues for me.

I made myself comfortable on the bench outside, and I was surprised as Mary arrived alone. Before I could even ask, she explained.

"Cyrus had to do something at home, we're going to go pick him up."

I nodded. I mulled over how I'd bring up what I learned in therapy, and I was about to speak up when Mary broke the silence for me.

"How was therapy?"

"Pretty good. We got through most of the list you helped me with."

"Nice, nice."

"I actually wanted to talk about that with you and Cyrus." I took a deep breath. "I appreciate how you have stepped up to help me with my car trouble, but I'd like to look at finding a way to solve my issues without forfeiting all of my agency in the resolution."

Mary bit her lip and stared at the road.

"That seems reasonable to me. How would that look to you?"

"I don't really know. I'm mostly kinda interested in the vibe feeling like I'm being guided to solve my issues in a more open manner, rather than just surrendering the entire ordeal to you and Cyrus.

Like maybe that would have been me calling the repair shop Cyrus recommended, rather than him arranging the pick up for me."

She continued to chew her lip, and I was surprised as she suddenly changed direction and pulled up to a coffee and donut shop. Once she was stopped in the drive-through, she announced she was going to see what Cyrus wanted. I browsed for interesting new drinks as she texted.

"Hypothetically speaking," Mary mused, "if the issue with your car was already resolved somewhat... how would you feel?"

"I mean I'd probably be relieved if my car was fixed. I don't think it would be a massive upset to be done with it... I'd just want to maybe handle things differently in the future."

"Cyrus is better at this stuff," Mary grumbled.

"We'll see him soon though. We can talk then."

She only nodded in response, and I struggled not to feel anxious as we neared home. I was getting the feeling my car repair was both expensive and well on the way to being completed.

In no time, we pulled up to the house. To my surprise, Mary parked in the driveway rather than the garage and walked to the front door. We greeted Cyrus at the door, and I was surprised to see Mazer on the couch with Ghost. The white fur complimented his black suit and plum skin exceptionally well.

I rolled my eyes as Mary and Cyrus shared a look.

"About your car..." Cyrus took a sip of his coffee. "It ended up being the transmission after all, and we have a few options going forward on how to fix it."

I sat next to Mazer on the couch and waited for him to elaborate. Sonia hopped into my lap and rubbed her face against mine.

"The shop wants about eight thousand dollars to replace your transmission."

"That's fucking stupid, the car isn't even worth that much."

Cyrus drummed his fingers on his cup.

"How would you like to proceed?"

I ran my hands through my hair. "I'd probably like to get my stuff out of the I-motto, sell it for scrap or something, and then look more seriously at what sort of replacement I can afford."

It was concerning how relieved Cyrus was by that idea.

Mazer broke the silence. "Car loans are rather predatory, so I offered to... finance the car so to speak."

It took a moment for the subtext to sink in. I set down my coffee, folded my hands under my chin, and opened my mouth to speak. However, I thought better of it and stood up. As usual, Sonia insisted she stay in my grasp. Ghost excused herself to her tower as Mazer moved to follow and Mary and Cyrus made half-hearted objections before following us to the garage.

I flicked the light on, and sure enough, a green sedan sat right where my car used to park.

I sighed heavily and shook my head.

"We can still return it..." Mary offered, but I shook my head again.

I turned to Mazer, who was, above all, amused at the mess he had helped my partners into.

"What's the finance deal?"

Mary rolled her eyes as Mazer pulled out a rolled-up piece of copy paper from his jacket. I traded Sonia for the contract and stepped over to what apparently would be my new car.

I flattened the paper on the hood and skimmed. My memory wasn't great, but the total to be paid was around a third the car's value. I had no interest rate. Any babysitting would pay into the car loan the same amount he would still give me in cash.

"You are all unbelievable," I mumbled as I fished a pen out of my bag and signed the bottom.

Mazer tossed me the keys as he received the contract. I took my time fitting it onto my key-ring as Mary and Cyrus struggled to find what to do with themselves.

"Thank you for pretending I solved my own problem, rather than having it fixed for me."

I hit the button to open the garage and stepped past them back into the house. "I'm going to grab my coffee, and then we can go finish our errands, I guess." I smirked as Mary hurried out to repark her car out of the way. I might feel different later, but it was kinda fun being taken care of at least this once.

# 41

## Closer

Nobody tells you how incredible being in a poly relationship is when you're monogamous. I mean, they may try, but nobody hears it, you know? Anyways, aside from having a consistent group for game nights and, in our case, an inflated household income, there were the little things. Like how driving around together was like having a small choir.

My new car had become the default outing car, and it rocked. Today, with Kimberly in town visiting, what was once a private concert listening to Mary was more like an acapella performance. I had gotten better at singing, and since Mary and Cyrus were already pretty experienced, it was even better when Kimberly came to visit.

Unlike in the smaller city, here, we needed a designated driver for our bar crawls. Even having lived here for three months, we were still chewing through the list of Cyrus's favorite places. Tonight would be a throwback since it was an Irish pub. Magical things always happened in those places: whether it be meeting a new love, kicking off an orgy with Mary's family, or whatever would happen tonight. I was hyped.

Tonight I was the designated driver, but I didn't mind so much. I would remember the good food this place was known for.

I found myself enjoying the looks we drew. Cyrus, Mary, and I showed some pretty fresh ink, and we looked like quite the harem: three ladies with one gorgeous man.

I had been kinda swept up in Mary and Cyrus's interests lately, so Cyrus designed a tarot card-themed tattoo for my left shoulder: the chariot, specifically. Cyrus had hopped on the bandwagon to make an event of it and got a combination of the emperor and the tower cards. Mary had acquired yet another woman with a sword. I suspected she was making a subtle pop culture reference given the resemblance to a certain princess of power, but she insisted it was just a Valkyrie.

Rather than line up at the bar, we piled into a small booth. For once, I managed to figure out what I wanted relatively quickly as I glanced at the menu.

"What can I get started for you tonight?"

The waitress looked around the table in turn as Mary, Cyrus, and Kimberly rattled off drink orders, but I got a meat pie. To my surprise, she informed me that I could get bottomless non-alcoholic cocktails for the night. It's always classy when a place caters to designated drivers. I almost requested a brown cow before I realized, without Irish cream, it would be milk. It took a minute to get her recommendation, but I ended up getting an Irish coffee.

I took in the scenery as the table conversation drifted from food to movies. Everything was pretty cramped with a cozy "hole in the wall" vibe. As a result, I had a painful lack of difficulty spotting a familiar face across the room. Rich. The dick himself. He had apparently been looking our way, and when he caught my gaze, he took that as his sign to come to say hello.

"Hey, Addison!" He slurred.

Jesus Christ, it was only seven PM.

"Rich." I glared up at him, and I saw Mary bite her lip as he dragged a chair up to the booth. I wished I had called him Dick. Nobody would have minded.

"Ish been like four years!"

"Sounds about right." I glanced from his shaggy mop of hair to his distressed graphic tee. "You look as good as the day I met you."

He beamed as if this was a compliment, but I heard Kimberly mutter "savage" behind me.

If I was being honest, I don't even remember how I managed to break up with him. I mean, technically he always ended it, but the roller coaster only really ended when I didn't get back on. How had I not seen him for the manipulative bastard he was?

"Who're your friends?"

I contemplated introducing them, but I found I couldn't quite count on him forgetting. If nothing else, Rich was an experienced drunk.

"Cyrus."

He half stood and held out his hand across the table. A small part of me felt sadistic satisfaction as Rich did his typical squeeze of dominance and swiftly had his bones crunched together by a much more impressive answer.

Nobody else offered their name, and he didn't bother asking.

Miraculously, the fucker recovered. "You get a new car? I didn't expect you could afford that little green thing on a kitchen girl salary."

I gave up. I rubbed my forehead and elected to ignore the question. Regrettably, I was too slow to notice his hand coming to poke at my shoulder.

"And a new tattoo? You're like a totally different person."

I hissed a breath through my teeth as he jabbed the tender skin.

I pushed his hand away and he looked like he was going to jab again just for fun, but Cyrus cleared his throat.

"Nice catching up as always." I grit my teeth and turned to stare him in the eye.

His response was interrupted by the return of the waitress. She took one look from us to him before rolling her eyes.

"Oi!" She kicked his chair hard enough that he nearly fell out. I noted her tray didn't shake to spill so much as a drop. "Bugger off to your stool ya filthy lush."

"Well, it was nice to meet y'all." He half sneered around the table, but he lost his nerve as we stared back.

"God," Mary murmured, "I hope we never see him again."

I wiped my shoulder with a napkin in case he had left residue. The waitress apologized for him.

"We do a three-strike thing here, and that was number two for him. The bouncer will be having a chat with him before he closes his tab."

I nodded and shrugged, pleased to be distracted by the curvy frothed cup she placed in front of me.

"That meat pie will be out in a minute, and let me know if you have any more trouble from him. Here, or anywhere else."

"Please tell me that wasn't Mr. Condom," Mary groaned, and I shrugged.

"He thinks they call him Dick for a good reason." I sipped my foam.

Cyrus shook his head as Kimberly looked like she wanted to speak up but refrained.

I filled her in anyways, and she shared her disgusted reaction knowing I had gotten my tubes tied for his sake.

"All I can say is I've developed better taste since."

"I'll say," Kimberly muttered.

We watched with mild interest as he started a commotion when the bouncer sat next to him. The predictable conclusion was reached as he was walked out the door by the elbow.

I groaned as he left. I wondered whether I should make sure he didn't vandalize my car.

"Do you want to talk about it?"

Now Mary was ignoring her drink to attend to my feelings. Damn it, I wanted to have fun tonight.

I looked up from my glass as Mary placed her hand on mine. She raised an eyebrow and tilted her head so I got up and followed her to the bathroom.

Once the door was shut, she took my hands. "What do you hear?"

"Your voice. Muffled drinking songs."

"Good. What do you feel?"

"Your hands." She nodded me onward, so I sighed and thought harder. "The ground, my clothes, gravity I guess. Air in my lungs."

"What do you smell?"

"Bathroom." I wrinkled my nose, and she giggled.

"Fair, what do you see?"

"A couple of stalls, checkered tile, a mirror, sink, and an empty soap dispenser."

"Good girl."

I managed half a smile and shrugged. I should have been able to ground myself but the help wasn't unwelcome.

"It's a bit early for Halloween."

I smiled as Mary looked over her shoulder, probably expecting out of season decor.

"I mean with the ghosts of the past haunting and all."

"Ah. Yeah, that's rough. It won't ruin your night though will it? He can't hurt you. Besides, I know his face and daddy can get me out of jail."

"It's not worth the hassle, he's out of my life."

"I agree. See? Ancient history. You're safe."

I rolled my eyes but nodded anyway. She swung our hands side to side a couple times and swayed in place until I smiled again.

"Do you need the bathroom before we head back?"

I shook my head and she danced her way out of the bathroom, thankfully though, she didn't dance across the bar.

A meat pie was waiting for me when we returned, and it was every bit as good as Cyrus hyped it up to be. He and Kimberly had become engrossed in tabletop game conversations again, and it was pleasant to slip into step with them.

Luckily for me, nobody overdid it. A couple of short hours later, I herded my kittens to the car, and the drive home proved uneventful. The singing quality had declined, but it wasn't remotely discordant.

Nobody fell on the step up from the garage to the utility room this time; yes, that was an actual thing we had to worry about with guests. To my surprise, Kimberly dragged me after Mary and Cyrus rather than to my room as she had the last couple of nights. I got to watch with mild amusement as Mary invited her to bed formally, and I rolled my eyes at the inevitable resulting make-out they spawned.

Supposedly, alcohol inhibited arousal, but Mary never let that stop her. When I got back with the pain pills, cups, and a small pitcher of water, Kimberly was engrossed and out of her depth.

It was funny to see a pecking order established. Mary and Cyrus were switches, and the idea was growing on me, but Kimberly switched more aggressively. She would only top me, but she was an absolute puddle to Mary.

I met Cyrus's eye across from the spectacle, that looked like a green light eye wiggle to me. It was to be an orgy, after all. I slipped out of my dress as I walked around the bed. I crawled over him to be his little spoon in the middle and my interest in watching Kimberly slipped away as Cyrus distracted me with his personal attention.

\*~\*~\*

A full bed.

This was always the better way to wake up. None of that empty bed crap for me, no way.

I crawled up to sit back against the headboard, and a sea of bodies surrounded me. Cyrus had helped himself to water and was flicking through his phone, so I amused myself playing with his hair as Mary and Kimberly appeared to doze. At some point Ghost had worked her way into the bedroom and that meant Sonia joined the fray as well. Ghost was satisfied watching from her bed on top of the toy shelf but Sonia stretched to touch as many people at once. She lay primarily in my lap now but her back paws were on Cyrus and she reached to hold one fore-paw on Mary's back. Mrs. Separation Anxiety indeed.

I had to wonder what could come of it all. When would I run out of love to give? I had prepared for my relationship with Kimberly to die, and yet here she was. Hell, I'd expected the same for Joshua but he had visited last weekend and things were as good as ever. Though, he was more Mary's golden retriever than a flame for Cyrus or me.

I had to wonder if this would end with Kimberly being a bunkmate. I was still daydreaming about more four- or even five player tabletop game nights when Mary stirred and sat on her knees.

She looked from me to Cyrus blearily before flopping across my legs next to Sonia. Cyrus poured her a glass of water, and I dumped out a couple of painkillers for her as she mustered the energy to rise again.

It started to matter less how permanent Kimberly was as a fixture in my life. I'd been content with Mary, and I'd grown content with more and more since.

I, for one, was looking forward to new frontiers of contentment.

**Mary, Josh, Cyrus, Kim, and Addie**
*Illustrated by: Claudia Cangini*